THE DEAL

THE DEAL

A NOVEL

LISA BRISKIE

ZONE PRESS
DENTON, TEXAS

THE DEAL
By Lisa Briskie

Zone Press
an imprint of Rogers Publishing and Consulting, Inc.
109 East Oak – Suite 300
Denton, Texas 76201
info@zonepress.com

Jim O. Rogers - Editor
Charlotte Beckham - Copy Edit
Lori Walker - Production and Design
Danielle Briskie - Original Cover Art

Any resemblance to actual people and events is purely coincidental. This is a work of fiction.

Printed in the United States of America
ISBN:0-9761706-7-1

I dedicate The Deal to:

My beautiful, intelligent and talented daughters,

Melisa Elena and Danielle Marie…

you're my greatest source of inspiration, pride and joy.

Heartfelt Thanks to:

My husband Dave whose sense of humor is a gift and whose enduring love is my life's greatest treasure.

My parents, Elena and Ettore Mutalipassi (Passi), whose guiding principles, love and support have shaped the woman I am today and allowed me to be all I can be.

Countless family and friends whose devoted friendship and faithful encouragement are such a blessing to me.

You, my readers, who have chosen to enter the world of The Deal and embark on this exciting journey of affluence, deception and intrigue. Enjoy.

Special Acknowledgements:

Danielle Briskie for the awesome original cover art

Lisa Guernsey for her excellent editing

Jim Rogers and the team at Zone Press for their belief in this project and efforts to publish The Deal.

Prologue

———◇———

The woman was barely visible as she stood hunched in the shadows of the doorway. Her hands shook uncontrollably as she shifted her weight on her walking stick and moved forward enough for the streetlight to cast a soft glow upon her aged features. It was the movement that caught Jaclyn's attention and she looked in the woman's direction.

"Change…Lots of Change!" With an unexpectedly forceful voice, the woman shouted at Jaclyn as she approached. Startled by her comment, Jaclyn was taken aback and paused briefly. It was then that the woman reached out toward her. The gesture alarmed Jaclyn, but there was something in the woman's eyes that spoke volumes to her…made her take notice. In her hesitation, the woman continued. "I see it…people, places…all changing around you."

Jaclyn's curiosity overtook her common sense. "Excuse me, but are you speaking to me?"

The woman did not hesitate. "Yes, I am. And I beg you to heed my warning. I know things…I see things."

Disturbed by her words Jaclyn slowly stepped sideways, increasing the distance between them, but the woman's urging continued. "Don't be afraid…be forewarned. There is trouble brewing and hardship in your path… use caution on your journey …and be careful who you trust…."

Jaclyn hastened her pace. New York certainly took on an air of mystery and peril in the dark hours. Tonight was no exception. As she continued walking home, the woman's words played on in her mind…change…trouble…caution… she found herself contemplating her warnings. Shaking her head as if to knock sense into her stream of troubling thoughts, she buried her chin in her scarf, pulled her coat closed tightly about her and jogged the rest of the way home.

THE DEAL

CHAPTER 1
—◇—

Jaclyn looked up from the files sprawled out before her on the handsome mahogany desk. As she stretched her arms above her head and arched from side to side, the richly paneled squares on the walls appeared to move. Her eyes scanned the room and came to rest on the beautiful 18th-century canvas that she adored. Along with the Persian rugs placed strategically throughout the office, it was one of the personal luxuries she had added to this plush and well-appointed office suite. When she had happened upon the landscape in a quaint antique shop in Dallas, she knew immediately she had to have it. Rarely did anything capture her heart as that painting did. A massive stone castle rose from green rolling pastures. A cloudy, deep blue sky peeked out over the round turreted towers. There were no people visible, but Jaclyn imagined them there. She envisioned the women in magnificent flowing gowns moving gracefully down the expansive stone hallways toward men dressed in formal dinner attire, who were waiting to escort them into the grand dining room. As pairs formed and entered the majestic hall, one young woman remained standing shyly in a corner. Her complexion fair and her young beauty striking, she remained alone and unescorted. After several moments of pacing about, the visibly saddened maiden began a solemn retreat down the immense passageway to return to her chamber. For more than a year now, this had been her routine. A distant sound caught her attention and she looked up. It was then that she saw him approaching. Clad in his princely attire, he moved purposefully toward her. His wide gate brought him to her swiftly and before she could steady herself, he was upon her. Suddenly, he stopped, fixed in one spot, taken aback by her beauty. Was she always so fair? Had she blossomed so in the time he had been away? Surely it had not been that long. As he moved closer to her, she caught her breath. He reached for her hand, knelt before her, and softly touched his lips to her knuckles as he peered up into her sultry eyes. At his sensuous touch, her skin flushed red and he smiled at her shy innocence. He stood slowly and extended his arm to her, offering her an escort into the party. She smiled tentatively at him, looped her arm under his and allowed him to lead her. She found it hard not to stare at him. It was difficult for her to believe he was truly standing before her. But as his touch reminded her, he had returned home at last.

Jaclyn sighed. She was a hopeless romantic, indulging herself in a fanciful fantasy in a rare moment of solitude. As she thought about the young couple in her daydream, she was certain they would ride off into the sunset to begin their lives together. It was imperative that there be a happy ending. She wouldn't allow it to conclude any other way.

Her attention was diverted by a knock at the door. "Come in," she called out.

Matt, her assistant, appeared at the doorway, "Sorry to interrupt, Jaclyn, but there is a delivery for you. I tried to sign for it, but the courier insisted you personally receive the package."

Jaclyn smiled at Matt. He was so eager to please and do all he could to avoid disrupting her work. "Thank you, Matt. I need an excuse to stretch my legs anyway. It's no problem."

He opened the door as she moved toward him and held it for her as she stepped through. She walked into the lobby, where the courier was waiting. She called out to him. "Hello, I am Jaclyn Tate."

The courier looked up at her as she entered the room and was visibly taken aback. He stared at her as if he had never seen a woman before. What was obvious to all who came in contact with Jaclyn was her striking beauty. Her wavy auburn hair fell freely about her shoulders. Thick, bouncy curls encircled her face like a decorative frame surrounding a spectacular work of art. Her fine features were laid out perfectly against a soft white complexion. Almond-shaped, deep blue eyes peered out from behind long brown lashes, and wide rosy lips added to her beauty and sensuous appearance. Her voluptuous breasts, slender torso and lean legs combined to complete her enticing look. The way she carried herself, with her shoulders back and head held high, made her look taller than her 5 feet, 6 inches. She accentuated her curvaceous physique with her manner of dress. Her wardrobe consisted primarily of soft silk dresses that clung to her body in all the right places and fitted suits that were as feminine as they were professional. She was stunning and when she walked into a room, she owned everyone's attention.

From an early age, Jaclyn learned that her looks were special, but as an adult, she was often underestimated or not taken seriously because of her appearance. Although few realized how her beauty could be anything but a gift, she found it an obstacle in the early years of her career, a hurdle she had long ago surmounted. As a summa cum laude graduate of New York University with a master's degree in business and an outstanding resume, she had, over time, earned the respect of her peers and established herself as a professional at the top of her field. At 32 years of age, she felt accomplished in her work. She had built an excellent name for herself among her associates and clients and was considered one of the best real estate brokers in the Northeast. Such growing esteem prompted new contacts to give her instant credibility. Although some continued to comment that her looks took them by surprise, Jaclyn was satisfied that they appreciated her business acumen, which was all that really mattered to her.

Jaclyn smiled at the man standing speechless before her. When the courier did not say a word, Jaclyn prompted, "I understand you have a package for me." As she extended her hand, the young man seemed to come out of his trance. Without saying a word, he placed the envelope in her hand and presented the log for her to sign. Jaclyn quickly scribbled her name and returned the pen to its holder. She then thanked him, turned on her heels and returned to her office. As she passed Matt's desk, she paused as she tore open the pouch and pulled out a stack of papers. She quickly scanned the contents. "Excellent," she commented. She turned to Matt and explained. "These are the final papers I need for the closing. Now everything is set." Jaclyn was smiling broadly as she walked into her office and closed the door behind her.

Refocusing her attention on the work before her, Jaclyn looked down at her desk. Cluttering the surface were many folders, each in a designated pile. Her organization made sense to her, but to anyone else it looked chaotic. This was, however, the only part of her that appeared so for Jaclyn Tate was the epitome of polish and reserve. Working since early morning, she had taken only a few breaks to sit back and stretch. She knew she had to concentrate to ensure that everything was in order. She had worked long and hard to market this building and it would mean a sizable commission. It would be her first big transaction since her arrival in Dallas nearly a year before. She could hardly believe so much time had gone by, and yet much had happened and her life was dramatically different. Looking back, she remembered how resistant she had been to the idea of the move, and yet it had turned out to be the best decision for her. She couldn't help but think fondly of Carl Toner as she reminisced.

Carl had been her mentor in New York. He was one of her favorite people although she knew of few others who felt the same way. Beneath the tough and stern exterior, she found a gentle and compassionate man. Not many were allowed close enough to see that side of him. From the day he and Jaclyn met, they held a common appreciation for each other. A string of difficult relationships had taken their toll on Carl and although he was only in his late fifties, his hair was completely gray and he appeared much older than he was. He never fought his aged appearance though and instead said it was good because it made him seem wiser than he really was. The crux of his problems centered on the fact that he had married the wrong woman twice in his life, but thankfully, he would add, neither marriage had produced children. As a result, Carl swore off commitments to women and devoted his undivided attention to his business. During this pivotal time in Carl's life, he met Jaclyn at a dinner party at a mutual friend's Park Avenue apartment. They met over the crab bar and found they had complementary circumstances; Jaclyn wanted to find a dynamic brokerage house at which to launch her career and Carl wanted to mentor a protegee to help him expand his real estate empire. Within weeks of the party, Jaclyn had a new job and Carl had an apprentice. In the more than six years since their first meeting, Jaclyn had become the top agent at Toner and Associates, all under Carl's watchful eye. And although he hated to have her leave New

York, it was he who pushed her to take over his upstart Dallas office and leave behind an unpleasant situation in New York. She thought back to the day Carl sat her down in his office, put on his most serious face and again reviewed the opportunity with her. "Jaclyn, I've been discussing the Dallas office with you for the past few weeks now, but you still haven't told me your decision. What is standing in the way of a commitment?"

Jaclyn took a deep breath before responding. She knew this was an exceptional opportunity Carl was offering her, yet it was a big move and she was having a difficult time deciding in the affirmative. "It's complicated, Carl. On the one hand, I am honored and thrilled that you would offer me this position. And you know better than anyone how I thrive on a challenge. It's just that I am so entrenched here in New York, and the thought of giving up everyone and everything I know is a little overwhelming."

Carl understood her concerns. Change was always frightening and uncomfortable. But he was convinced that if she stepped outside her comfort zone and made the move, it would be the right choice for her. His task now was to convince her of that fact. "Jaclyn, leaving what is familiar is never easy. There are a lot of unknowns with this move. But look at all the advantages. And remember, Dallas isn't on the other side of the world." As he spoke, he moved around to the front of the desk and leaned against it. He paused for a moment, then continued. "You have to admit getting away for a while would be great and you know you will have fun starting the new office."

She looked up at him but did not respond. Carl bent down and reached out to her, touching her hands that lay clenched in her lap. "Trust me, Jaclyn, if you go to Dallas and it isn't everything you expect it to be, you can always come back. I'm not asking for a lifetime commitment. I just want you to get the office started and put some key people in place. Then it's up to you whether you stay or come back to New York."

Jaclyn took a few minutes to consider Carl's offer. She had spent hours toying with the idea since the day he mentioned it, but now the time was coming for a decision and finalizing her answer was not easy. It was clear to Carl that she was still lost in her thoughts and so he spoke to break the silence. "Well, what do you say?"

In the quiet of the moment, she found her answer. She peered into his eyes as she spoke, "You're a hard man to refuse." A smile crossed his lips. She smiled too. "When do I leave?"

Although they had reached an understanding, it wasn't easy for Jaclyn to pick up and move to a city she had never even visited. Yet she trusted Carl and knew he would never steer her wrong. He had promised a fresh start; that sounded so welcome to her at the time. Besides being her mentor, he had become a dear friend and confidant. He knew she needed a change, and his Dallas office could use her skill and ambition. It made sense for both of them and before she could change her mind, she had a one-way ticket to the Dallas Fort Worth International Airport.

It took Jaclyn weeks to realize she was truly leaving New York, but the day the movers came to pack up her office and remove most of the clothing and furnishings from her apartment, she had to admit it was actually happening. She took off a few days of work before her departure to pack the remainder of her personal belongings and to spend time with her parents. Early on a Friday afternoon, she walked out of her apartment for the last time and, bidding New York farewell, drove to her parent's home in Pennsylvania. The three-hour drive gave her time to reflect on the past and think about the future. She knew she needed to regain control of her life, but she hated to let go of the full and successful life she had built in New York. Though a side of her was eager for the challenge a new beginning would present, she also dreaded the unknown. But what pained her most about leaving was the thought of being so far from her mother and father. Even though they only saw each other a few times a year, primarily on holidays, she had always felt close to them because she was only a three-hour drive away. Now she would be a three-hour flight away, but the physical distance that would be between them saddened her. By the time she pulled onto the tree-lined street that led to her childhood home, she was filled with emotion. Memories flooded her mind. It was as if she could see herself as a teenager again, walking her dogs down the winding road, looking up at the canopy of leaves formed by the branches that bent and touched above her. She recalled riding her prize horse, Champion, through the fields that stretched out before her. As she came over a rise in the road, Jaclyn spied her father in the distance riding his favorite horse, Pride. The two moved in perfect rhythm, as though one creature, traveling swiftly along the edge of the expansive Tate property. She slowed the car to watch her father. He was her everything. She adored him just as much now as she did when she was a little girl riding pony on his knee. His strong, athletic build had changed over the years and his hair had transformed from a striking auburn to a soft grayish-brown, but he was still her daddy and she loved him completely.

Slowly she drove through the open gates that marked the only break in the seemingly endless white iron fence surrounding the property and turned onto the long gravel drive that curved up toward the house. It was then that her father saw her. He quickly led Pride in her direction, pulled the tattered wide-brimmed hat from his head and waved it at her excitedly. She rolled down the window, stuck her hand out and waved back as she pulled the car alongside the house. As soon as she stepped onto the drive, she was nearly overwhelmed by her parent's two German shepherds, Max and Rex. They each stood on their hind legs so they could welcome her with a thorough licking. She couldn't believe how good it felt to be home.

Moments later, her father reached the fence, slid down from the horse and jogged over to Jaclyn. He wrapped his arms around her and gave her a firm bear hug. She took in the smell and feel of him and it was familiar, warm and wonderful. He spoke into her hair as he nuzzled her. "Welcome home, darling. It's so good to have our little girl here again." Jaclyn was overwhelmed by the moment. Tears stung the back of her throat. "It's great to be home, daddy." It wasn't until her mother came running down the steps, calling out to her, that her father loosened his grip. As Jaclyn embraced her mother, she realized how little things had changed. Her mom was wearing a basic cotton dress, sensible flat shoes and the print apron she always donned to tend the house and garden. Her smile could warm you on the coldest winter day and her hazel eyes sparkled like gems. Her light brown hair was teased into the same set of tight curls. She was one of the most wonderful, consistent and kind people Jaclyn had ever known and Jaclyn drank in her sweetness as she held her mom tightly.

The three of them walked arm in arm up the wide wooden steps of the front porch. Jaclyn sat on the porch swing while her mother went inside to get some lemonade and cookies and her father went in to wash-up. It was amazing how she felt as if she were twelve years old again; that was the magic of coming home to her parents. As Jaclyn took it all in, she noted how little had changed about the place, the only residence she had known until she moved to New York to attend college. The white wood siding that covered the two-story, prairie-style house still looked as if it could use a coat of paint. Hanging slightly crooked, the white frame, screen door opened stiffly and closed loudly behind you. The sun-bleached porch floorboards still creaked terribly and needed weather sealer. And in spite of it all, there was no question in Jaclyn's mind that this house was and always would be home, the most safe and welcoming place in the world.

Rocking gently back and forth on the porch swing, Jaclyn reflected back on all the memories wrapped up in her parents' home. She could recall the many special times on that very swing: counting the stars with her grandmother, knitting with her mom, discussing philosophy theories with her dad, getting her first kiss from Brandon Callo. She had a rural upbringing, devoid of many cultural experiences, but filled with affection and happy moments that were priceless. Remembering them warmed her soul. It was so therapeutic to be back in a place that she associated with unconditional love and never-ending kindness. Spending time with her parents in the familiar setting was just what she needed, and she immersed herself fully in its warmth.

***

Later that night, Jaclyn's father took her by the arm and led her down the hall to his favorite place in the house, his study. As they walked through the threshold, Jaclyn took her usual seat by the fireplace and her dad stepped behind the antique inlaid wood desk to sit in his regal-looking armchair. It had been many months since they had sat in that room together to talk, but as they sat there now, it felt as if it had only been yesterday. Both of them in the chair they favored, relaxed and looking forward to the conversation about to ensue.

Jaclyn's father was a theologian. Son of a pastor, educated at Notre Dame and Oxford, he was well-versed in matters of doctrinal significance as well as current, globally pressing sociological issues.

For years, he had taught divinity at several universities in the area, in addition to serving as pastor of a nondenominational church two miles away. Today, he continued to act as pastor but had recently retired as a professor. He was a gifted public speaker, extremely charismatic and the true inspiration and guiding light in Jaclyn's early years.

"Jaclyn, my darling. Tell me about this move." Her father sat back in his chair as if to express that he was getting comfortable and that he wanted her to feel free to speak her mind.

She smiled as she spoke. "I'm extremely excited about this opportunity, Dad. Carl has entrusted this new office to me and given me full rein to make it happen." She paused, as if considering her words carefully. "Besides the thrill of the challenge, I am happy to have a change of scenery. I didn't want to worry you and Mom with all the details, but things have gotten worse since I refused to let Andrew back into my life." Jaclyn paused and hung her head. It was as if speaking the words left her weak.

Sensing her pain, her father gently asked, "Do you want to talk about it?"

Jaclyn looked up into her father's eyes. He was so kind and unintrusive. "No, Dad, I'd rather not dredge up all those feelings tonight. Let's just say it will be good to be far away from him and start my personal life over. After so many years as a couple, we share too many friends and favorite places in the city, which can make things awkward. This is why, I am grateful for the move..."

Her father prompted her to finish her thoughts, "And..."

Jaclyn hesitated. "Well, it is just that I hate to be so far from you and Mom. When Carl and I first discussed this opportunity, it sounded perfect. I had a challenge for my career and a chance to start things over. Then it hit me. I would be so far away from you. It was enough to make me want to back out of it right away. Then I came around and once Carl seized the first hint of an agreement, he moved fast to organize things and plan for my move. Before I knew it, it was time to leave."

There were tears in Jaclyn's eyes and her father could see that the distance was truly troubling her. "And you shall leave your mother and father . . ." Her father stopped short of completing the biblical reference, but he knew she understood it fully. "Jaclyn, it's part of life. Didn't my father leave his parents in England, expecting never to see them again to travel to this country, a world full of promise? Back then it truly was a challenge to bridge the distance. I remember my dad telling me it had been ten years before he was able to return to see his family. Even so, he never regretted the move or the life he built here. Nowadays, if you get homesick or want to come home for the holidays, no problem, you just pick a flight and before you know it, you're home. It's the right thing for you to do. I am certain of it."

Jaclyn was amazed by her father's ability to make everything better. "I know you're right, Dad. I guess I just needed to hear that. How do you always know the right thing to say?"

He chuckled at her words. "That's my job, darling."

As the two of them were talking, Jaclyn's mom prepared coffee and dessert. After filling a silver serving tray with some of Jaclyn's favorite homemade cookies, she carried it to the study. As she walked into the room, she was touched by the sound of their laughter. It made her happy whenever the two of them enjoyed time with each other. They looked up as she entered.

"Mother, what do you have there?" Jaclyn's father asked.

"A few of Jaclyn's favorites." As she spoke, she lowered the tray so they both could see.

Jaclyn's eyes got big as she took in all her favorite treats. "Mom, I can't believe you did this for me." She stood, helped her mother place the tray on the desk, then gave her a big hug. "Thank you."

Then the three of them sat together to talk. Each took a cup of coffee and a few cookies and her father continued, "I know moving is difficult Jaclyn, but take your mother for example. She left her family in Illinois when she chose to marry me. I had been offered the position of pastor at our church and we had to move to Pennsylvania. Although it seemed the end of the world to her back then, we adjusted and made a good life for ourselves. I know you can do the same."

Jaclyn's mom added her thoughts. "Jaclyn, sweetie, I can remember the day your father and I met as if it were yesterday. I was studying in the library at Notre Dame and your father was sitting at a desk across the room facing me. He stared at me until I looked up and saw him. He was determined to get to know me and he did just that. We met in his senior year. I was a sophomore. Once we started dating we knew we had something special. Then I remember when he came to mother's home, a month after I graduated to ask my parents for my hand in marriage. They were happy until he explained that the wedding needed to take place quickly because he would be taking the pastor position at our church here in Pennsylvania. You should have seen the look on my parents' faces. They loved your father, but the thought of their little girl moving so far away nearly scared them to death. Still, they agreed and we all know it was the right decision. Now, I'm not saying it was easy. For the entire first year, I wished I could go home. But after I started teaching at the high school and we started making friends and getting familiar with the area, it became home to us."

Jaclyn looked from one parent to the other. "You two always know what to say. Deep down inside I know this is the right thing for me, but the uncertainty of such a big change is never easy."

This time Jaclyn's father replied. "I completely understand how you could feel that way, but I want you to stop being so serious about life. Roll with the punches a little less deliberately. Let things flow naturally and enjoy the curves in the road. Have fun with this Jaclyn. It's a great opportunity. And you know what? Your mom and I will love an opportunity to come for a visit. In fact, one of my best friends from Notre Dame, you remember, Peter Albright, is pastor in a Baptist church in Dallas. I would like the chance to visit with him when we come to see you."

Jaclyn's mom added, "That's right. My goodness, it must be five years since Peter came to see us here at the house. It would be great to visit him. See, Jaclyn, it's all going to work out."

The three of them spent the evening discussing everything from the challenge ahead of her opening the office to the real estate climate in Dallas. Her parents cared deeply for her happiness and wanted to share in this experience with her. It was well into the early hours of the morning when they finally gave in to their sleepiness and unwillingly retired for the night. Each of them cherished fully the moments of togetherness.

That weekend, Jaclyn did all the things she loved to do. She slept in her old bed, in a room that hadn't changed in all the years she'd been away, rode Champion II until she was sore, baked bread and prepared meals with her mother, took long walks and had long talks with her father. It was a terrific weekend and she felt thoroughly relaxed before it was over, and was looking forward to her move to Dallas.

The afternoon she left, the three of them held onto each other for a long time before they were willing to let go. Carl had arranged for a limousine to pick Jaclyn up at her parents' home and take her to the airport. As a surprise, Jaclyn gave her parents her four-year-old Cadillac Seville so trips to church on Sunday did not always have to be in her dad's vintage 1965 pickup truck. Her mom cried when Jaclyn handed them the keys. Her mom said it was the nicest thing anyone had ever done for them. Giving them the car made Jaclyn feel good, although it truly took very little in the way of material possessions to make them happy. It was their understanding of the true priorities in life that Jaclyn admired most.

As Jaclyn gave them one last hug before getting into the limo, it struck her how dramatically her life had changed. Before she left the small rural community, she had excelled in school and enjoyed ranch life. She was well known about town because of her father's position, and so she tended to be reserved in her conduct in order to uphold her father's firm rules for proper social manners. Life was simple then. Everyone knew what was right and wrong and people looked out for one another. It was almost surreal, as she looked back on it with her expanded perspective. Once away from it, she was quick to learn that the real world was vastly different from the caring community in which she had been raised. The rules had changed. Still, she learned to adjust and ultimately became a successful businesswoman who lived and worked in New York City, maintained a spacious and well-appointed Upper East Side apartment, wore pricey designer clothes, drove a luxury car, and regularly socialized with New York's rich and famous. It seemed hard to imagine that the little girl who grew up on this ranch in rural Pennsylvania would have become the powerhouse real estate agent that she was. It always amazed her when she thought about the contrast.

There were endless details on Jaclyn's mind as she left her parents. It was an hour drive to the airport and Jaclyn spent the time in quiet introspection. She thought about her father's advice that she take life less seriously and knew he was right. Jaclyn's personality had been molded by the fight she had waged to stake her claim in her male-dominated profession. She had fought her way into the complex world of commercial real estate and battled prejudices and obstacles along the way. The process had taken its toll on her character. She had become tougher and more reserved. Her father was right. It was time for a change. It was then that she vowed to enjoy life fully and learn to be more impulsive and free-spirited. With her fresh start, she would take with her a positive attitude and a brighter outlook on life. Suddenly, she was more excited than ever to embark on her new life.

Before long, she was boarding the airplane. It was a beautiful clear night for flying and the pilot took every opportunity to point out the brightly lit cities that appeared beneath the plane as they crossed the eastern half of the United States. Jaclyn sat relaxed in her seat, enjoying the tranquility of the moment and watching the cities approach and disappear beneath her. As they neared their destination, an odd but comforting feeling overtook her. She knew this city was home now and it felt good, as if living there was always meant to be.

CHAPTER 2

—◇—

On her first day in Dallas, Jaclyn set out to find a building for the satellite office of Toner and Associates. By the second afternoon, she came upon the perfect space. The moment she drove up to the complex she knew it was the one. Located on the outskirts of downtown, it was close to many excellent restaurants and blocks from the famous and lavish Mansion on Turtle Creek Hotel, where she would be staying until she found an apartment and where she planned to accommodate her out-of-town guests. The white stucco office building was only two years old and had the ideal setup for her business. Immediately inside the front doors was an open receptionist area from which two corridors branched off. Down the first hall was an impressive, wood-paneled corner office with a secretary's bay stationed in front and a small conference room immediately to the left, where a wall of windows overlooked a greenbelt. The other hallway led to six smaller offices that lined two walls, creating a border around an area of cubicles arranged in a square. The office space could easily accommodate more than twenty employees and perfectly matched Jaclyn's two-year business plan for the Dallas office. The landlord also offered furniture for rent, which Jaclyn considered and agreed to on sight. She selected matching light oak desks and credenzas for the six smaller offices and a large mahogany desk, burgundy leather chairs and a tall mahogany credenza and bookcase for her office. For the conference room, she selected a mahogany table and surrounded it with ten, high-back, burgundy leather chairs. She wanted to exude a sense of accomplishment and success and she felt that the office, its location and its furnishings achieved that well.

Once her office had been selected, she moved on to finding a suitable place to live. That proved more of a challenge since most of the nicer residences close to downtown had no vacancies. After several disappointing days of looking, she came upon an interesting opportunity at an Ebby Halliday office. One of the Realtors met Jaclyn at the door. "May I help you?"

Jaclyn shook the woman's hand as she began speaking. "Yes. I am interested in finding a townhouse or apartment for rent. I want to live within ten miles of this area."

The Realtor lit up. "It may be your lucky day, Ms...?"

"Tate, Jaclyn Tate."

"Well, Jaclyn, I may have just the thing for you. I live in Highland Park and have a guesthouse I want to rent. I have only recently begun mentioning the idea to friends and business associates, so, you see, it may just be fate that you came in here today."

Jaclyn agreed to visit the property and together they drove to the house, which turned out to be just minutes away from her office. Its setting and location were perfect. To the rear of a massive, red brick colonial, whose yard was heavily landscaped with mature oak trees, flowering bushes and seasonal blooms, was a small cottage at the edge of the property, facing the light blue lap pool surrounded by Roman fountains. As the two women approached the guesthouse, Jaclyn couldn't help but feel a little like Snow White. There was something about the white picket fence and English garden that led to the small stone structure, with its green shutters and severely pitched dark gray roof that reminded her of the fable she loved as a girl. Beyond the exterior charm of the cottage, once inside, Jaclyn was sold on her new home.

Immediately inside the front door was a great room covered in warm ash paneling. The room had a high cathedral ceiling, which was dissected by wood beams forming a crisscross pattern. Directly across from the entry was a floor-to-ceiling brick fireplace with a large, carved wooden mantel and built-in bookcases on either side. Off the living room was a country style kitchen with an adjacent eating area. Next to the kitchen were a cozy bedroom and a quaint bathroom with a pedestal sink and an old-fashioned, ball-and-claw footed white metal tub. Both the kitchen and bedroom suite were decorated in a simple, floral decor. The walls were covered with pale yellow wildflower wallpaper. The kitchen had ash cabinets, yellow Formica countertops, and a yellow and white ceramic tile floor. The same cabinets and tile were repeated in the bathroom and a coordinated yellow shag carpet covered the bedroom floor. Jaclyn liked the cozy feel and the character of the cottage. It didn't take her long to decide that this would be her new residence. Before leaving, the two women agreed on the rent and the move-in date. Jaclyn was excited about her quaint new home. It reflected the dramatic departure from her life in New York and she welcomed the contrast.

Having a wonderful place to live truly helped, especially during the times Jaclyn questioned her sanity for leaving behind everything and everyone she knew in New York. Unavoidably, some days were very lonely. Dallas was nothing like New York City, where she had walked everywhere and knew everyone in the neighborhood. Gone were the weekly walks to the bread shop, the Italian deli and the international cheese shop, her favorite Italian and Chinese restaurants, as well as the daily stop at the bakery next door to her apartment building for her morning coffee and muffin. On the way home from work, she often stopped at Harrigan's, the dimly lit Irish pub on the corner of her street. It was a gathering place for many of her friends and it was there that they met to swap stories about the day or grab a bite to eat. All that was a thing of the past, a fond memory that seemed attached to another person's life. In Dallas, she drove everywhere and hardly knew a soul. She had heard about Southern charm and hospitality but didn't know where or how to meet the people to experience it. It was all quite the opposite of what she had heard and thought prior to her move, but now that she was here, she was determined to make the most of her new life.

In between furnishing her home and buying a new car, Jaclyn turned her attention to staffing the office. She knew good employees would be critical to her success, so she began actively recruiting the first week she arrived. The process turned out to be incredibly smooth since she had contacted several employment agencies before coming to Dallas, which had lined up candidates for her to consider. Her first hire was a personal assistant, Matt Carlson, a recent honors graduate of Southern Methodist University who was eager to make a name for himself in real estate. Jaclyn liked him immediately because he reminded her so much of how she had been when she first graduated. As Jaclyn sat across the desk from him, she studied him intently. He was twenty-four years old although he looked several years older. He was a man of average height and build, with dark brown, conservatively cut, straight hair, a thick moustache, and bushy brown eyebrows and eyelashes that contrasted severely with his light complexion. On first impression, she decided he was not the type that won your confidence in an instant; instead, it was his personality that set him apart.

"So, Matt, tell me about yourself." Jaclyn liked to start interviews with an open-ended request. She felt that the reply provided insight into the person's priorities and self-concept.

Matt sat up straighter in his chair, cleared his throat softly, then replied, "Ms. Tate, if I may, I would first like to thank you for the opportunity to meet with you today. I have learned about you and your success with Toner and Associates in New York and am certain that you will be equally successful here in Dallas. In fact, to be considered for the position of your assistant is an honor." He looked into Jaclyn's eyes as he spoke and the sincerity in his face touched her. It was clear to her that he had come to the interview eager to please and he was succeeding. He continued, "In fact, I was most impressed with your sale of the Harbor Hotel last year. That had to be an incredible experience. And the price tag, now that had to make the seller a friend for life." His expression loudly attested to how in awe he was with Jaclyn's accomplishments. He had done a thorough background study on Toner and Associates and Jaclyn's personal success and spoke about his findings as if they were common knowledge. Jaclyn was pleasantly surprised to find he had taken the time to prepare so thoroughly for their meeting. It told her a lot about the man seated before her.

"Well, Matt, I must say I am impressed that you know as much as you do about Toner and Associates, but I would like to know about you. Tell me about Matt."

He smiled as he spoke, "Certainly, Ms. Tate. As you can see in my resume, I recently graduated with honors from SMU with a major in finance and a minor in marketing. It has been my intention for several years now to build my career in real estate. During my last semester, I worked as an intern for the Cinetail Group, which gave me great experience. I gained insight into the world of real estate transactions by being involved in all phases of the business. Having had that training, I am more intrigued by the profession now than I even thought I would be."

Matt paused and Jaclyn spoke. "Can you be more specific? What is it specifically about real estate that intrigues you so?"

Matt did not hesitate. "The stakes. The amount of money invested in commercial real estate deals is incredible. It also presents such a challenge. I thrive on challenges."

Jaclyn smiled at this young man who was clearly enamored with the industry. She thought it would be great to harness that passion and turn it into success. "I admire your ambition, Matt. Now tell me about you. The Matt who exists outside of school and work."

Matt took a moment to reply, almost as if he were uncertain of what to say or where to begin. "I play polo." He said it succinctly, as if his statement would meet with objection. He was surprised by Jaclyn's reaction. A big smile crossed her face. "Polo? How exciting. I grew up on a ranch in Pennsylvania, surrounded by horses. Riding is my favorite pastime, although I regretfully have done very little these days."

Matt jumped at their obvious common interest. His demeanor relaxed, changing dramatically as he replied. "Not many people I meet even understand horses, let alone enjoy them as much as I do. I have to admit that I didn't anticipate a person from New York City would have such a history."

Jaclyn was amused by his remark. If he only knew of her life on the ranch, he would see a very different person than the high-powered real estate professional he had learned about. They talked for more than an hour and the more they spoke, the more Jaclyn liked him and saw great potential in him. Before the end of their time together, she had planned to hire and train him as Carl had mentored her.

Matt started work the day Jaclyn opened the doors to the new office and had been a tremendous help from that moment. Together, they did everything from set up the office furniture to recruit personnel. Before the first month had passed, Jaclyn had hired a receptionist, two experienced real estate agents and two qualified administrative assistants. Toner and Associates Dallas was well on its way.

That had been many months ago. Jaclyn stretched her arms over her head again, bending from side to side, trying to work out a kink in her spine. For the past two hours she had reviewed the multitude of details in her file to ensure that every "t" was crossed and every "i" dotted. The abundance of detail was one of the few parts of the business she disliked. Most other aspects intrigued and challenged her. Matching a property with a buyer and working the deal to a close provided her with great satisfaction. It was thrilling and addictive. Especially when the stakes were so high. Today's closing would be the culmination of a tremendous amount of hard work and would result in the actualization of a longtime goal. Making deals happen in Dallas hadn't been as difficult as she had once believed. It was true that she had come to Texas during an economic lull, but that meant things were getting stirred up. Sellers were eager and buyers were out in droves looking for good opportunities. There was plenty of business to be done and with her optimism and determination, she was making it happen.

CHAPTER 3
—◇—

It had been only two days after her arrival that Jaclyn discovered Thanksgiving Tower, one of the most recognizable buildings in the Dallas skyline, was for sale. Her blood raced when she heard and it immediately became her goal to sell it. It would be the coup she needed to make a name for herself in this new market. Finding a buyer for the Tower in this depressed real estate market would not be easy, but it was possible. All Jaclyn needed to do was focus on an objective and she would be on her way. Before long, the challenge consumed her.

By the end of her first month in Dallas, Jaclyn had contacted every person she knew of who was capable of buying the Tower. She spent endless hours making hundreds of phone calls to contacts, networking the deal until she had narrowed the playing field down to the parties with the most interest or buying potential. Week after week, she contacted individuals whose net worth and current real estate portfolios made them potential buyers. Before long, a prospectus on the building was on the desk of every interested party, and by the sixth week she had several solid prospects. Her determination was beginning to produce some promising leads.

Jaclyn and her staff met in the conference room for her first monthly update. Since many of them had only begun working with her a few weeks earlier, the meeting centered around her strategy to sell Thanksgiving Tower. When she had everyone's attention, she began. "As each of you is aware, Thanksgiving Tower is my number one mission for this office. I want us to put ourselves on the map quickly and closing this sale will certainly let everyone in Dallas stand up and take notice." She paused for emphasis. The agents seated around her nodded in agreement. "I want this to be a priority for each of us. Please network, as much as possible and let me know when you have promising leads. I want to work all angles." She paused again to punctuate the importance of her statement. "I have three interested parties in the works. The first is a Louisiana oilman, Jed Hebert. He showed great enthusiasm, but since the pace of his actions seems to match the speed of his speech, a slow Southern drawl, I am anticipating a lengthy process just to get to the next step. As of our last conversation he hadn't gotten around to the paperwork yet, but assured me he would…sooner or later." Those more familiar with working with a slower Southern pace chuckled at Jaclyn's New York minute mentality. "Secondly is Mr. Sumitomo, who heads the real estate division of Mitsu. You may be familiar with the Japanese conglomerate. Recently they have purchased several high profile properties in Houston. Sumitomo had shown keen interest in the beginning, but his lack of willingness to speak English has made things difficult. When I employed an interpreter, he ended our discussions. Although no explanation was ever offered, I am lead to assume that it had to do with his discomfiture with my use of an interpreter. If any of you has any insight into this one, please let me know. At this point he is not taking my calls and has not returned my messages. I know he had originally been interested in the property, so if anyone has any contacts that could get us in with him, I am still hopeful that we can work with him."

Jim Barrett, Jaclyn's newest agent commented. "Jaclyn, I know one of the senior VP's of Mitsu. I'll give him a call and see what I can find out for you. I'll let you know."

"I appreciate any help you can offer. Please let me know what you find out."

"Will do."

Jaclyn then continued with her update. "That leaves me with my third interested party." Jaclyn paused briefly. "I don't know his identity." Jaclyn saw the eyebrows raise on the faces before her and commented on their reaction. "I know this is mysterious and somewhat odd, but I am eager to follow any lead and this one is actually turning out to be quite promising. I met with the buyer's agent and we visited the building. He took numerous photographs and I sent him back to his employer with a briefcase full of data. At first I questioned if this wasn't someone kicking tires, but yesterday I received a letter postmarked from New York, requesting additional details. Once again, however, no identity was revealed. I will continue to work this one as if it is real, because you never know, it may be. But I am strongly urging you to work this deal. It's a big one and it will do wonders for us and for the person who closes it. It will put you on the map." Everyone around her nodded in agreement. There wasn't one person in the room who didn't know what closing that deal would mean to their careers. They all wanted to make it happen, but they all recognized it wasn't going to be easy.

**

Outside work, Jaclyn had few opportunities to socialize or make friends, and although she had always been one who did well on her own, she often missed having someone to talk to or dine with, and she longed for her friends who were now far away. On a few occasions she accepted Matt's invitation to ride with him at the ranch where he boarded his horses. Although she thoroughly enjoyed the riding, it stirred emotions in her of the past and did not fill the void. Sensing her loneliness from a recent conversation, Carl made some phone calls and learned of a real estate awards gala taking place the following month in Dallas. He used his contacts to secure an invitation for her and called Jaclyn to ensure her attendance. The gala was being held at the grand Anatole Hotel, and from the time she had seen the Anatole on a telecast news report on President Reagan's trip to Dallas, Jaclyn had wanted to see it in person. The news report showed the massive and impressive lobby of the hotel, its extensive art collection and beautiful gardens filled with stone and bronze statues. When she arrived in Dallas, she had promised herself that she would spend time at the hotel and now she would have the opportunity. She was excited about attending the gala.

The night of the event came before she realized where the days had gone. Knowing it was to be a black-tie gala, she treated herself to a new evening gown. She had selected a black, fitted Victor

Costa creation with silver and black sequins that covered the thin shoulder straps and followed the band of the princess neckline. She liked the way the dress hugged her figure and set off her coloring. To make the most of the neckline, she wore her hair up in a mass of big, loose curls, letting a few soft ringlets fall against her temples and along the nape of her neck. To complete the look, she paired the dress with black, high-heeled, satin pumps and matching purse, added her Rolex watch and diamond tennis bracelet, which had been gifts from her former fiancé, teardrop rhinestone earrings and her grandmother's antique diamond wedding band, which she wore as a cocktail ring. When she stood before her bedroom mirror, she viewed herself from many angles before she gave herself the nod of approval. She was very pleased with the way she looked and glad she had agreed to attend this event. Having a night out on the town was just what she needed.

The Anatole was everything she had anticipated it would be. It left a great impression on her from the moment she entered the front doors. Its tremendous lobby and soaring ceilings left Jaclyn conscious of her small size. As she walked toward the guests congregating in the reception area in front of the grand ballroom, she marveled at the exquisite tapestries that hung from the glass-covered ceiling, one hundred or more feet above. As she neared the ballroom, she stopped to admire life-size statues of regal elephants that framed the entrance to the banquet area. Massive oriental rugs and soft cream and red chairs and sofas created inviting seating areas throughout the open lobby. Beautiful paintings, colorful statues and decorative vases lined each alcove. Along the walls of the enormous space were tiled walkways leading to the various wings of the hotel and marvelous artwork and collectibles on display. As she neared the reception area and the assembly of guests gathered under gigantic crystal chandeliers, she stopped to watch the flurry of activity before her. The men all sported a variation of the standard black tuxedo and the women wore exquisite gowns, each more glamorous than the next. Gold and diamonds glittered about her and she paused a moment to take in the feeling of wealth, power and social status that oozed from the crowd.

It was a half hour into the evening when she looked around

the room and wondered why she felt eyes piercing through her. She figured it was just her imagination and her self-consciousness at being alone at an event at which she knew no one. She was annoyed by her uncharacteristic lack of assertiveness, but her solitary existence since her move to Dallas was starting to have an impact on her social skills. As she turned toward the expansive hors d'oeuvres table, their eyes met and he flashed her a broad smile. She studied him intently. His captivating good looks sent butterflies dancing throughout her body. He stood more than six feet tall and seemed massive in comparison to the slender woman standing beside him. His light brown wavy hair was conservatively cut and contrasted with his athletic, boyish build and deep tan. Jaclyn could easily picture him surfing in Southern California. His strong facial features were so chiseled that he reminded her of the Roman statues she'd admired on her last visit to Florence. As their eyes locked into an inviting stare, she felt as if her feet were glued to the floor. Her legs refused to move. Emotion welled within her. It had been months since her breakup with Andrew and not even for a fleeting moment had she thought about another man. In fact, she had made a pact with herself to forget about men for a long time. They made life too complicated and exposed her heart. That was all forgotten now as she stared into this stranger's eyes. His eyes called out to her, beckoned her. She wanted to go to him and yet her feet remained fixed to the floor. Instantly, the spell was broken. The stranger's eyes left Jaclyn's as he looked down at the woman beside him who was pulling on his jacket sleeve. She was petite and slender, with obviously highlighted blonde hair in a shoulder-length bob that did not move even as she did. In a red, ankle-length, strapless dress, she stood out in a sea of black and white. Diamonds flashed on each of her fingers, dotted a band around her neck, covered her ears and fell loosely against both of her wrists. As she moved her arms, it was as if tiny flashes of light went off about her. She perfectly fit the stereotype of the typical southern woman Jaclyn had come to discover. Jaclyn turned her attention back to the gentleman as he leaned down toward his escort so he could hear her over the noise of the crowd. She said only a few words to him before turning his attention to the couple before them. He politely shook hands but Jaclyn surmised by his clearly cool manner that he did not appreciate the interruption. He looked up again, stealing a few seconds to scan the crowd in Jaclyn's direction, but their eyes did not meet again. Jaclyn wanted to wave her arms and shout, "Over here!" but she controlled the impulse. Just then, the dinner chimes sounded and everyone seemed to turn in unison toward the banquet doors opening before them. Her enchanting stranger was suddenly engulfed in a sea of elegantly dressed guests moving in the opposite direction. She stood motionless, wishing he would escape his escort's grasp and come to her. She waited until the last guest entered and the doors closed before she moved. Besides the bustling wait staff clearing the area, she was the only one left in the large reception hall. Before going inside the banquet room to find her assigned table, she chose to go to the ladies' room to freshen up. She needed a moment to compose herself. It had been the first time in a long time that a man had so captured her attention with his mere presence. She felt weak in the knees and slightly light-headed as she headed down the corridor.

She walked slowly down the hallway as a wave of forgotten feelings came crashing down on her and took her back to a trip she had made to Paris several years before. It had only been a year since she had begun working for Carl when he insisted she take a break and get away. At first she resisted, claiming she had too many irons in the fire to leave, but Carl fixed that. He personally took over all of her pending business so she would have no excuse. Realizing she had no option, she began planning a trip to Paris, something she had always hoped to do. Once her itinerary was set, she excitedly looked forward to her vacation. Before long she was there and enjoying every moment of it. She spent her first day exploring the Avenue Des Champs Elysees, shopping, eating at a sidewalk café and strolling along the famous boulevard. She stopped frequently to look around and take in the moment. She was in Paris and it was as beautiful and romantic as she had expected it would be.

Toward the end of the afternoon, she came upon the Arc de Triomphe and paused to admire it. She was lost in the moment, absorbing the fact that she was in the center of Paris when a police officer approached her. In a heavy French accent, he softly spoke. "May I tell you that you are the most beautiful woman I have ever seen?"

Taken by surprise, she turned to him and smiled. As she looked into his eyes, her knees went weak. He was gorgeous. He had

thick wavy reddish-brown hair, deep, sexy brown smiling eyes
dangerous smile. She was at a complete loss for words. Smiling b
at him, she simply said, "Thank you."

He was staring deep into her eyes. "I see you are admiring the
Arc. Would you like to go on top? You get a great view of the city."

Jaclyn was intrigued. She looked across the heavily trafficked
road that circled the Arc and asked, "How do you get on top?"

He smiled at her and pointed to a stairwell that disappeared
underneath the street. "There is a secret passageway and only I know
how to get there, but I will show you if you wish to go."

Jaclyn took a moment to think. It went against her instincts
to trust this stranger and go with him. Then again, he was clearly
a police officer and it was the middle of the day with hundreds of
people around them. She looked at the Arc, then back at him and
nodded. "Let's go."

As they walked, they talked and laughed. They stood at the top
of the Arc, admiring the view. He pointed out many famous sites and
gave her a short history lesson, which she truly enjoyed. They spent
the rest of the day together, taking a walking tour and enjoying each
other's company. It amazed Jaclyn how comfortable she was with this
stranger and how much fun she was having. At his insistence, they
spent the next five days together. It was her first romance in many
years and it was magical. Jean Philippe was so romantic and such a
gentleman. He treated her like a princess and showed her Paris and the
French countryside as only a Parisian could. They explored the Louvre
museum, Notre Dame and miles of the Seine. Another day they spent
at Versailles, enjoying the majestic palace and its endless gardens. One
evening they went to Montmartre and Sacre`-Coeur and watched the
sun descend on the skyline. Every moment was filled, as they enjoyed
the Parisian sites and lifestyle. The days passed quickly and before long
it was time for her to leave. Parting was difficult, but she knew when
it began that their brief romance was limited to the time she had in
Paris. They lived an ocean apart and their lives were worlds apart. But
she still thought back on the fleeting relationship fondly. Every time
Jean Philippe came to mind, her face changed. A tender smile crossed
her lips and her eyes sparkled. Thinking back on it now, years later, it
was almost as if it had been a fantasy, but she cherished the tender and
affectionate memories. Her time with Jean Philippe would forever be
part of the special romantic moments that lived on in her heart.

...ilippe was the last man she felt such an instant and
...1 for. The mysterious stranger she had seen across the
...d inspired that same pull and enticement. The feeling
...n she longed to feel again and the thought of having
...1d frightened her. As much as she tried to control
...ounting desire, it threatened to overwhelm her. She passed an
armoire filled with beautiful vases and colorful porcelain statues and
to distract herself stopped momentarily to admire the exquisite pieces.
She then continued to the end of the hall, where a set of decorative
lead glass double doors marked the entrance to a meeting room and,
immediately to the right, was the ladies' lounge. She pushed open the
ornate white and gold door and entered the sitting area of the restroom.
A full-length, gold-framed mirror came into view. Jaclyn studied the
image before her and was pleased with what she saw. She knew that
although a woman of average height, her posture and long, slender
legs made her appear statuesque. Her auburn hair looked stunning
in contrast with the black dress she wore this evening. There was a
soft rose tint to her china doll complexion and her blue-green eyes
shone like the waters surrounding the Cayman Islands. Looking at
her reflection made it easy for her to understand why that enchanting
stranger had been so captivated by her. Yet Jaclyn had learned early
in life that her looks could also pose the greatest threat to her true
happiness. That thought sent a chill down her spine and she quietly
went about her business, then slowly returned to the banquet room.

Negotiating the sea of round tables, Jaclyn zigzagged through
the immense dining room, scanning each marker in search of number
22. The dining room, decorated in a pale salmon and light green
paisley pattern that was repeated in the wall coverings, seat cushions
and carpeting, was spectacular. Suspended from the center of each
ceiling panel, large gold and crystal chandeliers cast a soft glow down
upon the guests. A peach satin tablecloth, fine china and brightly
polished silverware created a formal table setting, and in the center
was a beautiful bouquet of spring flowers. Just above the centerpieces
were the table numbers. Jaclyn finally spotted her table and made her
way toward it. Seated around the table for ten were four middle-aged
couples and a young man with an unoccupied seat beside him. The
gentlemen were all in classic black tuxedos except for one, whose
tails poured out the back of his chair. The women beside them were

all conservatively dressed in a variation of the basic black evening gown, which set off their abundance of jewels beautifully. Each of the women had blonde highlighted hair that had been teased into full curls. Jaclyn's auburn hair set her apart like a diamond among a sea of emeralds. The young man seated alone looked up at her as she approached. When she was clearly headed in his direction, he stood and held out his hand as she neared the empty seat.

He spoke softly and directly to her. "Tell me my prayers have been answered and that you are my dinner companion for this evening."

Jaclyn couldn't help but giggle at his comment, especially when she noticed how jealous the other ladies at the table appeared. She took his extended hand. "It appears that we are indeed dinner companions. I am Jaclyn Tate."

He continued to hold her hand as he spoke. "And I am the luckiest man in the room. Jaclyn, I am John Fitzgerald and it is an honor to meet you."

Jaclyn was flattered. "Thank you, John. The pleasure I assure you is mine."

Jaclyn could not help notice how the other couples had stopped their conversations and fixed their eyes on the two of them. Jaclyn turned her attention to them as she casually introduced herself and took her seat. Following a polite exchange of pleasantries, which were clearly more genuine coming from the men then their wives, the couples resumed their conversations. Jaclyn then turned her attention to John. He was about thirty-five, very charismatic and smooth, and certainly had a way with words. He was average looking, with a full face that contrasted with his slender build. His small, dark brown eyes were hidden behind wide black-rimmed glasses. His smile is what caught Jaclyn's attention. He had the nicest smile she had ever seen. As she made herself comfortable at the table, she turned to him. "So, John, what brings you to this gala?"

He looked pleased to tell her about himself. "I am a real estate broker with the Roger Staubach Company, as are several of my associates at this table. And you?"

"Same story, different company. I recently moved from New York to organize the Dallas office of Toner and Associates. It's been quite a work-intensive experience. In fact, this is the first real socializing I've done since I arrived."

John raised his wineglass and moved it toward hers as he made a toast. "May this mark the beginning of a much fuller social life." Jaclyn happily raised her glass to his.

Before long, the typical banquet meal of salad, roll, prime rib and baked new potatoes was served and, between courses, the guests made their way to the dance floor and moved to the sounds of the big band orchestra. John and Jaclyn danced and talked and laughed. She was having a very nice time. Toward the end of the evening, they were dancing a waltz. John held her closely and led her effortlessly with a firm hand against the small of her back. He moved them with grace and style. Jaclyn couldn't remember dancing with a better partner. He circled the entire dance floor several times and Jaclyn saw the ballroom swirl about her in a blur of color and sound as he led her from one turn to another. It was intoxicating. When she came to a breathless halt at the end of the song, John led her off the dance floor, his hand still on her back, gently guiding her. She was slightly dizzy and still smiling from the wonderful waltz when she saw the handsome stranger again. He was standing at the edge of the dance floor directly in front of her, staring at her once again. This time her eyes could not hold his, as she felt certain John would notice and follow her line of vision. She felt he had been too nice and too kind a dinner companion for her to reward him by staring into the eyes of another man. Especially considering how that man was looking at her. Instead, she glanced in his direction only long enough to catch his eye and smile. His eyes followed her intently until he could no longer see her through the crowd. He vowed then to find out who she was. And whenever he wanted something he always got it, no matter what it was.

It was shortly after the dance that Jaclyn decided it was time to go home. She had enjoyed a wonderful evening and met several real estate contacts who she felt certain she would have occasion to call upon as she grew her business. John was another story. He had been such a gentleman during the evening that she felt obligated to give him her telephone number when he asked for it. She knew she didn't want a romantic relationship with him, but having a friend and companion would be most welcome. As she stood to leave, he insisted on walking her out to the valet. They walked to the entrance and waited while her car was brought out to her. As her car was pulled up along side of them, she turned to say good-night to John and was surprised when he reached for her hand and kissed it gently. She smiled at him as she got into her new black 420 SEL Mercedes. Slowly, she pulled out of the hotel drive. He stood where she had left him until she turned onto the service road and he could no longer see her.

As she drove home, Jaclyn reflected on the evening. It had been so much fun to laugh and dance and just talk to people about things other than the deals she was working on or what had to be done at the office. She realized then how much she had needed this break. She also thought about that enchanting stranger. He had melted her with his eyes. Her body tingled at the thought of him. She wondered who he was and if she would ever see him again. He was the type of man that alarmed her, for she knew he would own her heart if he wanted it. She knew firsthand the pain of a broken heart and she never wanted to feel that anguish again.

CHAPTER 4
—◇—

Jaclyn spent the next month focusing on the buyers who had shown continued interest in the Tower while she continued to send out prospectuses to pique the interest of others. Despite her frequent phone calls, the Louisiana oilman put off making a decision on the property. Jaclyn's best possibility continued to be the mystery man from New York. And although the number of interested parties had dwindled, her hopes of selling the Tower were far from dead, as she truly believed that, like all things she put her mind to, she would succeed.

The breakthrough came nearly five months after he had initiated contact; the anonymous buyer was ready to meet. Early one morning a telegram arrived at Jaclyn's office stating simply,

```
        Meet   me   Monday,   10:05   a.m.,   DFW
Airport,
        American Airlines Flight 245 arriving
from LaGuardia.
        Coming in to do physical inspection
of Tower.
        JPM
        P.S. You will know me when you see
me.
```

Jaclyn reread the telegram. Even now that a meeting was

set, he only hinted at who he was. JPM… she repeated over and over, hoping to think of a clue to his identity. None came to mind. She dialed Carl to see if he might recognize the initials and help her unravel the mystery. Even though she had the number to his private line, she was usually unable to reach him on her first try. Luckily, this time he was at his desk and picked up the phone on the second ring. "Toner."

The sound of his voice brought a sense of calm and confidence to Jaclyn. She could picture Carl sitting tall in his high-back, black leather chair behind the massive black granite desk. Behind him a wall of windows overlooked the Hudson River and New Jersey. In front of him, pulled close to his desk, were two black leather swivel chairs and beyond them a cherry wood conference table on a shiny silver base with six matching black leather swivel chairs surrounding it. To the left, a tall cherry bookshelf held his treasured book collection and memorabilia he'd gathered on his travels around the world. One of her favorites was a replica of the Taj Mahal that Carl described simply as "one heck of a piece of real estate." To the right, a cherry credenza displayed the replica sailboat collection that was Carl's pride and joy. If you wanted to spend time with Carl, all you had to do was ask him about sailing. You were guaranteed at least an hour.

"Carl, hi, it's Jaclyn."

"Jaclyn, how are you? Listen, I just received the monthly numbers on the Dallas office. I knew you could make it happen, but in less than six months and in one of the toughest real estate markets, you're incredible."

It meant the world to her that he appreciated her business acumen, however that wasn't why she was calling and she hurried on to her purpose. "Thanks, Carl, we can discuss everything in detail on Friday during our weekly update. Right now I need your help to unravel a mystery."

Carl muffled a laugh. He had been tickled by Jaclyn's anonymous client, often wondering if someone were having a good laugh at her expense. He hoped for her sake that he was wrong. He tried to sound serious in his reply. "Sure, Jaclyn. How can I help?"

"The mystery buyer has made contact. I'm meeting him on Monday."

Surprised, Carl replied, "That's great. Who is he?"

"Well, that's the problem. He sent a telegram. All I know is he is coming from New York and he signed it JPM. Do you have any idea who he could be?"

Carl silently considered the initials… JPM… JPM… "Maybe it's J.P. Morgan." He couldn't contain his amusement at his own joke and he laughed as he spoke.

"Very funny, Carl. I guess you think his ghost is coming to meet me some seventy years after his death. I'm amused."

Carl could tell she really didn't find the humor in his remark so he changed course to a sober discussion. "On the other hand, it could be Joseph Phillip Mattes. He would certainly fit the bill. I read in the *Wall Street Journal* last week about his generous donation to the Met and to his alma mater, Fordham University. In fact, the article said he'd wanted his identity withheld and was appalled that his wish for anonymity hadn't been respected. Sounds like his M. O."

The thought was intriguing, but somehow, from what Jaclyn had read about Mattes over the last several years, it didn't seem like the right fit. It appeared to her that in the twilight of his life he was donating most of his money to his favorite charities, not adding to his real estate holdings. Although it certainly could be him, her gut told her it wasn't. "I guess we won't know for certain until Monday. If you think of anyone else, let me know and if I don't speak with you before then, I'll talk to you on Friday."

"I'll speak with you then, Jaclyn. Keep up the great work."

After the connection had been lost, Jaclyn paused, looking at the receiver. JPM…JPM… who could he be? Methodically she scanned the directory in her memory, trying to place the initials with a name. She didn't like surprises in business. There was no way to prepare for them and she didn't like being out of control of a deal. Those initials would torment her until Monday morning arrived.

***

Monday was a warm June day, with winds blowing steadily from the south. The enormous sky that sprawled out before her was a clear expanse of light blue. Jaclyn paused for a moment taking in the crisp morning air. As she looked about, she noted that there was not a cloud in sight. The sun was so bright that she had to shield her eyes when she walked out her front door and made her way through the gate and down the path to her car. With her mystery client arriving in an hour's time, she had difficulty controlling the great level of anxiety she felt and could hardly contain herself. Well before necessary, she left for the airport. Arriving half an hour early, she sat across from the arrival gate at a window seat in a small restaurant, drinking a cup of coffee while she perused the morning paper, but no article managed to hold her attention. She was totally distracted by the impending arrival of her buyer.

As she sat staring out at the many faces that passed, she suddenly realized she had been given no indication of what the man would be wearing or what he looked like. How would she recognize him? Panic momentarily set in. What if he expected her to know him and she didn't? It would embarrass her and insult him. In the middle of a mild anxiety attack, she began to laugh at herself. This whole thing was way out of hand. It would play itself out. She was shaking her head and laughing at herself when an announcement came over the PA. "Flight 245 has landed and will be arriving shortly at gate 23."

In great anticipation, Jaclyn hurriedly paid the cashier and walked to the arrival area, standing in direct line with the jet-bridge exit. Out of habit, she smoothed her suit jacket and picked imaginary lint from her sleeve. She had selected her royal blue Jimmy Gamba suit that wrapped snuggly around her waist and laid open at her neck to reveal the top of her cleavage. The matching fitted skirt hit her leg just above the knee. Black sling-back pumps and a black purse completed her fashionable look. Minimal jewelry added to the professional image she tried hard to create but was part of the feminine look she did not try to hide. As she saw a gate agent open the door to the jet-bridge, she put on her most welcoming smile and waited for the passengers to disembark.

The first passenger off the plane was a man of average height and weight, in his late fifties or early sixties, with salt and pepper hair cut conservatively above his collar, but left long and straight at the top. He was impeccably dressed in a double-breasted black tailored suit and a crisp white shirt. He completed his look with an understated beige and black paisley tie and a matching handkerchief that barely peeked out of his breast pocket. In his left hand was a slender burgundy leather briefcase and in his right, a brown distressed leather garment bag. His long stride insinuated pride and determination. He looked directly at Jaclyn and moved purposefully in her direction. The telegram had been correct. She did know him when she saw him, although she didn't know how since they had never met before. A broad smile came to her lips as she extended her hand to greet him. "Hello, I'm Jaclyn Tate."

Looking almost put out by her comment, he replied, "Well, of course you are. You would be surprised what I know about you, young lady, the least of which is what you look like."

Jaclyn was instantly offended although she wasn't certain why she should be. This man had obviously done more than just research the building. He had thoroughly investigated her as well. Then, it dawned on her that he must have liked what he'd discovered to be standing in front of her. She relaxed a bit before she replied. "Since you are here, I trust that your findings met with your approval."

Her comment endeared her to him. She was just what he had hoped she would be, tough and confident, but personable. That was his definition of a good businessperson. "Correct you are. Now I guess I should not keep you in suspense any longer. I am John Paul Morrison. I go by JP."

Jaclyn recognized the name immediately. "Morrison, as in the tobacco empire?" She did not like the way her question came across, but the words were out of her mouth before she could correct them.

He didn't skip a beat in his reply. "Precisely why I like to keep my identity a secret. It isn't easy being the benefactor to an industry that has gone from the epitome of class, to the worst carcinogen in history. I have never smoked and am not actively involved in the tobacco industry, actually never have been, but since my grandfather and father built the business and I inherited everything at my father's death, I am associated with it, much to my dislike."

Jaclyn could see his discomfiture was genuine. Sensing the need to change the direction of the conversation, Jaclyn took control. "Well, Mr. Morrison…"

He interrupted to correct her. "Please, call me JP."

"Very well, JP, I am very pleased to make your acquaintance and it is certainly my privilege to be working with you."

He was instantly put at ease and Jaclyn was reassured by the smile that slowly crept across his lips. They shook hands and Jaclyn led him toward the airport exit.

As they drove into Dallas they discussed the Tower in great detail. JP had come to do his physical inspection of the building. If all went well, and he expected it would, he planned to submit a contract on the property. Jaclyn let him lead the conversation. He was completely focused on business and never once delved into personal matters. That suited Jaclyn, who was eager to stay focused on her goal. As they neared downtown, she pointed out the huge structure to him. Jaclyn noted the pride swell in his chest as he imagined the building as his. They went directly to the Tower so JP could see it and get a feel for it. He expressed his desire to walk through the building, floor by floor, to get a sense of the culture and mood of the tenants and a feel for the environment. Although this was a far cry from the factual information he had requested during his due diligence, Jaclyn found his request intriguing.

As they walked toward the building, JP stopped to take in the fifty stories of glass that soared above him. He stood in that manner for several moments just staring at the structure while Jaclyn observed him. At JP's prompting, they slowly walked up to the front doors of the enormous building, where he again paused and reflected. Slowly, he opened the heavy glass doors and entered the lobby. He stood in the center of the rectangular space and took in long, deep breaths with his eyes closed. Jaclyn watched this ritual with much interest. A moment later, he opened his eyes, scanned the lobby area and then moved swiftly toward the elevators. Jaclyn followed on his heels in silence. They made several stops at what seemed to be random floors, but Jaclyn was certain this was part of his plan since he moved with extreme purpose and direction. On each floor he took time to chat casually with the receptionist, asking subtle but probing questions with such ease that he obtained more information from them than one could hope to uncover from a financial statement and an annual report. He learned which tenants were growing and in need of additional space as well as one that was downsizing and possibly going out of business. Overall, however, the mood of the tenants was positive and the building well maintained. Every person questioned about the office space, its comfort and facilities, was complimentary in reply. Jaclyn felt confident that this walk-through had met with his approval.

Three hours later they left the building. Jaclyn was eager to know what was JP's reaction. "Well, JP, what are your thoughts?"

He took a moment to reply. "I must say I'm impressed. It may have actually exceeded my expectations and that, my dear, is not easy to do."

Jaclyn smiled in response. "Then why don't we take a break and stop for lunch."

JP was quick to reply. "Actually, Jaclyn, I appreciate the offer, but I prefer to go to the hotel for an hour or so. I want to call my office in New York."

Jaclyn understood completely. "Very well. I have made arrangements for you to stay at the Mansion at Turtle Creek. I am confident you will find the accommodations to your liking. It is a very comfortable hotel and they have an excellent business center."

"Sounds perfect."

In a few minutes they were pulling in front of the Mansion. Before them unfolded an intimate hotel with a soft peach stucco exterior and Mexican tile roof that looked like an Old World Spanish estate. The property was nestled in a mass of oak trees and heavily landscaped with bushes and flowering plants. As they drove up the circular drive to the entrance, Jaclyn could tell by JP's expression that he was pleased. She left her car with the valet and accompanied JP into the hotel lobby. A few steps inside the entrance, JP paused at the entry table to study the massive fresh floral arrangement that covered the entire surface and stood almost six feet in height, towering above them.

"This is one magnificent arrangement." He held a tiger lily between his fingers and studied the bloom. "I have a large English garden. That's how I spend my free time, gardening. It's so relaxing and rewarding to look out at my garden and see all the beauty I've created."

For the first time he mentioned something about himself. It was clear to Jaclyn by the way he spoke that he had a true passion for the hobby. She admired anyone with any gardening acumen, as she had none. "I, unfortunately, do not have a green thumb."

JP turned abruptly toward her and brusquely commented, "Nonsense. You just haven't honed your skills." Jaclyn smiled at his strong opinion. He continued, "I'll let you in on a secret. You have to love what you're doing, and this doesn't just apply to gardening. If you put your heart and soul into something, whatever it is, it will flourish." He paused for a moment, then turned and walked purposefully toward the reception desk. Jaclyn shook her head as she watched him. He is certainly a complex man, she thought to herself.

                    ***

At exactly the time agreed to, Jaclyn was at the Mansion once again. JP was walking into the lobby when she arrived. Under his direction they immediately left the hotel and drove the area surrounding the Tower to assess vacancies in nearby buildings, rental rates, vacant lots and zoning ordinances. It was several hours of walking and talking to various people, gathering and analyzing data and both Jaclyn and JP were exhausted by the time they returned to the Mansion later that evening. As they pulled up to the front drive of the hotel, JP said, "Jaclyn, thank you for being so patient with all of my requests today." She nodded and smiled at him as he continued. "Your patience is going to be rewarded. I am ready to tender an offer."

Jaclyn was thrilled. Although she knew their findings had surpassed JP's expectations, until that moment, she had been unable to read him clearly enough to know whether he had reached a firm decision. Now that he announced he was ready to write an offer, she was elated. "Terrific, JP. Shall we go inside to prepare the offer, or would you prefer to go to my office?"

He was quick to speak. "No need to go to your office. I am very comfortable working here."

His decision suited her. "Of course. Let me leave the car with the valet and we can go inside."

JP waited by the curb while she left the keys with the valet. As soon as she joined him, they walked inside together and found a quiet table in the corner of the lounge. JP put his briefcase on his lap, opened it and pulled out a thick manila file marked "Tower Deal." He then closed his attaché case and placed it on the floor beside him. He laid the file on the table and opened it, revealing the contents to Jaclyn. "I have prepared an offer based on the details I had prior to my trip. Considering what I learned today, I am even more comfortable with my proposal." Jaclyn leaned in to get a better line of vision. She was anxious to see the deal points. She nodded, showing her understanding, and JP continued. "I am prepared to offer $145 million in cash." He paused to read Jaclyn's reaction, but she had a good poker face and revealed nothing. "When I say cash, I mean no banks or financing. I am able to close in 30 days."

This time Jaclyn chose to speak, as it was obvious to her that JP was looking for a positive response. "The cash will make your offer extremely clean and very attractive. And 90% of the listing price is extremely fair."

With a serious expression punctuating his words, he said, "There are conditions. A few, but I am very firm where they're concerned. I want clean structural and mechanical inspections and five years of guaranteed leases at the current occupancy and rental rates."

Jaclyn replied, "I wouldn't be concerned about the conditions. I believe your offer is solid. The cash makes it attractive, clean inspections are standard, so the only item that may meet with any objection is the guarantee on leases. However, if I recall, many of the tenants are under long-term leases that would extend beyond your five-year period. Barring bankruptcies and other unforeseen circumstances, we may be talking about only a few exceptions. We'll present the contract with the conditions you have indicated and see how the seller responds."

JP was pleased with her analysis. "Good. I want you to present the offer first thing in the morning."

His quick time frame surprised Jaclyn, although she did not think it presented any problems or conflicts for her. She quickly glanced at her daily planner before agreeing. "Tomorrow should not be a problem. I will call the listing agent and request a 9 a.m. meeting."

JP took a moment to note a further condition to his offer. "Before you call, I want to point out that I have added a 24-hour reply clause. When I make an offer, I want an answer in short order. I don't want to be strung along while a seller uses time to test my patience or to keep me on the hook while he weighs other offers against mine."

Jaclyn had worked with imposed reply deadlines before, but never one so short. "That should not present any problem, JP. I'll advise the agent on presentation so he is clear about the timing afforded the seller for a response."

JP added, "I learned a long time ago that you have to put a

time line on everything or you get nothing accomplished. The seller will know we are serious and ready and that's additional incentive for him to strongly consider my offer. I don't like to waste time."

Jaclyn took out her mobile phone, checked her directory for the listing agent's number and dialed. Although it was nearly 10 p.m., no time was too late to call a broker to announce a contract about to be submitted on a property. That unwritten law among real estate professionals was never questioned. The stakes on a deal this big were worth disturbance at any time. Jaclyn held the line. To her disappointment, the call was answered by an after-hours service, but when she explained to the operator that she was an agent calling to present an offer, her call was immediately transferred. Within moments of being put on hold, the line rang again. JP watched her intently. Finally there was a response. "Al Harris, may I help you?"

"Hello, Al. This is Jaclyn Tate with Toner and Associates. I'm calling to advise you that I have a contract to present on Thanksgiving Tower."

Al sat back hard against the cushion of his chair. He was blindsided. He had heard that a woman had called his office a few times recently asking for facts on the Tower, but he hadn't anticipated that the interest would turn into an offer. Realizing he was delaying his response, he cleared his throat and replied, "That's good news."

Because of the lengthy pause and his curt reply, Jaclyn assumed she had called at an inopportune time, so she immediately got down to business. "I thought you would be pleased. I would like to come to your office at 9 tomorrow morning. Will that work with your schedule?"

It was all happening so fast that Al had a difficult time thinking clearly. "Of course. Anything else will just have to wait."

She jumped at his agreement to meet. "Excellent. I will see you at your office tomorrow morning at 9 a.m. Have a good evening."

JP understood from listening to her side of the brief conversation that Jaclyn and the agent had agreed to meet as requested. He felt satisfied to have come this far so quickly and was now anxious to get the paperwork in the seller's hands. When Jaclyn hung up, she turned to JP and smiled. "Alright, JP. We're on our way. I'll have the contract in Mr. Harris's hands first thing in the morning."

Jaclyn could see the anticipation in JP's eyes. "Please call me as soon as you are through with your meeting. I want to hear what he thinks of our offer."

Jaclyn nodded as JP began packing his briefcase. As he organized his portfolio, he spoke, "Jaclyn, I must say that I'm very happy with the progress we made today. Tomorrow will be pivotal. Once the offer is tendered and in the hands of the seller, we are that much closer to the achievement of our goal and that feels good."

Jaclyn agreed and, knowing that the offer was as solid as it was, she felt confident the deal was well on its way. "My feelings exactly, JP, and with the 24-hour reply deadline, we can expect to know their answer shortly."

The seller was obligated to let them know by the day after tomorrow. That was all the patience JP would extend. This suited Jaclyn just fine. Her nerves certainly appreciated the short wait.

JP finished collecting his belongings from the table and stood. Jaclyn stood alongside him. Recognizing that he was ready to leave, she courteously asked if he wished to have a drink or something to eat, however, he declined the offer and promptly retired for the night. Jaclyn was somewhat relieved. Although she wanted to get to know JP better and learn more about this mysterious man, she too was consumed by their full day and graciously accepted his decision. Things had moved along so quickly. It had been a mentally exhausting day, but a very productive one. As she drove herself home, she felt a sudden adrenaline rush. She was in possession of an offer on Thanksgiving Tower. It didn't get much better than this.

***

Al Harris nervously ruffled through his business cards, taking all of two minutes to find Steven Cason's home number. Anxiously he dialed and waited for him to answer. He pleaded with the phone, begging Steven to pick up, but there was no answer, just ring after ring. Al's leg fidgeted nervously, rocking side to side at a frantic pace. Running a trembling hand through his hair, he mumbled to himself, "How do I reach him? Think! Think!" Then Mindy, assistant to Cason's secretary Diana, came to mind. He had casually dated her a year or so ago, if that's what you call having sex a few times. Where had he put her number? He hadn't been certain he wanted to keep it after she got upset when he told her it had been fun, but...He searched through his daytimer...Oh, here it was. Maybe it was too late to call her, but hell, there was too much at stake here to worry about the time. He would pitch it to her that she could score points with her boss if she helped him reach Cason tonight. Luckily, Mindy picked up on the second ring, her voice groggy and deep. Al guessed she was in bed and probably not alone. He chose to disregard the obvious.

"Mindy. It's Al Harris." He spit out his words rapidly so she would not hang up on him. "I'm going to make this quick Mindy. I need your help to reach Cason tonight."

In a deep and drowsy voice, she attempted a coherent reply. "What? Al, ... why are you calling me?" She glanced at her clock as she spoke, her annoyance escalating. "Do you know what time it is?" Her impatience with the disruption was clear in her tone.

Al kept calm but made certain the seriousness of his call was distinct. "Listen, Mindy. I'm sorry to bother you but I need to reach Cason tonight. This is very important. I tried his home number and got no answer. Do you know how to reach him or can you reach Diana at home? I have very important information for him..."

Before he could finish, Mindy rattled off Diana's home number and the line abruptly went dead. Al's fingers fumbled the numbers the first time, and then he slowed the pace and got through on his second try. Diana answered the phone in her usual upbeat and professional voice. "Good," he thought to himself, "it wasn't too late to call." He actually wasn't surprised that she was home and his call wasn't interrupting anything. In sharp contrast to Diana, Mindy was a blonde doll with a body to lose sleep over. He figured there weren't many nights he could call her that she would be home alone. Diana, on the other hand, was a nice girl with a pretty face, but she dressed like an old lady and looked like the fitness craze had missed her entirely. Al couldn't understand that about a young person. He spent every free minute he had at the gym. Calming his voice, he asked, "Diana?"

"Yes?" she asked in return, not recognizing his voice.

"Hi, Diana. It's Al Harris." At the sound of his name, her body instantly responded. She thought back to a year before when she had first seen him and hoped he would notice her. He was tall with a great build, deep olive complexion and dark wavy hair that fell somewhat haphazardly. She remembered those dark brown eyes that narrowed and tilted as he gave that sexy half smile. She was getting warm at the thought of him. But back then he chose Mindy to hit on for casual sex. Men, she certainly would never truly understand them. She could have offered him so much more, but she had to admit that she was considerably more woman a year ago than she was today. She had transformed herself over the last several months into quite the looker, as Steven often told her. Maybe Al would react differently on their next meeting. This was certainly interesting that he was calling her. "Al Harris, well, it must be a year since I've seen hide or hair of you. Where have you been hiding?"

Though Al was pleased that she was being so nice, he didn't have time for small talk. He did his best to keep it short and sweet. "Well, Diana, I've been very busy, especially representing Thanksgiving Tower. In fact, that brings me to why I called. I need to have a word with Cason tonight. It's an important matter that needs his immediate attention."

After five years as his personal assistant, Diana knew Steven's business style well. "Timing," he would say, "was equally important to location, location, location." If Al needed to reach Steven tonight, especially at this hour, it was because of timing. Even though she knew the importance of helping him reach Steven, she wasn't going to let this opportunity to speak with Al pass her by. "Well, Al, I can't say I'm not disappointed that business is the only reason for your call, but I understand. I will get a hold of Steven and pass along the message that he needs to call you urgently. Give me your number so he can return your call."

Al purposely ignored her come on, gave Diana his number and agreed to stay glued to the phone. Immediately after they hung up, she called Steven on his private line. Only three people in Cason's universe had that number and he hadn't expected to hear from any of them tonight, so he anxiously picked up before the second ring.

Diana didn't wait for him to say hello. "Steven?"

Sensing the seriousness in her voice, he gave her his full and undivided attention. "Yes, Diana, what is it?"

She got directly to the point of her call. "Al Harris called and said it was urgent that he speak with you tonight. I have a number for you to reach him."

Steven sat back hard against the rear seat of the limousine. As he listened to Diana, he had unconsciously moved away from the woman seated beside him and loosened his bow tie. A sense of urgency rushed through his veins. Al Harris, Thanksgiving Tower. Something was happening and before he anticipated. He was going to own the Tower, but when he was ready. He was holding out to get the seller ready for his offer. Make him wait. Sweat it out. And when he thought all hope of selling was lost, he would settle on a lower offer and Cason would be that much richer. Making deals was an art to Cason and he was the ultimate artist. Something was interfering with his plan; Harris's phone call told him that. Without wasting a moment's time, he made note of Harris's number, thanked Diana for her call, and then dialed. Al seemed to pick up before it even rang.

Anxiously, he said, "Hello."

Steven jumped in, "Al, it's Cason. What's happening?"

"Oh, am I glad to hear your voice. I've been trying to reach you..."

Steven cut him short. "Yes, Diana told me. Well, what is it?"

Al blurted it out as if he would burst. "I'm getting a contract on the Tower tomorrow morning at 9."

Steven's blood raged. His temperature and temper rose. Who would cross him? Everyone in his circle of influence knew the Tower was his deal. That meant every player in Dallas knew it was off-limits. Steven spoke through pursed lips. "A contract from whom?"

Al heard the anger in Steven's voice. "I don't know the buyer, and the agent is someone I've never heard of before, from Toner and Associates."

Steven's mind raced. "I know Toner and Associates, out of New York. Is he from out of town?"

"It's a she and she will be at my office tomorrow morning at 9."

"Shit." Steven's mind went in ten different directions. He hadn't prepared his formal offer, but he could do so before 9. He needed to be the first to the table, but with another contract coming in, his position was severely weakened. Damn it. In his plan, this was going to be as easy as taking candy from a baby. Now it wouldn't be as sweet a deal, but he would still get it. Of that much he was certain.

Al sat quietly waiting for Steven to say something . . . anything. Finally Cason broke the silence, choosing his words carefully as he spoke. "Al, let's meet at your office at 7. I'll have my contract in first. Some of the blanks may not be filled in until you know the details of the other offer, but you'll have my paperwork in first. You will present my offer to the seller accordingly. We'll work out the details when I see you in the morning. See you at 7."

The line went dead at Steven's last word. Al hung up the phone, noting the severe shaking in his hand. He sat back in his chair and breathed a sigh of relief. He did as he had been told and alerted Cason the minute he knew a contract was coming in. He thought back to the lunch he had had with Steven a year before when Steven had invited him to his office to discuss the building Al had just listed. Although it had only been a week since the property was put on the market, Steven made it exceedingly clear that he was going to buy the building, but on his time and under his terms. No one was going to come in the way of his deal. He gave Al explicit instructions to advise him immediately of anything newsworthy on the building and in the end, when the Tower was his, Cason would make certain Al was a happy man. No sum of money was discussed, but Al knew from Cason's reputation that he could reap some hefty benefits. Al felt that he was now officially in the player's circle. The rewards potentially great, the stakes high, but so was the heat. On this sleepless night, he would question yet again whether he had what it took to be a player in this game.

Steven slipped the phone into his breast pocket and sank deep into his seat. He hated to be caught off guard. A brush against his side reminded him that he was not alone. Damn it. Caroline. She was sitting there beside him completely upright, as if she had a stiff board attached to her back. Her arms were crossed severely at her waist and her lips were closed tightly into a thin, taut line. Her short designer dress clung to her bony body, making her look sickeningly skinny. Cason shook his head thinking about women who believed you could never be too thin or too rich, which in Caroline's case was wrong on both counts. She sat with her head held high and her attitude clear. She looked thoroughly put out by the interruption his business call had caused. From the moment the phone rang, he had completely forgotten her and the conversation she was forcing. In fact, he quickly pondered what she might have heard. Not good, he thought to himself, but hopefully she was smart enough to forget the conversation she was privy to. Without consulting her, he called ahead to his driver. "Change of plan, Carlos. Take us to Ms. Hunter's home."

Carlos always did as he was told without question. Politely, he replied. "Of course, Mr. Cason."

Caroline questioned Steven with her eyes, but he did not look at her. Instead, he fixed his stare out the window, avoiding her entirely. His mind and attention were a few miles away, at Thanksgiving Tower. She had had enough of his lack of concern for what she wanted. But he did not see the anger in her eyes. They rode the rest of the way in silence. As if trying to understand him, Caroline studied this man before her. Steven was the epitome of power and manliness. He had the looks of an Adonis: tall, muscular, ruggedly handsome and extremely virile. There was something about his eyes that drove ladies wild; she had seen their effect on many a willing young woman. For her, however, it was his power and wealth that drew her to him, though she admitted that his looks were a nice bonus. She had been most pleased with herself that she was able to maneuver her way into becoming his social companion, but she had to make certain that was not all he thought of her. Until now, however, he had rarely asked her to fill any other role in his life. Yet, having learned well from her mother, she believed that as long as she was the one he was with socially, that was all that really mattered. His money would make up for the rest. She would just have to work on the way he treated her in private. He might be able to dismiss her tonight, but she would see that things progressed between them and soon. She would not wait long to move on to the next phase of her plan, to become Mrs. Steven Cason.

CHAPTER 5
—◇—

Jaclyn moved about the cottage in a light and happy manner. Her deal was steps closer to becoming a reality and the realization gave her a great sense of accomplishment. Things were starting to go her way. New York seemed like another lifetime ago. As she sat down in her rocker recliner, she picked up a letter she had just received from her mother and began reading. As she had anticipated, it had been difficult for her to be so far away from her parents, but their frequent phone conversations and periodic correspondence made the distance more bearable. As she read her mother's letter, she felt pangs of remorse for having moved so far from them. Her parents had been so supportive and encouraged the move, but she could see that it was still a difficult adjustment for each of them. Her mother frequently expressed her fears about Jaclyn's ex-fiancé. In her mother's mind, Jaclyn's move to Dallas didn't remove her from the risk of Andrew's irrational behavior. For Jaclyn, her fears were lessening since she had not heard a word from Andrew in the many months she had been away. It seemed unlikely that he would show up in her home uninvited and unwanted as he had done in New York. She shook her head as if to rid herself of thoughts of him, but they stayed and played on in her mind . . .

Andrew Thorton was an established real estate attorney in New York. Jaclyn met Andrew across the table during a negotiation; she represented the buyer and he the seller. Their meetings were centered on intense business arbitration and no personal interaction came into play. Finally, following numerous heated proceedings, their clients reached an agreement. It was on the evening of the closing, that Andrew stepped outside of his adversarial role and invited Jaclyn out for a drink to celebrate. Relieved to have the details worked out, she agreed, thinking it would be strictly a business celebration. What she had not anticipated was Andrew's romantic interest in her. But by the end of the night, he made his attraction to her exceedingly clear. Although Jaclyn had some reservations about him, she agreed to go out with him again and again and before long, they were dating. In time, she grew to love Andrew. He became the man with whom she planned to build her future. He was tall and blonde with a trim athletic build. His sparkling blue eyes and warm smile drew her to him. He had the qualities she wanted in a man. He was attractive, ambitious and extremely successful. They also shared a passion for real estate deals and implicitly understood each other's work and dedication to their careers. All that added up to a comfortable and satisfying relationship. Maybe it didn't have the fireworks, but she didn't dwell on that. Andrew had been good to her and she anticipated he would make a good husband. For the last several months of their relationship, she had been planning their lives together, but then suddenly and without warning, her dreams were shattered. Tonight she remembered vividly, as she had so many times since, how it all fell apart.

It was within weeks of his 40th birthday that Jaclyn realized she had begun to see Andrew much less frequently. He was full of excuses why they could not get together more often, and initially, Jaclyn accepted every one of them. Then she insisted they meet to talk, not so much about their lack of time together, but more about the way things felt. She couldn't put her finger on it, but their relationship had begun to change dramatically. Andrew tried to avoid the meeting by reassuring her that the case on which he was assigned was a killer, needing his full and undivided attention and that was why he hadn't had more time for her. She knew how hard he worked so she was appeased for a while, but then a nagging, sinking feeling she couldn't quite understand began to gnaw at her until she could ignore it no longer. On the fourth week of having seen Andrew only once and briefly, she planned to surprise him at his apartment and make dinner. She learned from his secretary that he was in town and not scheduled to have any late meetings for that evening. Excited to spend time with him, she wore his favorite outfit, a short, tight navy wrap dress, and pampered herself so that she looked exceptionally beautiful. By 8 o'clock that evening, everything was ready; the dinner was perfect, the lighting dim and romantic and she looked fabulous. She waited patiently, but slightly apprehensively, for him to come home. Finally, she heard him at the doorway and positioned herself away from the entry, but close enough to see him enter. She recalled how she had felt, like a child at Christmas waiting to open a present. Her eyes were fixed on the door and she was ready to fly into his arms and tell him about her surprise dinner. As he came through the door, he was laughing and Jaclyn suddenly saw that he was not alone. He was with a young woman who was pulling at his tie as they came through the entry. Jaclyn wasn't certain if it was the mixed smell of food and scented candles or whether he just sensed her presence, but with a jerk of his head, Andrew looked around the room and saw her standing nervously before him. Their eyes met and panic washed over his face. In disbelief, Jaclyn stood waiting for him to say something, to explain the obvious to her, but only a heavy silence filled the room. The young woman accompanying him stood stiffly by his side. Slowly she looked up at Andrew with big, scared eyes. Jaclyn stood perfectly still as she watched them. After what seemed an interminable pause, Andrew broke the awkward silence. "Stacy," he spoke softly, "go on to the bedroom." His words echoed in Jaclyn's head. Unwillingly, the young woman loosened her grip on his arm, looked into his face with sad, confused eyes and left the room. Jaclyn felt as if she were in a slow-motion film as she watched the woman move apprehensively into the next room.

The scene before her played in her head like a bad dream. She was numb with confusion and shock. Andrew moved cautiously toward her, took her gently by the arm and guided her to the sofa. She walked slowly and clumsily as if she had forgotten how to command her legs. As they sat down, he began to speak. It was a blur, but she recalled him telling her something like, "I was just having some fun . . . she means nothing to me . . . I love you . . . everything is going to be fine between us . . .nothing has changed . . . in fact, I was going to tell Stacy . . . " Hearing the other woman's name used so familiarly made it more real and Jaclyn thought her heart would break in half right then and there. At that moment, she knew it was over between them. That's why his words felt so heavy on her heart. He thought she would get over it. He would come to learn she could not.

Jaclyn left Andrew's apartment in a fog. She vowed never to see him again. The days that followed were filled with grief and regret for what they had had and could have had. She would not take Andrew's calls and did not return his messages. At first, he decided she needed time and left her alone, but each day that passed made him more and more impatient. The less she allowed him in, the more he wanted her. He even showed up at her office and told her that she was being childish over this silly thing and that he would make everything right between them. But Jaclyn was a tower of strength and resolve, and although she had loved him, she would not take him back. He had done the unthinkable, had destroyed her trust in him and she could never forgive him for it.

That same night, Andrew went to her apartment after drinking heavily at his favorite jazz club and, using the key he still had, let himself in. Jaclyn had not yet come home from work. She had buried herself in her business as a way to deal with her sense of loss. As she approached her apartment, she was feeling exhausted and grateful to be home. What she didn't know was what was just beyond the door. Andrew waited patiently in the dark. Finally he heard her put her key into the lock and moved silently into the dining room, away from her line of sight. His heart pounded in his chest. He had to make it right between them and tonight was the night. He promised himself that he would not leave until she came around to see things his way.

Jaclyn juggled her briefcase, purse, newspaper and keys as she unlocked the front door and walked inside. Totally exhausted, she dropped everything onto the antique table in the entry and walked into the kitchen. Tonight she would settle on a frozen dinner from her favorite Italian restaurant. She preheated the oven, then went into the living room to turn on the television set. As she walked into the dark room, she removed her suit jacket and unbuttoned her shirt. She switched on the TV and a feature news story began. Interested, she watched as she continued to undress. Garbed only in her undergarments, she turned toward her bedroom to put on a robe, when suddenly, out of the corner of her eye, she saw the flickering image of a man reflected on the glass doors of the china cabinet. Trying to conceal her fear, she pulled her clothes to her chest and walked briskly out of the room. Sensing her apprehension, Andrew quickly moved into the kitchen to cut off her path. Jaclyn heard him coming toward her. She quickened her pace. They met in the hallway. Jaclyn's heart nearly stopped. Then she realized it was Andrew, and she became blinded with anger. She snapped at him. "Andrew, what on earth are you doing here? You nearly gave me a heart attack!"

He did not reply but instead pulled her toward him. The alcohol on his breath sickened her. The anger raging inside her was evident by the severe tone of her voice. "Andrew, let go of me. How dare you break into my apartment?" Jaclyn pulled away from him and crossed her arms about her body. She was determined to make him leave.

He leaned against the doorjamb across from her and smiled. He was trying to lighten the mood, but it only enraged her more. Her eyes flashed angrily at him.

He tried to remain calm and unfazed by her animosity. "Jaclyn, …I don't understand the hostility."

She laughed loudly. "You don't understand the hostility? Come on, Andrew, it's me you're talking to, not Stacy."

The words cut through him like a knife. He hung his head and looked down at the floor. "I guess I deserve that, but it still isn't easy to take." He tried to look into her eyes, but she avoided his gaze. "I came here to make things right between us, Jaclyn. You know we had a great thing. I can't just walk away from us."

Jaclyn's posture remained unchanged. "How dare you come here talking about what a great thing we had when you're the one who had the affair?"

Andrew reached out his hand, pleading with her to let him touch her, but she turned away. His voice softened as he spoke again. "Listen to me, Jaclyn. I told you that night and I'll say it again. She meant nothing to me. It was just a little harmless fun."

Jaclyn could no longer contain her disgust. "Harmless? Harmless to whom? I don't think it was harmless, or fun for that matter, at all. In fact, it hurt me a lot. But I can only guess that I wasn't on your mind when you decided to have your harmless fun." She paused only long enough to make the point stick, then she continued, "Now, I want you to leave."

Andrew had come with a purpose, to make everything better between them and he had no intention of leaving until he had accomplished it. He pleaded his case… "I will admit I made a mistake, a small indiscretion, but you're blowing everything out of proportion. We can get over this and regain what we had. What's it going to take for you to realize that I'm not going to give up? We will be together again. I promised myself that I would make everything better between us and I have every intention of fulfilling that vow."

Hearing his words appalled her. How could he stand before her trivializing what he had done and pledging to make things better between them? She turned away from him and walked toward the front door. She placed her hand on the knob and began opening the door, but her actions only made him more determined. He slammed his fist against the door, forcing it shut, and with his free arm pulled her toward him. Professing his love for her, he began kissing her neck and caressing her bare back. She squirmed away from him in disgust. Growing more and more furious by her response, he took her in his arms and pushed her down to the floor, straddling her torso. She struggled beneath his weight but could do nothing to free herself. Angrily, she reached up and punched his arms, trying desperately to get out of his grip. In response, he forced her forearms under his legs, pinning her arms beneath him. Trapped, she felt helpless, fear and anger filling her head. Tears silently streamed down her face and began to fill her ears. She tried to scream but Andrew muted her sounds with his mouth. He hurriedly unbuttoned his pants and awkwardly removed his clothes while atop her. Jaclyn could not believe what he was doing and pleaded with him to stop, but it was as if he didn't hear her. When he was naked before her, he tugged at her panties while he explained to her that he would show her how much he loved her. Unable to stop him, she lay still beneath him as he forcefully entered her unwilling body. Tears flowed continuously from her swollen eyes as she lay limp beneath his crushing weight. The more she struggled, the worse it hurt, so she lay there, helpless, numb and in disbelief. Andrew was like a wild animal. His eyes were glazed over and his movements fierce. He pumped inside her insistently until his body jerked in fulfillment and he fell lifelessly upon her body. He was satisfied with himself for showing her the depth of his love.

Jaclyn was utterly sickened. She felt violated, used and dirty. He had taken an act that had once been a beautiful part of their relationship and made it ugly. Finally, his grip loosened and she was able to work her way out from under him. He rolled to one side to let her up and watched as she walked slowly and stiffly down the hall. Her mind struggling to absorb what had just taken place. Her back was sore from the weight of Andrew's body crushing her against the hardwood floor. Her body ached all over. In the bathroom, she turned on the hot water in the shower and stood beneath the warm flow. Her thoughts were scattered and she cried out of anger and pain. Minutes later, Andrew followed her into the shower and stood behind her, tenderly rubbing her back and shoulders, caressing the red blotches that covered her shoulder blades and lower back. Her body tensed at his touch. She shrugged his hands off of her, but he persisted. He took her in his arms and pleaded with her to forgive him and set the date for their wedding. "Jaclyn, can't you see what you mean to me? We are great together. You know that and I know that. I can see now that what I did hurt you terribly. I'm sorry for that. I truly never meant to hurt you. I can't explain why it happened. All I can do now is ask for your forgiveness and promise it will never happen again." When she remained silent, he added, "Why can't you let me in?"

Jaclyn was unmoved by his words. She had already come to terms with the end of their relationship. Now he had invaded her intimately and she felt only anger and contempt for him. It was difficult for her to keep her composure. "You're amazing Andrew. You have excused yourself for your behavior and made me out to be the bad guy in all of this. Now you come into my home and do this to me. When will you be through hurting me? I want you to leave." She wanted to say so much more, but out of fear she tried to maintain a calm exterior.

"Jaclyn, I don't know what possessed me to do what I just did. I guess I'm just desperate to show you how much you mean to me." He tried to turn her to face him, but she would not budge. She stepped out of the shower and wrapped herself in a terry robe. He followed her and continued to try to persuade her, but she would not listen to his pleading. An hour later, exhausted and frustrated, he agreed to leave. Jaclyn hoped he understood that there was no going back for her. But there was something in his eyes as he was saying good-bye that haunted her for many nights to come. Although she was now miles away from him and many months had passed since that night, in the back of her mind, she still feared Andrew was not through with her. It was a very unsettling feeling and she wondered if she would ever truly be at peace again.

CHAPTER 6
—◇—

When Jaclyn's alarm sounded, the normally intrusive buzzer was a welcome respite from a restless night's sleep. Thoughts of Andrew had plagued her dreams, turning them into nightmares. On a day when she had desperately wanted to have had a good night's sleep, she felt fatigued rather than rested. Damn Andrew. Today was too important to ruin with thoughts of him. In a few hours she would present the offer on Thanksgiving Tower. Nothing was going to get her down. She lay in bed focusing on the Tower and rehearsed the presentation. She concentrated her attention on all the good things that were happening in her life. Soon her mood lifted and she relegated thoughts of Andrew to the recesses of her mind. In anticipation of the day ahead, she bounded out of bed and began to get ready for her meeting with Al Harris.

***

Steven pushed himself away from the desk at his home office and stretched his tired back muscles. He had spent a sleepless night planning his contract offering and thinking about the Tower. It would be the crown jewel in Cason's investment portfolio. Cason Tower, now that sounded good. Nothing satisfied him like his deals. Casey was a close second, but only late at night when she came alive in his bed. Too bad the rest of the time she was too young and too naïve to fit into his social scene. That's where Caroline came in. She was the right type of woman to be on his arm, socially connected, educated at Yale, daughter of an old-money player and attractive by social standards, not his. To him, she was a trophy and he used her only for his public affairs. He was certain she was using him too, probably to appease her father, and that suited him fine. He got what he wanted and he suspected she did as well. Beyond his public engagements, he couldn't stand the time he spent with her. She was plastic and shallow. Luckily for him, she never asked to end their evenings privately. It never dawned on him that she didn't want him, instead he assumed she was as frigid as her mother was rumored to be. Just as well for him, he had Casey to fill those needs. Oh Casey, he could not even think her name without having an erection. Casey and Caroline, the perfect pair. If only they could be combined into one woman. Crazy, he thought. That perfect woman doesn't exist.

Just before 7 o'clock, Steven pulled his Mercedes sports car into the rear parking lot of Al's office. He entered the building through the back door and wound his way through the maze of empty hallways until he came to Al's office. He found Al sitting at his desk shuffling through a stack of papers. Al looked up the moment Steven appeared in the doorway. Quickly, Al rose from his chair and made his way around the desk, his nervousness obvious. A weak man, Steven thought to himself, hopefully not too weak.

"Good morning Steven. Here have a seat." Al pulled out the chair across from him, then moved back around the desk. He waited for Steven to sit before he sat and waited again for Steven to speak before he spoke. Sad puppy, Steven thought, but fear and respect were essential for Al to perform as Steven needed him to, so maybe it was for the best. Steven pulled his chair closer to the desk, leaning his elbows against the edge of the shiny wood surface, and peering into Al's nervous face, he began his detailed instructions. "Harris, listen carefully, this is how we will work this deal. I have detailed my offer in this contract." Steven reached into his portfolio and retrieved the paperwork he had completed. He showed the document to Al as he spoke. "I have purposely left a few key items blank until we know the conditions of the other offer." Al remained silent but nodded at Steven's words. "I trust you're still comfortable completing the contract following the presentation of the other offer." Al nodded again. "Good, then let's review the deal points as they are to be presented."

The two men read through the document for the next hour. Steven wanted to ensure that Al was exceedingly clear on how to proceed. He would leave nothing to chance. Then he left Al's office with a cushion of time between his departure and the scheduled arrival of the other agent. He also wanted to be out of Al's office before his staff arrived for the day. Steven was a very public figure and his presence caused a stir wherever he went, especially where ladies were concerned. He didn't want anyone remembering he had been at Al's office this morning. Quietly, he made his way down the hall. No one was around. He was relieved. Thinking ahead to his morning schedule, he opened the rear door swiftly, and suddenly came face-to-face with Al's assistant Samantha. Shit… was all that came to Steven's mind. Samantha put on her broadest smile, tossed her long, dark curls back from her face, shifted her shoulders back and pointed her chest out at Steven as she greeted him. "Mr. Cason. What a nice surprise to run into you like this." She was oozing with southern charm and sex appeal. Her strong perfume made Steven momentarily nauseated. When Steven did not reply, she continued, "I didn't know you had a meeting scheduled with Mr. Harris this morning." Steven distanced himself from her and moved outside, holding the door open for her as she entered the building. He responded to her greeting with only a nod and continued on his way. Rarely did he stop to acknowledge a young, admiring girl; he had learned long ago that even the slightest bit of attention was enough to make her think that he was interested in her. He was not altogether comfortable with the way he was forced to behave. It was his nature to be friendly and open to relationships, but a man in his position had to be guarded. Early on in his successful career he was enlightened to the ways of leeches. It took a few hard blows for him to learn to be cautious and wary. Since then, he had become suspect of people who tried to get close to him until he fully understood their motivation. The life he had chosen had determined to a great degree what relationships he could have. A man with as much power and wealth had to choose carefully the people he let into his inner circle, but it was a price Steven was willing to pay. As he drove out of the parking lot, he focused on the day ahead. He didn't give Samantha a second thought.

***

Promptly at 8:45, Jaclyn arrived at Al's office. As she entered the lobby, the old and shabby building surprised her. The furniture in the waiting area was unmatched and visibly worn. The reception area was created by using two sides of two different color cubicles but appeared functional. Marks on the wall spoke to the length of time since the office had been painted and the dingy carpet was frayed and worn. It struck Jaclyn as odd that in the world of real estate, where image was everything, an agency would have such a poorly maintained office. She was suddenly puzzled at how Harris had landed the Thanksgiving Tower listing. It seemed rather curious. It was then that Jaclyn realized the receptionist was watching her, so she made her way to the desk and introduced herself. "Good morning. I'm Jaclyn Tate. I have a 9 o'clock appointment with Mr. Harris."

The woman smiled at her. "Thank you, Ms. Tate. Please take a seat and I will let Mr. Harris know you are waiting." Jaclyn returned her smile, then walked over to the two chairs against the far wall that functioned as a waiting area. The young woman waited for her to be seated before she rang through to Al's office to announce her arrival. Jaclyn watched her as she nodded several times in silent understanding, then hung up the receiver. She looked over at Jaclyn as she spoke. "Mr. Harris is on a conference call and will be with you in ten to fifteen minutes. While you wait, would you like some coffee?"

"No, thank you." Jaclyn replied. She didn't mind waiting as long as there was activity around her. Jaclyn was an avid people watcher. Lobbies and waiting rooms made for great entertainment, so Jaclyn made herself comfortable and began observing the activity around her as the office came alive for the day.

First there was the young man whose sole purpose for entering the lobby was apparently to say hello to the receptionist. Jaclyn was amused by his young and underdeveloped courting skills. Nonetheless, he was sweet. The receptionist clearly did not share her assessment of this young man. She promptly ignored him, busying herself with straightening stacks of messages in employee mailboxes, obviously in an effort to avoid him altogether. He walked away down one hall, visibly dejected. As he departed, a young attractive woman with long dark curls and wearing a tight, short black dress and spike high heels came rushing into the lobby from the back hall. Oblivious to Jaclyn's presence, she rattled on about her run-in with Steven Cason earlier that morning. She recounted how he had been walking out the back door at 8 that morning and had held the door for her. The women went on about him and how gorgeous he was and expressed some of their innermost desires about him before the receptionist's attention reverted to the phones and the young woman bounced back into the office area from whence she came. Jaclyn was amused by their excitement. It was as if this guy Cason were some kind of god.

Shortly thereafter the receptionist indicated that Jaclyn was to proceed to Mr. Harris's office. She gave Jaclyn rapid-fire directions to find her way through the office maze, then pointed toward the hallway as if giving her permission to proceed. Jaclyn gathered her briefcase and found her way to Al's office. When she arrived at his secretary's desk, she recognized the woman who had been talking to the receptionist moments earlier. This time, she was peering into her compact and powdering her nose. She quickly put her makeup away and sat up straight as she saw Jaclyn turn the corner and move purposefully toward her. She rose to greet Mr. Harris's guest. "You must be Ms. Tate. I am Samantha, Mr. Harris's personal assistant."

Jaclyn shook her hand in greeting. "Samantha, it's a pleasure to meet you. Is Mr. Harris ready to meet?"

Before Samantha could answer, Al appeared in the doorway of his office. Jaclyn was taken aback. He was very good-looking and very young. Somehow Jaclyn had pictured him as middle-aged, with a potbelly and a bald head. Why she had this image of him, she wasn't certain, only that she would have expected the man representing the Tower owner to have more…experience, that's what it was. The agency also looked so old and worn that she imagined the man who ran it had been there from the day he opened the doors for business, twenty or thirty years earlier. The athletic and attractive man before her was not who she expected to be meeting with this morning.

Al was having similar thoughts about Jaclyn. Under different circumstances, he would have definitely liked to get to know her better. He led her into his office with a wave of his hand and studied her from head to toe as she stepped in front of him. "Very nice," he said under his breath.

As Jaclyn took a seat, they exchanged business cards and made brief introductions. Jaclyn could not contain her curiosity and asked Al how he had won the opportunity to list the Tower. Al obliged her request and answered rather concisely, "My father and the seller go back many years. In fact, they were best friends in high school. Football buddies, you know. Anyway, this is the first property I am handling for him and I am very eager to make it the first of many."

Jaclyn was not surprised to hear the reasoning behind his listing of the Tower. It answered a myriad of questions she had had since the moment she entered his office. She had also come to learn that there was a strong internal network alive and well in the Dallas Metroplex. Even more so than New York, it was all about who you know and how connected you are. Breaking into this circle was a rather formidable challenge, but she was determined to find a way. Now she was eager to get down to business and moved the conversation along quickly. "Very well then, let's get right to the contract. I'm certain that the seller will be very pleased when you present him this offer. I trust you will find it extremely fair." As she spoke, she handed Al the contract.

He took his copy and laid it out in front of him. He listened intently to her as she began her presentation of the offer and animatedly elaborated on every point. Al was impressed. The contract was equitable and well presented. He felt certain that the seller would accept the offer and conditions… would have accepted, he corrected himself. He waited until she had completed discussing each term and condition before speaking. Choosing his words carefully he said, "Congratulations, Ms. Tate. This is a good offer. I appreciate the fair proposal and your hard work." Then, without warning, the tone of the meeting changed dramatically. Something in the way he nervously began tapping his pen on the desk and moving his chair from side to side gave Jaclyn an uneasy feeling. When he began to explain, she understood clearly the reason for his anxiety. "As I said, the offer is solid, extremely presentable. However, it is my duty to advise you that yours will not be the first offer presented on this property."

Jaclyn's mind raced. What was he talking about? A few days ago when she had checked with Al's office, she had been told that no contract had been presented on the building since its listing. How could this have happened? Was it plausible that for the longest time, no activity had taken place, then in a few days time, two contracts hit? Possible, she decided, but not probable.

Al paused, watching her grapple with her thoughts, before continuing. "In fact, I was advised of the other offer only yesterday. It was the first offer received and so will be presented accordingly."

Jaclyn was having a hard time believing in the coincidence of the contracts being submitted within such a short period of time. Regardless, she reminded herself, it was an obstacle that she would have to surmount. She gestured toward the pile of papers before her. "How does this offer compare?"

Al sat back in his chair. He could not offer her too much information. He needed to come up with a way to make it clear that she would have to accept second place. "Well, Jaclyn, it is solid, as I have already said, but that is inconsequential at this point. It is our policy to have the seller review the first contract presented and respond to it before even considering any secondary offer."

Al seemed pleased with himself and his position, but Jaclyn did not like what she was hearing. "That may be so, but you represent the seller and I am certain you would advise him whether to accept the contract or hold out for a better offer." Jaclyn knew she was treading on ethical ground, but she chose her words carefully to avoid any taint of impropriety.

He smiled at her in an attempt to keep the conversation light. "Of course. My loyalty is certainly to the seller; however, it is purely up to him to decide what to do with the offer I present today. As soon as he has refused the first contract – if that happens - I will submit yours for review. Please keep that in mind regarding your 24-hour reply stipulation; the clock will not start ticking on that clause until then. I will advise you as soon as I know when, or should I say, if, your offer will be presented." With his last word, he rose from the chair, putting an end to the discussion. He was not accustomed to acting this way and his body was responding with excessive sweating. He was grateful his suit jacket was concealing the bands of sweat forming on his shirt. He didn't know how long he could keep up this tough guy act, so he wanted her to leave and now.

Jaclyn's bubble was burst. She had gotten by on little sleep but her excitement about presenting the offer had invigorated her. Now she hit a low. Like air exploding from a popped balloon, her energy had instantly dissipated. She hurt as if Al had physically punched her in the stomach, and her head felt fuzzy and light. She stood as Al came around his desk to show her out. In almost a whisper, she acknowledged what he had explained to her and thanked him for his time, then walked out of his office and down the hallway. Al saw the change in her and even felt slightly sorry for her, but he had work to do and quickly turned his thoughts toward Cason and finishing the contract for submission. Things were progressing as planned. Cason would be pleased with the deal points. Al made certain Jaclyn had left the building before he returned to his office. He shut his door, sat at his desk, pulled the phone close, and dialed Cason's private number.

"Cason." His deep voice bellowed through the phone.

"It's Al."

"How did it go?" Steven was all business as usual.

Al stated the obvious. "I have the other offer."

Cason was short on patience. "Well, how does it look?"

Sensing his anticipation, Al hurriedly raced through the deal points. "The contract offers $145 million in cash but requires guarantees on leases for a period of five years and clean mechanical and structural inspections. Besides the cash offer, the amount and stipulations are well within the parameters we discussed."

Cason sat back hard in his chair. "Al, did you say cash . . . cold hard cash . . . money up front . . . greenbacks?"

Al had to reply, even though he feared his reaction. "Yes. Cash. No financing. Closing in 30 days as long as all inspections and further due diligence are clean."

Cason sat silently running numbers through his head. He had to one-up the deal to make it attractive to the seller and to ensure he would accept the deal right away. He could not risk the seller rejecting his offer, which would obligate Al to present the second contract. Al waited patiently for him to say something.

After what seemed an endless pause, Cason finally spoke. "Okay, Al. These are the deal points. $150 million, financed through limited partnership. Clean inspections as usual, but no lease guarantees. Closing in 90 days." Cason hoped that that would be enough. Matching the cash offer was impossible. There was no way he could raise that amount of cash in such a short time. "Fill in the blanks as we discussed and present the deal. I want to hear from you the moment you leave the seller. And, Al, make note of everything, even his facial expressions as he reads each part of the deal. I want to know what the sticking points are in advance so I can react accordingly."

Al made frantic scribbles and sounded short of breath as he replied. "Got it. I'll call you as soon as I leave Thompson's office."

Sensing Al's nervousness, Cason sought to help him regain his confidence and control. "You can do this, Al. I know you won't let me down."

Al was still searching for the right words to reassure Cason's faith when the line went silent. Immediately, he hung up and began filling in the blanks in Cason's contract. He didn't stop for a moment until it was complete and ready to go. He had already scheduled a 2 o'clock appointment with the seller, Milton Thompson, and now he had just enough time to get over to his office.

***

Milton Thompson, a second-generation multimillionaire, had obtained his wealth by expanding his father's holding company threefold. His father had taken a modest inheritance and used it to buy controlling interest in a small West Texas bank, First Southwest. Not long after Milton took over the business, he built the bank into a sizeable financial institution and bought out the remaining interests of outside investors. That led to other bank purchases. He then began using his financial holdings to flip real estate deals for his personal benefit. He also acquired substantial assets through defaulting mortgagors. Through his real estate transactions, he became a formidable player in Texas and the Southwest. One property that had recently come into the bank's holdings was Thanksgiving Tower, a prize piece of Dallas real estate. Built by Henry Hunter as a monument to himself, the glass, chrome and marble tower was a testament to his wealth and power. To those in real estate's upper echelon, it was more than brick and mortar, but to a banker, it was all about return on investment. Although the building was profitable, it was not Milton's philosophy to hold onto real estate. Instead, he preferred to lend against it with the anticipation that, as in this case, the mortgagor goes down and the property becomes his. Milton was pleased that an offer was coming in on the Tower in a declining real estate market. The sooner he turned this large property into cash, the better. He had often been told he was born lucky; he figured the sentiment was correct. No matter what Milton worked on, he made money, lots and lots of money.

Right on schedule, Al pulled up his BMW to the front of Thompson's ten-story, marble and glass office building, just on the outskirts of downtown. The structure reeked of success. There was marble and chrome throughout the lobby, leather furniture in small seating areas around a gray granite reception desk. Between the receptionist and the elevators, a modern art sculpture challenged visitors' imagination; whatever it represented, the piece was, no doubt, expensive. Al was given a guest badge and escorted to the tenth floor by a security guard. Thompson's secretary met Al at the elevator and led him toward Mr. Thompson's corner office suite. She showed him through two heavy glass doors and into a glass-enclosed conference room that looked out over part of downtown. One of the glass walls was shared by Thompson's office and Al could see him at his desk on the phone. Al took a seat and as he waited, watched Thompson intently. That, he thought, is what success looks like. He knew that closing the deal with Cason would be a major step to getting there. Then he could upgrade his image and his office and draw more big deals. This is just what he needed, to be known as the agent who sold Thanksgiving Tower. Then others would want him to represent their properties. Al sat back in the chair, shoulders pulled back and chest held out proudly. He suddenly felt extremely good about himself.

Moments later, Milton entered the room. Al stood quickly. As the two men exchanged greetings, Harry, Milton's CFO, and Mike, his real estate attorney, also walked in. "Harry, Mike, come on in. Meet Al Harris. He's Bill's boy."

Al shook hands with both of them. Following on their heels was Milton's secretary who carried a tray of refreshments. As they sat down, each man helped himself to a cup of coffee and a few cookies.

Milton quickly moved the meeting along, "Al, I believe we are ready for you to present the offer."

Al pulled a stack of documents from his briefcase and handed out copies of the contract. "Gentlemen, I am pleased to present you an offer for the Tower. I trust you will find it extremely fair and that it will meet with your approval." He paused for effect. "First, I wish to call your attention to the buyer, SC Investors. I anticipate that each of you is familiar with Steven Cason, the principal of SC Investors." Al hesitated as he gauged their agreement. They each nodded and Al continued. "Then, with your permission, I'll dispense with Mr. Cason's impressive biography which includes a multitude of successful joint ventures."

"Yes Al, you can skip the biography," Milton said impatiently. "We are all very familiar with Cason. Please continue."

"Of course. I imagine you are more interested in the terms, so please turn to the first page and note the offer amount. $150 million." Al paused for emphasis. "Cason will arrange the limited partnership under SC Investors and expects to close in 90 days. The stipulations include only clean mechanical and structural inspections. I think it is worth mentioning that he does not ask for lease guarantees or rebates." Al stopped speaking long enough for the others to consider the offer.

Mike was the first to speak. "What guarantee do we have that he will organize the partnership? You did not mention any escrow to bind the offer."

Al took a moment to formulate his thoughts. "I imagine Mr. Cason is accustomed to letting his reputation speak for itself. After all, he always does what he says he is going to do."

It was at this point that Milton spoke up. "Thank you for bringing this to us today, Al. I feel we have the details we need to make a decision on this offer, but I am not inclined to respond immediately. I will consider it, but I won't reply at this time."

Al had fully anticipated a reply for Steven today. He knew that's what Steven would expect. He needed to try to get an answer. "But, Milton, I believe you will agree, this is a very solid offer. It's close to 95% of your asking price and the conditions are negligible."

Milton chuckled at his impatience. He attributed it to Al's youth and lack of negotiating experience. "I agree, but I have advisors for a reason. I want to hear their thoughts before I reach a decision. I am not aware of any urgency in replying, are you?" Milton looked to Al, who shook his head. Milton then continued, "Very well then son, please inform Steven that we thank him for his offer and we will reply to him shortly."

Before seeing Al out, Milton conferred with the men seated beside him. "Gentlemen, do you have any reason to believe we cannot reply to the offer by, let's say, tomorrow afternoon." The men shook their heads. "Alright, then, it's agreed. Al, be back here tomorrow after lunch. Make it one o'clock. We'll have a response for you at that time."

Al wanted to plead his case for a quicker reply, but Milton was not giving him any room. He had already risen from the table and was walking toward the door. At the threshold, he turned and said, "Al, I will see you out."

Al promptly rose, gathered his belongings and bid a quick farewell to the men seated around the table. As he approached, Milton stepped outside the room and held the door open for him. Al followed closely behind. Milton turned toward him and put a fatherly arm around his shoulders. "Good work, my boy. Your father will be proud. I put a lot of faith in you by giving you this listing. I am pleased that it was not misplaced."

Al gave a nervous smile. "Thank you, sir."

At that, Milton slapped Al's shoulder, turned away from Al and headed back to his office. As Al waited for the elevator, he formulated his thoughts and rehearsed his discussion with Cason. Cason had instructed him to take detailed notes of everything discussed, especially points of contention, but Al had jotted down only a few words in their brief meeting. Things had moved so quickly and although no counteroffer had been alluded to, Milton made it clear he wanted time to think about the reply. Al knew Cason would want to know more, but all he could do was tell him what had transpired and hope it would be enough.

As soon as Al returned to his office, he dialed Cason's private line. To Al's surprise, he did not answer. He had understood that Cason would wait for his call. In the next half-hour, Al tried to reach him again and then again, but there was still no answer. Al figured he had had a change in plans or couldn't wait any longer and had left his office. That's when Al decided to go out to grab a bite to eat before trying him again. Al had been gone only ten minutes when his direct office line rang insistently. Annoyed, Cason sat listening to the rings. He had certainly expected to hear from Al by now. He rang through to Diana's desk to ask if Al had called on the main office line while he was away from his desk, but Diana confirmed that he had not. Cason then tried Al's mobile phone but could not get through. He did not like when things didn't go as planned. He could only wait a short time, and then he had to leave to attend a dinner meeting. Al had better call before it was time for him to leave.

***

Seated in a dimly lit corner of the county courthouse, Jaclyn sifted through endless property records, each identifying the owner of a parcel of land. Finally she came upon the history on the Tower. She scanned the file to find the information she needed...built five years earlier by Henry Hunter...sold after only a few years to the last owner on record, Mark Mettleton Holdings. That made sense. She remembered reading about the well-publicized bankruptcy of Mettleton. She surmised that his assets had either been taken back in foreclosure or were being sold to pay off creditors. Jaclyn wrote down all the details, including the name of the bank holding the mortgage and the office numbers for Mettleton, then returned to her office. Her first call was to Mettleton's office, but the number she had was no longer in service, nor did Information have any listing for a company under that name. She then called First Southwest, the bank holding the mortgage. The switchboard operator transferred her call to the commercial lending department. A very helpful young man answered the phone. "Cesar Hernandez, Loan Consultant, may I help you?"

"Hello Cesar, my name is Jaclyn Tate and I am calling you regarding Thanksgiving Tower. Would you be able to help me?"

"Certainly, Ms. Tate. How can I be of assistance?"

"I understand that the Tower has been taken back by the bank in a foreclosure, and that you are actively marketing it. Can you tell me who is handling the sale?"

"Yes, Mr. Milton Thompson, CEO and owner of the bank, handles the sale of large properties personally. You can speak to him to discuss the Tower. Would you like his direct fax and phone numbers."

Jaclyn was thrilled to have come this far with only one phone call. The young man eagerly provided her with the contact information for Thompson and felt satisfied with himself. As their call ended, he thought he should let someone know that he might have just helped the bank sell Thanksgiving Tower. That would certainly be worth a raise or at minimum, a bonus. Darn, he should have written down her name; who did she say she was? Oh well, it didn't matter, he would figure out how to parlay that phone call into some type of recognition. It wasn't coming to him just yet how he would do that, but he expected he would think of something.

Jaclyn knew instinctively that unless she informed the seller of JP's offer, he might never have the opportunity to see it. At first, she was tempted to call and speak with him directly, but after considering the perceived unethical circumstances, she decided to keep herself one step removed and notify him anonymously. She composed a one-page letter that advised Mr. Thompson of a second offer on Thanksgiving Tower and indicated that the other contract was in Al Harris's possession. It was signed, "an interested party." Jaclyn used the fax machine at the public library to send the letter. She waited eagerly until she received confirmation of its transmission. Once her mission was accomplished and Thompson's fax was sent, she immediately left the library and went directly to the Mansion. She had called JP following her meeting with Al and explained to him that she had presented the offer as instructed, but experienced an unforeseen hiccup in the deal. She explained that she needed to do a little research before she could advise him of exactly what had transpired and what they would need to do to remedy the situation. It had taken her most of the day to complete the investigation and send Thompson the note. Now, as she approached the Mansion, she considered what she would say to JP so he wouldn't walk away from the deal. She had to convince him to stay and fight.

***

Milton was gathering his daily planner and switching off his desk lamp when his personal fax machine began to hum into activity. He finished collecting his things, then passed the fax machine on his way out. He glanced at the paper as it was leaving the printer. His first thought was to wait to read the fax till morning, but then the style in which it was written intrigued him. It looked like a telegram, and he noted, there was no sender identified. Interested, he picked it up and read it aloud.

> *Dear Mr. Thompson:*
> *Please be advised that there are two offers on Thanksgiving Tower. One was presented to you today, the other remains in Mr. Harris's custody. I am certain he advised you of this fact, however, I believe it is in your best interest to review both offers before reaching a decision on either.*
> *Respectfully yours,*
> *An Interested Party.*

"How odd," Milton said to himself. "If this were true, why hadn't Al told me about the other contract?" Rereading the fax, he moved around to the front of his desk, sat down, opened his Rolodex and dialed Al's number. Al was returning to his office when he heard the phone ringing. He missed the last ring by only a few seconds. He assumed it had been Cason, whom he was planning to call right back.

Figuring Al had left his office for the day, Milton decided to try to call Al again in the morning before their scheduled meeting. He was keenly interested in learning whether there was in fact another offer. He could only hope it were true. That would be great news. There was nothing better than being in the driver's seat on a deal, and having two offers to work would guarantee him a good outcome on the sale of Thanksgiving Tower. Milton couldn't help but feel that it had been another lucky day.

With a sense of urgency, Al dialed Cason's private line. Steven was in his office pacing. The past two days had been full of surprises - just what he hated in business. As he reached the furthest point from his desk, the phone rang. The sound jarred him from his thoughts and he jogged over. Slightly out of breath, he answered, "Cason."

Al greeted him as usual. "It's Al."

Steven snapped at him. "Where the hell have you been? What happened today?"

Al took a deep breath before beginning. Steven was not an easy man to work with. He had less patience than anyone Al had ever come across. Referring to his sketchy notes, he began a synopsis of the meeting he had had with Milton and his advisors. Steven listened intently, stopping Al only to ask for clarification or additional explanation. Otherwise, he listened and made a few notes while he thought about how to manipulate their reactions into a better deal for himself. When Al was done, Steven asked for more, but Al explained that the meeting had been short and to the point and had left him with little opportunity to learn anything further. Steven was not satisfied. "I don't understand, Al. Are you certain you pushed the offer as hard as you could?"

Al wanted to appease Steven, but he was at a loss. "I tried, believe me, I did everything I could think of. I requested a reply to the offer, but Milton insisted on discussing it with his advisors. He did say he would have a reply for you tomorrow at 1 o'clock."

Steven did not like being made to wait. He wasn't accustomed to it. Then he remembered another concern. "Does the seller know about the other offer?"

Al held his chest out proudly as he spoke, "Let's put it this way, he didn't ask if there were any other offers and I didn't volunteer the information. As far as he knows, yours is the only one in on the property."

Steven sat back, pleased. "Good. Let's keep it that way. That it for now?"

"All I have."

"Alright, then call me tomorrow right after your 1 o'clock. And let me know if anything happens before then."

Once again, on his last word, Steven hung up. These days Al was unsure about a number of things, but he was clear about one, when Cason was finished with you, he hung up, no good-byes, no thank-yous, nothing, just the sound of a disconnected line.

***

Jaclyn sat across the table from JP and placed her briefcase on the chair between them. She adjusted a decorative flower arrangement that obstructed her full view of JP, then began to tell him about her day. He was eager to hear what had taken place and, pulling his chair closer, gave her his full attention. "I went to Al Harris's office this morning as planned and presented the contract to him." JP sat patiently, nodding to indicate his understanding and encourage her to get to the details that mattered. She continued, "He seemed very pleased with our offer and the terms and conditions didn't appear to create any major issues. Then, the meeting took the most unexpected turn." JP unconsciously moved to the edge of his seat and leaned his elbows against the table. "When I had completed my review of your offer, Al informed me he had another offer on the Tower that he would present to the seller first." JP shook his head in disbelief. His immediate reaction was anger, but she had anticipated that so she continued before he could collect his thoughts enough to speak. "I was, as you can imagine, surprised by this news since I checked personally with Harris's office just before you arrived in town and no offer had been submitted since the listing. That's an entire year without any activity and then, within a matter of days, two contracts hit. I don't know about you, but I am not one who believes much in coincidence, do you?"

JP followed her line of thought easily. For the first time since she began her explanation, he spoke. "I am of course disappointed, but like you, I don't like the way this smells. What happened next and why didn't you let me know earlier what had taken place?" His calm reply and open attitude relieved Jaclyn.

She elaborated, "I asked Al to advise the seller that he had two offers. His response was that it was his policy to present only one contract at a time and to have the seller respond to and work through one deal before presenting another. I reminded him that he works for the seller and that it was his responsibility to advise him of another offer. He assured me that he was well aware of whom he worked for and that he would do what was best for the seller, however, he was not willing to discuss my suggestion to present both offers. Then he ended our meeting rather abruptly." JP shook his head. He did not like what he was hearing. Jaclyn read his thoughts and continued explaining so he would be fully aware of what she had done. "When I left Al's office, I wasn't through. I went to do some research. I figured the only way to be certain the seller knew about both offers was to tell him myself." For the first time since she began speaking, JP smiled. He liked her style. Jaclyn was pleased by his reaction. "I went directly to the county courthouse and checked the ownership records on the property and traced it to Mettleton Holdings. I also noted which bank picked up the mortgage because I recalled reading about Mettleton's very public bankruptcy eighteen months ago." Jaclyn paused to allow JP time to digest all the information she had given him.

He was pleased with her work and knew they needed to take immediate action. "Okay, Jaclyn, good job. We need to contact Mettleton right away."

"Exactly what I thought," she said contentedly. "I have already done so."

Surprised, JP replied, "You have? Tell me. How? When?"

"My first attempt was to reach Mettleton, but the numbers I got from the courthouse records were no good. I checked with directory assistance but they had no listing under his name or the name of his holding company. Guessing that the bankruptcy took him out, I contacted the bank on record and learned from a young man in the commercial lending department that the bank had indeed taken the Tower back on a foreclosure. He also informed me that Milton Thompson, CEO and sole shareholder of the bank, handles the sale of large real estate holdings personally."

JP spoke before Jaclyn could continue. He was eager to tell her what a fine job she had done. "Jaclyn, this is excellent. Have you already contacted Thompson?"

From his obvious excitement, Jaclyn knew he would be pleased. "Well, let's put it this way, I am confident he is now aware there are two offers. Although I knew it would put him in the driver's seat and certainly in a position to negotiate, I felt it was our only chance to get our contract in front of him."

"Excellent work, Jaclyn. I don't think we had any choice but to advise Thompson if we wanted to get our offer on the table. If Harris was smart, he told the seller about our offer, even if he suggested that he counter the first offer before considering ours. If Harris wasn't that smart, I'm certain he has heard from the seller already or will hear from him soon. If I had to guess, I would say that Harris is on the take on the first offer." Jaclyn raised her eyebrows at JP's insinuation. He saw her reaction and added, "Come on, Jaclyn, look at the timing. You yourself questioned the probability of two offers coming in the same week. How does that happen on a property that has been on the market a year with no activity?" He paused to let Jaclyn think it through.

She sadly looked into his eyes. "I know, JP. It crossed my mind too that something underhanded had taken place. I just don't understand how people can be so unethical. I know business is business, but I can't fathom how people live with themselves when they step all over each other to get ahead."

JP sympathized with her sentiment. "I hear you. But I have learned that in business, ethics are often overlooked." He paused for a solemn moment, then continued, "In fact, they are overlooked most of the time."

Jaclyn thought about what he had said and had to agree with him. "I love the challenge and the rewards of this business, but it is a trade with high stakes. I guess when so much is on the line, people will do just about anything to come out ahead. Whenever I think I have seen it all, something else like this happens. I fear it will never change."

JP added, "Unfortunately, it's not just the real estate sector.

Take the industry I was born into. Should cigarettes be outlawed? Probably. Certainly it would save a lot of lives. But it isn't going to happen and we all know why. It's money, lots of it and it's lining the pockets of some highly influential and extremely powerful individuals. For that simple reason, it will continue. Sad but true. Money truly is the root of all evil. I think we have had a taste of that today."

Jaclyn looked up at JP and smiled. "I think my contact with Thompson will even the score a little. Tomorrow may prove to be a good day for our side."

JP lifted his wineglass in a silent toast to Jaclyn and her efforts. He peered into her eyes for a long time, saying nothing, just grinning at her. She had truly impressed him today.

CHAPTER 7
— ◇ —

Al was in his office with his secretary when a call came through on his personal line. He promptly adjourned his meeting with Samantha before answering the phone. She took the dismissal seriously and rushed out of the room, her long, dark curls bouncing freely as she moved. As soon as the door closed behind her, he lifted the receiver.

"This is Al."

"Good morning, Al. This is Milton."

Al relaxed. He leaned back in his chair and sighed with relief. He assumed Milton was calling to confirm their meeting. "Milton, good morning. Are we still on schedule for 1 o'clock?"

Milton noted Al's casual demeanor. "Yes, Al, but that's not why I'm calling. I understand that you have a second offer on the Tower. Is that correct?"

Al sat up abruptly, his mind racing in ten directions. How could Milton know about the other offer? Anxious not to hesitate too long, he responded, but this time his voice was strained. The change in his tone was obvious to Milton. "Well . . . Milton, . . . actually, yes, we received a second offer after the first contract was submitted, however…"

Milton was furious. He didn't hear anything after Al acknowledged that a second offer had come in. He shot back, "Why wasn't I informed of the other offer, Al? Or did you have a momentary lapse of memory and forget who you work for?" The words were said sharply and with distinct purpose. Al fidgeted in his chair as he grasped for the words to make his reasoning sound logical, but he couldn't think quickly enough and Milton was not giving him any room to remedy his error in judgement. "Al, I suggest you arrive at my office at 1 o'clock today, as planned, with the other contract in hand. I will see you then." The line went dead. Al sat anxiously at his desk, thinking about what to do. He was falling into a bad pattern. Powerful men calling him, barking out orders, and then hanging up on him. It was becoming unnerving, and he wasn't fairing well at all. Then his mind turned to Cason. What would he tell him? What should he do next? He sat at his desk for what seemed like a few moments, but an hour had passed before he had the guts to call him. Slowly, he dialed the number to Cason's private line and listened apprehensively to the rings, hopeful that he would not answer. When he heard Cason pick up, he could hardly find his voice.

"Cason." By his tone, Al knew he was extremely busy.

Al's spoke in slightly more than a whisper. He was a man who knew he was about to feel the wrath of Cason and he was anticipating the anger. "Cason, it's Al."

Steven was quick to respond. "Al, is this urgent? I have someone in my office."

Al wanted to tell him that it wasn't important, but he knew it was. Cason needed to know now. Putting off the inevitable would only prolong the agony. Al found his resolve as he responded. "It is important and I think it's worth a few minutes of your time."

Steven's voice turned serious. "Has something come up on the Tower?"

Al replied meekly. "Yes."

"Alright Al. Hold while I wrap up. I'll be with you in a minute."

Al listened to the music on the line for what seemed like an eternity. He hated being in limbo. His mind filled with unsettling thoughts…Would Cason blame him? . . . What would he ask him to do? He was breaking out in a sweat when Cason was suddenly on the line again.

In a hurry, Steven said, "Alright, Al, tell me what's up, but make it quick. I have ten things on my plate as it is."

Al didn't know any other way to say what needed to be said than to spit it out. He didn't try to soften the blow. He shut his eyes as he spoke. "Milton Thompson knows there is another contract…"

Steven lost control of his temper. "What?! How?!" He raised his voice to a muffled yell that sent Al to the edge of his seat.

Al knew he needed to explain, but what could he tell him? "I'm not certain…What I mean is I don't know how, but he knows about the other contract."

Steven was blind with anger. This useless man, what had he done? Steven wanted answers and now. He tried to control his temper as he spoke, but it was forced and Al knew it. "Al, explain. How did you find out that Milton knows there's another contract?"

Al took a deep breath and tried to relax enough to speak coherently. "Milton called me this morning. I thought he wanted to confirm our 1 o'clock meeting, but he was quick to tell me that was not the purpose of his call. Point-blank, he asked whether there was another offer on the building. I couldn't believe he was asking, so I knew he already knew and just wanted to see what I would tell him. I acknowledged the other offer and tried to explain that it was second to yours, but he cut me off to remind me that I work for him and ordered me to bring him the other contract at 1 o'clock."

Al took a breath and Steven jumped in at the pause. "How did he find out, Al?"

"I…I don't know…"

Al fumbled over his reply and Steven rephrased the question. "Al, have you told anyone about the deal?"

Al shot back a quick reply. "No one."

Steven followed with rapid questions and Al tried to reply in a similar fashion. "Who in your office knows about the other contract?"

"No one."

"Did you leave any paperwork around for someone to see?"

"I didn't have anything laying around. All paperwork relating to the sale is in my safe."

"Are you certain you didn't say something in your meeting to tip off Milton? He's a sharp guy. Think back."

"Believe me, I never mentioned another offer, contract, buyer or anything."

Steven sat back thoroughly frustrated. "Well Al, if no one but the two of us knew about the other offer and I sure in hell didn't tell him, then who did?"

Al felt like a defendant being cross-examined by a hostile

prosecuting attorney. "I don't know how he knows. I haven't told anyone. Samantha assisted me in the preparation of your contract, but she did not see the other one. It has been in my safe since right after I reviewed it with you."

Steven let his anger flow. "Shit. How did he find out?! This certainly throws a fucking wrench in the deal. My offer is sweeter, but their terms are super clean. If Milton's in any rush, their cash deal will win. Shit." He wracked his brain, trying desperately to think of a way to turn what had happened to his favor. Nothing came to mind immediately, but he had so much else to think about and he was very short on time. "Listen, Al," he barked. " I need time to think this through. Call me at noon on my mobile and we'll talk some more. In the meantime, find out everything you can and let me remind you that this is my deal and no one is going to screw it up for me, least of all you. Figure out how you are going to make this right. I don't accept people slipping up, not when so much is on the line. Someone knows something and that is not good. Find out who."

The line went silent. Al engaged the do-not-disturb feature on his phone and sat back hard in his chair. His hands were shaking and he was damp from sweat. As he tried to calm himself he reflected on the recent series of events and agonized over how Thompson could have learned about the other contract. Steven's words played over and over in his mind. How was he to find out what had transpired? What was he supposed to be, some kind of investigator or something? And he didn't like being threatened. He wasn't certain how he got himself into this mess, but he knew he had better start planning a way out of it and soon.

***

Jaclyn wasn't satisfied with only informing Thompson of a second offer. She was eager to learn about the first contract and who was behind it. Racking her brain, she tried to think of a way to get the information she needed. Suddenly it came to her. She would call Al's secretary. Samantha would have access to the paperwork and Jaclyn was certain she could maneuver easily around her young and inexperienced mind. She placed a call to Al's office. Jaclyn waited while the receptionist transferred her call.

"Al Harris's office, Samantha speaking. How may I help you?"

Jaclyn put on her most sincere southern accent to disguise her voice. "Samantha, hello, this is Marilu from Mr. Thompson's office."

Samantha immediately recognized Mr. Thompson's name from her work on the Thanksgiving Tower contract. She knew this was an important call. She replied in her most professional voice. "Yes, Marilu, how may I help you?"

Jaclyn tried hard to keep her accent flawless. "Well, you see, Mr. Thompson isn't clear who the buyer is on the Tower contract. Could you be a dear and give me that information off your copy?"

The request struck Samantha as odd, but she didn't want to offend Mr. Thompson by not obliging. She thought about checking with Al before giving out the information, but he had asked not to be disturbed, so Samantha took it upon herself to get her copy of the contract out of the file. She came back on the line. "Marilu?"

Jaclyn was eager to hear what she had to say. "Yes?"

Samantha held the contract in front of her and scanned down the front page, looking for the buyer's information. "I have the contract in front of me and the buyer is listed as SC Investors in Houston."

Jaclyn wanted to be certain she heard the letters clearly, so she asked, "S, Sam, C, Charlie?"

"Yes, ma'am."

Jaclyn probed for more information. "And who signed the contract for SC Investors?"

Samantha was turning to the last page to give Jaclyn the information she requested, when Al came out of his office. He began speaking to Samantha without noticing that she was on the phone. Quickly, she asked Marilu to hold and turned her attention to Al. "I'm sorry, Al. I was on the phone with Mr. Thompson's office. Did you need me right away?"

Al was puzzled. His voice rose as he spoke. "Why didn't you put the call through to me?"

She was confused. "You told me you didn't want to be disturbed."

Al was incredulous. "Yes, but this is different. If a buyer or a seller calls, especially when we are in the middle of contract negotiations, always let me know they are on the line." He pointed to her phone. "Well, who is it?"

Samantha sat up straight as she told Al. She was, after all, proud of herself for handling this call. "Marilu."

Al looked dumbfounded. He had met several of Milton's assistants, but had never met anyone named Marilu. "I don't know who that is. Well, what does she want?"

Samantha explained, "She was asking me who the buyer was on the contract and who signed the . . . "

Al went pale. Thompson knew all of those details. This was someone trying to find out information. Damn, this was one bad day. He angrily reached down and picked up the line. "Hello?"

At the sound of Al's voice, Jaclyn quietly put down the receiver. She could not risk him recognizing her. Damn it, she was so close to getting more information.

Al looked at Samantha with an impatient expression. His normally calm tone shook with anger and he wagged his index figure for emphasis. "Do not, under any circumstance, talk to anyone in or out of this office about the Tower contract. If a call comes in like this again, put it through to me immediately and without question. Is that understood?"

Samantha's eyes filled with nervous tears. This was her first real job and she didn't want to lose it. She had no idea she had done anything wrong. What was the big fuss about anyway? The seller just wanted to know who the buyer was. Why was Al so mad at her? As soon as he returned to his office and shut the door, Samantha rushed off to the bathroom to check her makeup. She had a lunch date in one hour and the last thing she needed was smudged mascara.

Al paced in his office. He desperately tried to get a grip on the events unfolding around him. What was happening? How did the deal get so out of control? Jaclyn suddenly came to his mind. Could she be behind this? Maybe Steven was right. He needed to do some investigating. Think, Al, think, he coaxed himself. Then, it came to him. Jack Brody. He rushed over to his desk and placed a call to his longtime buddy who was a private investigator of sorts by day and a nightclub bouncer by night.

***

As soon as Jaclyn hung up on Al, she placed a call to directory assistance in Houston and requested the listing for SC Investors. To her disappointment, there was no number available. Then John Fitzgerald came to mind. He had mentioned attending Texas A&M, so she figured he might have contacts in Houston who could help her. As she dialed his number, she hoped he would be the link to the information she desperately wanted. John's secretary answered his direct line. "John Fitzgerald's office, this is Nancy."

Jaclyn had spoken with John's secretary on several occasions and greeted her familiarly. "Hi, Nancy. This is Jaclyn Tate. Is John available?"

Although Jaclyn was certain the woman recognized her voice and name from previous calls, she was impersonal in her reply. "Ms. Tate, your company name, please."

Jaclyn chose to play along. "Toner and Associates."

As if on autopilot, the woman replied, "Please hold."

While she waited, Jaclyn pondered what John would think of her call. He had phoned her several times since they met at the Anatole, but she had declined each of his subsequent invitations to go out. After three rejections, his calls became further apart until they finally stopped. It had been weeks since they had spoken. She wondered what he would say to her or whether he would even take the call...

His voice broke into her thoughts. "I see...you like being the pursuer instead of the pursued."

Jaclyn laughed at his good humor. "Hi, John. Thanks for taking my call. I'm sorry we haven't had an opportunity to get together since our wonderful night at the Anatole, but seriously, things have been quite hectic around here. All good though, and that makes all this hard work worthwhile."

"Good to hear that things are going well, Jaclyn. I'm glad you called."

Jaclyn was relieved by his friendly tone, but was anxious to get to the purpose of her call. "One of the reasons I'm so swamped is that I'm working an offer for a building downtown and I've come up against another contract. The buyer is SC Investors, out of Houston. Since you went to school in Houston, I thought you might have heard of it or have a tip on how I might track the company down. I tried Information, but there was no listing."

John paused for a moment as he considered her request. "SC

Investors. The name doesn't ring a bell, but I can put some feelers out to see what I can dig up. I'll let you know in a day or two what I learn."

Jaclyn was pleased. "Thank you, John. I really appreciate your help."

He would not let her off the hook that easily. "For you, Jaclyn, it's no trouble, but what is my reward should I unravel this mystery for you?"

Jaclyn thought carefully about an appropriate reply. "How does dinner and dancing sound?"

John was very pleased with that prospect. From the night they had met, he had been hopeful they could begin seeing one another. His mood was suddenly light. "You have a deal, Jaclyn. Now let me go so I can do some digging. The sooner I uncover this SC Investors, the sooner I get to see you again."

Jaclyn was flattered. "Thanks, John. Call me when you know something. Good-bye."

Jaclyn hung up the phone and was planning her next move when the receptionist rang through to inform her that Al Harris was waiting to see her. Jaclyn was surprised but intrigued by his visit. She asked the receptionist to show him to her office. Hurriedly, she buried a sheet of notes she had been making on the Tower deal and scanned her desk for information she would not want him to see, then rose to greet him as he appeared at the door. With an extended hand, she welcomed him into her office. "Al, what a nice surprise. Please come in."

Al looked around the room as she spoke. He was clearly impressed. "Jaclyn, I'm sorry to barge in on you like this, however, we had a change in plans regarding your offer." Jaclyn fought through the urge to say, "Really?" and instead let him continue. "I will present your contract at 1 o'clock today. I wanted to advise you that the 24-hour reply clock will start ticking at that time."

Jaclyn was gratified by the turn of events. "This is very good news, Al. Am I to assume then that the seller rejected the first offer and is now considering our contract?"

Al nervously jingled the coins in his pant pocket and avoided her eyes as he replied. "Um, well, actually, I told the buyer about your offer, as you suggested, and he was willing to examine both at the same time."

She could not believe Al was actually saying he had told the seller about a second contract. She was beginning to dislike him immensely. There were few things she liked less than liars. At this point, though, the only thing that really mattered to her was that JP's offer was being presented. She also didn't want to alienate Al, since he represented the seller. It certainly wouldn't help her cause to have him working against her. She put on her best, forced smile as she replied. "I am pleased that you decided to tell the seller about both offers. I applaud your ethics and appreciate your effort. Thank you for going out of your way and coming all the way over here to give me the good news in person." She made it clear to Al that she thought his visit was unnecessary and unusual. There were many things one could infer about his visit. At this point, Jaclyn was unsure why he had come, but whatever it was, she was certain it wasn't good.

Al fidgeted as their meeting was apparently ending before he had the answers he had come to her office to find. He had been hoping to uncover clues that revealed her involvement in notifying the seller about her offer. He also wanted to learn if she knew anything about the other contract. He continued talking, in the hope that a prolonged conversation would offer him some hints. "I just wanted you to know as soon as possible and your office was on the way to the seller's office, which is where I am going right now." Although Jaclyn was making her way around the desk and toward him, Al remained in the doorway and continued talking.

Jaclyn had heard all she needed to for now and was eager to have him on his way to the seller. She took his arm and led him out of her office. "Well then, Al, I must not keep you from getting over to the seller. I look forward to the reply."

Before Al knew what was happening, he was steps away from the front door and being shown the way out. He damned himself the entire way. He just wasn't good at this type of thing. He was leaving with as little knowledge of what was going on as when he had arrived. Failure was beginning to feel familiar.

Jaclyn, on the other hand, was thrilled. Her fax had worked like a charm. Thompson must have called Al, insisting to know if there was another offer. Fantastic. Her plan couldn't have worked any better. The contract would be reviewed within the next few hours and they could expect to have an answer by tomorrow at the same time.

Just as she had hoped, things were turning their way. She would call JP and let him know. She was certain he would be pleased.

***

As agreed, Al called Cason at noon, reaching him on his mobile phone. Al had been hoping to have information to share with him from his visit to Jaclyn's office, but no such luck.

He was his usual brusque self when he answered the phone. "Cason."

Al cleared his throat and readied himself. "It's Al. I'm just leaving Tate's office…"

Steven impatiently interrupted him. "You just left where?"

Al wished now that he hadn't let him know where he had been. But it was too late, so he explained. "Tate, the agent on the other contract."

Steven's controlled anger was more than Al could handle. "Why did you go there, may I ask?"

Al felt like a little kid who had been caught with his hand in the cookie jar. "I thought I might dig up something…"

Steven interrupted, "And?"

Al meekly replied, "No such luck."

In total frustration, Steven slammed his hand against the steering wheel and shook his head in disbelief. He could not believe Al's incompetence. "I don't know why I have a boy doing a man's work," Steven said to himself but clearly enough for Al to hear. Al sunk into his seat. Now his manhood was being challenged, what next? His immediate response was that he didn't have to take that kind of abuse. Then he remembered who he was dealing with and realized he didn't have a choice.

"Need I remind you of our deal, Al?" Steven's question was rhetorical, for he paused for only a fraction of a second before continuing. "Now you listen carefully. I want you to go to Thompson's office and make a soft pitch of the other deal. Make certain you leave them with plenty of doubt about this buyer and his real net worth. I know the cash offer and quick close will be attractive, but if they doubt his ability to come up with the greenbacks, then they'll opt for my offer. Make it clear to them that I won't be a backup offer, it's either they take my deal or I move on to the next property. Do you understand?"

Al was relieved that Steven's tone had turned businesslike again. "Got it."

Steven tried his best to remain calm. "Good. And from now on, Al, consult with me on anything to do with this deal. Do you understand? Anything. Don't leave out any detail. Tell me everything, especially any investigating ideas you have. I will not lose this deal. Is that understood?"

Al thought he should probably tell Steven about the call that came into his office today with that woman trying to find out who the buyer was on the first contract, then he decided it would be better not to upset him any further. He was certain he would just catch more abuse. With only a slight hesitation, he assured Cason, "Understood."

Steven relaxed a bit. "Good, then call me when you're done meeting with Thompson." As his words ended, the line went dead. No surprise, but then, anything different and Al would not know how to react. He was beginning to feel like a robot, following orders and thinking less and less for himself.

CHAPTER 8
—◇—

Al fidgeted nervously as he sat in the lobby of Milton's office, waiting to be called in to their meeting. During this time, he thought about his precarious situation. He had to be certain he did everything he could to get Milton to work Steven's contract. There was no way he could go back to Steven and tell him the other contract had been selected over his. The thought of having to do that made Al sick. No, he reprimanded himself; he would not even consider that outcome. That could not and would not happen. Al coaxed himself to stay positive in his thinking, but it was becoming increasingly difficult. He turned his attention to Milton's secretary, who had picked up the phone to answer a page. As she put down the receiver, she looked at Al, stood, and made her way around the desk, toward him. As she approached, Al stood.

"Mr. Harris, Mr. Thompson will see you now." As soon as she finished speaking, she turned on her heels and walked slowly toward the door of Milton's office. Al followed her in silence. She opened the door for him, waited as he stepped into the room, then closed the door behind him. Al slowly entered into the room and approached Milton, who was seated at his desk, talking on the phone. Milton motioned for Al to come in and take a seat in front of him. A moment later, Milton hung up and turned his attention to Al. Milton had a serious expression on his face as he began to speak and his tone was controlled and patronizing. Al began to sweat. "Al, today is a good day. Do you know why today is a good day?" Al shook his head in silent reply. He could not anticipate the meaning behind Milton's question. Milton answered for him. "I'll tell you why today is a good day. Today I have two contracts to consider on one property, one very big property. That puts me in an excellent position, wouldn't you agree?" Al nodded and tried to find his voice, but Milton was apparently not anticipating a reply because he hardly paused before he spoke again. "Considering the position the second contract affords me, I fail to understand why you didn't tell me about it. Can you explain that to me?"

Al felt backed into a corner, but he knew the whole mess was of his own doing. He had no one to blame but himself. He could only think to apologize at this point. "You're absolutely right, Milton. I'm sorry."

Milton looked long and hard into Al's eyes. "Al, my boy, there is no room for apologies in business. We are not in first grade here. This is the big time. I have a lot riding on the sale of this property. I gave you a golden opportunity with this listing and I expected more allegiance from you. Because of my loyalty to your father, I will let it go this time, but don't let me down again. Is that clear?"

Al nodded his head as he replied. "Absolutely."

Milton rose from his chair as he continued. "Good, then let's get down to business. I am anxious to see the other contract." Milton pointed to a seat at his conference table. "Have a seat here and I'll see if Harry and Mike are ready to join us."

Milton walked out of the room, leaving the door open behind him. While he waited, Al opened his briefcase, took out three copies of the second contract and laid them down on the table in front of him. He couldn't help but think about what a mess he had gotten himself into by concealing information from Milton. He knew deception was part of the game, but he would have to be more careful in the future.

Moments later, Milton and his advisors came into the room. The men shook hands with Al and then sat down around the conference table. Al handed each of them a copy of the second offer and reviewed the deal points as they scanned the document. They didn't get far into the terms of the offer when Harry let out a howl. "Wow. Do I see correctly? Does that say cash?" As Milton's CFO, he was excited about the prospect of having such a large sum of money hit their balance sheet.

Milton had not yet read that far when Harry called his attention to the cash offer. Quickly, Milton scanned the document to find the payment terms. "Al, is Harry correct?"

Al's reaction was conservative. "Yes, Milton, he read it correctly."

Milton sat back in great satisfaction. "How sweet is that?"

Recognizing that Milton was thrilled with the bid, Al immediately began trying to discredit the buyer. "Milton, may I suggest we take a conservative approach here. I am not familiar with this buyer, JP Morrison. For all we know, at this moment he doesn't have the money. I have run into more than one character like that. I bet we all could swap stories about con artists who tie up properties by endlessly baiting the seller with the prospect of a cash deal. On the other hand, you have a great offer from Cason and you know he's good as gold on his ventures." Al felt vindicated when he saw Milton nodding in agreement. Maybe he had won back a few points.

They then resumed the review of the contract and when they reached the term regarding closing, Harry was quick to comment. "A 30-day close, now Milton, that's about as sweet a deal as we've come across in a long time."

Both Milton and Mike nodded in agreement. Al was damp from sweat. He had to say something. "Gentlemen, you know what they say about things that sound too good to be true."

Milton scrutinized him. "Al, you seem to have some serious concerns about this buyer. Is there something we should be aware of?"

Al fumbled over his reply. "Well, Milton, it's just that he's not from this area and I'm not familiar with him. Are you?"

Milton chuckled. "I don't know a lot of people, Al, but that doesn't mean they are incapable of closing on a deal. Let's continue our review."

The men read through the document together, noting the five-year guarantee on leases, which brought about adamant objection by both Milton and Harry. Al was relieved that they were displeased with that contingency and focused an exorbitant amount of time discussing that unreasonable requirement. Yet when they were through, Milton commented that overall, he was extremely pleased with the second offer. Although he and his advisors were also comfortable with the first contract, this was a cash deal and that diverted their interest. The sales price was insignificantly less than that of the first proposal, and though the offer contained a few stipulations about guaranteed leases and clean structural and mechanical inspections, they surmised they could probably work out those points to an agreeable conclusion.

Both contracts were acceptable to Milton, so now all that remained was the question of which offer to counter.

After Al was done presenting the second offer and had taken every opportunity to give the men his unsolicited opinion about which offer to respond to, Milton dismissed him. He wanted to discuss the offers openly with his advisors and decide on the best way to handle the two contracts. Al hated to leave the meeting but obliged Milton's request and took a seat in the reception area.

When the three men were alone, Milton spoke. "Gentlemen, considering the market, I feel extremely fortunate to have two contracts on this property. It certainly puts us in the driver's seat. Both offers are fair and appear very solid. What do you suggest we do?"

His CFO, Harry, was the first to volunteer his opinion. "I would counter the first contract with the cash offer you have in the second offer. First, Cason's offer is five million higher. That's a significant sum. Also, we know him and he is certainly someone with the means to close on any deal he signs his name to. If you get Cason to agree to the cash terms and the 30-day closing, the first contract is cleaner than the second and nets you the same result. The problem I have with Cason's venture is that he will tie up the deal until he can organize the partnership and raise the capital. I agree he's the best at putting together partnerships, but why wait 90 days or longer when we can have the money in 30? After all, with this market depressed and potentially declining, if anything falls through on Cason's venture and we are forced to put the Tower back on the market, we have lost a lot of time and may not get another offer as good. In addition, our building is currently nicely leased, and with all the empty office space in Dallas and occupancy rates declining every day, we don't want to wait and risk losing tenants and making this property less interesting to potential buyers."

Milton listened intently while Harry vocalized his thoughts. When he had finished, Milton said, "I follow you, Harry, and what you said makes a lot of sense." He then turned to Mike, his attorney, for his input. "What do you think, Mike?"

Mike scanned the notes he had compiled on the legal pad that lay square in front of him. He spoke slowly and looked at both men as he replied. "Milton, I agree with Harry. I suggest we counter offer number one, but I propose we add one million dollars in earnest money that must be put up within 24 hours of acceptance of the counter and that goes hard next Friday at 5 p.m. If it doesn't work out with Cason, we will know in one week and can always fall back on the second offer. If Cason chooses to continue with the deal, he will have 30 days to close from Friday's date and must put up an additional million a week in hard earnest money until the closing. That will guarantee Cason is serious and not just tying up the deal while he tries to get a venture put together. I agree that time is of the essence and we don't want to wait while the market continues to slide." Mike paused to check for agreement from the two men seated beside him. Both nodded and Mike continued, "I suggest you give Cason 24 hours to reply to our counter offer to keep a tight timeline and if he accepts, then give him until Friday to organize his cash offer. If we keep the offer open to Cason for only one week, we shouldn't lose the interest of the second buyer. We also need to respond to the second buyer by 1 o'clock tomorrow, so I suggest we inform him in writing that he is the second offer received on the property and we are currently in negotiations on the first contract. We will inform him on or before Friday at 5 p.m. whether we have reached an agreement on the first contract or will begin negotiations with him." Mike put down his pen on his legal pad as if to indicate he was done.

Milton took a moment to think through the advice he had been given. He agreed with their opinions, and as usual, was pleased with their analysis of the situation. Just as he suspected, the second contract gave him the power to go back to Cason and ask for a better deal. He turned to his advisors and said, "Very well, men, I believe we are all in agreement. We counter Cason's contract as discussed. I feel very good about our position." As he spoke, he stood and moved toward his desk. When he finished speaking, he dialed his secretary's extension and called her into his office. Within seconds, she was standing at the doorway with a pad of paper and a pen in her hand. Milton called her in and she took the empty seat beside him at the conference table. When she was seated and ready to take notes, Milton gave her explicit instructions of what to add to the counteroffer on the SC Investors contract and what to write in reply to the second offer.

Sitting outside Milton's office, Al watched intently for signs of activity. When he saw Milton's secretary go into the meeting, he knew a decision had been reached and a counteroffer was being prepared. Within fifteen minutes, the secretary returned to her desk and began typing. As soon as she had finished, she rose from her desk and returned to Milton's office. She knocked at the door and waited for a reply before entering the room.

Moments later, Milton was in the open doorway. He called out, "Come on back in, Al."

Al jumped out of his seat and walked gingerly back into the office. As he took his seat, he was handed a copy of the counteroffer. Immediately, Al scanned the paper before him to see how the letter was addressed. With total relief, he read Cason's name at the greeting line. He took a deep breath. As he looked further down at the paper in his hands, Milton briefed him on the points of the counter. "It's all there, but I want you to note the following: Cason has only 24 hours to respond and accept the changes and then only one week to present the parties of the venture to us. If he is successful at raising the capital in this short time frame, the deal is his. If not, we will begin negotiations on the second contract."

Al nodded. "Understood."

Milton then handed Al a letter addressed to JP Morrison and highlighted the main points in the response to the second offer. "As you can see, this letter fulfills the 24-hour reply requirement and states that we have elected to work the offers in the order in which we received them. It also explains that if the first offer is not executed by next Friday, then we will begin negotiations with him." Milton looked at Al and waited for him to look up from the paperwork before continuing. "I want you to deliver the counteroffer to Cason immediately and the letter of response to Morrison's agent at noon tomorrow. Is everything clear, Al?"

Al made a few notes in his daily planner, then sifted through the papers in front of him before replying. "I believe so."

Milton shook his head at his reply. He wanted more confidence from his broker; but then again, Al was proving to be nothing more than just a boy. He would learn, but Milton feared it might be at his expense. "Very well then, we will let you go so you can take this counter to Cason."

When Milton was through speaking, Al put the paperwork in his briefcase, stood, shook hands with each of them and then walked out of the room. Milton followed. As they walked past his secretary's desk, Milton put a fatherly arm around Al's shoulders. "Thank you for coming in today," he said as they stopped in front of the elevators. Then Milton moved within inches of Al's face. In almost a whisper, he said, "Al, your father and I go way back. I gave you this listing because of him. I had hoped you would earn my respect, but I have to say I'm very disappointed that you didn't tell me about the second offer." Milton's eyes looked deep into Al's and a serious expression crossed his face. "Not many men would be so forgiving, but I will forget this transgression for your father's sake. But I'm warning you, don't fuck with me again. Is that understood?" Al swayed nervously on his unsteady legs. Milton's tone and choice of words clearly told him how angry he was. Al also hated being reminded he only got the Tower listing because of his father. He desperately wanted to be successful on his own. He also did not appreciate being made to feel like a child. He didn't respond quickly enough and Milton repeated himself. "Al, do I make myself clear?"

Al looked nervously at the man standing before him as he answered, "Crystal clear."

Milton nodded at him, firmly patted him on the back and then walked away.

When Milton returned to his office, he was grinning from ear to ear and both his CFO and attorney knew he was very pleased with the deal. Negotiation was a game to Milton and nothing short of winning was ever acceptable. He had won again and they saw the satisfaction of victory in his face. Without saying a word, Milton went to a cabinet behind his desk, opened the panel that concealed a small refrigerator and retrieved a bottle of Dom Perignon Champagne. He checked the label, then popped opened the cork. The top shot out loudly and Milton let out a whoop. Laughing, he poured a glass for himself and then for his advisors. The three men held their glasses high as Milton spoke, tapping their glasses as he made the toast. "Gentlemen, we've done it again. All I can say is, we must be living right." They clinked their glasses together and laughed robustly as they sipped their celebratory champagne.

***

The minute he walked off the elevator and entered the lobby,

Al called Cason from his mobile phone. Steven was at his desk when the phone rang. He picked up on the first ring, hopeful that it would be Al.

Al blurted out the news. "I have a counter on your offer."

Enormously appeased, Steven let out a long, deep sigh. Al had redeemed himself for the moment. "How is it?"

Al was cocky and nonchalant in his reply. "Not bad. I did a good job letting them see what a solid offer you presented." Al paused long enough for Steven to praise him but, getting nothing, continued. "They only changed the payment terms and the closing time frame."

Steven was losing his tolerance again. He never wasted time when working on a deal. He wanted information, facts and fast. Impatiently, he prompted Al. "To what?"

Once again, Al answered casually. "Cash."

Steven nearly fell out of his chair. His voice rose several decibels. "Cash? As in how much and when?"

Al was suddenly nervous again. He thought that a big player like Steven wouldn't have a problem with the deal being for cash. He fumbled through his notes as he spoke to ensure he relayed the exact information to him. "One million dollars earnest money up on acceptance of the counter, which they want within 24 hours. That money goes hard next Friday. Then they want another mil in hard earnest money every week until closing which has to take place in 30 days. The full amount, in cash, at closing."

Steven shook his head in disbelief. What he had feared might happen, did. The second offer gave Thompson the ammo he needed to counter for a better deal. He anticipated the cash offer would get Thompson's attention. Now he had to figure out how to make it happen. He thought out loud. "The million is no problem. Having it at risk and adding to that risk every week is not so easy to swallow. A bigger concern is the full amount in cash in only 30 days. That's the challenge. Damn that other contract." Steven sat back and contemplated his situation.

"Actually Steven," Al interjected, "the cash commitment needs to be in place by next Friday."

Steven could not control his temper. "Al, what are you talking about? Are they insane? I need to arrange for $150 mil in cash and they expect that can be done by Friday?"

Al tried to keep the conversation calm. He explained, "Yes,

they want the commitment for the full amount in one week. If you don't put the deal together by then, you get your million in earnest back and they work the second contract. If you continue with the deal beyond 5 p.m. Friday, your million is at risk and another million becomes at risk for each week you are under contract. They appeared concerned that you would tie up the property while trying to put together the funds. They don't want to risk having your deal fall apart when they have another offer for cash on the table."

It took awhile for Steven to respond. He ran the scenario through his mind a few times before he spoke. "Alright, Al, deliver the counter and your notes from the meeting to my office this afternoon so I can have the details of their reply in front of me. Make certain you hand-deliver it to Diana, since I will be out for most of the rest of the afternoon. I'll need to get busy getting the cash organized. Bring me any leads you have or let me know if you hear of anyone interested in a piece of this deal. If it's the last thing I do, I'm putting this deal together." Once he had given his orders, Steven hung up. Al knew that if anyone could pull off this feat, it would be Cason. He only wished he could help. That would really win him some points with Cason. Maybe he *could* dig up someone interested in investing in this deal.

***

Late in the afternoon, the receptionist phoned Diana to inform her that Al Harris had arrived and was requesting to come up to drop off a package for Mr. Cason. Steven had informed Diana that Al would stop by with paperwork for him to review and since then she had excitedly anticipated his arrival. Now that she knew he was on his way up to her office, she was suddenly nervous. She quickly straightened her skirt and checked her makeup in her compact before she assumed the nonchalant position she wanted Al to see as he came up to her desk. When she heard the elevator doors open, she held her breath. As she heard footsteps moving toward her, she looked up and saw him approaching. He was as good-looking as she remembered and her heart skipped a beat as their eyes met.

Al stared at Diana. He was trying to decide if it were her. Finally, he asked, "Diana, is that you?"

She was pleased with his reaction. "It certainly is." She rose from her chair, held in her stomach and pushed back her shoulders, trying to stand tall and thin as she extended her hand to him. He reached out and took hold of her hand in a very tender handshake. He smiled provocatively at her. "Diana, I hope you don't take this badly, but you look fantastic. I don't think I would have recognized you if I passed you on the street."

She knew he meant well, so she chose to ignore the insult that tainted his compliment. "Thank you, Al."

He pointed to the chair beside her desk. "May I?"

Diana extended her hand to invite him to sit as she sat in her chair. She pushed her chair away from under the desk and turned toward Al, crossed her legs and leaned forward. He studied her carefully and she suddenly became very self-conscious. He made her feel naked. She wasn't comfortable yet with a man's attention, although it was happening more and more often, and she was beginning to manage her way through it. They sat a moment in awkward silence. Diana was the first to speak. "So, Al, you have some paperwork for Mr. Cason?"

Al shook his head as if he were awakened from a daydream, "Yes, Diana." He fumbled through his briefcase and retrieved a sealed envelope, which he handed to her. She took it from him and laid it on her desk. Then she looked back at him, anticipating that he might say something, but he just stared at her with deep and sultry eyes. Uncomfortable with the silence, she continued trying to make conversation. "Al, it's been a while. How have you been?"

His trance was unbroken and his facial expression did not change as he answered, "Great. Things are great. Diana, I know this may be awkward for you since I'm working with Cason, but would you be interested in going out to dinner with me?"

Diana was thrilled. Little did Al know that he had been a big part of her motivation to get in shape and change her looks. From the moment she met him more than a year before, she had set her sights on him and knew it would take a good figure along with a pretty face to make it happen. She was aware of why he had chosen Mindy, her assistant, to date at the time. A man with his looks deserved a woman equally attractive. That's when she recognized it would take a lot of hard work to get Al's attention, but she expected it would be worth the effort. Now that he was asking her out, she knew it merited every ounce of willpower she had used to achieve her goal. She gave Al a coy smile as she replied, "I would love to have dinner with you, Al."

***

Jaclyn was sitting at her desk working late, reviewing a contract, when her phone rang, jarring her out of a state of intense concentration. She sat back and stretched before picking up the receiver. In almost a whisper, she spoke. "Jaclyn Tate."

A man's loud voice boomed into her ear. "Jaclyn, hi. It's John."

Glad that he was calling and hopeful he had good news, she brightened up. "Hi, John. Tell me you are calling with word on SC Investors."

His voice sounded dejected, but he continued. "No…but I haven't given up yet. I called to invite you to an event I think you'll enjoy. Our firm is holding an open house Friday at 8. The reception will be held at Reunion Tower. It will be another good opportunity for you to mingle with more real estate players. I'm one of the hosts, so I'll have to share my time and socialize, but if you're interested, I'll have your name on our exclusive guest list."

Jaclyn thought about how nice he had been to her and she felt badly that she wasn't certain she would be able to go, especially because this time she had a legitimate excuse. She hoped he would understand. "John, it sounds like exactly the kind of evening I need, especially considering the crazy week I'm having, but I can't make any promises. I have a buyer in from New York and he is planning to stay as long as necessary to negotiate his contract. Can I say I'll try my best and hope to see you there?"

John was pleased. "That's the most promising answer you've given me so far. I'll take it and hope for the best."

Jaclyn smiled. "Thank you."

Before ending the call, John added, "Dress is formal. You'll have to show ID at the door to get in. I'll keep an eye out for you. Hope to see you then."

Jaclyn replied sweetly. "Me too and thanks for everything, John. Good-bye."

Jaclyn considered John's invitation. It was certainly the type of event at which she could meet the contacts she needed to know to grow her real estate business. At every turn she was learning the importance of a strong network and she needed to work on developing hers. She would do her best to attend.

Now that her concentration had been broken, she pushed her papers aside and looked at her watch. She was definitely working too many hours. Checking to see if any employees were still at the office, she peered out the wall of windows facing the parking lot. There was no car other than hers anywhere in sight. It came as no surprise to her since she was, as a rule, the first one in the office in the morning and the last to leave at night. As managing director of the office, she felt it was the right thing to do. As a matter of policy, she was the only one with a key to the office. That complicated her morning schedule, forcing her to arrive early every day to open the office, but it was her choice. In the evening, if she was out, her staff could close the door behind them on their way out and the door would lock automatically. Maintaining sole possession of the key was one of her control issues, but with the weight of the responsibility of the office falling squarely on her shoulders, she took every precaution to ensure things were secure. That included guaranteeing the integrity of confidential paperwork. With so many variables in business, she controlled every aspect she could and learned how to roll with the punches for the rest.

Before resuming her work, she wrote in her daily planner on Friday's page.

Reception, Reunion Tower, 8 p.m., Formal.

As Jaclyn returned her attention to her file, a good feeling began to overtake her. Things were going well: the Thanksgiving Tower offer was in the seller's hands, her social life was improving, and the overall profitability of the business was excellent. It had been a reach for her to take on so much on her own. Stepping outside of her comfort zone had both challenged and frightened her. But recognizing that this opportunity came with its share of risks and rewards, she had kept her sights firmly on the potential and did everything she could to make her venture successful. It was working.

CHAPTER 9
—◇—

It was only 6 a.m. when Jaclyn returned to her office, a meager 8 hours since she had left it, but she was anxious to get her day started. In a few hours, she would have the closing of a shopping center sale and then she wanted to follow up with Al on the contract presentation to Thompson. With the 24-hour clause, they were bound to a reply today. As she started to open the office door, she thought she heard a noise and froze in her tracks. Standing in the doorway, she looked around nervously as she listened intently. The lobby appeared eerie in the dark. Odd shadows were cast against the far wall. As she waited apprehensively, she heard it again. It sounded as if someone were opening file cabinet drawers. Her mind alternated between fear and rational thought. Cautiously, she propped open the door with her briefcase and slowly entered the reception area, listening intently as she moved slowly and quietly. She turned on the light and looked around. When a minute passed and she no longer heard any sounds, she called out.

"Hello…Mark? Candice?…is anyone there?"

Silence followed. At that moment, the only thing Jaclyn heard was the thumping of her heart, beating loudly against her chest and the rushing flow of blood which echoed in her ears. She paused for a moment, then cautiously moved back into the doorway. Something was telling her to get out. To run away. She fought against her instinct to flee. Her mind struggled to make sense of what she thought she had heard. Could she just have been paranoid? But she was certain she had heard something. As she questioned herself, she heard it again.

This time it sounded like someone moving toward her. Stunned, she called out. "Who's there?"

No one replied and Jaclyn knew she needed to get out. Quickly, she left the building and raced over to her car. She jumped into the front seat and locked herself in. Immediately, she reached for her car phone and called 911. She made a report with the operator, who put Jaclyn on hold while she called ahead to the police. Jaclyn fixed her eyes on the office door as she remained on the phone. The operator continued talking to her, repeatedly assuring her that help was on the way. Moments later, a police car pulled into the parking lot. Slowly, Jaclyn got out of her car and moved toward the officer.

As she neared him, he spoke. "Hello, ma'am. I'm Officer Weaver. May I have your name, please."

Visibly shaken, she replied, "Jaclyn Tate."

He took control. "Ms. Tate, can you please recount for me what transpired here this morning."

Jaclyn cleared her throat as she began. "I opened the door to my office and heard a sound. I stopped at the door to listen. When it was obvious to me that someone was there, I called out but no one answered. I was the last to leave the office last night and only I have a key, so none of my employees could have entered without my being here."

The officer made a few notes on his small black notepad, then placed it in his breast pocket. "Ms. Tate, did you see anyone?"

"No," she said, shaking her head.

"Do you know any reason why someone would want to break into your office?"

"Not at all."

"Alright, Ms. Tate, I would like to go inside and take a look around. I want you to wait here. My backup unit should arrive any minute." He paused to look around as if expecting to see the other police vehicle approach. "When they get here, please stay with them."

Just as the officer was entering the building, the other patrol car entered the parking lot. Officer Weaver paused and motioned toward to them that he was going inside. On his signal, two burly police officers exited their vehicle and came toward Jaclyn and asked her to wait by their car while they secured the perimeter. She watched their actions intently. The first officer entered the building with his hand close to his gun holster. Jaclyn was struck by how much the scene looked like an action/adventure movie. There was something very surreal about the events unfolding before her. One of the other officers waited in the doorway, the door open, while the third made his way around the far side of the building. It was nearly five minutes later when the first officer appeared at the door. He paused for a moment and spoke to the officer standing beside him, then walked over to Jaclyn.

A few steps away from her, he began speaking. "Ms. Tate, I checked around and found no one inside. I did, however, find the back door lock broken and files on the floor outside the office next to the conference room."

Jaclyn was nervous. That would be her office and she was certain she hadn't left any files on the floor. "That's very odd. I left late last night and there were no files on the floor by my office."

He replied, "The files appeared dropped. They were scattered across the floor."

Jaclyn shook her head. "Do you think whoever broke into my office was interested in my files?"

The officer nodded. "There may be more to this. I suggest we do a walk-through and check everything together. As we proceed through the office, please stay behind me and let me know if you notice anything missing or out of place."

Jaclyn nodded and the two of them entered the building. Slowly, the officer made his way down the hall toward Jaclyn's office. Silently, she followed. Her heart was beating rapidly and her hands trembled nervously. As they approached the end of the hall, she saw the files lying haphazardly on the floor between her door and Matt's desk. Chills ran up and down her spine at the realization that someone had been there and gone through her things. She felt violated and scared. As she stood there motionless, paralyzed by the fear that overtook her, the officer spoke. "Ms. Tate, is this your office?"

His words jarred her from her thoughts. She looked up at him, but her eyes could not focus and he appeared as a blur. She nodded at him and he entered the office. Cautiously, she followed.

"Please look around and tell me if you see anything out of place."

Jaclyn moved around her desk and looked at the documents and files stacked on it. Her eyes scanned the surface and came to rest on her Mont Blanc pen resting on her agenda just as she had left it the night before. Her Waterford crystal clock was also directly in front of her blotter. She looked up at her bookcase and examined the shelves. The fact that nothing of value had been taken was suddenly more troublesome to her than if a robbery had taken place.

She turned her attention back to the officer, who was waiting patiently for her assessment. "Besides my files, both on my desk and those on the floor, everything else appears to be in its place." She then made her way around the desk and out of her office. She bent to look at the files on the floor. "It seems that whoever came in here was looking for information, not things."

The officer took out his notepad and scribbled a few notes. "Ms. Tate, can you tell exactly what paperwork or files are missing?"

Jaclyn looked down at the piles before her. She picked up one file at a time and checked through a few before answering. "I can't say for certain. I'll have to look through my things thoroughly to determine what is missing."

The officer then asked Jaclyn to walk through the remainder of the office to verify what had been taken. They proceeded slowly and methodically through the entire office and, once again, Jaclyn confirmed that nothing of value appeared to be missing. When they had completed their walk-through, the officer spoke. "Alright Ms. Tate, I believe I have all the information I need. Do you have any questions?" She shook her head. When she did not speak, he spoke again. "Very well then, is there someplace I can sit and fill out the incident report?"

Jaclyn showed him to the conference room. She opened the door, switched on the light and held the door for him as he entered. "Please make yourself comfortable."

He pulled out a chair and took a seat. "Thank you."

"You're welcome." She was almost out of the room when she paused and turned back toward the officer. "I'm desperate for a cup of coffee. I'm going to start a pot. Can I bring you a cup when it's ready?"

"Thank you for the offer, Ms. Tate, but I will complete my report and then I'll be on my way."

"Very well," she said as she turned and walked out of the room.

Before going into the kitchen, she walked to the rear door and examined the lock. It was obvious that this was how the intruder had gained access. She made a mental note to have a locksmith come by today. She would also have him add a dead bolt to the door.

Before long, the officer had completed his paperwork and was ready to leave. As Jaclyn showed him out, he ran through a list of cautions for her to observe. When he was through, she thanked him and he left. She then returned to her office and sat at her desk. She dropped her head into her hands and considered the events of the morning. For some reason, of which she was not certain, someone had broken into her office looking for something. And it was clear he had come for information and not objects. What information did she possess that someone would so desperately want? The thought left her feeling very unsettled.

Although she began to feel better as her employees arrived, it was hours later when Jaclyn finally felt capable of speaking coherently. She asked Matt to gather the staff for a briefing of what had transpired. When everyone was settled in the conference room, she explained what had taken place and cautioned each of them to be aware of how important it was for them to keep their dealings confidential. It was clear to Jaclyn that they felt equally disturbed by the intruder.

After her staff meeting, Jaclyn called Carl. She was so relieved when he answered the phone that she didn't even wait for him to say hello. "Carl, it's Jaclyn"

His reaction was immediate. "My God, Jaclyn, what's wrong?" Carl was nervous. The last time he remembered her voice sounding that way was the morning after Andrew had forced himself on her and she had called to let him know she was taking the day off.

Emotion filled her at the sound of his voice. "Carl, it was awful. I came in this morning and heard a noise in the office. It was about 6 o'clock and I knew no one else would be here, especially since I was certain I was the last to leave. At first, I thought I was imagining the noise, then I heard it again. It was the sound of a file cabinet opening, that sliding noise. Anyway, I went to my car and called the police. I can't believe that someone was in here. What were they after?" Jaclyn spoke rapidly, hardly stopping long enough to take a breath.

Carl had listened intently. His first concern was for her safety. "Jaclyn, are you okay?"

She replied slowly, as if she had to apprise her condition before answering. "I'm shaken, but luckily, I didn't come face-to-face with him."

"Well, at least we have that to be grateful for. I still don't understand why someone would break into the office... Is anything missing? Was it a robbery?"

"That's actually the worst part. Nothing of value appears to be missing. In fact, I had left my Mont Blanc pen on my desk. Although a file beside it was taken, the pen was left behind. My crystal paperweight is on the edge of my desk, as always. No, Carl, I don't believe this was a robbery. The only things touched were some files from my desk. A few of those files were left behind outside my office door, but others are missing."

Carl couldn't believe what he was hearing. From her explanation, it sounded like intellectual sabotage. "Jaclyn, were only your files missing?"

She replied. "Only mine. Everyone did a quick check of their belongings and files and so far, only mine appear to be gone."

The questions mounted in Carl's mind. "Which ones, or can't you tell yet?"

Jaclyn was quick to answer. "An obvious one is my correspondence and activity file on Thanksgiving Tower. Luckily, I had the one with the contract and confidential paperwork with me, but the general communication file is gone."

Carl was angry. "Based on what you're telling me, Jaclyn, I would speculate that this wasn't a robbery at all. My guess is someone is trying to get information on your Tower deal. How are things going on your contract?"

There was something in his voice that concerned her. She had never heard him sound like this before. Although she had also had concerns when she realized the correspondence file was taken, she couldn't understand what good her file would be when her offer had already been presented. She realized then that Carl didn't know about the contract submission, so she gave him a quick update. "Our offer was presented yesterday at 1 o'clock. The 24-hour clause gives them until today to reply. I expect to hear their response within a few hours."

Carl felt he needed to caution her. She was dealing with bigger stakes than she had ever faced before and he knew firsthand how money made people do crazy things. He chose his words carefully. He didn't want to frighten her further, but he felt she needed to be warned. "Jaclyn, watch your back. I don't like the feeling I'm getting about this. The stakes are high and that can make even good people have bad thoughts if it can further their position. You're dealing with money, lots of it, and that amount of money can lead to some scary things."

Jaclyn listened intently to Carl's advice. "Carl, you're not suggesting that I should back off this deal, are you?"

"I'm not suggesting you back off, just to keep your eyes open and your back covered. Someone involved somehow in this Tower deal has enough money on the line to go as far as breaking and entering. If he would do that, what else would he do?"

Jaclyn did not like what she was hearing. "Carl, if you're trying to scare me, you're succeeding."

"I'm only telling you to be careful. Powerful and wealthy people have the most to lose and they can sometimes do the unthinkable to preserve their position. Moving in the circles that we operate in puts us in contact with some of the most powerful and wealthy people in the world. If things don't go their way on a big deal, they could resort to extreme measures to regain their position. I may be way off the mark here, Jaclyn, but I don't think I am considering what was taken from your office. A lot is at stake with the Tower deal, more than just money."

Something in the seriousness of his tone told her he was speaking from experience. That actually frightened her more than what had taken place that morning.

***

It was a few hours later when Jaclyn returned to her office. She was pleased the closing on the shopping center was finished and surprised the process had gone surprisingly well, considering her state of mind. She had just concluded the sale of a shopping center to a doctor who had become one of her best clients. She had met him only days after her arrival in Dallas. While waiting in line at the dry cleaner a few doors down from her office, she struck up a conversation with him. In only minutes, she had his business card, his parameters for investment properties and her first client. Today was the culmination of their second transaction and they were already working on a third purchase.

When Jaclyn walked through the door to her office, she couldn't help remember how frightened she had been earlier in the day. As she passed the front desk, the receptionist handed her the messages she had taken and a letter that had been hand-delivered an hour earlier. She continued toward her office while she scanned through her messages. She was hoping to see one from Al, but there was none. She laid her briefcase and messages on her credenza, sat down at her desk and opened the blank envelope her receptionist had given her. Inside, she found a letter from Milton Thompson responding to their offer. It read:

Dear Mr. Morrison,

Thank you for the offer you submitted for the purchase of Thanksgiving Tower. We are, however, in the midst of negotiations on a prior contract and so must conclude those discussions prior to entertaining your offer. It is expected that we will finalize our negotiations with the other party within one week. Until we have either reached an agreement with the other party or have concluded those negotiations, I am not at liberty to consider your offer. I therefore, respectfully request a one-week period in which to reply to your offer formally. We shall contact you on Friday at 5 p.m. to advise you if we are in a position to further our discussions with you. I look forward to receiving in writing your response to our request for a one-week postponement.

Thank you in advance for your understanding and cooperation.

Sincerely,
Milton Thompson
CEO

Disappointed, Jaclyn placed the letter on her desk and thought about the events that had transpired since she had submitted their contract only days ago. Someone powerful was in the mix. Too many things out of the ordinary were taking place. She wondered who it was. For now she would contact JP and inform him of this update. Since there was no reason for him to stay in town, she anticipated he would want to return to New York and await further communication from the seller. That is, if he was willing to wait. Men in such powerful positions often rebelled against the idea of being told to wait. It was her job to keep JP on the hook, learn what she could in the next week and do whatever possible to improve their position in the deal.

***

Steven sat at his desk intently reading the counteroffer. His partnership deal that would have taken him 90 days minimum to finalize was now a cash purchase and he had only one week to obtain commitments for the money before the stakes increased. "If only there had not been that other contract," he thought aloud. But then again, he assumed he had handled that. Al didn't do his job, damn him. The other contract screwed up his deal, but he couldn't give that further thought. He had to keep focused on the formidable task that lay ahead of him - putting together, in one week's time, parties that could ante up a portion of the $150 million. "Who?" he contemplated. He needed a plan. He began by making a contact list of his most promising prospects. He would call each one of them urgently. Then, he remembered his invitation to Staubach's cocktail party. There would be plenty of money in that room. Excellent timing and he was just the man to seize this golden opportunity and turn that reception into a victory celebration.

CHAPTER 10
—◇—

As Jaclyn had anticipated, JP decided to leave for New York immediately. To her great relief, he had had no objection to waiting in second position while the seller worked the first contract. In fact, he remained optimistic about owning the building. As they drove to the airport, they discussed the deal and the potential for closing on the building and it was almost as if JP were trying to convince Jaclyn to maintain a positive attitude. It became clear to her that JP was as determined as she was to make this deal happen. She had become so focused on her personal goal of selling the Tower that she had almost lost sight of how much JP had at stake. He made it exceedingly clear to her that it was his intention to see the deal through to the end and he had every expectation that they would soon be in Thompson's office discussing the closing.

It was well into the afternoon when Jaclyn returned to her office after seeing JP off at the airport. Waiting for her was a message from John Fitzgerald. It said simply:

No break on SC Investors, still searching.
Hope for better luck in seeing you tonight.

As she sat at her desk, she grappled over whether to go to John's party. Part of her was eager to attend because it had been such a long time since she had any fun and she knew she had to extend her contact list. The other part of her, tired, dejected and exhausted after this eventful and stressful week, just wanted to rest. At this moment, she wasn't certain which side of her would win. The good news was that she didn't have to decide until later on that evening.

Refocusing on her work, she began reviewing her messages and before long was consumed by phone calls, faxes and paperwork. It was nearly 6:00 when she decided she was too tired to do anything further and closed the last of the files she had been working on. As she gathered her belongings and moved out into the hallway, she stopped abruptly. She heard sounds coming from the boardroom. To her knowledge, no one was conducting a late meeting. She moved cautiously toward the room and slowly opened the door. As she entered, she saw two of her top agents and their assistants seated at the table. They looked up at her as she entered and spoke. "Sorry, I didn't mean to interrupt. It's just that I didn't think anyone had a meeting planned for this evening. I was just checking things out before leaving."

Jason, a middle-aged man with a strong real estate background, replied. "No problem, Jaclyn, come on in. We had intended on announcing our latest project during Monday's staff meeting, but since you are here, come have a look." He stood and walked over to an easel and lifted a flip chart onto the stand. She walked over toward him as he turned the page revealing an architect's rendering of an office building. Jason pointed to the image as he spoke. "This is Preston Sherry Plaza, scheduled for completion in six months, and you are looking at the exclusive leasing agents."

Jaclyn was thrilled. "Congratulations. This is excellent news."

Jason continued, "We are compiling our list of prospective tenants and reviewing the floor plans as we finalize our leasing strategy."

George, Jason's partner, agreed. "We feel we have a strong action plan, which we'll present next week. We'll need everyone's effort to maximize this opportunity."

Jaclyn felt fortunate to have such dedicated and talented professionals on her team. "That's terrific. I look forward to your presentation. I may have a few clients who will want first dibs on the space. I will call them as soon as I have materials to show."

Jason and George responded in unison, "Great. Look forward to meeting with them."

"Alright," Jaclyn said. "I won't interrupt further. I'm on my way out. Have a great weekend." Before she was out the door, she turned back toward them. "And, please, make certain everything is locked when you go." They nodded and she continued on her way.

As she stepped into the surprisingly cool air, she thought to herself what a beautiful evening it was. The refreshing breeze brushed against her cheeks, reviving her, and she wished she could walk rather than drive home. She still wasn't accustomed to the dramatic change in her lifestyle. When she was in New York she truly enjoyed walking home from work. It gave her a chance to clear her mind and refresh her senses. Somehow driving home just didn't offer her the opportunity to invigorate herself. It was one of the few things she still missed about the city.

Minutes later, she made her way into her dark home and suddenly began to feel exhausted. Overtaken by sleepiness, she was forced to lay down. Before long, she fell into a deep sleep. An hour later, she awoke startled. It took her a few minutes before she even remembered lying down. She felt drugged and drowsy as she stretched out and yawned. She forced herself to get up and, dragging her feet, made her way into the bathroom. Knowing a shower would awaken her, she put her hair up in a swirl of curls and stepped into the tub. She turned on the cold water and allowed it to flow over her body as she tried to regain her equilibrium. The stresses of the week had taken their toll. The cool water streaming down her body stimulated her senses. A smile crossed her lips for the first time that day. She felt alive again. She stepped out of the tub and pulled on a plush terrycloth robe. After she was dried off, she walked into the kitchen to make herself dinner. But after scanning the empty refrigerator and barren cabinets, she disappointedly realized she had nothing in the house to eat. Even a can of tuna would have sufficed tonight, but there was none to be found. She would have to go out or go hungry. Neither choice sounded appealing, but the latter was definitely worse. She was famished, but then, she had forgotten once again to eat lunch. It had become a bad habit of late.

As she stood at the door of her closet, deciding what to wear to run out to grab some dinner, her navy blue, sequined gown sparkled in the light, catching her eye. It was the dress she had bought last year for a formal banquet Andrew's firm was throwing for a senior partner who was retiring. Jaclyn had never made it to that party. It was a month after she had found out about Stacy. She pulled out the dress and held it against the light, watching it shimmer and shine. It was such a beautiful dress. She walked out of the closet with the dress and held it to her chest as she examined her reflection in the full-length mirror. Her mind spoke to her. "It would be perfect for tonight…Maybe you should go to John's reception…At least then you won't have to eat alone." She had to laugh at herself. She was trying to convince herself to go out and have a good time. Now that she felt rested, the idea of the party actually sounded very nice. It didn't take her long to decide she would go. She tossed up her hair in a bunch of loose curls, touched up her makeup and slipped into the dress. She selected a black evening bag and black heels, added a touch of jewelry and then stood before her mirror to study her image. Although she hadn't fussed much in getting ready, she had to admit that the end result was good. Before long, she was on her way out the door.

It was just before 9 o'clock when she arrived at the entrance to Reunion Tower. She pulled around the drive to the valet stand. Immediately, a young man opened her door, extended his hand and peered into her eyes as she stepped out of the car. The look on his face told her how attractive she was this evening. He gave her directions to the party and handed her a valet ticket as she began to walk away. She followed his instructions and took the elevator to the top floor. When the doors opened, she walked into the reception area and waited behind a couple who was being checked into the party. A gentleman sitting at a podium was verifying the invitations and identification of arriving guests. Jaclyn waited while the man and woman before her were shown into the party. When they moved inside, she approached the gentleman. He was very official in his behavior as he asked for her name. He then moved his finger down the list, *Sullivan, Sweeney, Tanner, Tate*. She followed his finger down the list and noticed that a note beside her name indicated she was a personal guest of John Fitzgerald. After the man checked her identification, he nodded toward the room where the party was well under way. She thanked him and made her entrance.

The restaurant was surprisingly dark, but despite the dim lighting, the mood was very festive. Decorations abounded in shades of royal, navy and silver. By coincidence, she perfectly matched the color scheme. She scanned the crowded room in hopes of seeing John, but he was nowhere in sight. It was not long, however, before she had company. Two young men made their way over to her and introduced themselves and quickly she was embroiled in a lively conversation with them. It was nearly an hour later when John finally spotted her. As soon as he saw her, he made his way over. She turned as she felt someone put his hands on her bare back. John bent to kiss her cheek and she gave him a hug hello.

"Jaclyn, I can't tell you how happy I am you came tonight." John's face showed he was truly thrilled with her presence.

She leaned toward him so he could hear her over the music and conversation around them. "Thank you for inviting me. I have to say I've had a pretty rough week, but now that I'm here, I'm glad I came."

To her disappointment, it seemed as if the words were hardly out of her mouth when John was summoned away. As he was being pulled from her, he pleaded with her to mingle, eat and have fun and told her he would get back to her as quickly as he could. Jaclyn understood and did as he suggested. She ate from the plentiful hors d'oeuvre table, talked with several guests and walked around the glass-enclosed round room that looked out over Dallas.

Her favorite view was out the north windows and revealed a panorama of downtown. She loved looking at a city at night, when the lights in the buildings sparkled like stars in the midnight sky. She had gone to the restroom and was returning to the festivities when she caught a glimpse of Thanksgiving Tower through the window before her. She stopped at the transparent wall, lost in her private thoughts, when a man approached her from behind. As he neared, she saw his reflection in the glass wall before her. As his image became clearer, she recognized him and caught her breath. He was the enchanting stranger from the awards gala at the Anatole. As she watched, she wondered whether she were imagining him. She had pictured his face so many times since the awards dinner that she wondered if she was just willing him to be there. She turned to face him as he came within a foot of her. Unbelievably, he was standing only inches away.

Her stomach turned flips and her breathing became rapid. Her body tingled and she felt a warm wave start at her feet and make its way up to her face. She could not speak or move. He was the most wonderful-looking man she had ever seen. It was almost like a dream. He watched her staring at him and knew at once that she recognized him. He extended his hand to greet her and she, lost in his eyes, touched his hand out of reflex more than out of coherent response. He spoke softly, as if not to ruin the magic of the moment. "I had to come over to meet you. I remember you from the Anatole."

At that moment, it was as if there were only the two of them in the room. The sparkling lights around them seemed like stars shining down on them and it was as if they were suspended on a cloud. Nothing and no one else mattered. His words registered on her and she realized that the impact of their distant encounter at the gala had meant the same to him as it had to her. It took her a moment before she could find her voice. "I am so glad you did. I'm flattered that you remembered."

"A woman of your beauty is not easily forgotten." He smiled sexily at her and she blushed at his words. "And she blushes too. Now that is an even rarer quality."

Jaclyn was so taken by the moment that she had difficulty remembering how to breathe. She was completely at a loss for words and felt like such a young and inexperienced girl. It was as if she were under a spell. She stood looking up into his gorgeous face, studying the lines that combined so perfectly. He returned the stare and lost himself in her eyes and perfect smile. For a long moment, neither spoke a word. Then Steven broke the silence. In a deep and husky voice, he said, "I'm Steven." Introducing himself was almost an excuse to reach down and touch her hand again.

She replied in a slow, steady voice. "Steven, I'm pleased to meet you. I'm Jaclyn." He reached down for her hand, but instead of shaking it, raised it to his mouth and brushed the soft skin of his lips against the back of her hand. The gesture sent chills up and down her spine and she tingled everywhere. He seemed to hold her hand for an eternity. "Jaclyn, Jaclyn…," he repeated several times in a very seductive voice. She was totally lost in this man. He had complete control over her.

Then the spell was rudely broken. A loud, boisterous man

walked up behind Steven and smacked him hard on the back. Steven turned abruptly, stunned by the violent intrusion on the wonderful moment. He excused himself to shake hands with the man who was loud and clearly drunk. Steven did not have the patience for his presence and ushered him away quickly. When he returned his attention to Jaclyn, he found her lost in thought, starring out at the skyline. He turned her gently toward him and asked her if she wanted to leave. He felt free to do so because he had already met with several key contacts and had his staff working the crowd. He was never one to bring up business at a social event. He left that to his well-trained and experienced staff. As he looked down at Jaclyn, he was infinitely relieved he had decided not to bring Caroline to the event. He asked Jaclyn again if she wanted to go and she responded with a simple nod of her head.

It wasn't until she was standing at the valet and the cool evening breeze was refreshing her mind, that she realized she had not said good-night to John. She made a mental note to call him first thing Monday morning. She then thought about her car and turned to Steven. "I also have my car parked with the valet. Should I follow you whenever we are going?"

He smiled at her as he replied. "Leave it to me. Let me have your valet ticket."

Without hesitation, Jaclyn handed him the stub and watched him as he walked over to the stand, handed the valet a few bills and returned with her keys. He dangled them before her as he spoke. "See, all taken care of. Now you have nothing to worry about until the morning." She went numb at the insinuation of his comment. Before she could respond, a limousine pulled up and Steven opened the rear door and helped her into the back seat. Jaclyn was surprised, as she had expected to see a valet bring his car around. It was then that she began to wonder about the man before her. He exuded such an aura of power and money. She found him most intriguing.

As soon as they were seated, Steven reached into the cooler and retrieved a bottle of white wine. He poured two glasses, handed her one and took the other himself. Before calling ahead to the driver to inform him that they were ready to go, he made certain she was comfortable. At his command, the driver pulled out smoothly and slowly and she was lost again in Steven's face. As she sat there staring into his eyes, her mind began to contemplate who he was, this man who had so captivated her. She felt a closeness and connection with him that frightened and excited her all at once. As they talked, they laughed and she giggled over the silliest things. She felt so wonderfully free from her world of responsibility and stress. For one of the few times in her life, she allowed herself not to overanalyze the situation and to abandon the safe and narrow path. She felt young and reckless, totally carefree. The events of this week were forgotten and Thanksgiving Tower was worlds away. She felt as if she were running naked along a beach with the wind blowing in her hair and caressing her body. It was the most exhilarating experience she had ever known.

Steven stroked her cheek gently. The tenderness in this man's touch was more loving than she had ever felt in her four years with Andrew. Who was this man? She marveled at him. He read her thoughts through the expression in her eyes and bent his head toward hers. Slowly and softly, he kissed her lips. The warmth of his skin melted her. She knew she was powerless in his arms. As Steven kissed her, he felt free. He could tell that Jaclyn did not recognize him and the discovery was refreshing. It was the first time he had felt a connection with a woman without wondering if it was only his money and social position that attracted her. At first, he wanted to take her to his home, but that would reveal too much. As it was, he wished he had taken his car rather than the limousine that evening. He could explain the limo as a perk from his company, but his home would reveal in a moment who he was. Instead, he planned to take her to the Turtle Creek condominium he maintained for his out-of-town buyers and frequent visitors. On occasion, it was where he brought a woman he did not want in his home, but with Jaclyn it was different. He wanted her there, but he needed her to know him for the man he was before she fully knew the extent of his success. Tonight, his apartment would have to do. It was beautifully appointed but understated. It would paint a picture of accomplishment, but nothing near the level of prosperity he had obtained. He called ahead to the driver and gave him the address. Steven felt it would appear more like a hired limo if he had to give his home address to the driver. Good old Carlos knew better than to ever question Steven; he just went along with whatever he said.

Before long, they pulled up to a fifteen-story apartment building in the heart of Turtle Creek. Carlos rounded the circular drive and stopped at the front entrance. Steven helped Jaclyn out, then thanked Carlos and asked him to put the bill on the company's charge. Carlos winked at Steven and stood by the vehicle until Steven and Jaclyn were inside. He was always on call and never far from Steven for those rare occasions when he was urgently needed. Steven paid him well for his allegiance and discretion, and Carlos was a trusted and valued employee. They had come to know each other through a car service that Steven used routinely years ago. After numerous trips back and forth to the airport, Steven proposed that Carlos work for him personally and promised him a limousine to drive. Carlos thought he had hit the jackpot. He could finally buy the home he always wanted and still care for his aging parents in Mexico. For helping him realize his dreams, Carlos was the epitome of loyalty and dependability.

Steven led Jaclyn quickly by the security guard, hoping he wouldn't greet him by name or strike up a conversation as he often did after not having seen Steven for a while. When the guard looked in his direction, Steven nodded and immediately turned his attention to Jaclyn to avoid further eye contact. Just past the lobby, a brass and glass elevator was open and waiting for them. Jaclyn was intrigued when he inserted his key into the command panel and pushed the penthouse button. She had looked at apartments in this area when she first came to Dallas and knew the high-dollar real estate in which he lived. But from the moment she saw him, everything about him told her that he was successful and not just ordinarily, but substantially. She had come to know the look of power, wealth and social standing and he had that look, without doubt.

A moment later, the elevator doors opened into the apartment. Steven took Jaclyn by the hand and led her into the living room. She was instantly in awe of the beautifully appointed apartment that unfolded before them. Its polished look impressed her. It seemed to her that a professional decorator had put the finishing touches on the decor. The main living area was a great room with an expanse of hardwood floors, sectioned off by Oriental rugs into distinct areas. To her far left was a brown lacquer bar with a large mirror and several glass shelves filled with a wide variety of bottles covering the wall behind it and black leather barstools lined up in front. Immediately before the bar, four brown velvet loveseats were grouped together to form a square around a large glass and iron coffee table. Beneath the seating, a beautiful plush area rug perfectly combined all the colors of the room. Opposite her, an ornate writing desk stood against a wall of windows overlooking a park, which was lit at night, creating a picturesque backdrop of muted green and brown tones. To her right was an informal dining table, which matched the coffee table across the room and was surrounded by eight wrought iron chairs with brown velvet cushions. In the center of the glass table, an enormous silk floral arrangement added color and warmth. Beyond the table was a fabric-covered wall with an opening encased by a pair of shutters. Beyond the wall, from what she could see through the narrow opening, was the kitchen.

Steven watched her take it all in, then he gave her a tour so she knew where everything was. He asked her to make herself at home while he went to get comfortable. He disappeared into a back room and Jaclyn was left to wander. As she walked around, it struck her as odd that there were no photos anywhere, not in an album, nor on the walls or in frames on his desk. In fact, the apartment was curiously devoid of personal touches that would give any hint about this man, his family, hobbies or life. It seemed to her as if the apartment were a hotel suite, beautifully appointed, but not homey in a personal sense. For the first time since their meeting, the identity of this man concerned her. Lost in her thoughts, she moved to the expanse of windows on the far wall that looked out over the park. While she was admiring the view, Steven returned to the living room wearing a pair of silk lounging pants with a matching smoking jacket casually tied at the waist and purposely left open at the chest. Jaclyn turned as she heard him enter the room. Her breath was instantly taken away. He was everything a man should be, extremely manly, but well groomed and polished. If Jaclyn could have designed the perfect look for a man, it would have been Steven just as he was standing before her. He moved toward her and she caught her breath. He reached out and caressed her bare arms. She melted at his touch. He offered for her to change into something more comfortable, but she declined, agreeing only to take off her high heels.

He took her hand and led her to one of the soft brown velour sofas on the other side of the room. He let her sit first, then sat down close to her. Using a remote control, he turned on soft, classical music. When he looked back at her, he smiled and she began to relax. He made an attempt at conversation, but he could tell that neither one of them really wanted to talk. Her eyes continually wandered down to his bare chest, making it difficult for him to resist her. When he could see she was comfortable and relaxed, he began caressing her arms and neck. He peered deeply into her eyes with a hungry, sensuous gaze. Jaclyn knew the look in a man's eyes when he wanted her; they glazed over and became fixed on hers. It had always frightened her before, but tonight, seeing that look come over Steven melted her heart. She wanted him as she had never wanted a man before. Prior to tonight, she always waited until she knew a man well before she became intimate with him. Steven was different. For him, she felt a pull and draw she didn't question but merely accepted. She wanted to be reckless. She refused to listen to her conservative voice of reason and instead chose to follow her heart and emotions. Being impulsive felt free and somewhat frightening, but she gave into the desire and allowed herself to enjoy the experience.

"Steven, I…" Out of nervousness, she initiated conversation, but Steven recognized that she didn't really want to talk.

"Yes, Jaclyn?"

"I don't know what to say. I'm glad we're here, but I feel odd…I mean, I don't know you…this isn't how I am…"

He smiled at her as he replied. "Jaclyn, I know. This isn't how I am either. But then again, how often have you felt like this?"

She laughed at his reply. She knew that what was happening between them was extraordinary. Stopping the evening at this moment was well within her rights, but well outside of her ability. The evening had taken on a life of its own and she was hesitantly, but happily going along for the ride.

When the look in her eyes showed her acceptance, he took her face in his large hands, held her close to him, then bent to meet her lips, kissing her ravenously. Their being together was completely impetuous and part of Jaclyn was terrified, but she was helpless to stop the direction of this evening. As he kissed her, he raised her hand to his chest, coaxing her to touch him, letting her lead in the furthering of their intimacy. The warmth of her hands sent waves of desire through him. It had been an unusually long time since he had been with a woman and the depth of his desire was evident by his firm erection. He had to reposition himself on the sofa to get comfortable. For Steven, tonight was a rare experience. For only the second time he could remember and the first time since his college love, he was drawn to a woman with an intensity that surprised him. It was more than a physical attraction. It was deeper, more meaningful. The feeling of being with a woman who only wanted him for the man she saw and not for what he could give her was so intoxicating he was having trouble controlling his desire to climax. They were strangers drawn to one another by a mysterious force and he basked in its eroticism.

Lost in the moment, Steven hungrily kissed and caressed Jaclyn to the point of self-induced torture. He could no longer resist having her. She was clearly lost in the moment as well. Her eyes were glazed over and she was melting into his arms. Gently, he took her hand and led her to the bedroom. As they approached the room, the smell of burning scented candles engulfed her. Crossing the threshold, the feel of a luxurious, plush carpet beneath her stocking feet welcomed her. Jaclyn took the room in as they walked inside. Before her was a four-poster mahogany bed, draped with flowing streams of a sheer, cream-colored fabric that looped around the canopy posts and fell softly to the floor. Beside the bed were mahogany nightstands and across the room a matching dresser completed the bedroom suite. The dark wood of the furniture contrasted with the soft, off-white tones of the carpeting, walls and curtains. The overhead lighting was very dim and, with the flickering candles on each nightstand, cast a soft glow on the bed. The romantic setting entranced her and complemented the mood of the evening perfectly.

As they neared the bed, Steven stopped and helped her out of her evening dress. Standing before him in lace undergarments, Steven drank her in with his eyes. She was ravishing. Her cream-colored body had soft curves and the small brown tuft beneath her white lace panties hinted at the pleasure he would find with her. Unable to control her mounting desire and needing him to take her, Jaclyn moved to the bed and motioned for him to join her. He shed his robe and pants and moved slowly in his nakedness toward her. Jaclyn took in his body. His physique was hard and well defined, with dark brown curls centered on his chest and covering the length of his legs. He was exquisite. His taught erection made it clear that his lust for her matched the desire she felt for him. He pulled himself alongside her and entwined his legs between hers. He moved slowly against her body, finding her hungry mouth with his and tasting all of her. He moved his soft but masculine hands along her curvaceous body. They kissed passionately and ravenously until Jaclyn reached down and stroked his groin. At her touch, he let out a soft groan and moved onto his knees, bending over her to remove her undergarments. As he unfastened her bra, her breasts fell into his hands and he caressed and kissed them. When Jaclyn's moaning heightened, he moved his mouth down her body, kissing her gently as he moved his lips and tongue along her stomach and hips and fulfilled her in a way no man had before. She was lost in waves of ecstasy. This man who was such a mystery to her had total control over her at this moment and was bringing her to a place she had never been. Uncertain if she could bear the urge to have him within her a moment longer, she pulled at his shoulders until he acquiesced and stretched out alongside her with his face close to hers once again. He looked deep into her eyes and smiled warmly at her pleased expression. Softly, she pleaded with him to take her. He smiled at her as he positioned himself on top of her and slowly entered her body, inching his way into her warmth. They groaned and moved in unison as they took each other to extreme passion.

The pleasure was powerful for Jaclyn and so complete for Steven. He pondered who this woman was and how she could enter his heart so quickly and completely. He had been with many women, but none satisfied him so completely as she did. Never before had he wanted to lie beside a woman after their intimacy. With Jaclyn, he wanted to be with her, touch her, talk to her, please her again and then watch her as she slipped into that wonderful and contented sleep that only follows consuming intimacy.

After they made love again, they remained side by side, fondling each other for hours. They spoke minimally. They mostly lay entwined in each other's limbs, stroking each other gently. And in the end, when they were completely spent, just as the light of early dawn crept into the room, they fell asleep in each other's arms as if they had been lovers for years. It was good and right and they both knew it, though neither understood it.

Later that morning, when Jaclyn stirred in bed and began to wake, she opened her eyes to find Steven lying beside her, propped up on one arm, studying her intently. Shyly, she covered her naked breasts with the sheet that was tangled around her waist. Softly, she spoke. "Good morning." The words were said with a giggle in her voice. In the light of the morning, she couldn't believe what she had done the night before and with a total stranger. What had come over her? She buried her head in the pillow to stifle a laugh.

Steven watched her with intrigue. He teased her. "Are you going to let me in on the joke?"

She looked up from behind the pillow with a wide grin brightening her face and making her eyes dance. She had mischief in her voice as she spoke. "I just can't believe what happened last night. I mean, I'm not like that, usually…oh, I bet that sounds so cliché." She shook her head and buried her face again.

Steven was tickled by her obvious discomfort with what had happened between them. She truly was different. It was clear to Steven this was not standard dating practice for her and he wanted her to know he understood. "Jaclyn, I'm not sorry it happened and I hope you're not either." As he spoke, he uncovered her face from the pillow and pulled her chin toward him so she would look at him. "I know this is not typical for you and that's what makes last night even more special." He knew just what to say and she smiled back at him.

"Thank you" was all Jaclyn could think to say. She sat up on the bed and looked at him. He was bare to the waist and looked so relaxed. The muscles in his arms were firm and toned and he looked like someone who could pose for a fitness magazine. He was incredibly, virilely handsome. After a moment of drinking him in again, she spoke. "Last night was incredible for me. It was as if I was someone else, somehow so free. It felt good and safe and wonderful. I can't believe I don't know you at all and yet, I have never been so comfortable with anyone before. I can't explain it. It was just so right and I knew it then. I have no regrets now, it's just that I feel so different, so reckless."

Steven laughed at her effort to make sense out of what had taken place. He knew better than to try to understand affairs of the heart. He touched her arm gently, as she lay back on the pillow and stared at the ceiling. As they lay side by side, wallowing in the memory of the night, Steven's stomach began to growl and they both laughed. Since he only stocked the refrigerator when he planned for out-of-town guests, he knew he didn't have any food at the apartment. The loud rumbling prompted him to discuss breakfast. "Jaclyn, I hate to even think about moving from this bed, but I'm starving. I'm afraid I don't have anything to offer you for breakfast. I was thinking we could go out for something to eat or I could have something delivered."

Jaclyn sat up, almost frightened by the prospect of having breakfast together. It was uncomfortable at the moment, although she wasn't certain why. "No . . . I mean, I can't stay, but thank you." Although the words came from her lips, they weren't the ones she wanted to say. She didn't want to leave him but now that she had said it, he was getting off the bed and leaving the room so she could have her privacy. Damn, she thought. After such a wonderful night, why was she running away? What was she afraid of?

By the time she was dressed, Steven had already called Carlos and instructed him to wait downstairs for Jaclyn. He did not want her to be uncomfortable with him, so he would not try to keep her from leaving if that is what she wanted to do. When she opened the bedroom door and walked into the living room, his heart nearly stopped. She was in that spectacular evening dress again, but this time, her hair was ruffled and her makeup kissed off. She was the sexiest woman he had ever seen. It took all of his self-control not to take her in his arms and devour her. Jaclyn saw the hunger in his eyes and was flattered. It crossed her mind to tell him she changed her mind, but remembering she had no other clothing with her, she concluded it would be better if she left for now. She broke the silence. "Steven, thank you for the incredible evening. I will never forget it. I hope you don't mind that I'm leaving you this morning, but considering the clothes I have, it probably wouldn't be the most appropriate thing to wear out for breakfast." She smiled at him and he smiled back.

His voice was tender. "I understand, Jaclyn. When can I see you again?" Although she was glad he had asked, she was unprepared for his question and hesitated. Her delayed response surprised him and he questioned her with his eyes. When she didn't answer quickly enough, he said. "Okay, let me guess . . . you're married."

Steven's comment tickled her and she started to laugh, "No, nothing like that, I'm just a little rusty on the dating thing and this is happening so fast, I guess I'm a little confused. But of course I want to see you again. Let me give you my number." She motioned toward Steven's desk. They walked over together and continued speaking as she wrote her work and home numbers for him. "Call me and we'll plan to get together again soon. I would really like that."

Steven took the paper and put it in the pocket of his robe and walked Jaclyn to the elevator. As they crossed the room, he explained to her that the driver was downstairs waiting and he would take her to her car or anywhere else she wanted to go. He turned her to face him and held her hands in his as he spoke. "Thank you for last night. I look forward to seeing you again, very soon again." He pulled her toward him and kissed her long and hard. She returned his embrace and long, passionate kisses and had to fight the desire to be with him again, right then and there. He pulled away as the elevator buzzer sounded. The doors opened before them and he led her into the elevator, pushed the button for the lobby, then kissed her good-bye. As the doors closed between them, she waved and he waved back. Both of them lost in thought about what had happened between them.

CHAPTER 11
—◇—

It was shortly after Steven stepped out of the shower that his mobile phone rang. He hurriedly wrapped a bath towel around his waist and jogged to the bedroom to find his phone. He followed the sound of the ring to the breast pocket of his suit jacket. Slightly out of breath, he answered. "Hello."

Al heard the breathlessness in his voice and suddenly wished he had not called. He thought about hanging up, but he knew Steven would want to hear what he had to say, so he found the courage to speak. "Hey, it's Al."

Thanksgiving Tower was the only thing Steven would allow to interrupt his thoughts of Jaclyn. He was eager to hear any updates that Al had to report. "Yes, Al, what is it?"

Al began rambling and, at first, Steven had trouble following what he was saying. "I got my hands on the names of a few prospects who may be good leads for us. I know how important it is to get the money pulled together as quickly as possible, so I thought you would want to hear about it first thing."

Steven almost didn't believe his ears. Could it be that Al had finally taken some initiative? He was eager to hear what Al had to say. "Okay, you've got my attention. Who are they?"

Al felt like a big man. He knew Steven would come around to see that he wasn't so bad after all. He would milk this one for all it was worth. "I actually have the names of quite a few contacts. Why don't we meet at your office and go through the list together?"

Steven had already planned to go into his office, so he agreed to meet Al there. "Okay, let's meet in my office in one hour."

The line went dead and Al hung up the phone feeling very good about himself. Maybe he did have what it took to be a player in this town.

***

Jaclyn moved about in a fog the entire day. After leaving Steven's apartment, she had asked the driver to take her to Reunion Tower to retrieve her car. As she drove out of the parking garage, she paused to remember the incredible feeling she had when she had first seen Steven. It all came back to her now and she felt warm and sensual. A smile came to her face and she had to shake herself from the memories of the incredible evening she had shared with Steven.

The first thing she did when she arrived home was to check her messages, then she undressed and stepped into the shower. She lingered, allowing the warm water to stream down her body, remembering the warmth she had felt in Steven's arms. She spent the rest of the morning and early afternoon relaxing at home, thinking about Steven and reliving the time they had spent together. It amazed her how comfortable she felt with this man she hardly knew and it excited her to think of him, his great body and incredible lovemaking. He was so warm and gentle, yet so manly. His mischievous smile stayed on her mind. Closing her eyes, she could feel him, taste him, and smell him. He had quickly become an obsession. She didn't tire of thinking about their night together and the recollection made her feel warm and wanted.

It was hours later when Jaclyn decided to go to her office. She had lounged enough for one day and figured she would either have to keep her mind busy or go crazy being away from Steven. When she arrived at her office, she picked up the mail that had been delivered earlier that morning. She sifted through the correspondence, then laid it on the receptionist's desk for distribution on Monday morning. She continued on to her office and sat at her desk. With her mind miles away, she pored through the files in front of her but was unable to concentrate. She tried several times to clear her mind of thoughts of Steven, but her attempts were futile. After trying to work but accomplishing nothing, she decided to leave.

As she stepped into her car and turned on the engine, she thought about where she wanted to go. As she sat there thinking, Steven was all that came to mind. She wanted to be with him again and suddenly it dawned on her that she had no way to reach him. She didn't even know his last name. She remembered the way his building looked, but having only been driven there in the limo, she didn't know exactly where it was. Suddenly, she realized how bizarre their evening together had truly been. Here was a man she didn't know except by sight at the awards gala and then their rendezvous last night. In the light of the day and without Steven before her, removing all rational thought from her mind, she found it hard to imagine what she had allowed to happen. It troubled her that she had been so intimate with a man she knew nothing about and she felt compelled to learn something about him. As she contemplated how, she remembered the party guest list. His name would assuredly be on it. She hurriedly turned off the ignition and returned to her office. Walking over to her desk, she flung open her Rolodex to F and dialed John Fitzgerald number. To her disappointment, his phone rang, until, finally, an answering service picked up the line. She left a message with the operator asking John to return her call. It was frustrating not to be able to speak with him at that moment, but she had no choice. She spent a few minutes trying to think of anyone else who would have access to that information, but no one came to mind. As she sat contemplating the odd situation, her thoughts turned to John and she was hopeful he would return her call soon.

John was at his desk when he heard the phone ring. He hadn't been expecting any important business calls, so he allowed the call to roll over to the answering service. It was unusual for him to be at his desk on a Saturday afternoon, but after the disappointing evening the night before, he had decided to go to the office and wade through some paperwork. He had built up so many expectations around Jaclyn's accepting his invitation to the party and then when she showed up dressed so beautifully, his hopes soared. He could hardly believe it when he went looking for her and learned she left the party with another man. His heart sank so low he had found it difficult to stay upbeat and social for the remainder of the evening. Now as he called his service and heard Jaclyn's message, he laughed out loud as he thought how foolish he had been to pursue her. She obviously wasn't interested in him. John figured she was calling now to apologize. At this moment, he didn't want to hear from her. He decided that he might return her call next week. Then again, maybe not.

***

Al and Steven sat across from each other at Steven's desk. Al was clearly pleased with himself. He was smiling ear to ear and sat tall with his chest held out as he waited for Steven to initiate the meeting.

Noting the change in Al and the confidence that was evident in his posture, Steven was eager to hear Al's list of prospective investors. "Alright Al, you've piqued my interest. Who's interested in a piece of this deal?"

Al wanted to savor this occasion. It was not often that Steven wanted to hear what he had to say. He sat up tall in his chair as he opened a manila folder on his lap. "I have done some research and compiled a list of prospective investors for the deal." Al paused for emphasis and looked at Steven, who was visibly eager to learn the identity of the prospects. "I want to do my part in helping you put the deal together."

Al paused again, but this time Steven interrupted. He was trying to be patient but he didn't like to waste time. "I appreciate that, Al, but now can we get down to business?"

Al nodded. "Of course. I thought I would begin by reading a list of potential partners. I will give you details about anyone you think is suitable. I have addresses and phone numbers if you wish to contact them. I will begin with those I consider prime candidates."

Steven acknowledged his understanding, "Very well." He took out a pen and a legal pad to indicate he was ready.

Without further delay, Al began his review. "First I call your attention to Mr. J. Hebert…"

As soon as Al said Jed's name, Steven stopped him. "Did you say, Jed Hebert?"

Al looked up from the file. "Yes, Jed Hebert, from Louisiana."

Steven sat back in his chair and put his pen to his lips as he thought about Jed. Steven and Jed were both on the board of directors at the Lone Star Bank. Steven recalled the old man with amusement. On the rare occasion Jed actually made it to a quarterly meeting, it was certain he would doze off noisily about halfway through. Steven was well aware that it was Jed's substantial net worth, much of which was deposited in the Lone Star Bank, that had earned him a seat on the board. The sound of money rang loudly in Steven's ears. He was certain Jed could easily come up with the cash for a piece of the Tower. Steven hadn't thought about that old man in some time. In fact, Jed had missed several board meetings over the past year, so it had been a long time since Steven had spoken to him. He decided he would call Jed immediately after his meeting with Al. Steven jotted down Jed's name at the top of his list and then asked Al to continue.

As Al read down his list, Steven made several notes, asking for phone numbers or additional information if a prospect sounded promising. After Al had read the last name, Steven thanked him for his hard work and showed him out of the office, giving Al a slap on the back as he left. At the gesture, Al stuck out his chest and held his head high. He felt good about himself. Maybe he could play at this game after all. As he left Steven's office and headed toward his car, he was lost in thought, dreaming about the money he would earn for helping Steven close the Tower deal. He was starting to spend the money as if it were already in the bank.

As soon as Al had left his office, Steven looked up Jed's home number and placed a call. Steven figured that on a Saturday afternoon, a man Jed's age was likely to be sipping lemonade on his front porch. He waited through several rings before a woman with a charming southern drawl answered the phone. When Steven asked for Jed, she cordially informed him that Daddy was taking a nap on the front porch swing. Steven's guess hadn't been far off the mark. When Steven mentioned to her that he was a business associate of her father calling from Dallas, she insisted on waking him. She was certain he would want to talk to an old friend from Texas. Steven thanked her and waited for several minutes until Jed picked up the phone.

Sleepily, Jed mustered his loudest greeting, which was little more than a whisper. "Hello?"

Steven decided to take it slow. "Jed?"

Jed replied a little less sleepily. "That's right, who's this?"

Steven smiled broadly at the old goat. Some things never change, he thought to himself. "Jed, it's Steven Cason."

It took Jed a moment to register Steven's name, then he replied with a chuckle in his voice. "Steven, how are you? What ya up to these days?"

Jed's apparent pleasure at hearing from him was a relief. "You know me, Jed, just trying to eke out a bare existence."

Jed broke into full laughter. "You're a sly one, Cason. So what's goin' on in Dallas? Did I miss another one of those daggum board meetin's again?"

This old character amused Steven. "No, Jed, I don't think so, but that's not why I'm calling. I want to talk to you about a property I think you might be interested in." Steven paused purposely to read Jed's interest.

Jed played along. "What prop'ty might that be?"

Steven continued. "Thanksgiving Tower in Dallas."

Jed shook his head in disbelief. "What in tarnation is all the fuss about that buildin' anyway? I got this girl, oh darn, what was her name? . . .well, it doesn't matter, anyway this girl's been callin' me on that prop'ty, sent me information I could hardly understand. You know me, I don't do business like that, but she sure as hell called enough for a while. I guessed she'd gone and sold it to someone else since I haven't heard from her in a spell. I don't have to tell you this, but I buy land by touchin' and smellin' the soil, not by readin' about it. City folk. I guess I'll never understand them."

Steven listened intently, picking up the interest and the manner in which he needed to proceed. "I'm like you, Jed, but I can tell you Thanksgiving Tower is one sweet deal. I am buying it as the showcase of Cason Properties. I'm going to do it with a partnership and I'm offering you a part of the deal."

Jed thought about it for a minute. He had all that money in CDs and his attorney had told him to get someone to invest it for him because interest rates were declining and he needed to diversify his portfolio. He had a few brokers working the market with some of it, even though he didn't like those investment types telling him what to do with his money. Who could trust them? Steven he trusted, and his involvement certainly indicated a safe investment. And wouldn't his daughters be proud of their daddy, owning a part of Big D. The thought started to excite him. "How much you talkin' 'bout, Steven?"

"Depends on how big a piece you're interested in. The purchase price is $150 million. SC Investment is taking 40%, the rest I will divide among other investors. What share are you thinking about?"

Jed wasn't one for particulars; he usually left the figuring to others. "Let me think about this for a minute, Steven." He paused and Steven remained silent. Jed thought through the money he had left over at the bank and how much he wanted to leave there for emergencies. When he had a figure in mind, he spoke again. "How 'bout you carve up that pie so I get a nice piece, let's say 20%. That would be around $30 million. I have that amount tucked away there in the Lone Star Bank. I bet those boys won't be happy if I pull that money out, but I've been lookin' for an excuse to get off their board anyway."

Steven let out a hardy laugh. "Alright, Jed, I appreciate your interest. I will reserve that percentage for you. Be happy to."

Jed was pleased. "Good, then it's all set."

Steven needed something in writing, but he was careful not to upset Jed with details. "Yes, Jed, it's all set. I do need to have your signature on a document to present to the seller. Is it alright if I have someone bring it out to you?"

Jed thought about what he should do. "Better yet, I'm gonna give you my attorney's number. You call him and work it all out. He can handle the rest for me."

Both men were equally pleased as they ended the call. Steven sat back and breathed a sigh of relief. He already had another part of the deal done. Now, 60% of the deal was done. Not bad, he thought.

Jed sat back on the swing satisfied and thought about his discussion with Steven. He felt good about the agreement. He sat on the porch, grinning. Later, he walked slowly into the house and down the hall to his office. He opened the worn leather book that sat square in the center of his old wooden desk and made a note in his daily journal. It said simply, 'Bought a piece of Dallas today'.

***

Steven's next calls to the leads given to him by Al were not as successful. Several of the individuals were flat-out not interested and some even asked that he not contact them again about the deal. Steven thought it odd that these individuals had already had the deal presented to them by someone and then he imagined Al might have initially contacted them. He also left detailed messages for others who were unavailable to take his call. His last attempt was to the final name on the list, Sumitomo. Steven knew Japanese investors well; they typically loved high-profile buildings. Like the Empire State Building in New York, Thanksgiving Tower in Dallas fit that bill perfectly.

When Sumitomo's secretary announced Steven's call, he took it himself. "Mr. Cason, to what do I owe the honor of your call?"

He spoke in perfect English, which surprised Steven. Al had informed him that a translator would be necessary. Steven questioned him. "Is this Mr. Sumitomo?"

The gentleman replied, "Yes, I am Sumitomo. Mr. Cason, what can I do for you?"

Steven explained his reaction. "I'm sorry for the confusion. I had been told we would need a translator. My mistake, for which I apologize."

Sumitomo was quick to explain. "No need to apologize. I do not need a translator, as you can see. However, I travel with my real estate advisor and attorney when I am negotiating a deal and only speak through him so I am certain my position is negotiated in the most favorable way for my business. I was educated at UCLA and, as you can tell, am quite proficient in English. Now, Mr. Cason, I am eager to hear the nature of your call."

Steven admired his candor and business tactic. "The reason for my call is that it has been brought to my attention that you may be interested in a position in the Thanksgiving Tower in Dallas."

Sumitomo's face lit up. This had been his goal, but that arrogant American woman had cut him short. What a stroke of luck that it was being offered to him again. He was clearly intrigued. "I'm very interested in the Tower. Please continue."

Steven was energized by his positive response. "I am currently under contract on the Tower and am planning to form a limited partnership. I will divide the ownership according to the interest I receive from each party. My company, SC Investors, has a 40% stake.

I also have a commitment from an individual investor for an additional 20%. I am discussing this opportunity with several prospects and will consider all interests with a minimum of 5% ownership. The total purchase price is $150 million dollars."

Sumitomo took a moment to formulate his thoughts. "Forgive me for the delay, it is just that I am running a few numbers. We are in the midst of closing several deals in Houston and I have just this week committed a significant amount of available funds to those purchases. I do want to be involved, however, and feel comfortable committing to a 20% stake."

In one day, Steven had almost enough money on the table to do the deal. Jed's 20%, and now Sumitomo's 20% left only 20% unaccounted for. A few more players and he would have it done. He returned his attention to Sumitomo. "Thank you for your commitment. I am pleased that we will be working together on this project and hope that it will be only the start to a mutually rewarding relationship."

Sumitomo echoed his sentiment. "I too am very pleased to be working with you. I hope that we will have many more opportunities to work together."

Steven continued. "As a formality, I need to present the partner's commitments in writing to the seller by this Friday. I will have a package detailing the specifics of the deal we agreed to sent out to you urgently. I also request that you fill out a few forms that guarantee Mitsu's cash position and allow me to act on your behalf in executing the contract. We are under a tight timeframe to finalize our offer and must have everything in order by the end of this week."

Sumitomo understood. "I know how urgent things can be when you are working under a tight deadline. I look forward to receiving your package and will review it, and barring anything unexpected, I will return the paperwork to you as you require."

Steven was thrilled. "Thank you. I appreciate your cooperation and look forward to our association."

When Steven was through with his call, he paused to consider the progress he unexpectantly made today. Although he was grateful things had gone so quickly and smoothly, it did dawn on him that neither Jed nor Sumitomo requested any details on the building. It was likely they were familiar with it, but enough to agree to a part of the deal without due diligence? Steven was curious but was not concerned. They both clearly expressed a strong interest in the deal and were eager to take part. He did, however, want their commitments in writing and the sooner, the better. That would remove any doubts Steven had about them following through with the purchase.

Before doing anything else, Steven called Diana. She answered her home phone, as he hoped she would. "Hello."

"Diana, it's Steven."

"Yes, Steven."

"Can you come to the office to type up partnership commitments for two investors who agreed to purchase interests in the Tower today? I want to be certain they have the paperwork in their hands first thing Monday morning."

Diana did not hesitate. "Of course Steven, I'll be right there."

Within a half-hour Diana was at the office and taking instruction from Steven. As always, she executed Steven's orders perfectly and managed all his correspondence flawlessly. When he was confident she was clear on his instructions and had the paperwork under way, he left the office and went to the gym. He needed to release some of the energy that flowed through his veins now that the deal was falling into place. He could taste it. The Tower was within reach. It was almost his.

***

That evening, Steven had a business dinner he had committed to attend weeks before. He had planned for Caroline to accompany him, but after his night with Jaclyn, he did not want to be with her, let alone spend an evening pretending he wanted her by his side. He wished there was a way to cancel on her, but she was friends with the host and would attend even if Steven did not accompany her. He felt suffocated by the thought of her. He knew it was time for a change.

Before Steven left his home for the evening, he called Jaclyn. He had wanted to phone her earlier to see how she was and hear her voice, but his day had turned busier than he had anticipated and his attention had been turned to solidifying his deal. Now as he placed the call, he listened disappointedly to the phone as it rang and rang, until, finally her voice sounded as the answering machine picked up. Following her greeting, he spoke softly and sexily into the receiver. "Jaclyn, hello. It's Steven. I wanted to hear your voice before I went out for the evening. I don't even want to go out after our night together, but I had already committed to this business dinner, so I must. I hope you had a good day and are having a good evening out. I hope to speak with you soon. Good night." Every time he had thought about Jaclyn, his body ached for her. It had been years since a woman had stayed on his mind like she did. She was definitely different.

***

Jaclyn had gone out to Blockbuster to rent a movie for the evening when Steven called. When she returned and found his message, she was upset that she had missed him but happy to know he had tried to reach her. She played the message over and over and saved it to listen to later. She couldn't wait to see him again. Their night together had been magical. Before last night, she had doubted she would ever let herself fall in love again or give herself to anyone completely. But having opened her heart to Steven, she now knew she could and wanted to. Loving Steven, she decided, would be worth the risk of a broken heart. She knew that instinctively.

CHAPTER 12
—◇—

Steven sat back hard against the rear seat of the limousine as Carlos pulled onto the driveway leading to Caroline's home. Lost in thought, Steven contemplated his life, considering both the good and the bad. Fortunate in so many ways, he lived a life of abundance. Regularly, he socialized with the upper crust, attending endless extravagant dinners, outings, and trips. Likewise, at work, he experienced boundless success, propelling him into elite status within his industry. Sadly, however, his personal life was shallow, meaningless and empty. Yet, he had accepted that until now. The catalyst for change, however, was Jaclyn. She made him believe for the first time in his adult life that he could have it all. Now, anything short of being with Jaclyn and completing his life with her was a farce and he needed desperately to find a way to correct his pointless existence with Caroline.

As they rounded the lengthy circular drive, Steven began to wish he had come up with a reason to cancel their evening together. He didn't know if he could stand being with Caroline after experiencing time with Jaclyn. His thoughts turned to Caroline's father, Henry. Steven knew all too well that Henry was a vindictive man and that hurting his daughter by ending their relationship would not be acceptable to him. Steven recalled hearing about Jacob Boswirt, a comptroller who shared too much company information with individuals outside Henry's inner circle. When Henry found out Jacob had publicized his business dealings around town, Henry made an example out of him. He ruined the man's name, forcing him out of Dallas. The man left with his tail between his legs, never to be heard from again. Henry's reputation preceded him. He was thought of as a ruthless businessman and a heartless individual. Those characterizations didn't phase Henry at all. All that mattered to him were money, power and social status and he would stop at nothing to possess any of them.

As Steven weighed Henry's vengeful streak, he knew he would have to handle Caroline with kid gloves and somehow let it be her decision to end their empty relationship. When the limosine came to a stop in front of the palatial house, Steven stepped out of the car and made his way up the flight of brick stairs. He rang the bell alongside the massive wood and lead glass double doors and waited. Shortly after the chimes had sounded, the butler opened the door and welcomed him in. The man showed Steven into Henry's study while he announced his arrival to Miss Caroline. When Steven walked through the massive oak door and into Henry's dark, paneled study, he was instantly relieved Henry was not there. He didn't want to face him tonight. As he took a seat by the massive mahogany desk, the butler asked if he wanted a drink while he waited. Feeling as if a Scotch might help him through the evening, he accepted the offer and asked for Pinch on the rocks. The butler nodded and retreated to the bar on the far side of the room. Just as Steven was getting comfortable in his chair, the door to the study opened. Anticipating that it would be Caroline, he stood to greet her but was instead surprised when the door opened fully to reveal Henry. Steven's body stiffened as he saw him. His jaw became tight with the contempt he felt for that man. Steven's eyes followed his as Henry walked toward him. As he neared Steven, he extended his hand. "Steven. How are you?"

Steven forced a smile and a casual reply. "Excellent, Henry. How are you?"

Henry moved around his desk and sat on the high-back, black leather chair. He motioned for Steven to sit, which he did on cue. Henry had a conniving smile on his face that Steven found repulsive. In his usual arrogant tone, Henry replied, "I'm terrific Steven. Any better and I'd be twins." Henry broke into a throaty laugh and Steven shot him a labored smile. When he was through laughing, Henry composed himself then continued. "Haven't seen you up at the club recently." It was a statement that asked for explanation and Steven hated to have to account for his whereabouts to anyone, especially Henry.

He chose his words carefully. "Actually, Henry, I've been rather occupied with the business. Things are going extremely well, but they require an enormous amount of my time. That leaves me little time to play."

Henry leaned toward Steven and spoke in the voice of a concerned elder. "All work and no play, Steven, makes for a hard and dull life. I wouldn't like to see you falling into a bad pattern so young. You need to get out with the boys more. Get in a few rounds of golf, shoot the breeze with the fellows, play a game or two of cards. Believe me, I get more business done at the club than I do at the office." He winked at Steven and sat back, satisfied with himself for his good advice.

Before Steven could reply, Caroline stepped into the room and Henry's attention was diverted to his daughter. Both men rose from their chairs and turned to see her enter the room. She was dressed in an ankle-length, sky blue taffeta dress that had a strapless, fitted bodice and a full, flowing skirt. She had draped a soft white, knit shawl about her. Her hair was arranged in the same straight bob as always and laid stiffly at the top of her shoulders. As Steven looked at her hard face, he felt nothing for her and wished he could vanish from where he stood.

Admiring his daughter as she entered the room, Henry walked over to meet her. Steven remained fixed where he was. Henry took his daughter by the hands, held her at arm's length before him and complimented her beauty. He turned to Steven, seeking his agreement. "Isn't she just beautiful, Steven? I have to say, you're one lucky man."

Steven just nodded his head in agreement. Caroline wanted more and she made it clear that his gesture was insufficient. "Cat got your tongue, Steven?" Her high-pitched, bitchy tone grated on Steven's nerves. He just smiled at her in reply.

She made her way over to him and presented her cheek. As usual, she expected Steven to kiss her, which he did to avoid a scene in front of Henry. Tonight he did not have the patience for her false pretenses. He hurried them along. "Well, Caroline, we should be on our way."

Just then, the butler appeared with Steven's drink on a silver tray. The man moved slowly toward Steven and presented him with the glass. Steven accepted the drink, chugged the contents in two gulps, and then turned his attention back to Caroline. She stood before him with a look of disapproval on her face. He smiled at her and spoke so that she could not comment on his action. "Caroline, shall we go?" He held out his arm for her and then led her toward the door. As he passed Henry, Steven patted him on the arm. Henry took hold of Steven and leaned in toward him, then whispered in his ear. "Take care of my little girl, Cason."

Steven didn't reply; he just continued to escort Caroline out of the house and to the waiting limousine. Henry stood at the windows of the study and watched them leave. He saw Steven help her into the rear of the car and then watched as they pulled away from the house. What he couldn't see was that they sat at opposite ends of the rear seat, not looking at each other and not saying a word. Caroline had become accustomed to Steven's lack of attention when they were alone, but she was convinced more than ever that she had to make her move tonight.

All week, Caroline had been making plans for this evening. She decided it was high time that Steven make a formal marriage commitment to her. She was no longer satisfied with being his trophy. She wanted more. Tonight's event, a cocktail party and business dinner at Senator Williams's home, where she would perform the duty of socializing with Steven's associates as his guest, provided the perfect setting for her to finagle a commitment from him. She waited for the right moment to present itself, then pounced on it like a hungry tiger.

She was discussing her brother's bid for congress with Senator and Mrs. Williams. They had been instrumental in her brother's campaign and were close friends of her father. Caroline expertly maneuvered the conversation. Before long they asked her about the seriousness of her relationship with Steven. It had been a full year now that they had been seen together at virtually every social event and there was speculation she would soon become Mrs. Steven

Cason, a coveted position amongst the eligible bachelorettes in Dallas. When the topic came up, Caroline pulled at Steven's sleeve to get his attention and dragged him into the discussion. "Steven," she paused to ensure she had his full attention, "Senator and Mrs. Williams were just asking me when we will announce our engagement. After all, as they correctly pointed out, we have been together for a year now and a girl can't be too concerned about her reputation." Caroline feigned a blush and an innocent look that sickened Steven.

He thought she had accepted her role in his life, but apparently he was wrong. This was not the time or place to discuss their future and he was not going to allow her to make him feel pressured into saying what she wanted him to say. He had never led her to believe they had a future together and after last night, he would rather spend the rest of his life alone than with a woman he didn't desire. He chose his words carefully as he responded. "Mrs. Williams, first of all, did I tell you how wonderful you look tonight? Did you do something different to your hair? You look at least ten years younger." Mrs. Williams raised her hand to her hair and puffed it up a bit. She thanked Steven for his compliment and held her head a bit higher than she had before. Steven turned to the Senator and in a half whisper told him to be careful because his wife was looking rather stunning. They both laughed and the Senator shot a loving glance at his bride of forty-five years.

Caroline was filled with fury. He was avoiding the issue altogether, but she wouldn't let it go. "Steven, Senator and Mrs. Williams are still waiting for you to answer their question about us." She glared at Steven as a warning that he had better answer this time. He wasn't amused by her behavior and didn't appreciate her making their personal life a public issue. Steven smiled again at Mrs. Williams as he spoke. "Of course, it was just that Mrs. Williams looked so beautiful that it completely took my mind off the conversation. What else can I do but apologize? I'm sorry. Now what was the question?"

Caroline was fuming. But before anyone could say another word, Senator Williams's press secretary called for everyone's attention so he could address the gathering. The entire group's focus turned to the man standing on the catwalk overlooking the living room. Steven used this opportunity to make a discreet exit. When the speaker began his speech, Steven pulled Caroline firmly by the arm and escorted her out of the party. She reluctantly followed his forceful lead.

When they were back in the limousine, Steven spoke his mind. "What was the meaning of putting me on the spot in front of the Senator about our private lives?"

She tried to act calm and sweet, but Steven saw through her unnatural demeanor. "Steven, it's a question on a lot of people's minds, including mine. After all," she reached for his hand and caressed it gently, "we have been together for more than a year now and we haven't once talked about our future together. Don't you think it's about time we did?"

Steven didn't want to have this discussion with her tonight. Especially when he had been unable to get Jaclyn off his mind all evening. He wanted Jaclyn by his side and he wanted her all night long. Then he looked at Caroline, studied her taut face and manipulative eyes and knew he had to end it now, regardless of the outcome of his relationship with Jaclyn. He couldn't continue the pretense any longer. "Caroline, I thought you enjoyed our friendship but understood that companionship is all we have between us." At his words, her eyes went cold and her body tensed visibly. Steven saw hatred in her stare, but disregarded it and continued, "I understand if you need a commitment, but you deserve to be with someone whom you love and who loves you. So, if you're telling me you need to move on, I understand."

Caroline was furious. How dare he twist this conversation to his benefit? Her eyes narrowed and she shot ice-cold glares at him as she replied, "You knew I expected a commitment from you. I have been by your side at every one of your social events over the past year and thought you wanted that to continue. I'm not stupid. You may have some floozy on the side to take care of your other needs, but that is of no consequence to me. I am prepared to be a good wife and look the other way at your indiscretions as long as they don't appear in the press." Caroline felt victorious as she spoke. She lifted her chin and held her head high. There, she had laid it on the line for him. What man could resist that offer, to have her on his arm socially and anyone he wanted in his bed? After all, wasn't that what all men wanted?

All Steven could feel was pity for her. What a shallow life she led. How could she sell herself so short? Money and social status. That's what it all came down to. That's all that mattered to Caroline and her parents. Falling in love was something that poor and uneducated people did; the upper crust chose their partners carefully according to their social position and financial worth. How sad, he thought. "Caroline, I'm not certain how to respond. Truthfully, I feel very sad that you would be willing to live your life in that manner. I would never ask you to make such a sacrifice for me. You are worthy of so much more than that. You deserve a man who will love you and treasure you for the woman you are."

Caroline crossed her arms and sat back in her seat with a huff. This was not going as she had planned. Before she could say anything further, Steven called ahead to Carlos and instructed him to take them to Ms. Hunter's home immediately. He had originally arranged to stop in at another function before retiring for the evening, but he knew they were in no condition to be out in public together.

Carlos's voice sounded into the rear compartment. "As you wish, Steven. In fact, we are only a few miles from her home."

Steven was grateful the evening would be ending shortly. He didn't know how long Caroline could contain her anger. He purposely ignored her piercing stare; neither of them spoke for the remainder of the ride.

Caroline sat in angry silence until they pulled into her driveway. The car came to a stop directly in front of the steps leading to the front doors. As she stepped out of the limousine, she turned back toward Steven angrily, her words pointed. "Steven, you should know better than to cross one of the most influential families in Dallas. Daddy won't be happy you upset me so. In fact, Daddy has told many of his friends that we would be announcing our engagement soon. After all, who would think anything less after all the time we have spent together. I will give you one last chance to reconsider before I go inside and tell Daddy how you've mistreated me."

Steven did not like being threatened and it was clear she was doing exactly that. Now his indifference turned to dislike. He grabbed hold of her wrist and pulled her within inches of him. He spoke slowly and put emphasis on every word. "Listen to me, Caroline, you're a big girl and big girls make up their own minds about who they see and what they choose to do. I never led you to believe we had a future together so you cannot hold me to plans you created in your mind. If you're frustrated, it's your own fault. You set yourself up for this disappointment." When he was done speaking, he let go of her arm and she stumbled backwards. She grumbled angrily, shot him a dirty look, then turned away abruptly and walked determinedly up the steps to her front door. As she waited for the door to open, she tried to regain her composure, but her anger was clearly visible in the way she shoved the door open and stomped inside. As soon as she had disappeared into the entry, Steven told Carlos to take him directly home.

Caroline almost knocked over the butler in her haste to get inside. She barked at the man standing by the door, "Benton, where is my father?"

The calm, elderly gentleman pointed toward her father's study but tried to warn her that she should not disturb him. Caroline took off in haste and did not hear a word Benton said to her. Upset, she barged into her father's private room without knocking. To her embarrassment, she interrupted him and a young woman who were sitting side by side on the large, leather sofa in front of the massive stone fireplace. A fire burned brightly, setting the romantic mood inside the dimly lit room. The only light came from the fire and at first Caroline had difficulty seeing clearly who was sitting by her father. As she neared them, she examined the young beauty by his side, estimating her age to be twenty, at best. She had dark brown hair that fell straight past her shoulders and big, brown, almond shaped eyes. She was a pretty girl, with a Barbie doll figure and a big broad smile. Her father's hand was resting on the woman's bare knee, her dress pulled up high on her thigh, exposing the length of her lankly leg. They were facing each other and laughing when she first saw them. Her unexpected entrance startled her father and for a moment, he didn't move. As soon as he regained his composure, he rose from the sofa. "Caroline, my dear, I didn't hear you knock."

She looked down as she replied, "I didn't knock father, I'm sorry." She looked up into his eyes before continuing, "It's just that I was so upset with Steven that I wasn't thinking clearly. I'm sorry."

Henry looked down at the young woman beside him, who was obviously uncomfortable with the situation. She had straightened her skirt to cover her knee and was smoothing her hair with her hand. He turned back to his daughter. "Caroline, darling, why don't you go upstairs and get undressed. Take a long, hot bath and get a good night's sleep. I'll see you in the morning and we can discuss then what is upsetting you." As he spoke, he walked her to the door. Caroline realized he was showing her, unwillingly, out of the room and she was furious at her father's obvious disregard for her feelings. How dare he bring a no-good tramp into her mother's home? Certain her mother was upstairs in her bedroom at that very instant, she suddenly hated all men. She pulled her arm angrily out of her father's grip and stomped out of the room. She crossed the marble entry noisily and flew up the grand, floating staircase in a huff. Her father watched her start up the stairs, then walked back into the study, shut the door and returned to his guest. Carolyn heard the lock on the study door bolted closed as she reached the second floor landing. Crying hysterically, she ran to her room and slammed the door behind her.

CHAPTER 13
—◇—

Jaclyn was sitting at the kitchen table eating breakfast when the phone rang. It was unusual for her to get a call so early on a Sunday morning, so her thoughts and hopes turned immediately to Steven. She cleared her throat before picking up the receiver. "Hello?"

"Jaclyn, honey, how are you?"

The sound of his voice sent chills up and down her spine. All she could think was how dare he call her and how did he get her number? "Andrew. I wasn't expecting to hear from you. How did you get my number?" She made it exceedingly clear that his call was neither welcome or wanted.

Andrew kept his voice soft and friendly. "Now is that any way to greet the man who was going to be your husband?"

Anger rose in her throat. "Past tense is correct. You and I both know that relationship is history. Why are you calling me?"

Andrew ignored her hostility. "I have a case in Houston involving a real estate company and I thought I could pass through Dallas to see you and catch up on old times. What do you think?"

Jaclyn was blinded by rage. "I think you've lost your mind."

He persisted. "Come on, Jaclyn. I know you've been busy, what with trying to sell Thanksgiving Tower…" Jaclyn momentarily froze. How did he know what she was working on? Her thoughts scattered. Andrew continued to speak, but she did not hear what he was saying.

When she didn't respond, Andrew said, "Jaclyn, are you there?" He waited for her to answer.

The lull in the conversation jarred her from her thoughts. "How do you know what I'm working on?"

She was irate and Andrew replied cautiously. "You know we run around with the same crowd, Jaclyn. Word gets around."

But that answer didn't cut it. She knew there was more to it. Was he investigating her? Following her? A sudden feeling of fear and dread consumed her. Andrew was frightening her again and a part of her was screaming that trouble was brewing. She tried to steady her voice as she spoke. "Andrew, I thought I made this clear to you before, but I'll say it again. I want you out of my life. What we had is over, dead and buried, finished. There is nothing between us any longer. End of story. There is no reason for you to call me ever again and even less reason for us to meet." On her last word she hung up the receiver. She sat there, numb. How dare he call her so casually and think she would want to see him? More disturbing, however, was his knowledge about her work. It was true they still shared mutual associates and a few friends, but she didn't think any of them knew about her business dealings since her move to Dallas. It didn't fit. And there was something more. She feared more than ever that he would not go quietly, and she was frightened to imagine the lengths he would go to get her back. She hated to be paranoid, but his being in the same state made her nervous. She registered a mental note to be more careful. The last thing she wanted was anything to do with him.

Andrew was surprised when she abruptly hung up the phone on him. He sat back in his recliner, stretched his arms over his head and thought about the conversation. The way she dismissed him was infuriating. He knew it was far from over between them, even if she wouldn't admit it. His plan was already in the works. He was going to win her back. He had no choice but to make certain of that. Since she had left for Dallas, his life had turned into a shambles. Stacy got cold feet after the confrontation with Jaclyn and refused to continue seeing him. The senior partners at the firm continually asked about Jaclyn and the wedding. Andrew was up for partnership consideration, but marital status weighed heavily in the final decision. Jaclyn was the perfect bride and the partners were all very fond of her. They often reminded him what a lucky man he was to have her on his arm. Recently, they were asking why she hadn't attended any of the firm's social functions. Andrew had finally run out of excuses and told them a half-truth about her going to Dallas to start the Toner and Associates office, but he assured them it was a temporary assignment and, aside from delaying the wedding, had absolutely no adverse effect on their relationship. Even thinking it to be an interim appointment, the senior partners were not happy with news of Jaclyn's absence. Andrew tried to soften the admission by saying it was working out well because he had been so absorbed by a few recent cases that required an enormous commitment of his time. The partners stood firm. If he was going to make partner, he needed a wife and Jaclyn was the expected choice. He needed to get her back and to New York, but how? He would stop at nothing to succeed.

***

Jaclyn sat at the kitchen table, considering the impact of Andrew's call. Her hands were trembling as she put down the receiver. She could not believe he would track her down and ask to see her. She jumped when the phone rang again, but this time she ignored it. It stopped, and then rang again. She was certain it was Andrew calling back and could not stand to hear his voice again. She needed to relax and get him off her mind, so she decided to take a bath to ease her tense muscles. She soaked in the tub for a half hour, allowing her mind to focus only on good things, like Steven and her deals and when she felt better, she got out of the tub, dried off and went into her bedroom to get dressed. She chose a casual navy short set and loafers and planned to spend the day walking through the mall. It had been a long time since she had spent any time shopping and she would definitely need lighter clothes for the hot summer ahead. A day out would certainly help take her mind off Andrew's call and the concern she harbored for what he would do. She was sure of one thing, she would hear or see him again, it was only a matter of when.

***

Steven was disappointed when Jaclyn did not answer her phone so early on a Sunday morning. She had not picked up the night before either. He wondered if he had misjudged her. Maybe she was more social than he had been led to believe. He had hoped they could spend the day together, getting to know each other better. At first he thought about leaving a message, but he had left one the night before and he didn't want it to be awkward if she were listening to her messages in front of another man. Steven couldn't believe how disappointed he felt at not being able to see her, but he busied himself with a long list of things that needed to get done and, before long, he was immersed in several projects he had put off for a long time.

***

Caroline was in the morning room having her coffee. She was lost in thought as she stared out the full wall of windows that looked out on the English gardens of their plush grounds. She was daydreaming when her father came into the room. "Caroline, good morning."

She somberly turned to him as he greeted her. "Daddy. Good Morning."

He bent down and kissed her softly on the forehead. As he leaned over her, she took in the sweet smell of his cologne. He sat down across from her and poured himself a cup of coffee.

"Daddy, I thought you would be at the club this morning. I saw Mother leave for her tennis match and I figured you were already playing golf."

He smiled at her as he spoke. "I had a game planned, but I saw how upset you were last night and I wanted some time alone with you this morning." She smiled back at him. He always made everything right for his little girl. He continued, "But first I want to talk about what you walked in on last night."

Caroline looked away. Her father waited for her to look at him before he continued. "I'm sorry for what you saw, but I hope I can count on your discretion."

Caroline could hardly believe what she was hearing. She had always suspected that her father had affairs, but in her mother's home? Such conduct was inexcusable. But that was her mother's business, not hers, and she would not interfere in their personal affairs. Her mother had made it clear to her on more than one occasion that her relationship with Henry wasn't perfect but that it suited her just fine and she had no intention of doing anything to change it. Caroline respected her mother's decision and, after all, she had enough to think about with her own life. She assured her father. "I can't say I agree with the obvious thing I saw you doing last night, but it isn't my place to judge you or make trouble for you. It won't go any further than the two of us."

Her father reached across the table and took her hands in his. "That's my girl. Now tell me what had you so upset last night."

She stood and paced the room as she gathered her thoughts. Her uneasiness with the situation was clear to her father. He listened patiently as she began ranting. "Well, Daddy, it's Steven. He's being impossible. We've been going together a year now and I felt as if it was time for him to make a public announcement of our engagement. I brought it up in front of the senator and his wife when they asked me about us and Steven completely sidestepped the issue and ignored the question. Then Steven insisted we leave the party. When we were alone, he yelled at me and told me he wasn't in a position to make a commitment and that if I wanted a commitment, I needed to find someone else to give me one. Can you believe it, Daddy? I have been by his side for a solid year and this is the thanks I get for my companionship." A solitary tear rolled down her cheek for effect.

Henry was furious. Steven had upset his little girl and that did not sit well with him. He would make him answer for that but first he had to reassure his daughter. "Now, now, Caroline, calm down. How did you leave off?"

Caroline took a moment to compose herself and dabbed at her eyes before continuing. "He told me it was over. Said he never promised me anything about a future together and that it was all my doing if I set myself up for disappointment. Can you believe that?"

Henry did not like what he was hearing, but he tried to make it seem less final for his daughter's sake. "Are you certain he wasn't just upset at the moment?"

Caroline continued pacing. "I saw the anger in his face. It's over."

Henry broached a sensitive subject. "Caroline, have you been there for him...in the way a man needs a woman?"

Startled by his question, she turned toward her father and then away from him as she replied. "Well, he was the one who decided what we did and where we went. In the very beginning, there were a few times when we ended the evening privately, but from then on, he just took me home. I never pushed it and he never asked."

Henry had hoped that wouldn't be her reply. He had plans for his daughter and Cason. Plans that he did not want to see changed. "Caroline, I want you to stop pouting and just relax. Let me do some checking around to see what I can find out and don't you worry your pretty little head over any of this. It will all work out. You just wait and see." He walked past his daughter, kissed her gently on her cheek and then left the room.

Henry drove his cream-colored Rolls Royce convertible Corniche a few blocks to his country club. Within ten minutes, he had pulled through its brick walls and was making his way to the clubhouse. It was there that he ran into one of his oldest and dearest friends, Cal Hanesly. Cal, like Henry, was old money and old money stuck together. Henry pulled up a barstool next to Cal and the two exchanged a firm handshake.

Cal instantly noticed something was wrong. "Okay, Henry, we're not best friends for nothing. From the sour expression on your face, I would guess that the missus found out about that pretty little thing you've been spending time with."

Henry shook his head, "No, Cal, it's not that. It's Caroline."

Cal knew that anything wrong with Caroline was the end of the world to Henry. She was his everything and he protected her happiness with his life. "What's wrong with Caroline?"

Henry took in a deep breath before he began to speak. "She had a confrontation with Cason about a commitment to their relationship. His answer was that there would be no commitment and that it was over between them. She is distraught. And rightly so, after all, she has invested over a year in that relationship and you know what happens to a girl dropped by the man she is linked to. At her age, her chances of recovering from that well publicized a breakup are slim to none. I need to find out what is going on with Cason and see what I can do to get their relationship back on track."

Cal had been at Staubach's party and had seen Steven there. He had also seen him leave with that spectacular woman. He was debating whether to tell his dear friend when Henry interrupted his thoughts. "Cal, you're miles away. What are you thinking about?"

Cal looked into his friend's eyes and said, "Listen, Henry, I know this is going to upset you, but I saw Cason the night before last at Staubach's party. He was there from the beginning. His guys were working the crowd, talking up a deal he is putting together. Appears he is looking for investors to put up cash. Anyway, later that evening, I was looking for him because I wanted to run a venture by him when I saw him talking to another guest, a woman. I didn't recognize her. I waited for a little while to see if they would end their conversation so I could go over, but before I could get the chance, they left the party . . . together. Obviously and clearly together. I didn't see him the rest of the night."

Henry listened intently. "Was she part of the entertainment?"

Cal was surprised by Henry's comment. "Knowing Staubach, he would never have those kind of women there. No, my guess is they either met there or she was his guest and met up with him later."

Henry was actually relieved by the news. "Another woman will not be a problem. I can handle that. I guess I need to pay Cason a visit." Henry stood and shook Cal's hand. He left the room, stopping briefly to greet friends he passed on his way out. Cal watched Henry as he departed. He could only think that the problem was significantly bigger than Henry anticipated. The woman he had seen with Cason was probably the most beautiful one that Cal had ever seen.

***

Henry pulled his Rolls through the gates of Steven's driveway. He paused and looked at the house, which he had been to a number of times for social events, and thought about how much he wanted it for his daughter's home. He knew Caroline would be a good wife for Steven. Maybe it was time he told Steven how things worked in their world. Love was not an issue. Henry rang the bell and waited. Steven came to the door in a casual pair of shorts and a T-shirt. He was clearly surprised to see Henry standing at his doorstep. He feared that he knew the reason why. "Henry, how are you?"

Henry nodded and walked passed Steven into his home. "Actually I've been better, Steven, but that's why I am here. I'll be just fine once we settle a small problem."

Steven did not move aside as Henry barged into his home. He was trying to make it clear to Henry that he did not have time to visit with him, especially if he had come to discuss his daughter.

Henry ignored Steven's unreceptive posture and took hold of his arm in a fatherly gesture. "I know you are busy, we all are, but we need to have a little man to man talk. It won't take long."

Henry tried to lead Steven toward his study, but Steven would not budge. He had no intention of having an intimate talk with Henry. He wasn't playing his game. "Henry, you're right about one thing, I'm really busy. Maybe we can get together for lunch one day."

Henry's face reddened with anger. How dare Steven disrespect him and not offer him a seat, a drink, a few minutes of his time?

Steven could see the rage grow in Henry, but was unaffected by it and remained fixed in his spot.

Henry broke the tense silence. "Very well, then I will speak my mind right here." He paused for effect. Steven remained unmoved. "Caroline was very upset last night. She is under the impression that things have turned sour in your relationship. I assured her she must be mistaken. After all, Steven, you two have been dating exclusively for over a year now. That certainly spoke loudly to your commitment to each other, wouldn't you agree?"

Steven had no patience for this man and what he had come to discuss. "Henry, with all due respect, what happens or doesn't happen between Caroline and me is just that, between Caroline and me. I'm sorry, but I'm not prepared to discuss this with you." When he was done speaking, he moved toward the front door and opened it wide enough for Henry to have a clear path to exit.

Henry was not through and had no intention of leaving until he made it clear where things should stand between Steven and his daughter. "As you know, Caroline means the world to me. If she's upset, I'm upset. Now, all I want to hear from you is that last night you two had a lover's quarrel and that everything will get back to normal. Caroline is a practical girl. She will wait until you are ready to make your engagement public." Henry was moving toward the door as if all was settled and agreed to when Steven stopped him with his words.

"Make no assumptions about Caroline and me, Henry. We won't be making any announcement about an engagement because there will not be one. Caroline and I agreed last night to end our relationship. There is nothing further to discuss."

Henry's face turned a bright red. His hands closed tightly into fists. He spit out venomously, "Make no mistake about this, Cason. You used my daughter for over a year and you can't just cast her aside. That will severely ruin her chances for another suitor. She deserves more than that. I strongly suggest you reconsider. She's a smart girl.

She will accept a lot more than you may understand. I'm certain she will be a good wife, just as her mother has been for me." When Steven began shaking his head in disbelief, Henry lost his temper. "Now hear me, Cason, if you hurt my little girl, you will be finished in this town. Finished, you hear me? And if you don't believe me, just wait and see." At his last word, he rushed out of the house, slamming the door behind him. Steven turned from the entry and went back to his project, unaffected by Henry's threats.

Henry sped out of Steven's drive, his mind a whirl of thoughts about how to force his hand with Steven. One way or another, he would convince Steven to continue seeing Caroline and ultimately, marry her. Nothing short of making Caroline happy again would suffice. Henry would make things better for his little girl and that meant convincing Steven that she was the woman for him. Come hell or high water, Steven would come to see that a future with Caroline was right. Henry would see to it.

CHAPTER 14
—◇—

Monday mornings were always hectic at Steven's office, but today was even more chaotic with only a week to secure the cash needed to close the Thanksgiving Tower deal. Per Steven's instructions, Diana had prepared the paperwork for Jed and Sumitomo to sign and sent it via courier to arrive at their offices by 8 a.m. Steven had already spoken to them following their receipt of the packages, reviewed the points of the contract and had their verbal consent. The paperwork was a formality required by the seller that legally spelled out their agreement. Steven asked them to return the signed paperwork to him by the next morning. If all went as planned, on Tuesday morning, he would have a written commitment for 80% of the deal. Things were looking good, but he knew he had to initiate contact with other prospective buyers urgently to put the final 20% in place.

As he sat at his desk, he reviewed his plan. First, he would begin calling his business contacts and present the offer to them. He would also run an article in the newspaper to lure investors. He had obtained permission from Jed and Sumitomo to advertise their involvement in the purchase to entice other parties. Now he needed to call Stefanie, his contact at the *Dallas Morning News,* and ask her to print an editorial piece about his contract on the Tower. The last time she did him a favor, Steven had arranged a weekend get away for them in St. Kitts as a thank-you for her assistance. She was a woman who knew how to please a man and Steven thought back on that weekend with a smile on his face and an erection in his pants. During his walk down memory lane, Jaclyn entered his mind. He could hardly believe he was feeling uneasy about something that happened long before he had even met her. He would have to be careful in what he promised Stefanie this time. He dialed her number and waited. She answered with her usual bubbly voice. "This is Stefanie. How may I help you?"

He knew she would be happy to hear from him. "Stefanie, it's Steven Cason."

A broad smile crossed her lips and she sat up in her chair, suddenly feeling very sexy. Her voice deepened when she spoke again. "Steven, how are you? It's been a long time since I've heard from you."

He moved quickly through the small talk. "As you know, I lead a crazy life. I'm calling to ask for a favor. I have a contract on Thanksgiving Tower and I need the story to hit the press in tomorrow's paper. Can you arrange it?"

She spoke sexily as she replied. "Considering the thank-you I received last time, you know you can always count on me for a favor."

Steven feared that would be her motivation for helping him, but he couldn't worry about that now. He would deal with the consequences at a later date. "Thank you, Stefanie. Here's the scoop. The headline needs to read something to the effect of Thanksgiving Tower is sold. Then I want you to explain that we are under contract for the purchase of the Tower for an undisclosed amount...The investors in the deal are SC Investors, Mitsu Industries and Jed Hebert. An additional investor is sought to complete the ownership of this premier property in Dallas. Interested parties are to contact SC Investors. Follow me?"

Stefanie was making frantic notes. "I'm with you."

Steven added, "Call Diana for the details, spelling of names, our contact person, and anything else you need. Fax the copy to me for review before you submit it. I would like to check it for content."

"Got it, Steven, but if it's going to hit tomorrow's paper, I need to get busy. I'll call Diana shortly to go over the details I need. And, Steven, you owe me."

Steven hung up the phone thinking only of what else needed

to be done to close the deal. He was reviewing his notes when his private line rang, interrupting his thoughts. He picked it up quickly, "Cason."

Steven immediately recognized his voice, but Al always introduced himself. "It's Al." After his greeting, he paused for permission to speak.

Steven prompted him. "Yes, Al."

He then began speaking rapidly. "I had a thought about the deal and I wanted to run it by you."

At this point, Steven was open to all ideas, so he indulged his request. "Go on."

Al added enthusiastically, "What if I contact the buyer on the other contract and see if he wants a part of your deal since he can't have it all himself?"

Steven studied his suggestion. He ran the scenario through in his mind before he verbalized his thoughts. "Well, Al, let's think about this. What is his motivation? If we fail to get the money by Friday, the deal is 100% his, so he could bet his money on that outcome and not be interested in working with us at all. On the other hand, if we get one more investor, and there is a strong chance we will, he is out 100%. Interesting idea, Al. How do you propose we contact the guy?"

Al continued. "I suggest that I call him as the seller's agent. I'll let him know I'm trying to make this deal work and thought he might like a part of the Tower since there is a strong likelihood that it will close under the first contract."

Steven took a minute to think it through before he commented. "Not bad, but I want to wait to contact him until our other options are explored. I would hate to get his agent up in arms about our deal and wake a sleeping giant. You never know what problems could come of it. I have an article printing in tomorrow's paper. Let's see who bites on that, then we'll call him if we have to. Not a bad idea, Al, not bad at all."

Al sat at his desk, grinning. He felt as if he were well on the road to Cason's good graces again.

***

Jaclyn was out showing properties on this busy Monday. The doctor that she represented had referred her to several other physicians and today she was presenting one of them, Travis Barber, a list of properties that fit his investment parameters. They drove from Farmer's Branch to Plano, evaluating retail strip centers and available land that had been zoned light commercial. Travis was representing a group of physicians who wanted to convert a shopping center into a clinic or find land on which to build a medical facility. Location was not as big a concern as finding the best property at the right price. Of all the properties they evaluated, he selected a site in Plano. Its adjacency to a small strip center would offer the finished space for a start-up practice and room for growth and expansion. Afterwards, they drove back to Jaclyn's office. On the way, she informed him of the next steps. "Now that you have selected the site, I will research the pertinent information and report my findings to you within the week. As we discussed, I'm a little concerned about the zoning on the vacant property, but even if it's unsuitable, we can always request a zoning change. Fortunately, I have made more than a few friends on the Plano P & Z committee, so we should be able to move it through quickly enough."

Travis was quick to reply. "Jaclyn, I don't know how to thank you for all of your hard work. I appreciate you spending the day showing me all of the sites. We saw enough options for me to feel comfortable making a decision."

She was pleased that he felt that way. "Good. Considering your parameters, I feel extremely good about this choice. I always like to show my clients enough properties so they feel they can make a good decision when they come across the right site. Like a lot of things, you may find the right one immediately, but you won't know it's right until you've seen others to compare it with."

He chuckled. "You are so right. Listen, Jaclyn, I would like to repay you for your effort."

She was quick to speak up. " No need to feel that way. This is my job and I'm happy to do it."

Her words, however, did not change the course of his thoughts. "I insist that at minimum you join me for dinner. I'm a member of the Las Colinas Four Seasons Club. Will you have dinner with me tomorrow night, say 8 o'clock?"

Jaclyn had a bad feeling that she was being propositioned. It wasn't the first time a client had made a move on her, and she feared it would not be the last, but every time it happened, it upset her. She was a businesswoman and when she was working, she felt there was no room for personal interaction. Although he was very handsome and distinguished-looking, he was also clearly married and Jaclyn found that situation unacceptable. But he was a client, so she chose a diplomatic response. "Thank you for your offer, but I must decline. I make it a rule never to mix business with pleasure. I hope you understand." She smiled at him in an attempt to keep the conversation light and friendly, but she could see he was disappointed by her reply. He bit his lower lip as he listened to her.

"Very well. I can't say that I'm not sorry, but I understand."

She jumped at the chance to change the subject and resume their previous discussion. He wasn't sure how she did it, but she had dismissed his offer and let him down gently and got them back on a business track without him hardly realizing what had just happened. She was sharp, he had to give her that.

When she was alone again, Jaclyn called JP. She wanted to make certain he had had a good trip back to New York. Part of her also wanted reassurance that he wasn't changing his mind about the Tower.

It was clear to her that he was pleased she had called. "Jaclyn, I've been thinking about you too. Thank you for calling. How are you?"

"I'm feeling better now that last week is behind us."

JP sympathized with her, "I know the outcome of last week was disappointing, but I have a really good feeling about who ends up with that property. And you know what, even if we don't get it, there are other class A sites out there."

She appreciated his attempt to make her feel better, but nothing short of her getting the deal back on track would appease her. "I agree. We need to maintain a positive outlook. Anyway, my primary reason for calling was to be certain you got back to New York okay and to hear that everything is fine."

"Thank you, Jaclyn. I appreciate your call. Now I must be off to a meeting. Let's plan to talk in a few days when we are closer to knowing if we have the deal in our hands again. Speak with you then."

Jaclyn hung up the phone and sat back in her chair. She so

wanted to have this deal work out for both their sakes. As she mentally planned out her week, she scanned her messages, hoping to see one from Steven. To her disappointment, there was none. Thoughts of him evoked a warm sensation inside of her. She rocked back and forth in her chair, lost in a daydream about him. If only he would call . . .

***

Stefanie worked hard rearranging the layout of the real estate page so she could feature Steven's article. She reviewed all the details with Diana and had everything set for print well before the deadline, but she had to cut out another story to add in Steven's piece. She knew she would catch grief over the change, but she also knew that Steven would make it well worth the trouble. She called him before leaving her office for the night. It took her a few tries to get through to him, but she was determined to remind him that he owed her.

Finally, Diana was able to put her call through. She spoke as soon as he answered. "Steven, you have no idea how much trouble you caused me asking for this favor. I hope you have a suitable thank-you planned."

Steven had known that topic was coming, but he wasn't certain how he would handle her at the moment. He figured he would buy some time. "I guess that means my gratitude alone won't do."

She put on a sexy voice as she replied. "It depends on how you express your gratitude. Last time was very acceptable."

Steven tried to keep it short. "I'll work on something agreeable. By the way, the piece looks great. I really appreciate all the work you put into this. We'll talk again soon and Stefanie, thank you."

As he hung up, he checked the time, then dialed Jaclyn's home number. He figured that at 7 o'clock she would be there, but again, her phone just rang and rang. This time he left a message. "Jaclyn, you appear to be as busy as I am. I tried you a few times yesterday morning with no luck, and again this evening, and you are out. I am beginning to think you were a figment of my imagination. I am regrettably out all evening at a dinner honoring the mayor. I'll try you tomorrow. Have a good evening. Bye." His tone was more businesslike than he wanted, but it had been a long and tiring day. As he thought about his message, he wished he had not said so much. He feared revealing his dinner plans with the mayor might raise questions in her mind about the circle in which he moved. Although he knew he would tell her more, he wanted to get to know her better before revealing too much of himself.

***

When Jaclyn arrived home, she dropped her briefcase by the door, slipped off her shoes and walked into the kitchen. The blinking red light on the answering machine caught her attention. She played the messages and was happy when she heard Steven's voice. Although she was relieved that he had called, she was upset she had missed him again. It also made her feel good to think he had also called on Sunday. Maybe the attraction she believed existed between them was as strong as she wanted it to be. At least his repeated calls gave her reason to hope.

CHAPTER 15
—◇—

It was early morning and as was her routine, Jaclyn would get a cup of coffee, sit at her desk and read the local newspaper and the *Wall Street Journal*. In order of relevance, she first read the front page of the paper, the front page of the business section and the real estate page before making a phone call or beginning the work of the day. It was her policy to be informed and avoid being caught not in the know. Her regimen took her only ten minutes every morning, but it gave her knowledge, which in her book meant power.

Following a cursory review of the front page and the business section, she turned to the real estate page. She took a sip of coffee as she glanced at the featured articles and nearly spit her drink across the desk. Before her, in the center of the page, was a picture of Thanksgiving Tower with a bold headline stating, 'Thanksgiving Tower SOLD'. Jaclyn read with intensity the article below the photo. The more she read, the more her disbelief and anger escalated. The parties named on the deal were…SC Investors… Jed Hebert!… and Mitsu Industries! That was Sumitomo's company! She reread it to ensure her understanding. How could it be that two of her three prime prospects were now in on the other contract? She tried to make the connection between them but the coincidence was too incredible. As she sat there grappling over what she had read, her stolen file came to mind. "My notes with all my prospects!" she blurted out. "That was it. The person who broke into my office was looking for details about my deal." Her mind raced. Who could be behind this? Was it SC

Investors, the party on the contract that beat hers in by mere hours? It had to be. Someone involved in the other contract had the most to gain and was more likely responsible. The lack of ethics sickened her. She knew she had to get to the bottom of this. With a sense of urgency, she called Bryan Taylor, the person identified in the article as the contact for SC Investors. She wanted answers and she wanted them now. A woman answered the phone. "Cason Properties. How may I direct your call?" As the woman spoke, Jaclyn made note of the company name. Cason Properties, she thought, another piece of the puzzle. Jaclyn read the contact name listed in the paper. "Bryan Taylor, please."

The robot-like voice of the receptionist almost made Jaclyn laugh. "May I say who is calling?"

In an instant Jaclyn decided to conceal her identity, in hopes she could uncover as much information as possible. If Bryan were at all knowledgeable about this scam, then he would surely recognize her name. Confidently, she said, "Janet Jones."

"Yes, Ms. Jones, one moment please."

Jaclyn waited several minutes before a gentleman came on the line. "I'm sorry but Mr. Taylor is not in the office at this time. This is Arthur Beard. May I be of assistance, Ms. Jones?"

Jaclyn was willing to speak with anyone who could provide her with information. She spoke slowly and carefully, so as to control her anger and not say the wrong thing. "I read an article in the paper this morning about Thanksgiving Tower and I understand your firm is looking for additional investors to complete this purchase, is that correct?"

She had his attention. Arthur had overheard Steven giving Bryan implicit instructions to follow should anyone call about the story. As Steven had hoped, a little press and someone interested in partaking in the acquisition of the Tower would come forward. With the strength of the three parties already involved, Steven knew others would follow. Although Arthur felt unprepared to take the call in Bryan's absence, he knew it was too important not to try. "You are correct, Ms. Jones."

Hoping she was speaking with someone who could clear away some of the mud, Jaclyn continued. "Good, then if you would be so kind as to give me the details about the investment and the shares of the partnership that we are discussing."

Arthur knew only sketchy details, and considering the importance of this deal, he wanted to refer her directly over to Steven. "I can do one better than that. Mr. Cason, our CEO and President, is meeting personally with anyone seriously interested in the deal as soon as is convenient."

Jaclyn hesitated. She wasn't certain she was ready to confront the man she believed was behind the contract suspiciously submitted before hers. At least not until she had a clearer understanding of what had taken place. She tried to steer the conversation in another direction. "Arthur, I appreciate Mr. Cason's personal interest, however, how do I know if I am interested if I don't have more information? For example, the mix of investors seems a bit odd, can you shed more light on the current parties involved?"

Arthur did not have the details on the other parties other than what was printed in the paper. He knew it would be better if she spoke directly to Mr. Cason. He didn't want to risk saying something that could turn away a potential buyer. "Ms. Jones, since you need more information than I have readily available, I would like to put you through to Mr. Cason's office."

Damn. Jaclyn did not want this Cason guy to know she was snooping around. She would have to find information another way. But how would she get out of talking to Mr. Cason? She tried to convince Arthur. "That may be premature…"

But Arthur was not willing to take no for an answer and cut her short. "We'll let Mr. Cason decide, please hold."

Without a choice, Jaclyn was put on hold. While she waited, she thought about what she had learned. Cason, she thought. Somehow that name was familiar, but she couldn't place it. She imagined he was the unethical excuse for a man behind the SC Investor contract who cheated her out of her deal. Maybe it *would* be good to speak with him…

Arthur returned to the phone and apologized that Mr. Cason was regrettably unavailable. Just as well, Jaclyn thought, she wanted more information prior to speaking with him anyway. Before Arthur could ask for her details, she hung up.

Her next call was to John Fitzgerald. Although he had not yet returned her previous call, she thought he was still her best source for information and she wasn't giving up on talking to him. She waited anxiously to be put through to his office. When she heard his voice, she was relieved. "John, hi, it's Jaclyn."

There was a heavy moment of silence and Jaclyn knew then that her leaving the party the other night had indeed hurt him. She would have to make it up to him.

His voice was low and lacked energy. "Jaclyn...how are you?"

She tried to elevate the mood. "I'm fine, John, how are you?"

He did not return her cheerful attitude. "Busy, to be honest."

His short replies and obvious desire to limit their conversation disappointed her, but she needed his help and had every intention of asking him for it. "Well, John, then I'll get to the point of my call. First, I want to apologize for leaving the party without saying good-bye. I'm sorry and I hope I will get a chance to make it up to you. I had a fantastic time and am so glad you invited me. Thank you." She paused, but John only mumbled something under his breath, so she continued. "I'm also calling because I need your help. Remember I asked if you knew SC Investors? Did you ever find out any information on them?"

He replied in a very businesslike manner. "No Jaclyn, I called several friends, but no one knew of them. Sorry I couldn't be of more help."

She was quick to respond as he sounded as if he were ready to end the call. "Well, maybe you can. What do you know about Cason Properties?"

This time there was no hesitation in his reply and the tone in his voice changed considerably. "Cason is only the biggest fish in town." John said it so matter-of-factly, expressing surprise that Jaclyn did not know that by now.

Bingo. She was on to something. "Do you know anyone over there that could be a resource for me? I need to get some answers. Did you see the paper today about the Thanksgiving Tower deal? I suspect someone at Cason Properties did something underhanded to get that deal out from under my nose. It might be the biggest fish in town, but its business practices stink."

John moved to the edge of his chair. He thought about Jaclyn and how over her head she was. His voice was suddenly very serious. "Jaclyn, listen to me, you don't know who you are dealing with here. Cason can make or break you in this town. Don't mess with him."

Cason, where had she heard that name before? Why did Cason Properties sound so familiar? She knew that name, but from where?

He interrupted her pause. "Jaclyn?"

Hearing her name snapped her out of her thoughts. "Sorry, John, I was just thinking that I've heard that name before. Tell me what you know about this Cason guy."

John's voice was solemn and businesslike. "I'm not surprised you've heard his name. You can't be working real estate in Dallas for long without bumping into him. He's the king pin. If he wants a deal, it's his, no questions asked and don't get in his way. Word on the street was that he was planning to buy Thanksgiving Tower from the day it went on the market. He was probably letting the seller sweat it out a bit before making an offer. The timing on your contracts could have been a coincidence, but more likely it was someone looking out for him, tipping him off that an offer was coming in so he could get his in first. There are a lot more people trying to get on his list of friends than off it, so if I were you, I wouldn't go head to head with this guy."

Jaclyn's blood boiled. No one told her what to do. She never backed away from anyone. That good-for-nothing, low-life Cason was a cheat and deserved to have someone stand up to him and tell him so. She wasn't afraid of him and she wasn't in business to make friends anyway. She had heard all she needed to hear from John. "Thanks for the information and the warning, John, but I don't play the game that way. I'll speak with you soon."

John looked at the receiver as she hung up on him. Boy, he thought, she doesn't know what she is getting herself involved in. He thought it better to stay out of it from here on in. The last thing he wanted was Cason thinking he got in the way of one of his deals.

Jaclyn hung up and sat back in deep thought. Her mind had taken over and what it was saying loud and clear was, "Okay, Cason, you've met your match. You want to play dirty, then watch out, I'm getting in the game." Her first move was to call JP. She dialed his office number, but when informed that he was not in, asked his assistant to have him call her at his earliest convenience. She was eager to give him this update. While she waited to hear from him, she delved into the work laid out before her. Absorbed, she did not realize hours had already passed when JP finally returned her call. She was at her desk when her private line rang. Her voice was deep, "This is Jaclyn."

"Hello, Jaclyn. It's JP. I understand you were trying to reach me earlier today."

She did not hesitate to tell him why she had called him. "JP, it's time we fight fire with fire. If you're game, I have an idea."

He laughed at her words. "Alright, Jaclyn. What's going on? What's your idea?"

She first explained to JP what she had learned earlier that morning when she read the newspaper. He was as furious to hear the details as she was. As soon as he heard the facts, he was as determined as she was to even the score. He listened intently as she detailed her thoughts to him about how they could further their position. He liked her style. He assured her that if it resulted in his winning, he was all ears. When she was finished and he gave her his full support, she was thrilled that he was willing to go along with her plan.

***

Henry's secretary laid out his morning paper along with his coffee and muffin as usual. Upon his arrival to the office, he routinely sat at the conference table and enjoyed his breakfast while perusing the newspaper. Today's article on the sale of Thanksgiving Tower held his attention. He read through it twice with great interest. Thanksgiving Tower was like another child to him. It had been his goal to erect a monument to himself, a testimonial for all to see, speaking loudly to the man he had become. When he achieved the means to construct such a building, it became his obsession. Overseeing every detail with a watchful eye, he built Thanksgiving Tower, one of the most recognizable buildings on the Dallas skyline. It was to be a monument representative of his power and wealth. It was during the construction phase, however, that problems with his oil holdings crept up on him. His sole focus on the completion of the Tower had almost been his demise, and was certainly partially to blame for substantial losses. Eventually he had to face mounting concerns about his ability to operate the building and the thought of the embarrassment of losing it, overwhelmed him. It was then that he caught a break. Mettleton approached him about selling. Maybe Mettleton smelled blood. Maybe he just wanted to make a very visible real estate play in Dallas. Either way, he had Hunter's attention. The deal happened quickly and quietly. It was reported by Hunter's press secretary that despite his personal attachment to the project, it was an offer too good to refuse. Since everyone knew the pride Hunter had in that building, no one questioned it, assuming that once again, Hunter had scored big on a sale.

Now he sat reading about the purchase of the Tower. Cason would make it his. Knowing this was greater motivation for Henry to keep Steven and Caroline together. How fitting that the Tower would be in his family again. The thought of it inspired him to come up with a plan. He needed to ensure Cason's relationship with his daughter at any cost. He started formulating his thoughts and as he considered his options, a smile brightened his face.

***

Steven was in the conference room finishing a long meeting with several of his key investment analysts when Diana came in and handed him a note advising him of an interested party, Arnold Carnley, calling regarding the Tower. Eager to speak with the investor, Steven dismissed his staff and took the call in his office.

He sat at his desk and eagerly picked up the receiver. "Steven Cason."

The man on the line cleared his throat, then said, "Yes, this is Arnold Carnley. My investment office informed me that you are seeking a buyer for Thanksgiving Tower. I am interested in learning more about this opportunity."

Steven's plan of advertising the sale was working just as he had hoped. "Excellent. Since this is of course confidential information, can you give me more details about you and your company."

The man did not hesitate. "This has nothing to do with my company. I have recently inherited a large sum of money and am looking to take some of the cash and convert it to real estate. My advisors have been searching for properties that fit my parameters and today they informed me of the sale of Thanksgiving Tower. They conducted a precursory analysis and informed me that it is a class A property, just the type of deal we're looking for."

Cash, Steven thought, just what I need to make this happen. His pulse quickened as he felt the final piece of the deal falling neatly into place. If this guy wanted a class A property, then he found one. Steven replied, "Fair enough, then let me give you some of the details. The partnership will be split 40% SC Investments, 20% Mitsu, 20% Hebert, and 20% to a fourth investor or any percentage split with a minimum of 5% ownership. The 20% ownership equates to a $30 million stake. All contingencies need to be removed by this Friday. I know that doesn't leave a lot of time for due diligence, but I have all the information compiled and you or your advisors can review the files immediately." Cason paused to gauge the potential of this interested party. If the numbers didn't chase him away, then Steven was certain he could close him on the property.

The man repeated the details as he considered the numbers. "$30 million cash for 20% ownership." He paused for a moment, then continued. "Is the building under contract right now?"

Steven was quick to reply. "Yes."

The man continued his questions. "Is your only contingency the financing?"

"Yes."

"And this contingency has to be satisfied by this Friday?"

"Friday at 5 p.m." Steven didn't want to waste time on the details. He had the deal under control. "Listen, Arnold, I understand you have a lot of questions and need more information to make a decision, but you don't need to worry about the legalities of the deal. It's under my control. There are several interested parties who want a piece of this high-profile property and, in terms of due diligence, you are way behind the others. I'm prepared to answer all of your questions and afford you every opportunity to conduct your evaluation, but I suggest you get in here quickly. We don't have any time to waste."

Although Steven had no one else interested in the deal, he wanted to give this potential buyer a sense of urgency. And there was a sense of urgency - for Steven. He had only four days left to find the final investor, have them judge the worth of the property and make a commitment to a share. With each passing minute, Steven grew more determined to make it happen, but was realistic in knowing that time was not on his side.

To Steven's disappointment, the man continued to ask for more information. "What's the cap on the deal?"

Steven had to put his foot down. He would only provide more

information if the man was willing to meet. That way, Steven had an audience with him and would not let him go before he committed to a share. One thing Steven was confident of was his salesmanship. "Come to my office and I'll share all the pertinent facts. Rest assured, you will find that the cap on this deal is well within an acceptable range for such a high-profile property. In fact, I would go so far as to guarantee that after reviewing the details, you'll want to take the final share."

The buyer expressed his interest. "I have to say, you have my attention. Just so you know, if I like what I see, I'm in for the remaining share. I'll have one of my advisors in your office tomorrow morning."

Steven organized the meeting time and gave him all the details of his office location. When he hung up the phone, Steven was feeling as if the deal were done. His decision to announce the deal in the newspaper had worked brilliantly. By this time tomorrow, Carnley's advisor would have all the necessary information. Steven knew the details would only strengthen the buyer's interest in the deal. And yet, despite the fact that the man on the other end of the phone had asked all the right questions, there was something about him that gnawed at Steven to do a background check. His next call was to Al.

Forgoing a greeting, Steven began speaking as soon as Al picked up the phone. "Al, I have something for you to do. Get on your investigator hat and check on an Arnold Carnley." Steven looked down at the note that Diana had handed him to check the spelling. "C...A...R...N...L...E...Y. His story is that he just inherited bundles of cash. He sounded like a middle-aged man from the Northeast, but I couldn't place the accent exactly. Find out everything you can on him and fast."

Al tapped his pen nervously against his desk. "This isn't a lot to go on Steven. I don't know how quickly I can get you the information without more details."

Steven didn't care about what Al couldn't do. He was only interested in what he had to do. "Al, you have until 5 p.m. tomorrow. Don't let me down."

Once again, Al was left holding a disconnected line, following orders he didn't fully understand but knew he had to follow. He sat wondering what would be the best way to get information on this Carnley guy.

Steven's next calls were follow-ups to potential buyers who he or his staff had met with at the Staubach reception. He would have to turn over every stone to make this deal happen. The clock was ticking loudly and Steven knew that someone would have to step up to the plate soon. He was encouraged by the call from an interested prospect, but he couldn't count on it. He needed to have more than one iron in the fire. The possibility that the deal would not happen wasn't something he wanted to consider, but he knew that each passing hour was bringing him closer to that possibility. With that thought, Steven became even more determined. He made calls to several former investment partners but became nervous after they acted especially elusive and noncommittal. It was as if they had shared notes, because they all had the same story. They either told Steven that they had other deals in the works or weren't in a position to move as quickly as Steven needed to get the deal done. Steven was baffled; it wasn't as if they had lost money in partnerships that Steven initiated and managed. Why was this deal proving to be so difficult? In Steven's circle, $30 million dollars for 20% ownership in a class A property was everyday business. But several hours of phone calls to his closest contacts were leading nowhere promising, and Steven was feeling that something unusual was going on. It was only after it was too late to reach anyone further for the day that Steven left to go home. As he drove, concerns about closing the deal plagued his thoughts. Why wasn't anyone jumping at the deal...his involvement basically guaranteed a secure investment... and the Tower...something was going on...he needed to find out what.

It was only after he was home and relaxed, sitting by the pool sipping a cold beer that his thoughts turned from the deal to Jaclyn. He reminisced about the night they had spent together. He shut his eyes and remembered the sweet scent of her hair and the softness of her skin. Her face was so vivid in his mind's eye that he opened his eyes thinking she was standing before him. Wanting her near, he walked inside to call her. He entered his study, opened his briefcase, pulled out his daily planner and found her home phone number. He dialed it, hopeful that this time she would answer. It only rang once when he heard her voice on the other end.

"Hello."

The sound of her voice excited him. When he spoke, his voice was deep and raspy. "Jaclyn?"

She recognized him instantly. Her heart began beating rapidly and a warm sensation worked its way around her body. A smile spread across her lips as she said his name. "Steven, how are you?"

He could hear the pleasure in her voice. "Insanely busy, but I've been thinking about you and wanted to hear your voice. You haven't been easy to reach."

She was smiling ear to ear. "I have been busy as well, but I'm so glad you called again. It's so nice hearing from you."

Steven wished he could touch her. The sound of her voice was making him ache for her. She was just what he needed to take his mind off the deal. "I thought we could spend some time together this weekend if you're free."

Jaclyn was thrilled that was why he was calling. "I am and I would like that very much. What do you have in mind?"

He knew exactly what he wanted to do on their date. He had thought it through and didn't miss a beat when she asked. "I would like to take you to my favorite restaurant. It has a great atmosphere and fantastic food. I also enjoy it because it's quiet and we can enjoy a nice conversation without having to yell at each other. I was thinking about Saturday night at 8 o'clock. How does that sound?"

Jaclyn was touched that he had planned such a nice evening. "It sounds perfect. I'm looking forward to it."

She gave him directions to her home before they said good-bye. She could tell he was looking forward to their evening together as much as she was. The timing was perfect too. She could get this crazy week over with and then celebrate her getting back the Tower deal. She was certain it was going to be a perfect evening.

Pleased with the outcome of the call, Steven went to his bedroom to change into his running shorts and T-shirt. He would take a quick jog before dinner. Afterwards, he wanted to spend time reviewing his list of prospects and planning his calls to them in the morning. He thought about Jaclyn as he changed. Instinctively he knew she was different, the type of woman with whom he could spend the rest of his life. She was beautiful and sweet and innocent in many ways, yet seemed worldly in others. He could see her moving comfortably in his circle. She was the embodiment of everything he wanted in a woman, the type of woman he had thought only existed in his mind. He could relax now that he had spoken with her and she had accepted his invitation for Saturday night. He needed the rest of the week to concentrate on making the Tower his. Then he could celebrate his victory with Jaclyn.

CHAPTER 16
—◇—

Arnold Carnley had one of his key advisors, Sam Banyon, at Cason's office at 8 a.m. Sam waited in the reception area for Steven to be available to meet with him. Steven was surprised by Banyon's presence so early in the morning and was unprepared to meet with him, so he quickly arranged for one of his analysts to review the file with him. Banyon did not take to being relegated to an analyst and took a lot of Cason's time before he would sit with the man Steven had appointed for him. Before long, Steven had spent a good part of the morning meeting with Carnley's guy instead of calling prospective investors. Finally, he told Banyon he couldn't stay any longer, insisting that his analyst could answer any of his questions. As soon as he was free, Steven returned to his office. Diana called out to him as he approached to review with him the messages she had taken in his absence. Steven signaled for her to follow him into his office. She jumped up from her chair and walked a step behind him, reading the messages in the order they had been taken. "I followed up with the individuals you wanted me to call to get their thoughts on your deal. Peter Smelton of DPI indicated he met with his real estate department and they have too many projects in the works to invest in another. He asked me to let you know he cannot entertain your project at this time but to keep him in mind on future deals." Diana paused to make certain Steven did not want to comment on the message. When she saw him turn his chair toward the window and sigh out of frustration, she continued. "Next was Dave Wintrop. He gave me a message to pass on to you because he is flying to Europe this afternoon and will be unavailable to speak with you for the next two weeks. He thanked you for thinking of him on your partnership, but explained that his company just made a major purchase of a pharmaceutical company in Germany and is not currently in a position to invest in Dallas real estate." This time she paused a little longer as she saw Steven getting visibly agitated. He indicated that he wanted her to continue, so she did. "Anthony Catalano's secretary called to advise you that Mr. Catalano is on vacation with his family in Hawaii and would not return until next Wednesday, at which time she will let him know that you called…"

Before she could continue, Steven held up his hand, stopping her stream of information. "Diana, I am so short of time, just give me the good news. The thanks-but-no-thanks messages aren't getting me anywhere. I need interested parties and fast."

She scanned through the stack of messages in her hand before looking up at him disappointedly. "I'm sorry, Steven. They are all pretty much the same."

He stood and walked over to the windows. He stared out while he thought through his next move. After a moment's pause, he spoke. "Alright, Diana, take the list of people I've called on this project and note who has called back. For the others, call their secretary and find out if they received my message and if they have time to speak with me right now. Put any of those calls through to me immediately. If anyone else calls, take a message or forward the call to someone else who can help. I need to focus all my time on organizing the final piece of this deal." Steven turned to assess Diana's understanding. She nodded at him, picked up the prospect list from his desk and left the room.

Steven walked over to his desk and pulled out a yellow legal pad from his briefcase. He quickly reviewed the notes he had made last night. Diligently, he began making calls to the people on his list. This was his 'B' list. He had already called everyone on his 'A' list and Diana's lack of success told him he was getting nowhere fast. His first call was to Neil Segalstrum III, the son of one of Dallas's wealthiest families. The reason he was on Steven's 'B' list was because he was consistently arrogant and obnoxious and Steven disliked dealing with him. They occasionally played a round of golf together at the Dallas Country Club because they were about the same age and handicap, but their equally large egos made it a challenge for them to work well together on business deals. Neil was the heir apparent to his family's oil business and was anticipated to be the next CEO and President. For the moment, his father maintained that position, but word was that it would not be long before Neil took over that role. Steven swallowed hard as he dialed Neil's private number.

"Segalstrum." Neil seemed preoccupied, but Steven chose to disregard the impatient tone in his voice.

"Neil, you lousy golfer, how the hell are you?" Steven tried to sound casual.

"I was fine till you called. What do you want, Cason?" Neil was his usual irritating self and Steven cringed.

"$30 million dollars, that's all. Pennies for you, Neil." Steven laughed as he spoke.

"Oh, this is about Thanksgiving Tower." Neil's tone changed and Steven did not like it. For one, why did he say it that way?

"So you've heard about my deal?" Steven was probing.

"You could say that." Neil snickered and Steven's blood was at the boiling point.

Steven put it on the line even though he anticipated more arrogance in return. "Well, I guess you've saved me from having to do the pitch. Since you know about the deal, what do you think? Interested?"

Neil paused for effect. "Sorry, Steven, I have the presidency on the line here and I can't risk it on a deal like this."

Steven lost control. What was he insinuating? A deal like what? He tried to regain his composure as he responded. "Thanksgiving Tower is class A. The investors in this venture are top-notch. If it wasn't that we need a commitment by Friday, I would have more than enough investors ready to take a piece." Steven stopped. He had already said more than he wanted to.

Neil was thinking of a way off the phone. "Listen, Steven, I wish I could help you, but I can't. Good luck, guy. See you at the club. Maybe we can play a round the next time you're out there." Neil waited for Steven to reply, but he didn't. He just hung up. Neil thought about what he had heard about Steven's deal. It may have interested him were it not for all the rumors flying around the club about the deal being questionable. Neil couldn't afford to take any risks. He was anticipating being announced president at the next board meeting. It was what he had waited his entire life to achieve and nothing was going to come in the way. Steven stood up angrily at his desk. Disturbing thoughts filled his mind. How dare that arrogant, good-for-nothing Segalstrum cast doubt on the deal. What was he implying anyway? Just then, the buzzer on his intercom sounded. He reached down and pushed the intercom button. "Yes?"

It was Diana. "Steven, I have Phil Anderson on the line."

Steven sat back down. "Very good, Diana, put him right through."

Steven checked his attitude, then picked up the phone. "Anderson. How the hell are you?"

Phil was pleased to hear Steven's voice. It had been almost a year since they last spoke. Phil primarily focused his investments on theaters and restaurant chains. Last time Steven and he had spoken was to finalize the lease of one of Phil's restaurants in one of Steven's buildings. It had turned out to be a great deal for both of them. "I couldn't be better, Cason. How about you?"

Steven chose his words carefully. At the moment, he wasn't feeling great, but he knew he had a solid deal, and once it was complete, he would be feeling fantastic. He was careful not to let any doubt or concern come across in his voice. "Good, Phil, I'm doing well."

"Glad to hear it. I had a message that you called on Friday, something about Thanksgiving Tower. What's up?"

Steven wanted nothing better than to tell him about the deal. "It's a great deal, Phil. I have Thanksgiving Tower under contract, but the seller is looking for cash, and a 30-day closing."

"How much cash are you talking about?"

"I have 80% of the deal done. I need $30 mil for the remaining 20% share."

"Wow. That's a little steep for me. I have so much money tied up in the restaurant expansion that $30 million is more than I have available to invest, especially considering the tight time frame."

Steven's mood changed dramatically and although he tried to hide it, Phil heard it clearly. "Well, Phil, thanks for giving me the time to run it by you. If you think of anyone who might be interested, please let me know. I only have until Friday to get the final commitment. I'm gonna close this deal if it's the last thing I do."

Phil wished he could help him, but at this moment there was nothing he could offer him. "You got it. If I think of anyone, I'll let you know. And next time you're down in Houston, give me a little advance notice and we'll have lunch."

"Sounds great. We'll catch up soon. Take care."

The men hung up and Steven thought about the last two calls. He knew Phil was genuine, but Neil's attitude bothered him. There was something about that call that stayed with Steven all day.

Diana spent the entire day chasing down people on Steven's list and when she was finally finished, she went back to Steven's office. She found him standing at his wall of windows staring out at downtown. She knew it had not been a good day. Quietly, she placed the list back on his desk with all of her notes attached. Softly, she asked Steven if he needed her to do anything further. Without turning toward her, he thanked her for her hard work and dismissed her. After she had left, he went to his desk and scanned over her notes. Damn it. Nothing promising from all the contacts she called. Then he walked down the hall to the conference room where he had left his analyst with Carnley's advisor reviewing the details of the Tower. When Steven entered the room, the analyst was alone, organizing papers into various files. He looked up at Steven as he entered the room.

Steven was surprised that he was alone. "Where's Banyon?"

The man stopped working, giving his full attention to Steven as he spoke. "Hey, Cason. Banyon left about a half-hour ago. Said he had all the particulars he needed."

Angrily, Steven's voice rose. "Why didn't you call me to have a final word with him? I would have liked an opportunity to ease any doubts he might have had or at least take his temperature before he reported back to Carnley."

The man was surprised at Steven's hostile reaction. "I can assure you that you answered most of his questions this morning and I addressed anything that came up as we reviewed the documents. I'm confident that all of his questions were answered and he was very impressed with the information. He said he would speak with Carnley in the morning and expected that he would get back to us by tomorrow afternoon."

Steven settled down a little. It was just that he was hanging onto a thread and time was moving so quickly. He spoke in a whisper as he left the conference room. "Alright then, good job."

***

Jaclyn was feeling good because she had had a very productive day and made some progress on the deal. Early on, she made two calls regarding the Tower, one to Milton Thompson and the other to JP. She had called Milton to speak with him directly about their position in the deal. She was grateful when he took her call. His secretary checked with him before putting her through.

He was very pleasant when he spoke. "Hello, Ms. Tate, this is Milton Thompson. What can I do for you?"

"Thank you for taking my call, Mr. Thompson. I wanted to speak with you to verify our position on the Tower. It is my understanding that at 5 p.m. on Friday, the first contract must meet its contingencies or become null and void. At that time we would move from secondary position to first, is that correct?"

"That is correct, Ms. Tate. As our letter stated to your buyer, we will only be in a position to negotiate the contract he submitted at such time that the first contract becomes null and void, which at the soonest would be Friday at 5 p.m."

"Then, Mr. Thompson, I would like to set an appointment for Mr. Morrison and me to meet with you at 5 p.m. on Friday."

Milton chuckled as he responded. "Aren't we being a bit presumptuous, Ms. Tate? After all, the buyer in the first contract is a very well-known businessman and I'm inclined to believe he will remove the contingencies and see the contract through to a successful close."

Jaclyn was quick to respond. "Let's just say I'm optimistic."

Milton was impressed by her attitude. "I guess we could always cancel if need be. Very well, Ms. Tate, we'll meet at 5 p.m. on Friday in my office unless you hear otherwise from me. I will put you back through to my secretary, so she can take your phone number and arrange for security to let you up to my office. Thank you for calling, Ms. Tate." Before she could thank him for the appointment, she was transferred back to his secretary.

Immediately upon hanging up with Thompson's office, Jaclyn called JP. After all, the Friday deadline was now less than 48 hours away and she wanted him to know that she had scheduled their meeting with Milton. "JP, how are you?"

He spoke in his usual calm tone. "Very well, Jaclyn. How are you?"

Jaclyn was enthusiastic. "Fine, thank you. JP, I wanted to let you know that everything is set with Thompson as discussed. We'll meet with him on Friday at 5 p.m. Did everything go as planned with your arrangements to arrive in Dallas on Thursday evening?"

"Everything is set on my end. I look forward to seeing you then. And, Jaclyn, thanks for taking care of everything."

She hung up the phone feeling good about her plan, but she wanted to be certain she had things well in hand. She needed to do some digging. She left her office with her mind focused firmly on her mission.

An hour later, she pulled up in front of a large glass and chrome building. The CP logo, in imposing shiny silver letters, was positioned several stories above street level. She waited for a parking space to open up in front of the building, then she left her car and walked up the massive slate steps leading to heavy mirrored glass doors which marked the entrance. As she neared the entry, she lost her nerve and chose to walk along a path that circled the building and led to a landscaped area with benches. She checked her watch out of nervous habit, paced along the walkway and tried to work up enough courage to enter the building. It was the first time she had put on a disguise and it didn't suit her well. Her palms were sweating, her heart was beating rapidly and her breath was short and choppy. She didn't think she could go through with this damn plan, but if she didn't, she would not have any more information about Cason and she wanted that more than she wanted to leave. She stopped pacing and urged her inner self to find the courage to go inside. She closed her eyes as if to shut out the voice of fear sounding loudly in her ears. When she opened her eyes again, she was ready. Without further debate, she strode purposefully inside the building and up to the receptionist, who was staring at her inquisitively. The woman had seen Jaclyn through the mirrored glass and thought she was acting peculiar. She noted the obvious black wig and dark shades, which seemed out of place on this otherwise attractive, well-dressed woman.

Seeing that she had the receptionist's attention, Jaclyn spoke as soon as she reached her desk. "Hello, my name is Maggie Andrews and I am with the *Fort Worth Star Telegram*. I would like to have a few minutes of Mr. Cason's time to discuss his purchase of Thanksgiving Tower." She had rehearsed her lines several times before entering the building and the words flowed a bit fast, but effortlessly from her lips.

When she finished speaking, she took a deep breath and tried to relax. Her greeting sounded so sincere she was beginning to think that just maybe she could pull this off.

The receptionist cracked a forced smile as she replied, "Your press badge, please." She extended her hand to Jaclyn, beckoning the identification from her.

Jaclyn momentarily froze. She had not foreseen that request. In an attempt to respond quickly, she thought up an excuse. "Oh, I'm sorry. I didn't believe I would need my press badge to get an appointment with Mr. Cason. I'm sorry, I don't have it with me." She smiled at the woman in a hopeful plea that she would accept her excuse and permit her to go up to Cason's office.

Instead, the receptionist was annoyed. Her tone changed to impatience. "Very well, then your business card will do." The woman held out her hand again.

Jaclyn started to perspire. She had not anticipated this level of scrutiny by the lobby receptionist, but the presence of one guard close by and another at the elevators, told her this was not going to be easy. Jaclyn opened her portfolio and checked a few pockets as if looking for something but did not produce anything. She looked at the receptionist and smiled, but the woman did not return the pleasantry. She continued to look disturbed by Jaclyn's presence. Jaclyn checked her trouser pockets before turning her attention back to the receptionist. "My goodness, I seem to be all out of business cards, I'm sorry."

The receptionist groaned in displeasure. She was clearly annoyed. "Any ID will do, Ms…"

"Andrews," Jaclyn said. She then looked for the woman's nameplate, and added, "Ms. Moore, I don't have my purse with me. In fact, I never take it with me on assignment, so I'm afraid I don't have any ID. I just want a few minutes of Mr. Cason's time. Could you please ask him if he would be willing to speak with me? I saw his article in the *Dallas Morning News*, so I am confident that he is not opposed to speaking with the press."

Tired of dealing with her, the receptionist picked up the phone and dialed Diana's extension. The phone rang only once before Diana picked up. Although the receptionist had turned her back to her, Jaclyn could hear clearly what she was saying.

"Yes Diana, this is Ashley. I have a Ms. Maggie Andrews at

the front desk requesting an appointment with Mr. Cason. She says she is with the *Fort Worth Star Telegram* and is asking to speak with Mr. Cason about the Thanksgiving Tower deal." Ashley listened as Diana responded. Jaclyn held her breath through the silence. Ashley replied, "Yes, I did ask for her identification, but she does not have any on her… That's right." Jaclyn wished she could hear the other side of the conversation. During a long pause, Jaclyn began to feel a sense of urgency. She glanced at the guard standing in the corner of the room, who had been watching her since she walked through the front doors. She turned her attention back to the receptionist as she spoke again. "Very well, Diana. I'll ask Ms. Andrews to take a seat." The receptionist hung up and turned back toward Jaclyn. "Ms. Andrews, please take a seat. Mr. Cason's secretary is checking his calendar and will let me know if he has any time to speak with you." There was something in her voice and in her cocky smile that Jaclyn did not like, but she felt as if she had no choice. She nodded at the woman, then turned toward the chairs lining the floor-to-ceiling windows at the front of the building. As Jaclyn sat nervously in the waiting area, the receptionist frequently glanced at her, which made her more apprehensive. A little voice in Jaclyn's head pleaded with her to get out and fast. As she was contemplating an escape, four gentlemen entered through the front doors and approached the receptionist. The woman's view of the chairs was blocked and Jaclyn knew this was her opportunity to leave. Quickly, she stood and walked toward the doors. She was careful not to allow her heels to touch the marble floor for fear that they would alert the receptionist of her departure. Slowly, she swung open the door and as she did, a young woman entered. The receptionist peered around the men before her as the door opened, but all she saw was an employee entering the building.

Jaclyn walked at a fast pace until she was down the first flight of stairs, then jogged the rest of the way to her car. Immediately upon sitting in the driver's seat, she tore off the wig and tossed off the bulky sunglasses. She took a deep breath as she tried to steady her nerves and slow her racing pulse. Her heart was pounding against her chest. She sat for a moment wondering how she had turned into the woman she saw reflected back at her through the rearview mirror. How could she allow this deal to take away her dignity? She had never stooped so low. Things had gotten out of hand and she was feeling desperately out of control. This deal had taken on a life of its own and she found herself placing too much importance on its outcome. It was as if this deal signified her ability to be a success in Dallas. Although that pressure was self-imposed, she felt the burden of it and was slowly breaking under the stress. Deeply disappointed, she drove off slowly and headed back to her office.

***

It wasn't until the men before her took their guest badges and walked toward the elevators, that the receptionist noticed Jaclyn was gone. It merely confirmed her belief that the woman had been a fraud. She stood and glanced out the glass wall in search of her but did not see her anywhere. She picked up the phone and dialed Diana's extension. "Diana, it's Ashley. I wanted to let you know that the woman who wanted to speak with Mr. Cason left the building while I was helping other visitors."

Diana was not surprised. "Ashley, I checked with the *Star* and after speaking with two editors, I'm convinced there is no Maggie Andrews. I was waiting to speak with Mr. Cason to see what he wanted to do about her, but he is still on his private line and I didn't want to interrupt his call."

Ashley was even more upset now that she knew the woman in that awful wig was an imposter. Her mind raced, thinking of all the bad things the woman could have done had she let her up to see Mr. Cason. She was so glad she had adhered to procedure and followed her instincts. She tried to compose herself, but Diana could hear the nervous tremble as she spoke. "Diana, what should we do now?"

Diana tried to calm her. "Don't worry about it, Ashley. You did the right thing and now there is nothing we can do. However," she cautioned her, "if she does come back, let me know immediately. Okay?"

"Okay," she said and hung up the phone. Ashley remained tense the rest of the afternoon and didn't once take her eyes off the front doors.

CHAPTER 17
—◇—

Wednesday evening came too quickly for Steven. He had anticipated that by now he would have had at least one prospect committed to the remaining share. The fact that no one had jumped at the opportunity disturbed him. He began to wonder if the real estate plunge was more than some could handle and speculated they feared the market had not yet hit bottom. For Steven, the deal was a slam-dunk. The Tower was priced right and had great upside. Whether he had a stronger belief in the future of Dallas or simply had a more fervent gambling spirit, either way, his confidence had served him well. Every investment he had made since the real estate decline had turned out to be an excellent purchase.

As he sat at his desk reviewing his telephone directory, scanning names of contacts, he spotted the name of his longtime friend and fellow real estate aficionado, Ross Parish. He knew that, like him, Ross would be at his office late so he made the call. As an independent real estate broker, Ross had earned a reputation of integrity and ability and was sought after by many property owners. He had accumulated an impressive list of clients over the years and amassed a nice fortune for himself along the way. Yet, he was different than the typical nouveau riche entrepreneur, who had to possess every material status symbol as a monument to his success. Instead, Ross remained down-to-earth and grew to be a trusted business associate and friend.

"Hello?" Ross's greeting was posed as a question and Steven

figured it wasn't often that he received calls this late in the afternoon on his private line.

"Ross, it's Cason."

Ross's tone changed immediately to friendly and upbeat. "Cason, how are you?"

Steven tried to relax. "Things have been better, like that night you and I went out on the town and didn't come home until the next morning. Now that was a good time."

Ross let out a hardy laugh. "Now you just don't go bringing up that night around Lizzy and that will continue to be an awesome memory."

Steven laughed along with his friend. "Your secret is safe with me. Speaking of your beautiful bride, how is she?"

Ross's voice took on tenderness. "Fantastic. Had I known marriage would be so wonderful, I'd have taken the leap years ago. I might have been reluctant to give up my bachelor status, but I can tell you, I've never been happier."

Steven was genuinely happy for his friend and having met Jaclyn, he could now understand the way he felt. "That's great to hear, Ross. I'm really happy for you. Please give Elizabeth my regards." He paused for a moment to gather his thoughts. "Ross, I want to talk to you about my deal on the Tower. Last time you and I spoke, I was waiting for the right moment to put the contract on the property. As you know by now, that moment came last week. I now have a contract on the Tower, but the terms have been countered from my original proposal to a quick close, $150 million cash deal. On top of that, earnest money goes hard on Friday and I have only 30 days to close."

Ross interrupted. "Nice chunk of change to have lying around. Where are you coming up with the money?"

Steven replied, "Actually, things have fallen into place rather nicely. In fact, I have 80% of the deal done. I only lack a commitment for $30 million, which I need in place by Friday. There lies my challenge."

Ross sighed. "Not so easy when you have such a short window."

Steven agreed. "Not easy, but it shouldn't be impossible either, not with all of my contacts. I'm a little frustrated right now, to be honest with you. I can't let $30 million dollars stand in the way of owning the Tower. I've called everyone I could think of and even spoke with my two investors, Hebert and Sumitomo, to see if they could increase their stake. Hebert is at the max for his cash position, and Mitsu just bought several buildings in Houston and is only able to commit to the 20% position originally agreed to. Apparently Mitsu is in it for the bragging rights, as their other deals are sweeter. I've run into dead ends everywhere else. All I can figure is that this down market is hitting people harder than I realized."

Ross chose his words carefully in response to his friend's dilemma. "Steven." That was Cason's first tip that Ross was going to tell him something he didn't want to hear. Ross only called him Steven when he had something serious to say. "Word around the Dallas Country Club is that you've fallen out of Hunter's graces." Ross's words fell heavy on Steven's ears. The words stung and Steven felt as if Ross had punched him in the gut. Ross continued, "Seems like he's been using his influence to drag you through the dirt and I heard something third hand about 'questionable business practices.'"

Steven's temper rose. "What are you telling me, Ross?"

Ross tried to keep the conversation on a calm and even tone. "I'm telling you that Hunter has a bone to pick with you and he's using his influence to discredit you. With all the deals available in this market, why would someone get involved in yours when Hunter is making it clear to everyone that you may be falling out of the circle. It will only complicate their lives if they get involved, so no one wants to touch it."

Steven could not believe his ears, but then his conversation with Segalstrum came to mind. It all made sense now. He spoke softly as he replied, almost as if he were trying to gather enough strength to speak, "All because I told his precious Caroline there were no marriage plans."

It was now clear to Ross why Hunter was out for Cason's blood. "Oh, so that's what was behind this. I didn't know what Hunter's motivation could be at first, but now it's crystal clear. I'm certain others will understand too when they hear the news about you and Caroline, but it will take time and right now, you don't have that luxury."

Steven was blinded by anger. "Shit, Ross. Hunter will pay for this."

Ross cautioned his friend. "Look, Cason, you can overcome this like you have other political obstacles. This is temporary and will pass. Don't make it worse by seeking revenge on Hunter. Don't stoop to his level. You're above that. Others will come to learn the reason behind Hunter's yapping and dismiss it as nonsense. You wait and see. As soon as word is out about you and Caroline, everyone will understand Hunter's sour grapes."

"I hear you, Ross, but I can't wait that long. I'm under a very tight time line on this offer and I will not lose the Tower. I've been planning on it being the showcase of Cason Properties for too long. I need to make the deal happen by Friday. Listen, thanks for the info. Let me know if you hear anything else, and if you think of anyone who might be interested, call me. I'd also appreciate anything you could do to disperse these rumors."

Ross understood. "You got it. And, Cason, good luck. Let me know how it turns out."

Steven's head was swimming. "Will do, Ross. Talk to you soon."

Steven put down the phone, sat back in his chair and took in what he had learned. Incredible, he thought to himself. Caroline ran home to Daddy and he made certain he got revenge on big, bad Steven. He shook his head in disbelief as he thought about this ridiculous turn of events. He would think of a suitable response to Hunter later, for now he had to focus his attention on the Tower and raising the remaining $30 million. Since most of the potential local investors would be tainted by Hunter's lies, he had to focus on outsiders. That's when his mind turned to his most promising investor of the moment, Arnold Carnley. Which reminded him that he had not heard back from Al on what the investigation had uncovered. He picked up the phone and called Al's direct line. There was no answer. He tried Al's mobile phone, but again, no reply. Steven checked his rolodex for Al's home number and tried him there, but again, there was no answer. "Where is that little…" Before he could complete his thought, his private line rang. He picked it up quickly, anticipating it would be Al, but instead, it was Milton Thompson.

"Cason, it's Milton. Just checking in with you. How are things progressing?"

Steven tried to sound optimistic. "Good, in fact, one investor had his analyst in my office all day. Not to worry, Milton, things are moving along just fine."

Milton offered no leniency. "Glad to hear, but I want to make it exceedingly clear that if you don't have your deal together and I mean signed parties committed to the cash by 5 p.m. on Friday, then I'm going on to the second contract. I'm certain you can appreciate my position. This is nothing personal. Business is business, Cason. Let's plan on meeting at 4 o'clock on Friday, my office. Okay?"

Steven hesitated for a moment, then agreed. Being put under such tight and unforgiving time constraints was complicating everything. For the first time since he began his pursuit of the Tower, he had a sinking feeling that the time frame would prove too short for him to get the deal done.

***

Al's investigation of Arnold Carnley had turned up nothing, zippo, nada. He knew he needed to update Steven, but he couldn't bear to call him with nothing to report. He phoned every person he could think of to help him dig up information on this guy, but no one turned up anything and everyone told him they needed more information about the guy to start a search. He needed a driver's license number, a social security number, an address, something more than just a name. Al hid in his office all afternoon, refusing to pick up his direct line. It wasn't until Samantha buzzed in and told him that Steven Cason was on the office line that he knew he couldn't avoid him any longer. He was certain Samantha had already told Steven he was there. It didn't help to have an assistant infatuated with the person you were hiding from. He could just hear her now, "Of course, Mr. Cason, anything for you..." Reluctantly, he picked up the receiver.

Steven didn't wait for his greeting to speak. "Al," he barked, "where the hell have you been?"

Al responded quickly but uneasily and it was apparent to Steven he was lying. "I was in a meeting."

Steven maintained his angry, impatient tone. "Like hell, Al. What did you find out on Carnley?"

Al fumbled his words. "Well, Steven, like I told you yesterday, I need more information. All my sources told me they need an address or a driver's license number or..."

Steven cut him short. "And if I don't have that information?"

Al's reply was just above a whisper. "Then, we can't get you the scoop on this guy."

Steven was not happy and Al was going to take the brunt of his anger. "I told you I needed information urgently and now you tell me you have nothing. Maybe you don't understand. I guess I need to spell it out for you. If I don't close this deal, you aren't going to be sitting so pretty. Remember our deal?" Steven paused momentarily to give his words a chance to sink in. "Al, get me info on Carnley and I'll double our deal."

Al interjected, "But, Steven, I tried. . ."

Steven wasn't willing to listen. "No excuses, Al. Results. Next time I hear your voice it better be you telling me what you know about this guy. Do I make myself clear?"

"Understood."

And at Al's reply, the conversation abruptly came to an end. Al sat in disbelief. Steven was willing to double his take. Wow. He would be set for a long time. But first he needed to do everything he could to help Steven close the deal. Now how could he find out about that guy Carnley? His fingers got busy searching through his directory for the number to a New York police detective he had met years ago. If anyone could help, it would be Pete. Al had heard he was an expensive source, but this was an emergency situation. With the heat turned up and his sweet deal with Cason on the line, he knew it was time to make that call.

***

Steven immediately began trying to remove the doubt that Hunter had cast on his deal. He called back several of his best prospects whom he was certain had heard the dirt Hunter was flinging around the club. To his disappointment, the calls were proving futile. Either he could not speak with them personally or they denied declining to invest in the Tower because of Hunter or any rumors he was spreading. Either way, he had had a very unproductive afternoon. When he was about to call it quits for the day, his phone rang. He answered in a less than enthusiastic tone. "Cason."

The man on the other end was full of energy. "Cason, it's Arnold Carnley."

Steven did not hold back his thoughts. "Carnley, I was hoping to hear from you earlier today. Nevertheless, I'm glad you called. I was beginning to think you were just wasting my time."

The tone in his voice spoke loudly to his concern with Steven's reaction. "I don't understand. We said we would talk after I had an opportunity to fully review all the information my analyst gathered. Was this not your understanding?"

The man sounded annoyed and Steven suddenly wondered if he had misjudged this man.

He settled down a bit before replying. "Of course, it's just that we don't have a lot of time."

Carnley was sympathetic. "I understand your concern for the short time frame; however, I still have some questions. I would like to meet tomorrow to discuss the open issues."

Steven was quick to respond. "Tomorrow is so close to the deadline. Couldn't we discuss your questions tonight?"

"I'm afraid not. I have a dinner engagement for which I am already late. I will take an early-morning flight to Dallas and should be at your office by 1 o'clock at the latest."

Recognizing that he had no choice, Steven agreed, "Very well, can I send a driver to pick you up at the airport?"

"No thank you, that won't be necessary. Sam Banyon will pick me up and we'll come to your office together. See you tomorrow afternoon."

Steven did not like waiting until then to hear his concerns, but he had no choice. Carnley was in the driver's seat and Steven would have to be patient. It would all come down to a few hours tomorrow afternoon. He would have to just play it out and see what happened. He was running out of time to find another prospect. Carnley was it. Frustrated and tired, he sat at his desk mulling over his options before deciding to head home for the night. He fought the urge to call Jaclyn and share his difficult day with her. He wanted to hear her voice and have her help him feel better, as he knew she would, but how could he tell her the part about Caroline and Henry? What would she think of him? He couldn't risk her turning from him before she truly knew the man he was.

As he drove home, he passed the street that led to Caroline's house. In an instant he knew what he needed to do. He turned the car around and drove toward the Hunter residence. As soon as he was at the end of their drive, he rushed out of the car and up the stairs. He rang the bell and waited. As expected, Bentley answered the door. He was his usual cordial self. "Good evening, Mr. Cason."

Steven kept his tone even, attempting not to tip him off that anything was amiss. "Hello, Bentley. Is Ms. Caroline at home this evening?"

Stiffly, Bentley replied, "No, Mr. Cason, Ms. Caroline and her mother took a week retreat at the Greenhouse Spa. They're not expected to return until Sunday night. May I give her a message?"

Steven maneuvered his way inside the doorway as he took hold of the old man's arm in a friendly gesture. "No, Bentley, but thank you. Is Mr. Hunter at home this evening?"

Bentley cleared his throat, then replied, "Yes, Mr. Hunter is in residence. However, he wishes not to be disturbed."

Steven hoped that meant what he thought it did. He moved far enough into the foyer to see into the study and, noting it was unoccupied, determinedly climbed the staircase two steps at a time. By the time Bentley could react, Steven was at the second story landing and was making his way toward Hunter's bedroom. Bentley called after him, but Steven ignored him. As Steven disappeared down the hallway, Bentley hurriedly made his way over to the house phone and dialed the extension to Mr. Hunter's room. The phone rang insistently, but no one answered. Steven could hear the phone ringing as he approached the bedroom. He did not check if the door was locked. Instead, he threw his shoulder at the door, which with a loud popping noise opened to reveal the scene before him. On his king-sized, four-poster mahogany bed, Henry was lying naked on top of a young woman. Both were startled by Steven's entrance. Henry sat up in an instant and covered himself and his guest. His face turned a bright red, more out of anger than embarrassment. The young woman beside him moved up onto the pillows and rested against the headboard. Steven looked into her eyes. He figured she could be no more than seventeen.

Henry broke the silence, his voice reverberating through the immense room. "Cason, what is the meaning of this?"

Steven stood before him with a satisfied smile on his face. "I hear you have been slinging mud, my friend, and I thought you and I should have a chance to speak, but I see you are busy."

Henry was fuming. "How dare you break into my home like this? You'll pay for this, Cason."

Steven turned his attention to the amused young woman. He

smiled at her broadly. "What's your name, sweetheart?"

She found interest in his smile. Before Henry could stop her, she blurted out her name. "Stevie and if you're interested, I have a twin, Barbie." As the words came from her lips, Henry moved his body in front of hers, blocking her view of Steven. Angrily, he yelled, "Cason, get the hell out of here or I'll call the police."

Steven just leaned against the doorjamb and smiled. "I wonder what the police would do? I think it would be quite entertaining to have them come here and find you with a minor. Why don't you just give them a call Henry, I could use a good laugh."

Stevie piped up from the background. "I'll be eighteen in two months." She pushed Henry aside and flashed Steven a great big smile. She thought Steven was one good-looking man and maybe he was interested in her. He would certainly be an improvement over this hairy old man. She had to admit, though, that he was the most generous of all the men she had worked for.

Steven could not contain his laughter. "Revenge is so sweet, Henry. Don't you agree?"

Henry grabbed his robe from the foot of the bed and covered himself as he stood. Steven caught a glimpse of his naked old body and his limp dick. The pitiful sight was gratifying and Steven couldn't resist commenting, "I'm sorry to see that I came in the way of your good time, Henry."

Henry stomped over to Steven. His fury was raging. "Okay, Steven, the show is over. It's time for you to go." He pushed on his arm, but Steven did not budge.

Steven was not going to leave until he had an agreement with Henry. "I will go on one condition, that you retract what you said about me and stop your slander campaign. If you do, then none of what I know will hit the press. If you don't, my friends at the *Dallas Morning News* would love to get their hands on this juicy bit of dirt. And correct me if I'm mistaken Henry, but isn't your son running for congress next year? Now I bet he would be very angry with you if this came out at such an inopportune time. Don't you agree, Henry?"

Henry took a firm hold of Steven's arm. He spoke through pursed lips. "Okay, Steven, you've made your point loud and clear. I'll retract my comments at the club. But this is all forgotten, is it a deal?"

Before agreeing, Steven added, "It's a deal if it all stops . . . the slander campaign . . . the attempts to reunite Caroline and me . . . "

Henry interrupted in his urgent desire to end the confrontation, "Yes, yes, I agree."

Steven extended his hand, which Henry reluctantly shook. "Good then, I think we understand each other perfectly."

Steven looked over Henry's shoulder and saw Stevie leaning toward them, straining to hear what they were saying. "Good night, Stevie," he said as he turned to Henry and patted him on the back. "Good night to you too, Henry."

Totally satisfied with the outcome of his visit, he headed for the front door. Bentley was standing at the top of the stairs. He didn't say a word as Steven passed. When Steven's back was to the man, he said with a chuckle in his voice, "Good night, Bentley." The old man did not reply.

***

Jaclyn could not sleep. Her mind was on Thanksgiving Tower. She knew it would work out favorably, but the waiting was nerve-wracking. Closing the deal wasn't even a question in her mind. She was confident it would go her way and the deal would be theirs. Still, she tossed and turned in a vain attempt to sleep. Finally, she went to the living room to lie on the sofa and watch television. She hoped that the television would distract her enough so she could fall asleep. It worked as she had hoped, but as light filtered into the room at dawn, she woke up, startled. She momentarily panicked. What time was it? Why was she sleeping on the sofa? She sat up straight and stretched her back as she remembered why she had slept in the living room. Her body ached from the awkward position in which she slept. She rose from the sofa and checked the clock on the mantle. Gratefully, it was only six and she had plenty of time to get to the office early enough to open the door before anyone else made it in.

As she approached her office, she noticed an unfamiliar car parked in the far end of the parking lot. From her vantage point, it looked unoccupied. She kept one eye on the car as she moved toward the door to let herself in. The break-in at her office had her on her toes. She opened the door, listened for unfamiliar sounds and looked down the empty halls before locking herself in. She stood at the door momentarily, listening for the slightest sound. When she was convinced she was alone, she walked down the hall to her office. As she flicked on the light, she stood in the doorway and examined the office. The break-in had certainly taken its toll on her. She was too paranoid for her own good.

As she sat at her desk and opened the newspaper, she heard a knock on the office door. That's when she remembered she had locked the door behind her. She moved quickly down the hall toward the entrance, anticipating it would be the first employee arriving. As she approached, she could make out the figure of a man, but she could not tell his identity. In the recesses of her mind, she thought he looked like Andrew, but she dismissed the idea as impossible. Then he turned around and faced her. It was Andrew. He waved at her and flashed her a tooth-filled smile as their eyes met. She stopped dead in her tracks. Her mind raced, wondering why he was there and what he wanted from her. She hesitated while deciding whether to let him in. In that moment, Matt pulled up in his car. She waited for Matt to come over before opening the door. The two men walked in together.

Matt was the first to speak. "Good morning, Jaclyn. I see we have a visitor first thing this morning." He turned toward the man as he spoke.

Jaclyn answered, "Good morning, Matt. Yes, Mr. Thorton is here to see me."

Matt was moving toward his office as he spoke. "Excellent. Shall I make a pot of coffee?"

Jaclyn watched him move across the room. "That would be great, Matt. Thank you."

When Matt was down the hall, Jaclyn turned toward Andrew. Her expression was severe and he was taken back by her disdain. She spoke through a clenched jaw. "May I ask what you are doing here?"

He forced a smile as he spoke. "Jaclyn, darling," he said, leaning toward her. "I've missed you and wanted to come to see you."

She was filled with contempt, but she kept her voice low in an effort to keep their discussion private. "Andrew, I made myself exceedingly clear that I did not want to see you. What makes you think you have a right to come here?"

Andrew tried to touch her hand, but she pulled away from him. Taken aback by her gesture, he retreated, but his smile never faded. "I know you were upset, but I figured you would get over it. I mean, how do you just throw away four years of a great relationship and not look back?"

Jaclyn was angry at the way he trivialized what he had done with that woman, what he had done to cause their breakup. "I don't know, Andrew, how do you throw away four years of a great relationship? You're the one who did it, so you tell me."

"Point made, Jaclyn. I told you I was sorry. Okay, I'm human. I made a mistake, but why does my error in judgement have to force you to make a bigger mistake that both of us have to live with."

He was pleading with her, but it didn't have an impact on her. She knew her decision to leave him after what he had done was not a mistake. Now that Steven was in her life, she knew her breakup with Andrew was the best thing that could have happened. "I don't see our breakup as a mistake. It was the result of your error in judgement, but it was the right decision and I have no regrets."

Panic began to set in for Andrew. She could see it in his face. He continued pleading his case. "You may not have regrets, but I have many. How can I make this right between us, Jaclyn? Do I have to beg?… plead with you?… Tell me how to make it better between us, Jaclyn, please."

She could see he was a desperate man and she felt a pang of sorrow for his troubled soul, but she would never forgive him for what he had done and she would never go back to him. "I'm sorry, Andrew, there is nothing you can do." As she finished, Matt walked into the room again. Shaken, Jaclyn turned toward him. Matt saw the emotion in her face and became concerned. Sheepishly he remarked, "I'm sorry to interrupt, but I thought I would let you know the coffee is ready."

Jaclyn smiled at Matt. "Thank you, Matt, but Mr. Thorton won't be staying after all."

Matt nodded and silently retreated. Jaclyn turned toward Andrew once again. "I think it would be best if you left."

Andrew looked into her eyes searching for a glimmer of hope. "I came here to reason with you and I'm not leaving until I speak my peace." He took her silence as permission to continue. "I know it got crazy at the end and it was all my fault, but remember our plans? We were going to set our wedding date. You can't believe the people in my office pushing me to announce our wedding. Mr. Grant asks me everyday how you are. I've run out of excuses for why you aren't at the social events. You know how particular those senior partners can be."

In an instant, it all clicked. He was not letting her go because of what it meant to his career. That was it. Andrew may have regrets, but they most likely centered on what he did to ruin his chances for partnership. After a few moments of silence, she spoke again. It was all clear to her now and she wanted to let him know she was on to his game. "Andrew, I'm certain you explained to everyone that I moved to Dallas."

He looked down at the floor as he replied, "I did, but they assumed it was a temporary assignment. I didn't tell anyone our relationship has ended because I still feel like we can get over this." He looked back at her as he finished speaking, optimistic she would say something to give him hope of their future together.

Instead, she shook her head in disbelief. He just wasn't getting it. "I don't know how else to say this to you, but to just come out and say it again." She spoke slowly, giving every syllable emphasis. "It is over between us. It has been since that night at your apartment. It wasn't easy for me either, but I have moved on. I suggest you do the same. You need to tell the partners the truth."

Andrew hung his head and ran his hands through his hair. He was frazzled and depressed, but he had not given up. He would try one more angle. It was worth taking one more shot at it. "Would it make a difference if I moved here? We could have a fresh start. I would be willing to give up New York, my career, everything, Jaclyn, everything, if it meant I would get you back in my life."

She began to feel deeply sorry for him. She could not even imagine the regret he must be feeling. It dawned on her then how sad it was for anyone whose life was so dramatically altered by one error in judgement. But no one had forced Andrew's hand and she wasn't going to feel like the bad guy in all of this. "I guess there is a moment in everyone's life when we wish we could turn back time. But short of that, there is nothing either of us can do to make this right between us." At her words, Andrew began pacing frantically. He moved toward her and she backed up. She realized he was getting irrational and losing control, so she tried to calm the brewing storm. "Andrew, I don't think there is anything further for us to discuss. I think you should leave."

He came within inches of her, put his hands on her upper arms and pulled her close to him. She was momentarily stunned by his forceful grasp. "I will not give up on the idea that we will be together. I know it is meant to be. In time you will know that too."

She pulled away from him but did not say a word. She could see that he was trembling. For a moment, she feared him again. She wondered what he might do, as he was clearly on the edge. She chose her words carefully. "Listen to me, Andrew." She waited for his eyes to focus on her before she continued, "Your life is in New York. Mine is in Dallas now. When I left New York, I left behind a lot, including us. I have moved past all of that and you need to as well."

He shook his head and began pacing again, like a caged animal dwelling on its lack of freedom. After an uncomfortable pause, he moved toward the door and looked back at her. "I'm going to leave for now, Jaclyn, since that is clearly what you want." He stared deeply into her eyes as he continued, "But we will be together again, and that's a promise." At his last word, he turned abruptly and stormed out of the building. Chills ran up and down her spin as she watched him leave. She knew she could not trust him and she feared what actions he would take to win her back.

                    ***

Henry walked nervously down a dark, narrow alley in the Deep Elum section of Dallas. He continually checked behind him as he walked hurriedly toward a back door marked with a rusted sign that hung crocked on a twisted wire. As he had been instructed, he knocked three times, then waited. It seemed a long time before the door open before him, revealing a scantily dress young woman. She peered at Henry for a moment, then questioned him. "Why have you come here?"

Henry remembered the code words he had been given. "Ramon sent me to see the Master."

At his words, she stepped into the stairwell and allowed Henry to enter. She gestured to him to follow her. Cautiously, he crossed the threshold and entered the musty hall. It was dark and dingy and Henry questioned his safety. At the top of the stairs, the woman opened a door and instructed Henry. "Wait here," was all she said as she disappeared into the room, shutting the door behind her.

As he waited, Henry apprised his situation. He was in a dark stairway in the warehouse district in a bad side of town, waiting for a man he was told could handle anyone who needed an attitude adjustment. Had he gone too far with this one? Was he in deeper than he should be? The little voice inside his head told him to leave. His pulse began to race and his palms became clammy. He was about to head down the stairs for a quick exit, when the woman appeared before him. "Follow me," she said as she turned and walked back into the room from where she had come.

Henry entered the room behind her. The lighting was so dark that Henry had trouble seeing where they were going. They walked through an empty room, through another door and into a second room. It was then that Henry saw the form of a man seated at a large desk at the far end. The woman stopped a distance from the man, told Henry to sit in the only chair that Henry could see and left. Henry's panic began to increase. His heart was beating so loudly that he feared the man across the room could hear it. He tried to calm himself for fear of giving himself a heart attack.

The man's deep voice boomed in the cavernous room. "Why have you come here?"

Henry cleared his throat. "Ramon sent me. He said you could help me."

"That depends. What kind of help are you looking for?"

Trying to stay calm, Henry took a deep breath before replying. "I want pressure applied on a man. He promised to marry my daughter, now he has cast her aside for another woman. I want him to be made to understand that he needs to reconsider his decision."

The man was silent for a moment. Henry began to sweat. Finally, the man spoke. "Explain pressure."

Henry had to think about his response. This was not familiar territory. He had never gone directly to a hit man before. Any other time he had resorted to this type of persuasion, he had hired an intermediary. But this time was different. He could not afford any mistakes or risk anyone finding out about his role in this plan. Henry chose his words carefully. "Enough to make him see things my way."

"Then death is not out of the question."

Henry's heart nearly stopped. "Wow. Wait a minute. No one said that. I mean, that's not my intention."

"Well, sometimes, no matter what we try, the person doesn't come around. What then?"

"Let's cross that bridge when we come to it. I would like to start with threats, or whatever you think is best to persuade Steven Cason to honor his commitment to my daughter."

"Did you bring the cash?"

Henry pulled an envelope out of his breast pocket. "Yes. I have the cash right here."

The woman reappeared from the shadows, retrieved the envelope and brought it to the man behind the desk. While he waited, Henry could hear the rustling of bills.

"Alright. I have what I need. We will pay Mr. Cason a visit in the next few days. Call Ramon at the end of the week for an update. That will be all."

Henry did not know what to do, but the woman came to his side and instructed him to follow her. As he stood to leave, he turned to thank the man, but he was already gone. In silence, he followed closely behind the woman and with a sense of urgency left the building. Hastily, he jogged down the alley and jumped into his car. He was drenched in sweat and was shaking from the nerve-wracking experience. He was a desperate man employing desperate measures. There are times, he convinced himself, in everyone's life when one has to put all else aside to obtain the correct outcome. He didn't believe in sitting back and hoping for the best. Creating destiny was his motto. This time was no different. Things always worked out as he planned. He always saw to it.

***

Steven had a full morning of meetings that had been scheduled for weeks and couldn't be changed. Several investors from Hong Kong were visiting to finalize a limited partnership that had been negotiated during the past six months. He was able to delegate part of their time to several of his key employees, but he felt obligated to spend some time with them discussing their plans. He had to use all of his self-discipline to stay focused on them when he desperately wanted to be spending time on finalizing the purchase of the Tower. Although Carnley was his best option, he never stopped working a deal until the money was in the bank. He didn't ever leave anything to chance. That philosophy had served him well on many occasions. So while he was tied up with meetings, he had asked Diana to continue to phone prospective partners. In spite of himself, his mind frequently wandered to the Tower and the progress he optimistically hoped Diana was making.

Just before noon, Steven adjourned the meeting for lunch, excusing himself from the meal and sending the investors and his employees out for an American version of Chinese cuisine. Once the group hustled onto the elevators, he immediately returned to his office. As he approached Diana's desk, he could tell she did not have good news for him. She avoided his eyes as he neared. "Okay, Diana, let's have it. Any prospects?"

She looked up at him and only shook her head in reply. Her face showing the frustration she felt after a long morning of doors slamming in her face.

He asked again, as if this time there would be a different answer. "Not one?"

"I'm sorry, Steven. I tried, but I couldn't get anything remotely close to interest."

Steven knew she was feeling the weight of his problem and he didn't want that. "Now you listen to me, young lady, nothing and no one is going to stand in the way of Thanksgiving Tower being the premier Cason property. Don't you worry about a thing. You know me, I always manage to pull a rabbit out of my hat." He winked at Diana and she smiled at him as he walked into his office.

As he sat at his desk, he checked his watch. It was noon and Carnley was scheduled to arrive in an hour. He called down to the commissary and ordered a box lunch to be brought up to his office. Desperate to have all of his ducks in a row for the meeting with Carnley, he cleared his desk of everything except his file on the Tower. He buried himself in the details as he waited for Carnley to arrive. Impatiently, he frequently checked his watch. As one o'clock rolled around, Steven called Diana into his office. As she appeared in the doorway, he said, "Advise reception that Mr. Carnley and Mr. Banyon are to be arriving momentarily. I want to be certain they are shown to my office without delay."

Diana was quick to reply. "I have already alerted reception to their arrival, but I will be happy to call again."

Steven nodded. He knew better than to ask Diana to confirm

a guest's arrival with the front desk, but then again, something didn't feel right. He couldn't quite put his finger on it, but he had this gut feeling that something wasn't going to go well.

As he waited, Steven busied himself with reading the mail that had just been delivered. Before long, he realized it was nearly 1:30 and there was still no Carnley in sight. He began to get antsy. He called Diana into his office again. As she appeared, he said, "Diana, check with the airlines to see if there were any major delays affecting flights due in Dallas this morning."

She nodded, then returned to her desk. Within minutes, she was back in his office. He looked up as she entered. "I'm sorry, Steven, there were no delays reported. Is there anything else I can check?"

He smiled at her. "Not at this moment, Diana, thank you."

She returned his smile and left the room. He rose from his desk and started pacing. He was thinking about what to do next when his private line rang. He picked it up quickly, hopeful it was Carnley. To his disappointment, it was Al. Steven was in no mood for his incompetence. "Al, whatever you have to say, it better be good."

Al believed Steven would want to hear his news, so he continued. "I have news on Carnley."

Steven went still. "What is it?"

Al continued without pause. "There is only one Arnold Carnley on file with any government agency. He is a retired army sergeant, living in a mobile home park on the outskirts of Las Vegas."

"That can't be." Steven vocalized the disbelief that raced through his mind. "Where did you get this information?"

Al was sure of himself. "Believe me, Steven, it's a trusted source. This guy has access to all government records. He assured me that if all I had to go by was a name, the best he could do was run a databank search for individuals with that identity. Then it would be up to us to see if anybody he found was the guy we were looking for."

"When did he inform you of the results?"

"I just got off the phone with him. He said he could fax me the findings if it would help, but he guarantees his work. He told me his search took all morning to complete and only resulted in two individuals. I thought with a name like Carnley there would be more, but he found only two."

Steven interrupted him. "I thought you said there was only

one match."

Al clarified. "There was another guy, but he died two months ago. His file indicated no living relatives, so his belongings were turned over to the state."

Steven's blood boiled. He immediately thought of Hunter. Maybe this was another of his revenge tactics. He also knew the sweetest retaliation would be winning, which was exactly what he was intent on doing. Slamming down the phone, he flew out of his office, yelling at Diana as he left. "You can reach me on my mobile phone if Carnley miraculously shows up or if anything else regarding the Tower deal needs my immediate attention. Otherwise, I am out of the office for the remainder of the afternoon."

She called after him, "Don't forget your 5 o'clock appointment with Mr. Spellman."

As he stepped into the elevator, he replied, "Cancel it. Reschedule him for next week."

***

Following her encounter with Andrew, Jaclyn had a hard time focusing on her work. Thinking back on it, she still couldn't believe he had come to see her. He was clearly desperate and that frightened her. Trying to rid her mind of thoughts of him, she went home early to refresh herself before going to the airport to pick up JP. She had to stay positive and sharp, as the next twenty-four hours would prove pivotal in the deal.

JP's flight was scheduled to arrive at 8 o'clock that evening. Jaclyn left for the airport with enough time to be waiting at the gate when he arrived. As she did on their first meeting, she positioned herself in line with the jet-bridge doorway where the deplaning passengers would exit. Once again, JP was the first to enter the terminal. When she saw him, she called out to him, "JP!" He turned in her direction and headed toward her. As he approached, she added, "Or should I say Mr. Carnley!" The two shared a hearty laugh.

JP added, "I would have given anything to have seen Cason's face when one o'clock came and went and no Carnley. This was truly a brilliant move, Jaclyn. I really enjoyed fighting fire with fire. He got exactly what he deserved." To her surprise, JP gave her a very fatherly hug.

She wanted to believe they had led Cason down the wrong path, hoping he had put his last hope in Carnley. "Do you think he really bought into it?"

JP assured her, "I feel as if Banyon spending the day at Cason's office made it credible. I only told Banyon that I had concealed my identity, which didn't surprise him. He knew I was using the name Carnley, but that was the extent of his knowledge of our plan. I wanted it that way so he would be thorough and confident instead of self-conscious and nervous."

Jaclyn was eager to hear more. "How did he say it went?"

JP had a smile on his face, "Without a hitch."

Jaclyn was afraid to be too confident. "I guess we really won't know how well it worked until tomorrow afternoon, but it sounds promising."

JP agreed. "Let's put it this way, I spoke to Cason last night. He was very eager to get the deal done. In fact, by the way he sounded, I would say Carnley was his only hope."

A feeling of accomplishment raced through Jaclyn's body. As she and JP walked out of the airport, she held onto the belief that the next day, the Tower would be theirs.

CHAPTER 18
—◇—

Steven was at his desk, finalizing his business for the week before leaving for Milton's office when Diana appeared at his door. He nodded, giving her permission to enter.

"Steven, Amanda at reception said there are three men in the lobby asking to see you."

Steven, whose patience was extremely low these days, had no time for ineptitude. "Well, Diana, do you know who they are?"

She blushed at his unusual impatience with her. "No Steven. When Amanda called, she sounded very nervous. They would not give her any information, just told her they needed to see you on a very important business matter."

It seemed odd to Steven, but regardless of whom they were, he had no time to see them. "Tell Amanda to have them leave their business cards and to inform them that I will contact them when I have time to meet."

"Very well, Steven. I'm sorry to have disturbed you, it's just that Amanda said they conveyed a sense of urgency."

As Diana left his office, Steven momentarily pondered who the men could be, but quickly refocused his attention to the Tower. He would allow nothing to come in the way of being ready for his meeting with Milton.

***

Jaclyn knew exactly what she would wear today. She had

selected her red, double-breasted suit because it exuded a sense of power and strength and it was those two qualities she would take with her to Thompson's office at 5 o'clock. Jaclyn spent her morning organizing her file to take to the meeting with Thompson. As members of her staff arrived for the day and ran into her, each commented on her appearance. Matt's remarks were her favorite. As customary, he would arrive shortly after Jaclyn, go directly to his desk to consult his daily planner, then walk into Jaclyn's office to greet her. This morning his salutation was unusually personal. As he entered her office, he stopped speaking mid-sentence. "Good morning, Jaclyn. How . . .?"

She looked up to see him standing before her, staring down at her. He was clearly at a loss for words. She spoke instead. "Good morning, Matt. Is everything okay?"

Her question snapped him out of his trance. "I'm sorry, Jaclyn, it's just that you look so..."

Once again he was at a loss for words and Jaclyn saved him. "Thank you, Matt. I'm meeting with Thompson this afternoon."

Matt complimented her. "You certainly look wonderful. If looks are part of the equation, you'll win hands down."

She laughed at his remark. "Thank you, Matt. Now, if you'll excuse me, I have a full morning before I leave to get Mr. Morrison."

Matt understood and was quick to oblige. As he walked away, he said softly, "Please let me know if there is anything I can do for you."

Jaclyn had already returned her focus to her paperwork and did not respond.

***

As Steven drove the short distance to Milton's office it became clear to him that he was being trailed. From the moment he pulled out of his parking garage, a black Mercedes followed closely behind. To test the possibility of a coincidence, Steven purposely circled a building, returning to the street he had previously been on. When the trailing sedan mirrored his moves, it become clear to Steven that he was being followed. He wondered why. It was unnerving. He thought back to the men who had come to his office to see him. Something was going on, but he didn't know what. All he knew was that he didn't like the way it felt.

Moments later, he pulled up to the headquarters of First Southwest Bank. He pulled his car around the circular drive, stopped directly in front of the entry and quickly exited his car. As he made his way into the building, he took note of the black car parked on the street, just a few yards away.

When he arrived at Thompson's office, his secretary showed him into the conference room. As he entered, Milton rose and met him with an extended hand. The two men exchanged greetings and took a seat across from each other at the conference table. Al had been asked not to attend, as Steven wanted to deal directly with Milton on the final negotiations. Milton agreed. However, he made it clear to Steven that he would involve his advisors at some point in the discussion. Steven acquiesced.

Milton was eager to commence the business at hand and so opened the meeting. As he spoke, he sat forward in his chair, clasped his hands on the table and looked into Steven's serious face. "Well, Cason, how successful were you in putting the deal together?"

Steven pulled a file out of his briefcase and laid it out on the table in front of him. He opened the file, took out a commitment letter and handed it to Milton. As Milton took hold of the letter, Steven spoke. "This is the commitment of 40% ownership by SC Investments. The cash is at the bank and can be verified. The details are explained in the letter signed by myself on behalf of SC Investments and by the bank. SC Investments is capable of closing in 30 days."

Milton took the letter from Steven and read it thoroughly. Everything appeared in order. When Milton was done reviewing the document, he looked up at Steven and nodded to show his acceptance. Steven then pulled out the next commitment letter and handed it to him. Again, he summarized what the letter stated. "This is the commitment for 20% by Jed Hebert. The cash is at the bank listed on the commitment letter. I verified that the cash is at the bank and was informed that the funds are being held per this agreement. You can likewise verify the funds by calling the bank contact listed on the letter. As you can see, it was signed by Hebert and the bank and was duly notarized. The 30-day closing is no problem for Hebert."

As Milton took hold of the letter, he smiled. He looked up at Steven. "I go way back with Jed. Does he know I took the property back on foreclosure?"

Steven chuckled to himself thinking about Jed's informal business practices. "I couldn't say for certain, Milton, but if you know Jed, you know he doesn't get caught up in the business end of things. If a deal feels good to him, he goes with it. I think he took a piece of this deal just to say he owns a piece of Big D. I really believe that's the long and short of it, simple as that."

Milton smiled thinking about Jed and then turned his attention back to reviewing the document before him. Meanwhile, Steven pulled out the next commitment letter and waited for Milton to look up before presenting it. He then concisely summed up the next letter for Milton as he handed it to him. "This is the next commitment for 20% by Mitsu Industries, signed by Mr. Sumitomo, CFO. Again, I verified that the funds are being held according to the agreement, but as with the others, feel free to verify the information yourself."

Milton reviewed the commitment, then looked up at Steven. "This bank guarantee is issued by the Bank of Tokyo. Will the funds be immediately available at closing?"

Steven was confident in his reply. "The bank issuing the letter is actually the San Francisco branch and the funds are in the U.S. If you want to be assured of same-day availability, we can have the bank amend the letter to state that. The bank also confirmed that a 30 day closing is no problem."

Milton was appeased. "Very good, but before we continue, I want to call in my secretary and ask her to begin contacting the banks to verify that the funds are available in the amounts listed per the attached investment commitments." He paused to read Steven's reaction, but Steven smiled at Milton's caution. He could hardly blame the man.

Recognizing that Milton was waiting for him to say something, Steven added, "Of course, Milton. I anticipated you would want to check with the banks. That's why I included the direct phone number for the bank officer who signed each letter. I even informed them of our meeting so they could anticipate your call."

Milton was impressed. He appreciated Steven's thorough handling of the details. Without delay, Milton called in his secretary, who was at his side in seconds. He handed her the commitment letters and gave her perfunctory instructions. "Call the bank officers listed on these three letters and ask them to verify that they in fact issued these letters and guarantee the sums are available. In addition, tell them that should the contract contingencies be removed, we will want these letters converted into bank guarantees. Ask them for the procedures to get that done."

The woman scanned the papers in her hand, nodded at Milton, then turned to leave. As she stepped away from the table, Milton called after her. "Let me know as soon as you have spoken to each of them." She turned back toward him as he spoke and nodded, but continued walking out of the room.

As soon as the door closed behind her, Milton turned his attention back to Steven and spoke. "Sorry for the interruption, Steven. I just want her to begin calling the banks before they close for the day. Please continue."

Steven replied, "There is no reason to apologize, Milton. Whatever it takes to get the contract to closing is okay by me." Milton nodded in appreciation of his understanding. Steven then continued. "The commitments you have account for 80% of the cash you require." Milton sat back with a concerned look on his face. He hoped that Steven was not going to ask him for more time to come up with the balance or ask him to finance the remaining 20%, as he was prepared to accept nothing less than 100% cash and a 30-day closing.

Steven read his thoughts perfectly. "The remaining 20%, I have to admit, was not easy to come by. In fact, in the short time allotted, I did not find another investor."

Milton fidgeted in his chair. Steven remained silent for dramatic effect. Milton could not stand the anticipation and broke the silence. "Are you telling me you are $30 million short?"

Steven paused as if that was exactly what he had to say but didn't know how to say it. Then as he began to speak, his demeanor changed. "No, Milton, not at all. I'm just letting you know I couldn't get any other investors, but I have the full commitment."

Milton was confused. "Can you explain?"

Steven took a long, deep breath before he spoke. "I have leveraged my shares in Cason Properties, my home on Beverly Drive and . . . essentially, I have leveraged everything I own. I have a separate personal commitment from my bank, for the remaining $30 million."

Milton was shocked. Why would a man like Cason put everything he owned and worked for up as collateral on this building?

He could have any other property he wanted and on his own terms. Why Thanksgiving Tower and why under these terms? The way he had it laid out, he could lose it all on this deal. The only reply Milton had was simple. "Why?"

Steven sat back with a big smile stretched across his face. He looked at Milton and explained as much as he was willing to share. "It's something of a matter of pride. There are a lot of people who tried to ruin this deal for me. I had to make it happen, even if it meant risking everything I have. If I lost the deal, I lost my reputation and pride. This is bigger than brick and mortar. The stakes are too high." What Steven left out was that he never lost, ever, at anything. And this was the building Henry Hunter had built for himself, a monument to the power and wealth he had acquired. Owning such a status symbol would signify that Steven had acquired that level of success. It would also be the ultimate revenge on Hunter - to own what Henry had built for himself, and have it bear Cason's name. In his business, status and position were everything and he wanted to be at the pinnacle more than anything else. It was worth the risk all right. It was worth everything to him.

Milton shook his head. This man obviously had a tremendous amount of pride and for that he had to admire him; otherwise, he thought he was nuts. As Milton reviewed Steven's personal commitment letter, his secretary buzzed in. Milton picked up the receiver. "Mr. Thompson, the commitments were verified as per the agreements. I spoke to the three bank officers personally. I also obtained their bank guarantee procedures, which should present no problem and can be done well within our time constraints."

Milton thanked her, but she was not through. "Your 5 o'clock appointment has arrived."

Suddenly Milton remembered the other party. Since he had no way of knowing in advance that Cason would remove the contingencies, he had not canceled the appointment. Milton checked his watch and noted it was only 4:45. "Please ask them to wait in the boardroom and tell them I will be there shortly."

He hung up and looked at Steven. He was amused to find him still grinning from ear to ear. He looked like a cat that had just caught a mouse. "Well, Steven, I believe we have a deal." He leaned across the table and shook Steven's hand. "I will call Mike, my real estate attorney, and ask him to join us. I want him to review the paperwork and if everything meets with his approval, we'll finalize the contract tonight. If you don't mind, I will meet my five o'clock appointment while Mike is reviewing the documents. I won't be long. In fact, I bet I'll be done before Mike is through."

Steven understood. "Of course, Milton. I'm very pleased that we have reached an agreement and am looking forward to closing this deal."

Milton rose and started walking out of the room. Steven followed him. He showed Steven to a waiting area outside of his office and across from his secretary's desk. He told his secretary to call Mike and ask him to come and review the paperwork, which he had left for him on the conference room table. She acknowledged her understanding and immediately called Mike as Milton headed for the boardroom. Before he turned the corner, Milton called back to Steven and told him to help himself to a drink from the refreshment center behind his secretary's station. Steven stood and walked over to the counter and selected a soda from the refrigerator. As he walked by her desk, he could clearly hear Milton's secretary speaking to Mike. She explained to him what Milton had told her. "Hi, Mike. Mr. Thompson needs you to come to his office to review the paperwork that Mr. Cason brought in to satisfy the conditions of the contract. If your review is satisfactory, then Mr. Thompson wants to document the removal of the financing contingency." After a short pause, she continued. "Yes, Mike, he is in with the other party now. I imagine he is informing them that the contingencies were met on the first contract."

Steven looked at her in surprise as she disclosed the purpose of Milton's other meeting. At that moment, he felt great satisfaction for having won. He found it interesting that the vultures were circling. The party behind the other contract obviously thought he would fail to meet the contingencies. He had to admire their gumption. But none of that mattered now. Thanksgiving Tower was his.

***

Inside the boardroom, Jaclyn and JP waited patiently. Since they had not heard from Thompson, they were convinced that the other contract was now null and void and that they would move into first position. Eagerly, they awaited Thompson's arrival. To pass the time, they spoke about the hot summer that was just around the corner. Jaclyn was unaccustomed to the Texas heat and she wasn't certain how well she would fare. JP shared with her some of his experiences as a young man spending summers in the sweltering heat of the tobacco plantations. "I remember my days in South America. Father and Grandfather would take me to the plantations so I could understand the business. There was no relief from that stifling heat. I'm not certain how I managed to make it through those trips."

Jaclyn watched him as his face reacted to the vivid memory, then added, "I have lived in the Northeast my entire life and never liked the summer because of the heat. I understand though that your body adjusts, so I'll have to hope for the best in making it through." They were in the middle of their conversation when the door opened and Milton stepped into the room. He was extremely cordial and immediately put Jaclyn at ease. They exchanged introductions, shook hands and then each took a seat on opposing sides of the long rectangular table. Milton allowed everyone to settle before he began to speak. "Ms. Tate, Mr. Morrison, first I wish to thank you for your interest and offer on Thanksgiving Tower." Jaclyn suddenly felt ill. That opening sounded like a soft way to begin bad news. She tried to stay positive as he continued. "Since your interest in the Tower is clear by the fact you are here today, what I must tell you is not easy for me to say." Jaclyn's heart sunk. She glanced over at JP, whose eyes did not meet hers. He kept a steady eye on Milton as he continued speaking, "I must inform you that the contingencies on the first contract were met."

Jaclyn heard the words, but her mind did not want to accept what they meant. How did Cason do it? She was certain the deal would be theirs. JP watched Jaclyn intently, knowing she had taken the deal personally and was set on closing it. When Jaclyn did not speak, JP answered for them. "Well, Milton, we gave it the old college try. We certainly are disappointed. That is one great property and we are sorry to have missed out on it, but I would like to say that if for any reason things don't work out for your buyer, I hope that you will call us."

Milton replied, "Thank you for the offer. I appreciate your understanding." As he spoke, he rose from his chair and extended his hand to JP. The gentlemen shook hands, then Milton turned to Jaclyn to shake her hand and thank her for her presentation of the contract. She acknowledged him with a forced smile and a nod.

She was blindsided, but she acknowledged that she might have set herself up for the disappointment. She was angry with herself for taking it all so personally. There was an empty feeling inside her and she felt the energy drain from her body. She had put so much of herself into the deal that losing it felt like she was losing a part of herself. JP saw the anguish in her face. As they walked out of the room and followed Milton down the hall, JP reassured her they would find another deal, one that would be even better, but Jaclyn felt defeated. It was rare that she did not achieve a professional goal. This sale had also been important to her because it would have guaranteed the success of the Dallas office for Carl. Carl had put his faith in her and she wanted him to know it had not been misplaced. She desperately wanted to make the Dallas office a winner; no business goal had ever meant more to her.

Before Milton turned the corner, Jaclyn called after him, "Mr. Thompson." He paused and turned to her. "Who was the final investor to complete the buy?"

Milton smiled at her question. "Mr. Cason personally took the final stake in the Tower."

Jaclyn was surprised. "What a bold move."

Milton's smile revealed that he had had a similar reaction. "I thought it was quite extraordinary that someone in his position would risk it all on one deal, but it must mean a lot to him to bet so much on it."

Jaclyn nodded in reply. She knew how Cason must feel, as she had been willing to do just about anything to get this deal done. The difference was that Cason's tactics had netted him a win and the deal was his.

When Steven heard people approaching, he looked down the hall and saw Milton walking toward him. A man and a woman followed, but Steven couldn't see them clearly from that distance. As Milton turned toward Steven, he revealed the two people behind him. To Steven's disbelief, one of them was Jaclyn. He stood as they approached. It was seconds later that Jaclyn looked at the man standing a few feet away. She was momentarily stunned.

Milton followed Steven's stare and decided to introduce him. He called out to Steven and Steven walked to his side. Before Milton could say anything, Steven spoke. "Jaclyn, hello. What are you doing here?"

She looked up at him and a smile came to her lips, "Steven… hi."

Milton was surprised. "Am I to understand that introductions are unnecessary?"

At his words, JP extended his hand to Steven to introduce himself. "Hello, I'm JP Morrison."

Steven gave him a firm handshake. "JP, it's a pleasure to meet you. I'm Steven Cason."

As the words left his lips, Jaclyn's blood ran cold. In an instant, the color drained from her face and she had to lean against JP to steady herself and keep from fainting. Steven did not understand her reaction until Milton explained who JP was. "Steven, Mr. Morrison was the buyer on the second contract."

At that moment, all Steven cared to know was why Jaclyn was there and what she had to do with the other offer. Although his mind feared the answer, he found the courage to ask, "And Jaclyn?"

Milton explained, "Oh, Ms. Tate is Mr. Morrison's agent." Confused, he added, "But I thought you two knew each other?"

Steven did not take his eyes off Jaclyn as the facts unfolded before them. All he could think was that she must hate him. He had won, but his victory was her defeat and he was suddenly overcome by anxiety. He watched her intently as he replied to Milton. "Yes, Jaclyn and I have met before, but I wasn't aware of her involvement in the deal until now."

Jaclyn remained silent, uncertain of what to say. Her head was pounding and all she wanted to do was run . . . run fast . . . run far.

Milton did not follow Steven's thoughts and, concerned about the time, tried to hurry the introduction along. "Very well, Steven, we have work to finish. Good-bye, Mr. Morrison, Ms. Tate. Thank you for coming in this evening." Milton walked toward his office and motioned for Steven to accompany him, but Steven did not follow. Instead, he turned toward Milton and called out that he would be with him in a few minutes. While Steven's attention was turned to Milton, Jaclyn excused herself quietly and retreated down the hall toward the restroom. She couldn't stand the pressure mounting in her head and she desperately needed some air. The beating of her heart was so loud in her ears that she felt as if she would pass out. As she

walked away, scattered thoughts raced through her mind. It all started
to come together . . . Steven Cason had been at Al's office the morning
of her meeting with him . . . that name, she knew she had heard it
before . . . the timing on the contract . . . the terms of the offer . . . his
contract beating hers by only hours . . .the break-in at her office and
her missing file . . . my God, she thought, did he break into my office?
. . .the newspaper article and her buyers in on his deal . . . where did
this nightmare begin or end? Her mind continued to race and her
thoughts were muddled. Her stream of consciousness continued. Had
he got close only to get information on the deal? . . .had she been
played for a fool? . . .A fool . . . A fool. Her head was swimming with
negative thoughts. It was hard to stop the musing that overtook her. It
wasn't possible, this man whom she had fallen for, believed in, given
herself to . . .He was Cason. That underhanded, conniving excuse of
a man... and what a fool she had been. He played her...she lost the
deal because she was played. Her thoughts were overwhelming her
and she knew she had to get out of there and fast. She didn't want JP
to know what had happened and she couldn't face Steven. In fact, she
never wanted to see him again. Seeing his face would only remind her
of the fool she had been played for. Why had she let him in? Hadn't
she learned her lesson from Andrew? She reprimanded herself for
letting emotions override prudence and common sense. She could
not believe that this man who in an instant had won her heart had, in
another moment, torn it to shreds. She was so overwrought when she
left the restroom that she was momentarily disoriented. She looked
down both ends of the hallway before deciding which way would lead
her back to the lobby. She walked slowly, staying close to the wall for
support and balance. As she turned the corner, she could see JP and
Steven talking by Milton's office, their backs to her. She hastened her
pace as she passed unnoticed and took the elevator downstairs to the
lobby. When she reached the entryway, she asked the receptionist to
phone Mr. Thompson's secretary to relay a message to Mr. Morrison.
She scribbled a note for him. The message read, 'Ms. Tate apologizes
for her urgent departure, but it was unavoidable. She will call you at
the hotel tomorrow morning.' As Jaclyn hurried out of the building,
the receptionist called Mr. Thompson's office and read the message
to his secretary. The woman then interrupted the two men in front of
her and gave Mr. Morrison a hand written note that relayed word for
word the message Jaclyn had left. JP took the note and read it, then

turned to Steven to share the message with him. Both men were very concerned about Jaclyn and her decision to leave so abruptly.

Steven felt compelled to make some sense of her reaction. He began by telling JP how he had met Jaclyn, but how little he really knew about her. JP shook his head in disbelief. He now understood completely why Jaclyn had been so upset. He then felt obligated to reciprocate. "Steven, do you realize why Jaclyn is so upset with you?"

Steven took a stab at the answer. "I imagine it's because she didn't end up with the deal and I did. We were obviously working against each other without knowing it and only one of us could end up with the deal. It was unfortunately a no-win situation."

JP nodded. "Certainly, but that is only part of it. There is a lot more. She was convinced that there were unethical business practices involved when your contract beat ours by mere hours. On top of that, your offer involves two of her most promising prospects, names that she is convinced came straight from a file that was stolen from her office during a break-in. Need I go on?"

Steven looked at JP in disbelief. He felt compelled to explain his side. "JP, I can see how all of this circumstantial evidence weighs heavily against me, but please hear me out. First of all, until this very minute, I had no knowledge of a break-in at Jaclyn's office. When did it happen? What exactly was taken?"

JP didn't know whether or not to believe him, but Steven's bewilderment sounded so convincing that JP continued. "Last week, someone broke into her office and took her file on the Tower. It contained her prospect list, which clearly noted Hebert and Mitsu as two of her three top prospects."

Steven was shocked. "Do you remember the exact day?"

JP tried to think of the morning he had called Jaclyn and her assistant explained that she couldn't take his call because she was completing the incident report with a police officer. "I'm almost positive it was exactly a week ago. Yes, it was last Friday."

Steven then recalled Al's telephone call on Saturday morning, telling him he had come up with prospects on the Tower. Steven hoped he was wrong, but suspected that Al had had something to do with the break-in. If Al were behind this, he would have hell to pay. Steven looked back at JP and said, "My world is very complicated and I can't expect you or Jaclyn to understand the tight circle in which I operate. We share information and make certain deals happen at the right time and for the right party. If we hear that a contract is coming in on a property we have dibs on, we rush in and present ours first. It's kind of like a brotherhood. Jaclyn was not in our circle and outsiders usually don't fare as well when competing against one of us, especially on a deal of this magnitude and in our backyard. No one in our circle wanted Thanksgiving Tower to go to an outsider. It's too much a part of Dallas's identity. Then there are other things I didn't even know about, like the break-in at her office. The names of the two buyers in my deal came to me through an interested party. I didn't question him about how he had obtained those leads. I didn't have reason to." Steven paused and considered what Jaclyn must be thinking of him at that moment. He ran a hand through his hair in frustration as he continued. "I imagine that right now Jaclyn believes this was all my doing. She must hate me. I can't stand the thought. The whole thing is unbelievable." Steven dropped his head into his hands and tried desperately to come up with a way out of this mess.

JP felt compelled to tell him the entire story. "It gets better." Steven looked up at him, curious to hear what more he could possibly add. "I was posing as Mr. Carnley."

Steven looked at JP in disbelief. "What?"

JP hung his head and nodded. "After the break-in, we thought it was time to fight back. Jaclyn was frustrated, so we thought we would give you a dose of your own medicine. I guess it was her attempt to play your game and gain back some ground for our side, but she wasn't very comfortable with the whole idea. Now keep in mind that she saw this as minor in comparison with the break-in."

Steven laughed a nervous laugh out loud and JP shot him a surprised glare. "I'm sorry, JP. It's just so unbelievable. I meet a woman like no woman I have ever met in my life and she turns out to be the agent on a competing contract on the most significant deal I've done in my career and we end up trying to screw each other out of the deal. Now tell me that isn't comical."

JP could see the irony in it, but his thoughts turned to Jaclyn and his fears for what she must be feeling. As if Steven could read his mind, he added, "Okay, JP, now we need to fix this mess. I have an idea."

The men sat and talked until Milton came out and called

Steven into his office to finalize the contract. Steven explained to Milton that there would be a slight change in the deal and asked if JP could join them to discuss it. Milton looked concerned but led the men into the office where Mike was waiting. As soon as they were all seated, Steven immediately began, "Gentlemen, I am pleased the deal is about to be finalized. Although the modification I am about to discuss with you in no way affects the bank's position, it does change the make-up of the new ownership. Mr. Morrison will take on my personal position, 20% for $30 million in cash plus an additional 10%. I will reduce SC Investments's position by 10%, thereby providing Mr. Morrison with a 30% stake." Milton gave JP a curious glance, then turned his attention back to Steven. "Mr. Morrison is prepared to call his banker at this moment to verify that the funds are available, but given his previous offer of $145 million in cash, I assume you will agree that $45 million will not be a problem. However, I will keep my guarantee in place as backup until you receive Mr. Morrison's bank documentation." Steven looked at the men and awaited their acknowledgement and agreement. Milton looked to Mike, who leaned in to whisper something. A moment later, Milton looked at Steven and nodded, acknowledging that he had no objection to the change. Steven jumped all over the first sign of agreement. "Excellent, gentlemen, then let's close this deal. Oh, yes, one other item. I will not be acting as the agent for the buyers, that will in fact be Ms. Jaclyn Tate. I advise you of this so the paperwork can be corrected." Milton raised an eyebrow. He was curious about the changes, but his deal was done and that was all that really mattered.

In the next hour, the men amended the offer and finalized the paperwork so the contingencies could be removed. The closing was now only a month away. Steven could taste it, Thanksgiving Tower was his and Jaclyn was in on the deal.

As JP and Steven left the building, they discussed what to do about Jaclyn. They decided it would be best to call to check on her and ask if she would meet with them. Steven used his cell phone to call her at home and then at her office, but she did not answer at either place. The men were concerned but felt unable to do anything further. Steven then insisted on driving Milton to his hotel. As they drove, they discussed when the next opportunity would be to speak with Jaclyn. Since she had promised to call JP in the morning, they agreed that he would ask her to come see him at the hotel before he left town. With any luck, she would agree to a visit. Steven would plan to be there as well. Together, he and JP would talk to her and explain the series of events. Both men wished they could speak with her immediately and help calm her down, but they accepted that she wanted to be alone. They would have to wait until the morning to make things right. It would be a long night for all of them.

***

The three men lingered close to the exit, anxious for Steven to return. Only steps away, they positioned themselves close to Steven's car and waited. They watched intently as each person came through the doors and each time they readied themselves, but repeatedly it was not Steven. Antsy, they contemplated an alternate plan, but decided it was best to just stick it out. The Boss would not be happy if they had not been able to have a chat with Cason. Now as Friday afternoon was quickly passing, they grew desperate. One of the men had just lit up a cigarette when finally, Steven came bounding through the door. Quickly, the men made their move, then paused short of reaching Steven when JP and several other men exited along with him. There was suddenly a group of men gathered at the doors, shielding Cason. Before the men could react, Cason and JP were in his car and pulling away. Hurriedly, the men ran to their car in an attempt to follow Steven, but they had lost him in the afternoon rush hour. They were pissed. It was not going to be easy calling the Boss and telling him they had failed on their assignment. There would be hell to pay.

***

Jaclyn sat in the middle of her bed, her arms wrapped tightly around her as she rocked back and forth. In the distance, she heard the phone ringing, but chose to ignore it. Over and over again she replayed the incidents that had led up to that moment. The more she thought about them, the more she loathed herself for being so innocent and foolish. How had she let her guard down so completely and allowed this stranger to steal her heart and, with it, her dignity and common sense? She imagined how satisfied Steven was now that his plan had worked so perfectly. She was convinced that she had only been a pawn in his game. What she could not believe was how genuine and caring he had appeared to be. She rationalized that he was the ultimate con artist and she his latest, unsuspecting victim. She categorized him as the kind of man who justifies the means by the end and wasn't the least bit troubled by his disregard for her as a person. It was clear to her now that she had meant nothing to him. He had used her and she had been foolish to permit it to happen. She hated her naivete. How could she have cast aside her prudence so easily? She knew better and this disappointed her more than anything else.

Her thoughts continued to torment her as night descended. Giving in to her fatigue, she climbed under her sheets, trying to rid her mind of further anguishing thoughts and will herself to sleep. As she felt herself drifting away, she thought about the pain she had fought through when she learned about Andrew's affair. It had been many months since she had experienced that pain, but it came back to her now, as if it had happened only yesterday . . . that familiar feeling, deep inside. . . tearing at her heart . . . What kind of fool was she to allow it to happen again?. . . When would she break this habit of being the victim? . . . She had to find the strength to get through yet another destructive relationship. Her thoughts continued to plague her until exhaustion overtook her and she fell into a troubled sleep.

***

Steven was restless all night long. He knew if he could only reach Jaclyn he could explain all that had happened. He tried calling her repeatedly, consumed by the need to speak with her and clear up this ridiculously incriminating series of events, but she did not answer. He thought of going to her home and pleading with her to listen to him, but he feared that she would be angered by his decision to go to her when she clearly wanted to avoid seeing him. He desperately wanted to hold her in his arms and let her understand the truth. It tortured him to imagine that she was thinking the worst of him. Signing the Tower contract was bittersweet for he feared it might have cost him his relationship with Jaclyn. He could not bear that thought. It would have to work out between them – he would see to it. He stared at the clock, willing the minutes to pass, eager to usher in the morning hours, when he would make things all right again. It was one of the longest and loneliest nights of his life.

CHAPTER 19
— ◇ —

When she woke, Jaclyn had to pry herself from the tangled covers that bound her legs. She had endured a disturbed sleep and crazy dreams that confused her as she recalled them in the morning light. Freeing herself from her sheets, she became conscious of the aches and pains afflicting her entire body. It was as if she had been in a fistfight during the night. She gently rubbed her shoulders, which seemed to have taken the brunt of the attack. As she moved slowly and stiffly from her bed, she thought about the day ahead. It wasn't going to be a good day. She turned toward her nightstand to check the time; it was already 8 o'clock. Then she remembered her promise to call JP. Unwillingly, she shuffled over to the phone and dialed the number to the Mansion. When the operator answered, she said, "Good morning. Mr. Morrison please."

"One moment, please."

Expecting to hear JP's voice, she was surprised to hear an unfamiliar man speak. "Good morning, may I help you?"

Jaclyn repeated her request. "Yes, I am calling for Mr. Morrison."

The gentleman replied, "And may I say who is calling?"

Jaclyn thought it odd that his call was being announced, but she obliged the request, "Ms. Tate."

The man's demeanor changed. "Ms. Tate, yes, Mr. Morrison has been expecting your call. He's in the dining room having breakfast and asked me to bring him the phone as soon as you called. Please hold while I take the phone to his table."

Jaclyn was taken aback by JP's eagerness to receive her call. She stopped to think about him for a moment. In her hasty retreat from Thompson's office, she had not considered him. Suddenly she felt sorry for her irrational behavior. What must he think of her now? JP's voice interrupted her steam of consciousness. "Jaclyn, good morning."

She was at once relieved by his clearly good mood. "Good morning, JP."

He heard the suffering in her voice and took control of the conversation. "How are you this morning?"

She hardly had the strength to reply. "Exhausted actually. I feel as if I lost in the twelfth round of a championship bout."

JP felt for her. "Jaclyn, I can understand that you are upset, but I have some things I need to discuss with you this morning . . ."

She interjected, "JP, I hope you understand when I say I'm in no condition for discussing business . . ."

He stopped her before she could finish. "I do understand, Jaclyn, and that's why I must insist we meet." He paused to allow her an opportunity to speak, but she remained silent. "I would not ask you to meet if I didn't think you would later be pleased you made the effort."

She took a moment to think through her options. She could refuse to go, but that would alienate him further, which she didn't want to do. It was clear what she had to do if she wanted to limit the damage she had caused by abandoning him. She mustered up her strength. "Very well, JP. I will meet with you, but it will take me an hour or so to get over to the hotel."

JP was relieved. "Thank you, Jaclyn. I will be waiting." He hung up the phone promptly, avoiding any opportunity she might find to change her mind. He turned to Steven, who was sitting beside him. "She will be here in one hour."

Steven had been unconsciously holding his breath through much of the phone call and, suddenly, he let out a long sigh of relief. He looked at JP with gratitude. "Great, JP. I don't know if I could stand to wait any longer."

JP smiled at the anguished man beside him. In the few hours he had spent with Steven he had come to see a vastly different person than the man Jaclyn perceived Cason to be. His thoughts then turned to Jaclyn. He hoped he could help her see past the circumstantial to the reality of what had taken place. When she learned the truth, he couldn't see how she wouldn't be pleased with the outcome.

***

At 9:20, Jaclyn left her apartment for the Mansion. It was less than a ten-minute drive, but this morning she wished it were much longer. Now that she would soon be facing JP, she was filled with a sense of remorse for leaving him so abruptly at Thompson's office. To her disappointment, she had to admit that she had acted unprofessionally and irrationally and was embarrassed by her emotional behavior. Seeing JP would be difficult, but she knew she needed to make amends and apologize.

As she pulled into the drive of the hotel, she composed herself. She stepped out of the car and gave her keys to the valet. As she walked toward the entrance, she smoothed out her outfit. She chose to wear a simple pant and vest set, her customary weekend attire. She slowly walked up the steps and entered the lobby. Once inside, she scanned the open area in search of JP. He was nowhere in sight. She was walking toward the house phone when a bellman approached her. "Excuse me, ma'am, are you Ms. Tate?"

She turned to the man. "Yes, I am."

He explained. "Mr. Morrison asked me to keep an eye out for you. He has reserved a small business suite for your meeting this morning. If you follow me, I will direct you."

Jaclyn was curious why JP would arrange a private meeting room, but anticipated it was because he needed to speak with her confidentially and didn't want to be overheard.

She followed the man down the hall toward a door marked with an oval plaque. He stopped in front of the entrance and extended his hand toward the door. She stepped forward and, putting a hand on the doorknob, thanked him for his assistance. She waited for him to leave before knocking. Almost immediately, she heard JP call out to her, "Jaclyn?"

She replied, "Yes, JP, it's me."

The door opened before her and JP held out a hand to greet her. "Good morning, Jaclyn. Please come in." He stepped aside so she could enter the room. She moved slowly and looked around as she entered. It was a small room with four armchairs positioned in a square around an oval glass coffee table. In one corner was a stocked wet bar and in another a door, which she presumed led to a restroom. The lights were rather dim, but Jaclyn assumed that that was how JP had set them. JP stood by her side as she studied the room. She turned toward him and he extended his hand towards the chairs, offering her a seat. "Please, Jaclyn, make yourself comfortable." She nodded at him as she sat down. Once she was settled, he took the seat to her left. JP looked at her and she forced a smile, but he could see it was less than heartfelt. He hesitantly took one of her hands. The action surprised her.

"Jaclyn, thank you for coming to meet with me." He spoke softly and slowly. "Jaclyn, I know you were upset yesterday and I understand completely. It wasn't easy for you to accept that we weren't going to get the deal. It wasn't easy for me either."

She stared into JP's eyes, but it was clear to him that her thoughts were elsewhere. He paused for a moment, hoping to gain her full attention, but it was she who broke the silence. "JP, let me apologize for leaving you so abruptly. It's just that there is so much more to this situation than you could imagine. It goes beyond the loss of the deal. It's being faced with unethical business practices that led to someone else's closing the deal." She paused for a moment, shook her head, then looked down at the floor.

JP tried to reach her with reason. "I understand your reaction completely, but I want you to consider that there are always two sides to every story. For example, couldn't the presumed unethical business practices actually have been coincidences or good networking?" Jaclyn gave JP a skeptical glare, but he was not deterred by her inflexibility. "I think you owe it to yourself to hear the other side of the story before passing judgment."

When Jaclyn realized what JP was intimating, she looked up at him with a shocked expression. There was fire and ice in her voice as she spoke. "Are you suggesting I give Cason an opportunity to explain what happened? I know what happened. It's crystal clear to me. Anyway, how would we benefit from knowing his side of the story? The deal is done."

Out of frustration, Jaclyn pulled her hand from JP's, but he continued to try to rationalize with her. "Jaclyn, listen to me. I bet you spent the entire night last night thinking about this from your perspective, but I believe you owe it to yourself to hear what Steven has to say." At that moment, Steven walked out from the door in the corner of the room.

Jaclyn was stunned. She turned to JP, angry with him for setting her up. "JP, how could you?"

JP tried to explain, but she would not look at him or listen to what he was saying. She stood and turned to leave, but Steven moved between her and the door, blocking the exit. He pleaded with her to stay. "Jaclyn, please don't leave. Give me a few minutes to explain. Believe me when I say this is one big misunderstanding. I promise you will feel better when I'm through explaining everything."

She avoided his eyes for fear of their power over her and instead looked at JP, who silently pleaded with her to sit down and give Steven a chance. After a few moments of weighing her options, she acquiesced and returned to her seat.

Steven sat down in the chair to her right and leaned toward her as he spoke. "Jaclyn, I'm only asking you to give me a chance to explain. After I've spoken my peace, if you still want to leave, I'll see you out." He reached out to her and gently touched her chin, raising her eyes to meet his. Her facial lines softened as their eyes met. "Yesterday, after you left Thompson's office, JP and I discussed all of the circumstances around this deal. Considering everything, I can understand how you could misinterpret some of the events. I'm not going to pretend that I didn't do what I thought it would take to make the deal happen, but it was never with any knowledge of your involvement or with any intent to hurt you." She continued to look at him, giving him unspoken permission to continue. He never took his eyes off of hers as he spoke slowly, trying desperately to say the words that would accurately convey his thoughts. "I've been working the Tower deal since the day it was put on the market eighteen months ago. I was the first interested party to meet with the selling agent, Al Harris. We agreed then that I would present my offer, the only question was when. I admit I decided the time was right when I heard another contract was coming in, but I had no knowledge of the other buyer or agent, nor was it ever my concern. The only issue was that it was my deal and I was going to make it happen." Jaclyn had to admire his honesty, but his explanation wasn't making it any easier to accept. He continued, "As for what happened next, I didn't have anything to do with the break-in at your office, nothing." He paused for effect and to be certain she knew he was telling the truth. "In fact, until JP told me about it, I had no idea one had taken place."

Her expression changed to one of disbelief and she chose to

speak her mind. "Then what kind of coincidence is it that my Tower correspondence file was taken, which listed all of my top prospects, including Jed and Sumitomo? How do you explain that parallel?"

Steven took a deep breath, then continued. "I was contacting everyone I knew to get the deal done. I had been given several leads from my associates, but those two individuals came to my attention through Al Harris. In fact, it was last Saturday that he called to tell me he had a list of promising investors that he wanted to share with me. I was open to all ideas, so I agreed to meet him. We met that morning to review the list and I felt he had some good leads, so I contacted them immediately. I had no idea how he had come up with the names. That didn't seem important at the time, but now I have every intention of confronting him about the list and I welcome you to be there so you can hear his response firsthand."

Jaclyn wanted to believe him, but doing so was difficult. After all, he had the most to gain from obtaining those names. She wanted to know more. "Al Harris gave you that information?"

Steven elaborated. "Yes, I got a call from Al on Saturday, about mid-morning. He asked if we could meet at my office to discuss potential prospects on the building. Of course I didn't question him, I just agreed to go. When we met, he had a list prepared that he reviewed with me. I made notes of the people I agreed were worth contacting and then he left. As you know, he stood to gain a lot if he could sell the Tower. He was highly motivated."

Jaclyn took a moment to digest what Steven had said. She thought back to the day Harris had unexpectantly showed up at her office to tell her their offer was being presented. She had noted then that he could have just as easily called and speculated about his true motivation for being there. She looked up at Steven and he took the opportunity to continue, "Jaclyn, I think you can appreciate that I move in a tight circle. We all share information that can further our positions in a deal, but that is the nature of our business. I'm sure you know that firsthand."

Jaclyn knew he was a powerful man and probably had many people who owed him favors or who wanted to be on his good side, as she recalled John telling her. It seemed credible that Al would do something so underhanded for him, simply because of who Steven was. She also had to admit that she had had a similar network in New York. There were occasions when she had been tipped off about other deals or 'slipped' pertinent confidential information to help her close a contract, but she had accepted that as a part of the business. When she realized he was speaking about the same type of favor, she began to soften. There was also something very sincere about the way he spoke that made her want to believe him.

Steven watched her as she sat thinking through what he had explained to her. He paused for a few moments before continuing. "I also had no idea that you had anything to do with the deal. If you think I did, then I could assume the same of you." Jaclyn looked up at him in surprise. He had made a point she had not considered. He was right. She could have been just as guilty as Steven for trying to get close to the person on the other side of the deal. It was almost comical. He waited for her to speak, becoming hopeful as he watched the lines around her mouth soften and the tension around her eyes relax.

She paused before responding. "Let me get this straight. You didn't know who I was in relation to the deal?"

Steven was quick to respond. "How could I?"

She wasn't giving in so easily. "I have come to learn you have a lot of friends in this town. I'm certain it wouldn't take you long to uncover someone's identity."

He looked frustrated as he replied. "Let me play devil's advocate for one minute. Let's say I did know, what benefit would it have been for me to get close to you?"

She smirked, "Information is power, isn't it?"

He was not pleased with the turn of the conversation. "What information did I obtain from you that furthered my position?"

She pondered the idea. The only information that had helped him had come from her file and not from her, so unless he took the file, he didn't benefit from getting close to her. "If it's true that you did not take my file, then nothing. But if you did take it, then it got you your deal."

Steven stood and began pacing. "Obviously my word is not enough to make you believe I had nothing to do with the break-in at your office or taking your file. I'll have to prove it to you and I will." He would phone Al later for an explanation about the list of contacts, but that would wait until she had aired all of her grievances. He probed her. "What else?"

Jaclyn was confused by his question, "What do you mean, what else?"

Steven was growing frustrated, but he tried to maintain a calm and open tone to their discussion. "I want to know everything that is disturbing you so we can clear the air once and for all. I don't want you to have any doubts left when we leave this room today."

Jaclyn took a few minutes to think it through. When she was ready, she looked up at Steven, who was still pacing the floor. "In the end, Steven, I guess the thing that hurt me the most was the idea that you got close to me to undermine my side of the deal. I want to believe that you couldn't have known who I was, just as I didn't know who you were." He looked at her and nodded, and she continued. "The lack of business ethics is another story. Our professional philosophies and tactics may differ, but in the end you won, so who is to say that mine are better?"

Steven listened to her but wasn't certain if she were cynical or sincere. Sensing that the conversation was moving in the wrong direction, JP spoke up. "Jaclyn, I have news for you that I think will shed more light on Steven and the type of man he is." She turned to face JP as he spoke. "Steven offered me the final 20% of the deal that he was going to buy personally and another 10% from the share SC Investors had taken, making me an equal partner." Although she was thrilled for JP, something concerned her about the turn of events.

Steven saw the uneasiness in her eyes and commented, "Jaclyn, you don't seem happy with the news."

She glanced toward Steven. She took a deep breath before speaking. "It's just that so much has come together over the past 24 hours and I'm just trying to digest it all. Of course I am pleased for JP." She turned toward JP and put a hand on his. "And it's good news that you have a part of the deal. I guess I'm just a little skeptical about everyone's motivation at this point."

JP tried to help her work through it. "Believe me, Jaclyn, when you left yesterday and Steven and I began discussing everything, I too was very apprehensive. But the more we spoke, the more I understood we were just two sides working toward one goal. I agree we need to get to the bottom of the break-in at your office, but Steven was plainly surprised when I told him about it. And when I informed him that your file on the Tower had been taken and that Hebert and Sumitomo were clearly identified in it, he understood completely how anyone could conclude he had taken it. Beyond that, it was just him doing what he always does to close a deal, working all the angles until he makes it happen." JP paused briefly. "But, there is more."

Jaclyn looked at JP in disbelief. How could he possibly have anything more to add to this complicated story? A big smile crossed JP's lips as he excitedly said, "After you left yesterday, Steven and I spoke about everything in detail and this entire situation began to make sense to both of us. That's when Steven offered me his interest in the building. Not only that, when he learned that the names of his buyers came from your file, he insisted that Milton change the buyers' agent to you. Jaclyn, you are the agent on the deal."

A look of doubt shadowed Jaclyn's face. She looked from JP to Steven, trying to assess if what JP had said was true. Steven nodded and JP added, "It was all Steven's idea and like he said, it was only the right thing to do and the one thing that would allow each of us to end up with what we wanted and worked so hard to achieve."

In disbelief, Jaclyn turned to Steven. "Is that true, Steven?"

Steven smiled at her warmly as he responded. "Well, the way I see it, Jaclyn, after I understood your involvement, the arrangement seemed only fair. After all, you brought Jed, Sumitomo and JP to the table. It's your deal to close."

Jaclyn couldn't believe what she was hearing. She had been on an emotional roller coaster but was relieved that everything was ending up so favorably. It was hard to control her emotions. Everything had turned around full circle. She took some time to let it soak in before she spoke. "I can't believe it. After all of this craziness, JP ends up with a share in the Tower and I get to close the deal. I still have some unanswered questions, but I guess I couldn't ask for better news."

Steven jumped in. "Then we need to get those questions answered, because I'm not satisfied until you are 100% clear on everything." He pulled over a phone from the credenza and dialed a number. JP and Jaclyn waited in anticipation. "Al, it's Cason. I need you to come to the Mansion right away. I'm in a meeting and need your input."

Al's chest swelled. Steven needed him. He had never felt more a part of the circle than now. For Al, it didn't get much better than that. He spoke with confidence. "Actually, Steven, I'm not far from the Mansion now. I'll swing by right away."

Steven was pleased he could be there shortly. "The sooner, the better. " Steven hung up and turned his attention to Jaclyn and JP, who were watching him intently. "Alright, he'll be here in a few minutes. We can question him together about his source for those leads."

Jaclyn nodded. JP stood and walked over to the wet bar, pulled out beverages and a tray covered with an assortment of appetizers, and carried them over to the table. Jaclyn appreciated the offer. She had not eaten since mid afternoon the day before and was starting to feel the effects of hunger. They conversed casually over their snack while they waited for Al to arrive. Within ten minutes of Steven's call there was a knock. Steven stood, walked over to the door and opened it. As Al entered the room, he was surprised by the people gathered there.

Steven quickly brought him up to speed. "Al, you know Jaclyn." Steven paused while Al shook her hand. "And this is JP Morrison, the buyer on Jaclyn's contract." Al turned and shook his hand. "Please, Al, have a seat." Steven continued as Al sat down. "First, thank you for coming here so quickly. We were discussing events that transpired recently and there is one incident we are having a hard time understanding. We need you to clarify a few things for us." Steven turned the questioning over to Jaclyn. "Please feel free to voice your concerns."

Jaclyn chose her words carefully, so as not to accuse Al of any wrongdoing, "Yes, Al, Steven informed us that you were the source of a list of potential investors for the Tower. We understand that that is how Steven learned of Jed Hebert's and Mr. Sumitomo's interest." Jaclyn watched his reaction closely.

Al sat tall in his chair, clearly proud of his contribution to the deal. "That's right."

Jaclyn continued, "How did you come by that information?"

Al's demeanor suddenly changed. Jaclyn remembered a similar transformation in him at their first meeting. He was clearly nervous, and she wanted to know why. She prompted him for an answer. "Al?"

He shot a glance at Steven but did not find comfort in his face. He took a moment to compose himself before he began to speak. His words were said under his breath and succinctly. "I know people. I put the word out that I needed investors and got the names from a… source."

Jaclyn chuckled. His response sounded like something out of a bad cop movie. "And who might that source be?"

Al looked at Steven and leaned toward him, speaking only to him. "Steven, I don't understand. Why is this important?"

Steven replied stoically, "It's important because the leads you provided me were stolen from Jaclyn's office."

Al shot Jaclyn a concerned look. "But this source had nothing to do with Jaclyn."

Jaclyn questioned him. "How do you know that?"

Al confessed, "I . . . I guess I don't . . . but I got this call from a guy staying over at the Fairmont. He told me he had leads on the Tower deal and that it would be worth my while to go see him." Al paused and swallowed hard. "I was surprised by that stroke of luck, but I really wanted to do right by Steven, so I felt I should see what this guy had to offer. And it wasn't like I had to meet him in a dark alley. We were meeting at the Fairmont."

Steven probed him for details. "What happened next?"

Al continued, "I went to the hotel like he told me to. I was to go to the main entrance and wait outside by the doors. He would meet me there."

Jaclyn stopped him. "When was your meeting?"

Al thought back. "It was last Friday night at about 10 o'clock."

Jaclyn prompted, "OK, go on."

Al took his time retracing his steps. "I went to the hotel. Got there about fifteen minutes early and waited until almost 10:15 before this guy showed up. He asked if I was Al. I told him I was. I asked who he was and he said it didn't matter. He said all that mattered was the information in the envelope. He instructed me to give it to SC Investments so they could close the deal. I went to open the envelope and he put his hand on the flap and shut it. He said I should open it in private. Then he turned to leave. I was really confused. He didn't ask for money or favors or anything." Al paused, but no one spoke, so he continued. "I went to my car and ripped open the package. Inside was a file with a lot of notes about the Tower and a list of prospects. I knew I could win points with Steven, so I called him in the morning."

Jaclyn sat back hard in her chair. The story was still very mysterious and somewhat implausible. "What did this man look like?" she asked.

"Well, we didn't talk for long, but it struck me as odd that he was wearing a raincoat. I've never met anyone from Dallas who owns a raincoat, so I figured he was from out of town."

Jaclyn wanted to know more. "Was he short, tall. . .?"

Al took a moment to reflect. "He was about my height, maybe a little taller. He had brown hair. I remember thinking he was kind of intellectual-looking, you know the kind, well-put-together, glasses. I did notice when he stopped me from opening the envelope that he had a scar on his hand. It looked like it had to have been a pretty nasty cut."

Suddenly, Jaclyn was at the edge of her seat. "Which hand?"

Al looked confused by her interest in what he considered a small detail. "I don't know, let me think about it." He paused and reenacted the exchange. When he was convinced of the correct answer, he replied. "It was definitely his right hand."

Jaclyn looked at Steven. Panic washed over her face. "Steven, can I use the phone?"

He pushed the phone across the table toward her as he spoke. "Are you alright, Jaclyn?"

"I will know better in a minute."

She called directory assistance and was given the number for the Fairmont. She dialed the hotel and waited for the operator to answer. "The Fairmont, how many I direct your call?"

She did not hesitate. "Hello. Andrew Thorton, please."

The men around her sat in silence waiting for her to explain what she was doing. The operator returned to the line. "I'm sorry, but Mr. Thorton checked out of the hotel earlier this morning."

Jaclyn suddenly felt sick to her stomach. She thanked the operator for the information, then turned her attention back to the men seated around her. "Al, would you say the man you met was in his early 40's, had no facial hair, blue eyes, and thick wavy hair?"

He agreed. "Yeah, that sounds like him."

She added, "And was his raincoat a beige color, belted, and square-knotted in front?"

He seemed surprised by her uncanny description. "Yeah, exactly."

Emotion welled up in her chest. Tears stung her eyes, but she fought them back. It was Andrew. He had stolen her file. He had been behind this, not Steven. She had been a fool, but not about Steven. Andrew's motivation to get her back was clear. He wanted her to fail so she would return to New York. He was desperate to win her back and continue on the partnership track. She was amazed at the length he went to ensure his future. It frightened her.

Steven could wait no longer. "Jaclyn . . ." She turned to him. "Are you going to fill us in?"

She then realized that only she knew what had transpired. "I'm sorry. I know who took my file. It's a long story, but it has nothing to do with you, Steven."

He was extremely relieved. As Jaclyn sat still, lost in thought, Steven thanked Al for coming and showed him out to the lobby.

Meanwhile, JP turned his attention to helping Jaclyn through this mess. "Jaclyn, is there anything I can do?"

She was grateful to him for arranging the meeting so she could learn the facts. The way she had worked it out in her mind last night, Steven was entirely to blame, which couldn't have been farther from the truth. She had come up with many uninformed conclusions, but given her emotional state the day before, she forgave herself for allowing it to happen. She was just thankful that the mystery had been cleared up. "JP, you have already done so much. Without you, I never would have known the truth. Thank you."

JP took advantage of their time alone to speak his mind. "Jaclyn, I must tell you it was clear to me yesterday and even more so today that Steven cares deeply for you. He was like a caged tiger not being able to speak with you right away."

Jaclyn smiled for the first time. "JP, it's kind of crazy, but I have never felt a connection with anyone the way I did with Steven. That's why it hurt so badly when I thought he betrayed me. I felt so foolish, so used, and I thought I had let you down."

JP was sympathetic. "Of course you would, but aren't you glad you let him clear it up and make things right for both of us?"

Jaclyn did feel better. "I couldn't ask for a better turn of events. I owe both of you."

As she finished speaking, Steven entered the room. He was pleased to see Jaclyn and JP smiling at one another. There was no more tension in the air.

JP rose. "Steven, I must say I'm glad things worked out so well for all involved. Thank you for your part in the outcome. Now I must be on my way, or I'll miss my flight home. Call me first thing next week about the paperwork you need me to forward from the bank."

The men shook hands. JP then turned to Jaclyn, who rose to stand by his side. "Good-bye for now, Jaclyn. We'll talk next week."

She was quick to interject. "But JP, I can take you to the airport." "No, thank you, Jaclyn. Steven has arranged for his limousine to take me. In fact, I imagine your driver is wondering where I am."

Jaclyn gave JP a hug and thanked him for arranging their meeting. JP then shook Steven's hand and left the room. When they were alone, Steven reached out and touched Jaclyn's arm, gently stroking the length of it. She was feeling weak from stress and his touch felt so reassuring. They stood in silence for a few moments, reconnecting at a different level than their talks of that morning.

Steven was the first to speak. "Jaclyn, are you okay with everything now?"

She looked up at him, then turned away as she replied, "I will admit I was pretty overwhelmed yesterday when I learned you were Cason. It was hard to accept that you were the man behind the other contract."

Steven hated having caused her such anxiety, but all he could do now was try to make up for it. "It was a surprise for me too to learn you were the agent on the other contract. After all, what were the odds of that happening?" He smiled, pulling her toward him as he continued. "Yet, despite what has happened, there is something I will admit to; business is business to me. I don't make decisions based on how they impact other people. My only concern is doing whatever is necessary to make a deal happen. You know this world of real estate. If you don't look out for number one, no one else will." He paused momentarily, checking Jaclyn's reaction before continuing, "But, for the first time, you made me think about the other side. Knowing you had lost the deal made it so much less sweet. That's why I was grateful to JP for staying and talking it through with me. He helped me understand all the circumstances that led to you being so upset and together we came up with a win-win situation. I could not have accepted it if the Tower had cost me a relationship with you."

She looked at Steven and tried to separate the man from his work. She had a great deal of respect for what he had accomplished in business, but that hadn't been what attracted her to him. Knowing what she knew now, however, she was having a hard time seeing him in the same light as before. She struggled to rid her mind of the bad-guy image she had painted of Cason and remember the wonderful person she had known as Steven.

When she remained silent, Steven added, "From the moment I saw you across that crowded reception hall, something was drawing me to you. I couldn't get your face out of my mind. I was certain I would see you again. When it happened, I believed it was meant that our paths cross. Somewhere deep inside, I knew you were different . . . special . . . and that's what made me so eager to get to know you before revealing who I was. I knew that the only way to know you were interested in me for the man I am and not for the things I have, was to conceal my full identity. You have to understand that a man in my position is a target for many women. I have experienced my share of eager ladies who were only interested in what I could give them materially and not the least bit interested in me as a person. That may sound pompous, but the one thing that someone like me never really knows is the reason why a person tries to get close. Can you appreciate what I'm saying?"

Jaclyn smiled at him as he explained a situation that was obviously sensitive and important to him. She tried to assuage his concerns. "I do understand. I never envied celebrities or public figures because I felt they risked ever having true relationships because of their notoriety. I guess it's a price you pay for amassing wealth or gaining fame." She added, "Some would say it isn't that bad a trade-off."

He smiled back. "Thank you for understanding. I need you to know I never meant to hurt or deceive you."

She laughed, shaking her head in disbelief. "I still can't believe the way this all worked out."

"There is something else very important to me." He paused to emphasize his words. "I want to know that you can see me as the same person you met last weekend."

She nodded at him and, with a mischievous smile, replied, "I'll work on it. Maybe you'll have to give me a refresher course."

At her words, Steven took her in his arms and hugged her forcefully. He had so hoped this is how the morning would end. He would do everything in his power to let her see the man she had come to know. After a few minutes had passed, Steven returned to an earlier concern. "Jaclyn, who was the man you called the Fairmont to find?"

Jaclyn pulled away from him and turned to face the back of

the room as she replied. "The description Al gave made me think of Andrew . . . my ex-fiancé." Jaclyn looked at Steven to gauge his reaction, but his face remained unchanged. "When the hotel verified he had been there until this morning, I knew he was the saboteur."

Steven walked toward her and touched her arm. "But why? What would he have to gain by furthering my position in the deal, and why would he do it at your expense?"

Jaclyn nervously tapped her foot as she began her explanation. "Andrew and I were planning to be married. Then things between us started to change. I ended up learning that Andrew was having an affair." Jaclyn paused, as if working through the pain her memories had caused. "Looking back, I realize how naive I was not to suspect there was someone else, but being as gullible and trusting as I am, I tend to believe in the good in people. One of these days I will smarten up, but for now, that's me." Jaclyn wrapped her arms tightly around her waist as she spoke. "I walked away from the relationship, but Andrew would not go quietly. He tried to persuade me to go back, but I held strong in my conviction. One night . . ." Jaclyn paused and took a deep breath. She steadied herself, then continued, "One night, he came to my apartment. He arrived before I got home. Using the key he still had, he let himself in and waited for me. He was determined to convince me to give us another chance. Of course I was furious when I came home and found him there. I asked him to leave, but he refused. When I wouldn't see things his way" - Jaclyn paused and finished in almost a whisper - "he forced himself on me."

As the words came from her mouth, Steven moved toward her, but she held up her arm to keep him away. When she felt she had the strength to go on, she spoke again. "You see, what Andrew didn't bargain on was that I am nice until someone crosses me. I am by nature very kind and giving, but abuse that compassion and you see a different side of me. I thought I let Andrew understand it was over between us, but he wouldn't accept that. He expected easy going Jaclyn to come around, but he was wrong. He came to me that night to convince me to change my mind. He thought that with a little coaxing I would forget his affair, forgive him and resume our relationship right where it had left off, as if nothing had happened. What he didn't count on was that I could never allow that, not after he had destroyed the trust I gave him so freely. It was shortly after that night that I decided to make a major change in my life. That's when I accepted Carl Toner's offer to come to Dallas and open the Southwest office for Toner and Associates." Jaclyn stopped and shook her head in frustration and disbelief. "You would think my move would be enough to convince Andrew that we were through. He apparently will stop at nothing." Jaclyn paused, leaned against the back of a chair and stared at the floor.

Steven watched her as she recounted the difficult tale. He felt deeply for her. When it was apparent she was finished, he added his thoughts. "His actions are unforgivable. I'm sorry you have to endure such pain. But one thing strikes me, this man must love you very much to go to such lengths to get you back."

Jaclyn let out a nervous, sarcastic laugh. "Love me? No." She turned toward Steven. "He's up for partnership consideration at his law firm. It's an unwritten, but strictly adhered to policy that partners must be married. I was the perfect bride. The senior partners were all very pleased with Andrew's choice. It looked as if his partnership was in the bag. Then came our breakup and my decision to leave New York. I'm certain Andrew explained my absence as temporary. However, as time passed and the date for our wedding passed too, I imagine the questions started flying and Andrew felt enormous pressure. I actually learned how hopeless he was just yesterday. He came to my office unexpectantly. Out of desperation, he rambled on and said too much. It all became clear to me and I knew instantly why he wanted me back in New York. So you see, Steven, although it would be incredibly romantic to think that this man is so lost without me, that he would stop at nothing to win me back, it is in reality for purely self-serving reasons that Andrew needs me in his life."

Steven shook his head as she explained the complexity of the relationship. It was hard for him to imagine that any man could treat a woman like Jaclyn in that manner. "Jaclyn, I'm sorry. One thing is clear. He is not through trying to get you back to New York. Did you ever report what happened in your apartment to the police?"

Jaclyn turned to look at him. "The police? No. I thought about it, but consider the circumstances. He was my fiancé. I had willingly given him a key to my apartment. Four years into the relationship, I claim rape? Add that to the fact he is a well-respected attorney in New York and I have a prominent name and position in the real estate community. Do you follow my line of thinking?" She looked to Steven and he nodded. "If I felt it would have done some good, of course I would have gone to the police, but I knew it would only have led to a media circus. Besides, I was ready to move on, not tie myself down to New York and a long and hard fight. In my mind it was over. I had no reason to believe Andrew would become dangerously obsessed with winning me back."

Steven moved closer and put his arm around her. Softly, he said, "But what has happened since then presents an entirely different scenario. Do you feel you might report him as a suspect in the robbery at your office?"

Jaclyn thought it through before answering. "I have to admit, his determination frightens me. However, reporting him to the police may just add fuel to the fire. Besides, I have no proof, just a strong suspicion that he did it." Steven gave her a doubtful look and she added, "I don't want to cower either, but I do want to be careful."

"Let's not worry about that for now. There is time to make those decisions. Even if you choose not to pursue legal remedies, there are other ways to make him pay." Steven turned her toward him and encircled her with his arms. Jaclyn remained still, luxuriating in the caring and affection evoked by Steven's warm embrace. As they stood sharing a tender moment, they were surprised by a knock at the door. Steven reluctantly let go of Jaclyn and went to open the door.

"Hello, I'm Mike, the concierge. Will you need the room for much longer? We have another meeting scheduled, but I can make other arrangements if necessary."

Steven turned to Jaclyn to confer with her. She spoke softly, "I'm ready to go if you are."

Steven looked back to the man before him. "We'll leave momentarily."

The man responded appreciatively. "Please take your time and thank you."

Ready to leave, Jaclyn leaned over and picked up her purse. She scanned the room to make sure nothing had been left behind, then walked over to the door. Steven held the door open and led her out into the hallway. As they began walking toward the lobby, Jaclyn turned toward him. "What now?"

Steven was feeling very lighthearted following their successful meeting. "How about we start our date right now?"

Jaclyn smiled at his remark. "As long as you take me somewhere to eat, that sounds good to me."

Steven knew she must have been feeling better if she had regained her appetite. That was good news to him. "I know just the place."

Jaclyn added, "I hope it's close."

Steven laughed as he took her by the arm and quickened their pace as they left the hotel.

CHAPTER 20
—◇—

After lunch, Steven took Jaclyn back to the Mansion so she could pick up her car. They had agreed to go their separate ways until dinner, when they would meet again for the date they had originally planned. As Steven pulled away from the Hotel, he couldn't help but notice a black Mercedes that appeared to duplicate his every move. It was then that he realized the same car had been around him for days. In disbelief, Steven acknowledged that he was being followed. Purposely, he entered Central Expressway in hopes of getting lost in the traffic. Without concern for the speed limit, he sped ahead and within several miles, managed to exit without the car following him. As he drove home, he frequently consulted the rear view mirror. He didn't like being paranoid, but this unexpected twist had him considering the motivation behind the people tailing him. Although a man in his position accumulated enemies along the way, he wasn't aware of any one with a particularly urgent vendetta. As the thought crossed his mind, so did Henry.

***

Jaclyn spent the rest of the day preparing for their date as if it were her first. She excitedly tried on several outfits until one seemed just right. As the time approached when Steven would arrive, she stood before her mirror, evaluating her look and wondering whether the fitted black slacks and formfitting, low-cut black vest were too provocative. No, she decided, it was just the look she wanted. She was organizing her purse when the doorbell rang. She shot a glance at the clock. It was only 7:45, but she figured that like her, Steven must also be eager to be together again. Smiling, she walked over to the door and excitedly opened it toward her. She stepped back in shock. Angrily, she reacted, "Andrew, what are you doing here?"

He stepped toward her, but she moved square into the doorway, blocking his entrance to her home. "Well, Jaclyn, I must say, it wasn't easy tracking down where you live, but I found you. Now what do you say you invite me in for a drink."

Jaclyn's face grew red with fury. "Andrew, there is no reason for me to invite you in. I have already told you that it's over between us." She intended to stand her ground, but he moved uncomfortably close to her and she unconsciously took a step back.

His hand possessively circled her waist as he spoke again. "I told you once and I'll tell you again, we're going to be together. That's a promise I plan on keeping." He reached up to caress her cheek, but she instinctively slapped his hand away.

Her anger rose to new heights. She tried to stay controlled, but her exasperation was more than she could contain. Her voice was filled with rage. "If you don't leave immediately, I will call the police." As the words left her mouth, she tried to shut the door between them, but Andrew held out a stiff arm and kept it open. Suddenly, his attitude began to change. He took hold of the door and threw it back toward her, sending her stumbling back a few steps. He reached out to her and grabbing her by the waist pulled her into his chest. He bent his head down toward her and tried to kiss her mouth, but she turned her face away and his kiss fell upon her hair. As she struggled to free herself, she determinedly and repeatedly told him to let go and get out. Then she heard a voice. It was firm and serious. "Do as the lady says and let go."

Startled, Andrew turned. The large man in the doorway had clenched fists and his jaw was tight. Andrew could see the wrath swelling inside him. Reluctantly, he relaxed his grip on Jaclyn's waist but continued holding her as he spoke. "Can we help you?"

As Andrew loosened his hold, Jaclyn freed herself and rushed over to Steven. She fell into his chest and whispered to him, "It's Andrew."

Slowly, Steven guided Jaclyn safely behind him as he moved toward Andrew. "I think it's time you got out of here. In fact, if you come anywhere near Jaclyn again, I'll have you arrested. Is that clear?"

Andrew tried to reason with the irate man towering over him. "I don't know who you are, but she is my fiancé and you have no right to tell me what I can or can't do where she is concerned."

Steven looked back at Jaclyn. She shook her head vigorously in disagreement. He then turned back to Andrew. "Looks like the lady does not concur with that statement. It's time for you to leave." He forcefully took Andrew by the arm and led him outside the house and down the path to the driveway. Andrew tried in vain to free himself from Steven's powerful hold. The more he struggled, the more determined Steven's grip became. When the two men approached the end of the path, Steven cautioned Andrew never to come near Jaclyn again. This time he left Andrew no chance for misunderstanding the consequences. Through gritted teeth, Steven spoke. "Get this straight, if you try to come near her again – you're mine. I have my share of favors to cash in on and I promise you, you will regret your actions if it comes to that. Be forewarned and stay away."

As Steven loosened his hold, Andrew shrugged off Steven's hand and called back to Jaclyn who was standing in the doorway watching them. "It's not over, Jaclyn."

Steven waited till he got in his car and started the engine before walking up the path toward Jaclyn. As he reached the doorway and embraced her, Andrew spun his wheels on the loose gravel and roared down the driveway.

Jaclyn remained snug in Steven's arms until she had the strength to speak. She looked up into his face. "Steven, thank you. I don't know what I would have done if you hadn't shown up when you did." He stroked her hair, giving her time to calm down. She found strength in his embrace. "Maybe it's time to go to the police. It couldn't hurt if I had a restraining order that prevented him from coming anywhere near me. Maybe that would be enough to convince him that he and I are finished." Jaclyn shook her head and buried her face in Steven's chest.

He held her tight for a few minutes, then held her out in front of him. He looked deep in her eyes as he spoke. "You're an incredible woman, Jaclyn. You're so beautiful and such an accomplished businesswoman. Women like you are rather rare. I can't blame him for not letting you go. But let's put him out of mind for tonight." She nodded in agreement. "What do you think about packing an overnight bag and spending the night at my home? I think you will be more relaxed if you are somewhere he can't find you. How does that sound?"

She looked up at him and smiled. "Thank you, Steven. I don't think I could have slept here tonight after what just happened. Give me a few minutes to get ready." She hurriedly walked toward her bedroom, calling out to him just as she disappeared into the room. "Please make yourself at home. I'm afraid it's nothing like your place, but it's very comfortable."

Steven thought about her comment. He would have to prepare her for his real home if she thought the apartment was impressive. While he waited, Steven wandered around her living room. On the mantel, a photo collage caught his attention and he studied the captured moments from Jaclyn's past. He smiled at the picture of her riding a handsome horse in a picturesque pastoral setting. In another, she stood grinning ear to ear between two people he figured were her parents. In each snapshot, she appeared happy and carefree.

As he was lost in Jaclyn's photographs, she called out from her bedroom. "I'm almost ready."

He took a seat as he patiently replied, "Don't rush. We have plenty of time."

She smiled to herself at his considerate manner. She returned to the living room with a small leather suitcase in hand and placed it on the floor beside her. "I'm ready."

Steven stood as she entered the room. He was smiling at her. "You know something? In the craziness of my arrival tonight, I neglected to tell you how fantastic you look."

Jaclyn smiled at him. He was melting her heart. "Thank you, Steven."

He picked up her bag and offered her his arm. She placed her forearm snugly under his and let him lead her out of the house. When she stopped to lock up, he took the keys from her and locked the door, before escorting her down the curvy, cobblestone path to his car.

Before long, Jaclyn was seated across from Steven at an intimate table for two, positioned by the windows of Nana's grill at the

Anatole. Steven wanted to return to the place of their first encounter. Jaclyn was touched by the sentiment behind his choice. The wine steward had just presented Steven with the wine list and was waiting patiently by his side as Steven perused the pages in search of a choice. Jaclyn studied Steven's face as he took seriously to his task. He had chiseled features that made him look like the model for a roman statue. The wavy hair about his face was graying, giving him a mature appearance, yet his eyes were youthful and captivating. She was lost in his face when he spoke to her, interrupting her thoughts.

"I'm certain you will enjoy the wine I've selected. I have only had it one other time, but it was memorable. Today is the perfect occasion to have it again."

Jaclyn smiled at him. "I bet it will be terrific, although I must admit I'm not quite the connoisseur."

Steven returned her smile. "Neither am I. This particular wine, however, was very good, and like you, when I find something special, I don't forget it."

Jaclyn's heart swelled. She had always hoped to find someone romantic and caring with his words and ways and Steven was proving to be just that man. Her expression told him that she appreciated his words. He continued, "Tell me about yourself."

Jaclyn looked surprised by his question and took a moment to reply. "I guess I don't know exactly where to begin, except to start at the beginning."

Steven laughed, "Usually the place I choose to begin."

She gave him a sideways glance. "Okay, very funny. Let's do a little time travel. I grew up as an only child in a small community in rural Pennsylvania. My Dad was a minister, my Mom, a schoolteacher. Consequentially, I walked a straight and narrow path through my youth. I excelled in school, dreamt big dreams and had what I consider a charmed childhood."

She paused and Steven commented. "Sounds great. What'd you do for fun?"

"My passion was riding. Oh, how I loved our ranch and horses. They were, for all intents and purposes, my siblings. I had a few good friends in high school. We went to the two-screen cinema from time-to-time, or met at the local diner, but mostly we got together at the church youth functions."

Steven was amazed at her upbringing. "That explains the photo of you on a horse that I saw on your mantle. Hearing you describe your life makes it sound as if you grew up in a different era. It sounds so much more like what my Mom would tell me of her youth."

Jaclyn smiled. "I have come to understand that as an adult. As a child, that is all I knew and I never questioned it as anything but normal." She paused for a moment, deciding in which direction to continue. "In High School, we had career days. I remember it as if it were yesterday. An elderly gentleman gave a presentation on his job; he was a commercial real estate broker from Philadelphia. I was spellbound. That's when I began forming my thoughts about my future. Ultimately, I chose NYU for my studies. I wanted to get a business degree in New York and NYU offered me a scholarship, so off I went. It was hard at first, as you can imagine, being away from my parents and living in such a big city. The contrast was somewhat stark, but I grew to love it. I was a very dedicated student and worked internships at several corporations to get as much on-the-job experience as I could. I was driven to be top in my field. I would be satisfied with nothing short of that goal." She paused and took a sip of water.

Steven was eager to know more. "Did you get into real estate immediately after graduation?"

"I did. I began with a few smaller firms, but my big break came when I met Carl Toner."

Steven remarked, "What a success story he is. I've heard fantastic things about him."

A tender look crossed her face. "Carl is fantastic. We met by chance, or as I like to think, by destiny's hand. We hit it off instantly and Carl insisted that I come to work for him. Shortly after I started, he became my mentor. He always made me feel like his protege. My relationship with Carl has been one of the greatest gifts of my life. I treasure our friendship and value our business association." Jaclyn momentarily became lost in her thoughts.

Steven watched her. "What do think about Dallas, now that you have been here for some time?"

She first avoided his eyes as she spoke. "At first, it was an escape. I saw it as temporary, but necessary." She then stopped and looked deeply into Steven's eyes as she continued. "Now I see it differently."

He smiled at her remark. Then the wine steward approached

the table and presented Steven with the bottle. Steven checked the label and nodded. The man expertly removed the cork and handed it to Steven. He lifted it to his nose, then turned it in his fingers as he inspected it. When he was satisfied that it was in good condition, he nodded toward the steward who then poured him a taste of the wine. Steven lifted his glass and viewed the contents through the light of a candle, then swirled the wine in a circular motion under his nose. He closed his eyes and took in the aroma, then touched the rim to his lips and slowly sipped the contents. It took him a moment to open his eyes and comment, but when he did the steward was pleased. "It's even better than I remembered, which is difficult to do, but this time it is superior." He looked at Jaclyn and remarked, "It must be the company."

She smiled tenderly at him as the steward poured the wine for them. When they were alone again, Jaclyn spoke. "Enough about me, tell me about you."

"Alright, let's see. I grew up in Dallas. I was, like you, an only child. That was not Mom's choice, but after numerous miscarriages, she reluctantly gave up trying. Each time it happened, it seemed to take a little more of her happiness with it. Our lives were rather trying. Dad was not well. When I was ten, he fell a few stories on his construction job. He never recovered fully and died just before I turned thirteen. I don't think about that time in my life much, I guess because of how sad a period it was. It was incredibly hard on my mother. She didn't know how we would make ends meet. She worked many hours a week at odd jobs and to help out, after school and on weekends, I did anything I could to earn a few extra dollars. I didn't want her to feel alone in our struggle. We managed. The good that came of it is that I became determined. I never wanted to worry about money or where my next meal would come from." Steven paused, his gaze far from where they were. In a solemn voice he continued. "With a scholarship, financial assistance and student loans, I was able to attend SMU. I truly believe I appreciated my education more than most. I graduated with honors. I feel as if that was the happiest day of my mother's life. Unfortunately, she passed away only a year later."

Jaclyn spoke softly, "I'm sorry."

Steven looked at her and smiled. "Time has a way of healing, but I appreciate that. Every time something good happens, I think of my Mom and wish she could have lived to see it and enjoy it with me.

That's my one regret."

Jaclyn wanted to lead the conversation onto a lighter subject. "How did you get into real estate?"

Steven laughed. "I, like you, was intrigued by the potential. I got a taste of it when I took a part-time job running errands for a title company. The people who worked in the industry impressed me. They all had plush offices, drove dream cars. I saw it as a way to gain the financial freedom I so desperately sought."

Jaclyn commented. "It looks like mission accomplished."

"It has been better to me than I could have ever hoped for, but I don't forget my past. I am involved in inner city improvement projects and work with high schools in low-income areas to try to inspire students to strive to achieve a better life. My story is very powerful for them. If I make a difference in even one of their lives, I have succeeded beyond my biggest real estate deal."

The compassion and sincerity in his conviction, touched Jaclyn. He was a complex man and the more she learned about him, the more he endeared himself to her. She was eager to know more. She began speaking when a waiter approached with their salads and she waited for his retreat before she continued. "What do you enjoy doing for fun?"

"I never had an opportunity to get involved in school sports since all my spare time was spent working, but I have always loved basketball. Whenever possible, I would get into a three-on-three game. I still enjoy a good workout, but now it's in the gym and I try to go whenever I have free time. On rare days, I go to the club. I belong to the Dallas Country Club. I enjoy a round of golf, but even that ends up being about work. Everyone I know there is involved in my business in one way or another. These days, my social calendar is closely related to my work. I end up having to attend endless dinners and social functions, all related to business in some form or fashion, but that is how our industry works. I'm certain it's the same for you."

Jaclyn nodded, "Much more so when I was in New York. I haven't quite entered the Dallas social circle just yet."

Steven was quick to add, "But with your participation in the sale of Thanksgiving Tower, you will have an engraved invitation."

She smiled at his remark. She took a moment to eat a few bites of salad, before she found the words to ask him about his personal life. "Steven, the first night I saw you, you were with a woman. Who is she?"

The look in Steven's eyes changed. The lines around his mouth tightened. Jaclyn noted the change with interest. "Caroline Hunter." Jaclyn waited for him to elaborate. Steven took his time. "She is the daughter of Henry Hunter. I am certain you have heard of the Hunters." Jaclyn nodded as he continued. "We have been," he corrected himself, " . . . had been social companions for about a year now."

Steven did not expand further and Jaclyn commented. "I'm sorry, I have no right to pry." Steven was quick to correct her, "No, Jaclyn, that's not it at all. Caroline is not my girlfriend, in fact, she never has been. It was a relationship of convenience, that's the long and short of it."

Jaclyn sensed the change in his mood, which spoke volumes about his feelings for Caroline. She chose to change the subject. Their entrees had just been served and she commented on the food. "This is an excellent meal Steven and the wine is as good as you said it would be. I always appreciate a wine that complements a meal so perfectly."

He was pleased. "I'm glad you're enjoying it. Luckily, Dallas is filled with excellent restaurants, but this is one of my favorites."

When dinner was finished, the waiter presented each of them a dessert menu. Jaclyn did not look at it and placed it at the corner of the table. Steven looked at her disapprovingly. "Am I to understand that you do not want dessert?"

Jaclyn laughed at his comment. "I'm full."

"Nonsense. Dessert is one of this world's greatest pleasures. Don't ever skip dessert. Life is too short."

She giggled at his remark, opened the menu and consulted its offering. She tried to sound serious in her reply. "You're absolutely right, Steven, this is too good to pass up. What are you having?"

With no hesitation, he said, "Crème Brulee. If it's on the menu, it's always my choice. If not, I have ice cream, chocolate ice cream. Dessert is one of my weaknesses. You, I fear, are another."

Jaclyn was touched by his words. "Let's make it two Crème Brulees. I believe our weaknesses are the same."

He gave her a sensual smile as he motioned for the waiter.

Immediately, the man appeared by Steven's side. Steven informed him of their selection, added two cups of coffee to the order and asked him to also bring the check. When the man was outside of hearing range, Steven spoke. "Suddenly I have the urge to take you in my arms and show you all of my weaknesses."

Jaclyn laughed a nervous laugh. She was lost in him. He was so much more than she could have ever hoped for in a man.

***

It wasn't until he drove through an elaborate set of wrought iron gates and onto the long circular drive that Jaclyn questioned him. "Where are you taking me? I thought we were going to your home?"

Steven smiled. "This is my home."

Jaclyn was completely confused. Steven stopped the car, turned toward her, took her hand and explained. "Jaclyn, as I told you this morning, a man in my position often has women interested in him only for his wealth and social position. I'm not saying you were one of those women, but I wanted to be certain we had a chance to get to know each other first before I revealed myself fully. Because you didn't know anything about me when we met, I felt incredibly free thinking you wanted me for who I am and not for the money I have. I didn't want to spoil that, so I took you to the apartment I keep for my out-of-town guests. I hope you don't mind."

Jaclyn appreciated his honesty. "Although it's hard for me to put myself in your shoes, I do understand how difficult it is to know if someone is genuinely interested in you as a person or by what they think they can garner from the association."

Steven was relieved. "You do understand. Good."

Steven continued down the drive, stopping the car at the front entrance. He jumped out and walked around to the passenger side to open her door. As she stepped onto the drive, she took in her first full view of Steven's home. Before her was a large, two-story, pale-brick, traditional style house accented with cast-stone columns and window casings. Lights set high in the trees cast a soft glow on the massive facade.

As Steven led her slowly down the stone walkway she commented on the beautiful landscaping and charming stone bench surrounded by colorful seasonal blooms. They stepped up onto the covered front porch and as Steven unlocked one side of the massive wood and lead glass double doors, Jaclyn peered through the opaque glass. As he opened the door, he stepped aside to allow her to enter first. As the interior unfolded before her, Jaclyn was in awe. A seven-tier crystal and brass chandelier sparkled and shone over the beige travertine marble floor. Antique furniture dotted the expansive hallways that extended to the left and right of the entry. Before her was a large formal living and dining room, decorated in soft white neoclassical style. Beautifully upholstered furniture formed an intimate conversation area centered on a large cast stone fireplace. Beyond the seating area was a formal dining table surrounded by 12 majestic looking armchairs. Casting a soft glow onto the table was a larger version of the hall chandelier. The two-story windows that framed the immense room were left free of window treatments and revealed a patio and heavily landscaped pool area. Tiered brick flowerbeds encircled the far end of the pool and a wooded backdrop made the backyard look like a garden paradise.

Steven watched with pride as he saw her appreciation of his home and appointments. He let her soak it in while he went to open a bottle of wine for them. When he returned to her side, he didn't think she had even noticed his departure. He extended a glass of wine.

"Oh, Steven, thank you. Everything is just beautiful. You have such a gorgeous home. I have to say, I'm very impressed."

He led her to the den and made her comfortable on a large, soft brown leather sofa. He walked to the stereo and turned on classical music. As she waited, she took in the light ash paneling, the brick fireplace and large entertainment center. The room had shiny caramel-colored wood floors and a plush Oriental rug that anchored the two sofas which met at a 90-degree angle. Apart from the end table between them, the sofas were the only furniture in the room.

When Steven sat beside her, they resumed their conversation. For hours they shared stories about their lives, their plans and hopes for the future. They were like soul mates, finding one another and feeling immediately at ease, as if they were always meant to be. Steven took advantage of a lull in the conversation to bend down toward Jaclyn and kiss her neck. As she responded to his touch, he began unbuttoning her vest. Before long, she was sitting beside him wearing only her lace bra and matching panties. Steven positioned himself above her. Slowly and gently, he kissed her neck and shoulders and methodically worked down the length of her body. She was lost in the sensual experience, her mind free and totally relaxed. When he reached her toes, he leaned back on his knees and removed his shirt and belt and unbuckled his pants. When he was naked from the waist up, he slowly came down on top of her, resting his weight on his side, but placing his chest on hers. Their faces met and their eyes locked in a passionate stare. She reached up and gently ran her hand through his hair and along his neck. Slowly he bent his head toward her, bringing his lips down onto hers and parting them with his tongue, allowing them to explore each other's mouths. As they kissed, Steven caressed her body with his warm hand, coming to rest on the mound beneath her panties. He pressed against her until she moaned with pleasure and pleaded with him to join her.

At her urging, he stood, removed his pants and helped her out of her undergarments. When she lay back down, he took in all of her; the soft curves of her body and the beauty of her face framed by a magnificent mane. Seeing her lying there wanting him made it difficult for him to control his mounting desire. Before lying down beside her, he knelt at her knees, spread her legs gently and bent over her, giving her pleasure that she had never felt free enough to experience. The warmth of his tongue brought her unimaginable sensations. When she was lost in a wave of ecstasy, he pulled himself up to her chest and slowly entered her willing body. She wrapped her legs snugly around his waist and pulled him into her deeply. They rocked back and forth, finding a rhythm and holding each other tightly, kissing each other ravenously until she arched her back in fulfillment and he joined her in reaching the peak of pleasure. The soft sounds emanating from her throat became screams from her chest and her body spasmed along with his. They moved together as one until they were suddenly still, enjoying the warmth and pleasure they found in each other's embrace.

CHAPTER 21
—◇—

Carl hurriedly made his way across his large kitchen to answer the phone. His live-in housekeeper had just set out brunch for him when it started ringing. He jumped up quickly from the sunroom table, hoping he would reach the phone before the ringing stopped. Out of breath, he answered, "Hello."

Jaclyn was warmed by his voice. "Carl, good morning. I hope I'm not disturbing you early on this Sunday morning. I know this is the one day a week you allow yourself to rest."

Carl was doubly pleased he had made it to the phone in time knowing Jaclyn was on the other end. "Jaclyn, hello. You never disturb me. It's always good to hear from you. How did things go on Friday? I've been anxiously awaiting your call."

Jaclyn felt remiss for not calling him earlier. After all, this deal meant a lot to Toner and Associates. "Well, Carl, if you have a few minutes, I'll tell you all about it."

Carl was eager to listen. "Let's have it. How did it go?"

Jaclyn leaned back on Steven's bed and started her account. "It was quite unbelievable actually. Although it was a crazy ride for a while, I think you will be very pleased with the outcome."

Carl urged her to give him the details. "Enough suspense, Jaclyn. What happened?"

She took a deep breath before beginning. "Well, you know what the plan was. JP and I had scheduled the 5 o'clock appointment with Thompson and when he didn't call to cancel our meeting, we assumed the first offer had fallen through. However, when Thompson met with us, he was quick to inform us that the contingencies had been met on the first contract and they were inking the deal that afternoon. Of course, JP and I were disappointed, but it appeared there was little we could do." As Jaclyn spoke, Carl began pacing the kitchen floor. Although she had said it turned out well, he was beginning to wonder how. "Then we were walking down the hallway and Cason approached us because he recognized me."

Carl interrupted. "Wait a minute. Cason recognized you? Did you know him?"

A smile came to Jaclyn's face as she thought about Steven. "Well, it turns out that Cason is Steven Cason, a gentlemen I had met a few times at real estate functions and let's just say there was a definite mutual attraction between us. The strange part was that I only knew him as Steven. You can imagine my surprise when I realized that the guy I was friendly to was the same guy cheating us out of the deal. I was initially in shock."

Carl couldn't help but comment. "My goodness, Jaclyn, that must have come as quite a disappointment to you. Especially with the break-in at your office and . . ." Jaclyn interrupted him. "That's exactly what was going through my mind. In fact, I left Thompson's office thinking the absolute worst. I thought I had been a fool about this guy Cason and that it had cost us the deal. Let's just say I wasn't feeling so good about things Friday night. But, thankfully, it gets better."

Carl was still confused. "I hope so."

"The next morning, I called JP as I had promised. He asked me to come to the Mansion so we could talk. As you can imagine, after the disappointment of Friday afternoon, I was in no mood to even think about business, but I felt obligated and so I went to see him. JP began telling me what he had learned from Cason after I left, which cleared up the circumstantial evidence against him. In fact, Steven was there to address each one of the issues personally. I felt so foolish for having run away the day before and not sticking around to hear his side. Bottom line Carl, JP ended up with a 30% stake in the deal, the final 20% we didn't think Cason had organized, which we later learned he had personally guaranteed to get the deal done in time, and 10% of SC Investments' share. The topper was that Steven insisted I be named as the agent for the buyers since the majority of the deal was done with parties I had brought to the table."

Carl shook his head in disbelief. "What a development. I guess, first and foremost, congratulations on getting the deal done, but did you ever get to the bottom of the break-in? I mean, it all sounds fine, but how can you be certain Cason wasn't behind it?"

Jaclyn was quick to explain. "That's the incredible part. Cason got the leads from the listing agent and you will never believe who he got them from."

"From whom?"

"Andrew."

Carl was furious. "You're kidding. How would he have leads on the Tower deal?"

"I could hardly believe it either, Carl, but Andrew is clearly far from giving up trying to get me back to New York. I guess he figured if I lost the deal, I would leave Dallas and come home. Somehow, Andrew got a hold of my file and arranged to meet the listing agent and give him the paperwork. Can you believe it?"

"You bet I believe it. After what he's done in the past, I wouldn't doubt he would do just about anything. It appears that he was the one behind the break-in. Like I told you earlier, desperate people can resort to desperate measures."

Jaclyn turned the direction of the conversation. "I agree, Carl, but the important thing is that net, net, the deal is ours."

Carl regained his positive attitude. "Jaclyn, that's absolutely great news. The deal is done and you did it. I am so proud of you."

Jaclyn was smiling from ear to ear, hearing his praise. "Thank you, Carl. I wanted to tell you right away, but things were pretty crazy around here yesterday. But you know I wouldn't let you leave on your trip without telling you. That's why I'm calling you so early this morning. I wasn't certain when you'd be going."

Carl consulted his watch. "I'll be heading to the airport in a few hours. I'm really looking forward to this trip. Hearing your good news will certainly make this an even better and more restful vacation. And while I have you on the phone, Jaclyn, Peters has the power of attorney for you to stand in for me during my absence, should anything urgent come up. I don't foresee anything; however, business being what it is, I want you to know that I trust your judgment implicitly and know you'd do whatever needs to be done."

Jaclyn understood completely and saw it as a great honor that Carl had for the past few years been leaving her in charge during his extended absences. He occasionally went on vacations to faraway and remote locations and thus needed someone who could stand in for him pending his return. It was a precaution he took seriously, even though she had only encountered one incident on which she had to exercise the right. When that time had presented itself, he later applauded her decisions and actions and informed her that she had acted exactly as he would have. Since then, she remained more at ease with the idea of providing leadership, albeit it temporary, for Toner and Associates during Carl's hiatuses.

She turned her attention back to Carl. "Thank you, Carl. Now, listen, you have a wonderful time in glorious Virgin Gorda. I am so envious. Enjoy your sailing and don't give us poor souls slaving away back here a second thought."

Carl let out a hearty laugh. "What poor souls?"

Jaclyn joined in on the laughter. "Good to know we are forgotten so easily. All kidding aside, Carl, have a great time. Call me as soon as you get back to New York. I want to hear all about your trip."

"Will do, Jaclyn, and thanks for calling and sharing the great news with me. You take care and I'll call you on my return."

"Take care, Carl. Safe trip. Good-bye."

Carl hung up the phone and smiled broadly, thinking about Jaclyn. As he sat alone, glancing at the Sunday paper and eating his breakfast, he mused fondly on his protege. She meant so much to him, and more than just as a business associate. In many ways, she was the daughter he had never had and always wanted.

CHAPTER 22
— ◇ —

The start of the week had been extremely busy for both Steven and Jaclyn. Each had returned attention to work that had been put aside during the Tower negotiations. For Jaclyn, it meant hours of updates from each of the agents working in her office. When her morning meetings were finished, she called her clients to review any further action needed on their purchase or sale. Occasionally, throughout the day, agents from the New York office interrupted her meetings to seek her counsel. She took those calls seriously because she felt obligated to give them the time and advice she believed Carl would have given. It made her feel good to be able to stand in for Carl while he took a much-needed break. Before she had joined his agency, he had not been on a lengthy vacation in the preceding five years. It gave her great satisfaction to know he trusted her with his business and that his confidence in her gave him the freedom to go away. She knew how much he had wanted this change of scenery and was happy he had decided to take advantage of the opportunity.

When she finally had a quiet moment, she sat at her desk and reviewed her messages from the morning. As she was about to return calls, her private line rang. "Jaclyn Tate."

The man, who answered, spoke in a deep, slow voice. "Ms. Tate?"

"Yes?"

"Leave town."

"Excuse me."

"You heard me. I said, leave town."

"You must have the wrong person. Who are you looking for?"

"Jaclyn Tate."

"Then there is some sort of mistake..."

"No mistake, just a warning that I strongly suggest you take seriously. Leave town or else."

The line went dead. Jaclyn was in shock. She stared at the receiver as if willing it to offer her an explanation. Why would this man call her with such a threatening message? Who was he? What was this all about? Questions swirled about in her mind, but no answers surfaced.

***

The peacefulness that Carl found on this tranquil and remote island was heaven to him. He knew he needed to get away from the daily grind. His patience had grown thin over the past few months and his blood pressure had risen dangerously high. Although he had faithfully taken his medication, his pressure remained elevated and that's when his doctor insisted he take a holiday. Carl knew a vacation was exactly what he needed, so he heeded his doctor's advice and made plans to do the one thing he longed to do: go sailing. His love for the sea transcended everything else in his life. Sailing was his first love. That's why he sought a retreat at the Bitter End Yacht Club on Virgin Gorda. He wanted to indulge his passion. Take to the sea. Feel the swift breeze across his face and the sensation of being taken by the power of the wind.

This morning he had risen early in anticipation of the day ahead. He walked gingerly from his tropical retreat, down the stone pathway, to a seaside restaurant. He selected a table at the patio edge so he could have an unobstructed view of the bay. After a quick breakfast, he headed excitedly down to the marina. It would be his second day out sailing, but today he would be without the captain, who had joined him for his maiden voyage. On their first day out, the experienced seaman showed Carl how to maneuver around the islands that dotted the waters and how to follow the channels deep enough for the vessel. The experience exhilarated Carl and he was eager for his next day at sea, when he would set sail alone. Immediately upon the completion of his instructional sail, he had returned to the yachting office and reserved a sailboat for the next day. He had selected a midsize sloop that he could handle on his own and planned to spend the following day exploring the deserted islands and taking in the expanse of sea before him.

Now as he walked eagerly toward the marina, he searched for the boat he had reserved. He stopped at the edge of the pier and looked out at the boats moored in the cove. In the distance, he could see the *Unforgettable* swaying rhythmically amid several other vessels. As he stood there, a man approached and diverted his attention. "Mr. Toner, good morning." Carl turned to see the captain who had taken him out the day before.

"Good morning, Joe. I see her. She certainly is a beauty."

"Yes, she is. As promised, she is ready and waiting for you." Together they walked briskly down the wooden slats of the dock to a tender tied up and waiting to take them to her. Carl did not take his eyes off her as they slowly made their way in between the piers and past other boats. As they approached, Carl smiled broadly. He admired her beauty as they neared the aft of the craft. He could see that she was polished and ready for his trip and his heart raced in anticipation of his journey on the sea.

As they pulled against the rear platform, the deeply tanned man gestured toward the *Unforgettable*. "Please, Mr. Toner, go aboard."

Carl did not hesitate and stepped carefully onto the deck. He immediately put his hands on the beautiful wood steering wheel and stared out at the calm water inside of the lagoon.

The man joined Carl. "Mr. Toner, I put the food you requested in the cabin. Please check to make certain you have everything you need."

While the man waited, Carl conducted a cursory examination of the equipment and supplies. The food and water he had requested were down in the galley. When he saw everything in good order, he confirmed that he was ready to go. "Joe, it appears I am all set. Everything looks good."

As the man replied, he handed him a map. "Excellent. Please

take this. It shows the surrounding islands and will help you navigate easily through the waters."

Carl took a few minutes to study the map and plan his course. It was not long before he was telling Joe he was ready to depart. At his command, Joe stepped onto the tender, effortlessly released the boat from the mooring and waited nearby as Carl turned on the motor and steadily pointed the bow into the still water. Instantly, Carl was exhilarated. His adrenaline was rushing as he crossed the buoys that marked the marina. As he headed for the open sea, his heart soared. He hoisted the sails and took control of the vessel. She was handling perfectly and Carl felt right at home at the helm. The wind filled the sails, taking him out to sea at a brisk pace. The bow cut through the waves easily which were increasing in height the farther he moved from the island. He stood behind the steering wheel and basked in the sensation of the swiftly moving air brushing against his face and body. It was cleansing and freeing. It was as if the passing air took all the cares of the world with it. He was at complete and total peace. Nothing crossed his mind except the beauty surrounding him. The color of the sea defied definition. Tones of deep emerald, striking sapphire and vibrant turquoise combined to form spectacular hues of blue and green. The strong smell of ammonia emanating from the sea, the soft wind against his body and the sound of sea gulls squawking in the distance added to the perfect experience. Waves thumped the sides of the boat and the sail's clamps banged against the masts as the canvas blew taut by the wind. The sounds combined in harmony with the rhythm of the movement of the craft. Experiencing the thrill of the moment was invigorating, stimulating and Carl was happier than he could ever remember.

As Anagonda, a small, uninhabited island neared, Carl decided to drop anchor. He was eager to take a swim in the spectacular water. He had brought along his snorkel and fins to explore the coral reefs and underwater life. He slowly approached the shore, eased into a cove and secured the boat in the still bay. He eagerly ripped off his T-shirt, moved swiftly to the teak swim platform, placed his snorkel gear beside him and positioned himself to enter the water. He took a moment to balance himself as the boat rocked beneath him. When he felt steady, he jumped feet first into the sea. As his legs hit the warm water, he let out a loud yelp. He swam around the boat, diving at random deeper into the sea. It was then that he spotted a school of fish and raced back to the boat to grab his mask and fins. Quickly, he placed the fins on his feet, positioned the snorkel on his head and returned to the area where he had seen the fish. To his amazement, the school swam toward him as he approached and he was instantly engulfed in a flurry of neon yellow and electric blue. He swam with the school for as long as he could, enjoying the randomness with which they moved. Finally, he gave up the pursuit and focused on the colorful coral, rock and moss beneath him. He was fascinated by the plethora of ocean creatures, fish and sponges around him. He felt at one with the sea. Lost in the moment, he did not realize how long he had been in the water. Only when his stomach called out to him was he reminded of the passing time. It had to be approaching noon. At the realization, he headed back to the boat with a swift breaststroke.

As he arrived at the sloop, he took hold of the platform, removed his snorkel gear and climbed up the ladder. As he stood on the platform, it took him a moment to regain his balance. Once the rocking subsided, he moved carefully onto the deck. He rested against the rear of the craft, taking a few minutes to dry off and enjoy the scenery before going down into the cabin for lunch. He watched pelicans soaring along the shoreline and noted the sense of freedom he experienced watching them. But once again, his hunger pangs prompted him to move. Otherwise, he could have remained there for hours enjoying the tranquility of the moment.

His hunger satisfied, he returned to the deck to relax. He placed a towel on the sun lounge on the bow and laid down. He propped his head up so he could enjoy the panorama before him. He stretched out, taking in the warmth of the sun on his face and chest. It had been a long time since he had felt so relaxed. His mind focused on nothing but the view. He marveled at the islands jutting out from the emerald sea and the deep blue sky dotted with small, puffy white clouds. It was so beautiful that he felt it should be preserved on canvas for all time. He was lost in the moment when, without warning, a sharp pain gripped his chest. The spasm within his rib cage forced him to pull himself into a tight fetal position. As his body contorted, his head swam with unintelligible thoughts. The agony took away all his senses. He was delirious from the severity and shock of the attack. He grappled to make sense of what was happening but could not think clearly. The plight of pain was like nothing he had ever experienced before. He was barely able to catch his breath when it struck again. This time the pain was so severe that he lost use of his arms. They dangled lifelessly at his sides. His head fell back with a thud and his body spasmed uncontrollably against the hard surface, making a loud thump that reverberated in his ears. Carl desperately tried to understand what was taking place. His weak hands instinctively groped at his chest. That's when he realized where the pain was originating. He struggled to sit up and then slowly inched his way along the side-rail toward the cabin. His body was unwilling to cooperate, but his mind tried to stay strong. He slowly crawled along the side of the boat and finally was close enough to the rear to swing his legs onto the aft deck. The sudden shifting of his weight caused him to fall onto the wood platform. Simultaneously, another attack hit and he was once again lost in a wave of suffering. He grimaced through the episode, trying to will it away.

Thoughts of dying entered his mind. He closed his eyes tightly, trying to stop the pain and fear that was overwhelming him. He would not die, he insisted. He had to live. Moments later, when the discomfort subsided, he tried to move again. He pulled himself along the wall of the cabin, reached the opening to the salon and stumbled down the narrow steps. As he hit bottom, he sat on the floor and reached for the two-way radio, which was hanging within reach. He turned the knob to raise the volume and with barely sufficient strength to depress the talk button, began to speak, "*Unforgettable* to Base, do you hear me?" His voice trembled and his speech was slurred. When no one replied immediately, he tried again. "*Unforgettable* to Bitter End, do you read me?" He waited a moment.

To his great relief, a man's voice sounded, "*Unforgettable*, this is Bitter End, how can we help you?"

Carl closed his eyes out of total relief. He felt safe knowing that help was now within reach. He tried to steady himself as he replied, "Bitter End, please help me. I'm not well." The reply was delayed and Carl tried again, "Bitter End, do you read me?"

A few seconds passed before he received a reply. The words were distorted by loud static, "Come 'gain, *Unfor. . .able,* . . . we . . . trouble. . . hear . . . you."

As Carl tried to reply, another wave of pain seized him. He could not answer and the strength in his hand was gone. The mouthpiece fell from his hand as he was momentarily paralyzed. In the distance, Carl vaguely discerned a man's voice. *"Unforgettable, do you read me? . . . Unforgettable?"*

In one final attempt, Carl reached toward the mouthpiece but could not find his voice. Out of desperation, he reached up to the control panel and felt around for the anchor release trigger. When his fingers passed over it, he pulled it toward him. Instantly, the anchor motor sounded. As he lay back, he heard the mooring returning to its storage cabinet. Within moments of the sound of the cabinet doors shutting, the boat began to rock. He then released the main sail and heard the canvas flutter as it rose up the mast. Suddenly, the sloop jolted forward. Without a captain at the helm, the boat was embarking on a haphazard course. Before long, the bow was hitting swells at an awkward angle, tossing Carl from side to side. He tried to pull himself toward the steps in an attempt to reach the deck, but his exertion was in vain. He had limited use of his limbs. In one final attempt, he lay on his belly and tried to inch his way up the steps, but he was too weak and suddenly the pain came crushing down on him again. This time his face distorted in agony and all of his strength left him.

The brightness of day turned into a golden dusk and Carl remained lifeless and still, his limp body pressed against the floor of the cabin. The *Unforgettable* continued on its journey despite the absence of a captain, navigating the perilous waters on an uncharted course.

***

It was a sunny day in Dallas. As she drove to work, Jaclyn noticed how blue the sky was. Maybe it was just because she was falling in love that the world seemed so beautiful to her, but it did and she didn't look for reasons why. She just enjoyed the wonderful feeling that consumed her as she moved about in a light and carefree manner. As was customary, Jaclyn sat at her desk and read the paper to start her day. Before she had finished the business section, Matt came in and wished her a good morning. He was becoming so important to her, had developed into such a good assistant and she couldn't help but feel he was her protege, just as she was Carl's. Although she usually went back to her paper after Matt's routine greeting, she instead put her paper aside and called out, "Matt, when you have a minute, please come into my office."

"Of course, Jaclyn." It was unlike her to break her morning routine, but Matt did not question the request.

When he appeared at her door, pen and paper in hand, Jaclyn smiled at him. "Matt, come on in and have a seat. I just wanted you to know I think you're doing a great job."

Matt was surprised with the unexpected compliment. A smile crossed his lips, although it was clear he was trying to hide the apparent pleasure her comment brought him. "Thank you, Jaclyn. I really appreciate your saying that, but I feel incredibly lucky to have been given such an unbelievable opportunity to work with you. Through your experience and talent for getting deals closed, I have learned so much. If I'm doing a good job, it's because you gave me the means to accomplish it."

Jaclyn found his humility endearing. In the world of inflated egos in which she worked, it was refreshing to find someone so humble. "Matt, you deserve the praise. You're doing a fine job. In fact, I think it's time you had a promotion and a raise. I will work out the details for you, but consider it done."

Matt's face lit up. His eyes widened full of anticipation. The excitement he felt came across loud and clear in the tone of his voice. "Thank you so much, Jaclyn. This means so much to me."

Jaclyn simply nodded as she replied. "You've earned it."

Before either of them could say anything further, Jaclyn's private line rang and she excused herself before picking up the phone. Matt knew the routine. He left her alone to take the call, closing the door behind him as he walked out of the office.

Momentarily Jaclyn relived the call she had received a day earlier from the mysterious man telling her to leave town. The man's tone and his message left her with an uneasy feeling, but she would not allow it to distract her. It was part of the game she had come to learn to play. Refocusing her attention, she removed an earring as she lifted the receiver. "This is Jaclyn."

A solemn voice came across the line, one that Jaclyn did not immediately recognize. "Jaclyn, I'm afraid I must ask you to come to New York immediately."

Dread filled Jaclyn's body. There was some unspoken bad news behind this man's statement and she feared what it might be. Her thoughts instantly centered on her parents, but then why would she need to go to New York? She tried to calm her rising fears. "I'm sorry. Who is this?"

The man was quick to reply. "Forgive me, Jaclyn. It's Stan Peters."

Jaclyn was relieved to discover it was clearly a business matter. But why would Carl's attorney need her to come to New York so urgently? "Stan, what's going on?"

Stan chose his words carefully. "Jaclyn, you are aware that Carl left you in charge in his absence, aren't you?"

Jaclyn didn't miss a beat. "Of course, Stan."

"Then, Jaclyn, you need to trust me when I say you are needed in New York. I wouldn't ask this unless I felt it were imperative and, Jaclyn, the sooner, the better. In fact, I've taken the liberty to book you on a 9 a.m. flight. I'll fax you the itinerary as soon as we hang up. A driver will be waiting for you at LaGuardia airport. Please come directly to the office on your arrival."

Jaclyn was waiting for more information, but none was given. "Alright, Stan. Can you at least advise me if I need to bring anything with me or how long you anticipate I'll need to stay?"

Stan's voice was suddenly trembling. "Pack for a week. I made reservations for you at the Plaza."

Jaclyn was taken aback. "A week?" Her mind raced. Then she remembered that Carl was due back in a week. Maybe Stan was just being cautious and wanted her there until Carl's return. Without waiting for a reply, she agreed. "Very well, Stan. I'll see you at the office."

Relieved by her agreement, he thanked her and ended the call.

She hung up the phone and hastily looked at her watch. It was already 7:15 and she needed to go home, pack and then fight rush-hour traffic to make the flight. She grabbed a few files, stuck them in her briefcase, picked up her itinerary off the fax, and rushed out of her office, taking a bewildered Matt with her as she got into her car and headed home. As she drove, she explained the urgency to Matt and gave him detailed instructions of what to do in her absence. Within fifteen minutes, she was home, haphazardly packing her garment bag. Matt waited for her in the living room, responding to the questions and orders she yelled out to him as she thought of things that he would need to do. She was leaving him in charge, which meant giving him the key to the office. It was a big step for Matt and he understood its significance. He would prove to Jaclyn that her trust and confidence had not been misplaced.

Once she was packed and was ready to go, she tossed Matt the car keys, got in the passenger seat and dialed the number to Steven's private line as they pulled out of the driveway. Steven picked up before it even seemed to ring. "Cason."

She took a deep breath to steady herself, but the panic and stress in her voice was obvious. "Steven, hi, it's Jaclyn."

Hearing the urgency in her voice, he asked her to hold while he excused the staff in his office so he could speak to her in private. Nervously, he came back on the line. "Jaclyn, what is it? What's wrong?"

She did not hesitate. "First thing this morning, I got a call from Carl's attorney and he insisted that I come to New York immediately. He would not give me any details, just told me that I was needed urgently. He booked me on a 9 a.m. flight, so I am rushing to the airport. Matt is with me and he will drop me off and then take my car back to the office."

Steven took advantage of her pause to interject his thoughts. "Do you have any indication of what is going on?"

Jaclyn tried to remain calm as she spoke. "No, Steven. That's what is so unnerving about all of this. The issues I have dealt with during Carl's other absences were certainly manageable via the phone or teleconferencing. I'm certain Stan wouldn't rush me up to New York unless something critical had happened."

Steven shared her concern. "I understand. Is there anything I can do? Can I contact Stan or do something for you while you're in transit?"

"Thank you Steven, but I doubt Stan would disclose anything to you. He wasn't even at liberty to tell me anything until I arrive in New York. He said he would advise me fully when I get to the office. He arranged for a driver to meet my flight and take me directly there."

Steven was serious in his reply. "Well, it certainly sounds urgent. Let me know what's going on and, Jaclyn, if there is anything, and I mean anything I can do, just ask."

She was grateful for his support. "Thank you, Steven. I'll let you know if I think of anything."

He sensed she was ready to hang up but he wanted to know one more thing before he let her go. "Do you know how long you'll be away?"

Jaclyn let out a heavy sigh. "No, not fully, but Stan said to be prepared to stay a week."

"A week!" Steven said, surprised. "Why so long?"

Jaclyn could only speculate. "I'm guessing that whatever it is, someone in authority is needed to tend to it, and until Carl's return next week, I'm that person."

Steven was disappointed she would be away for so long. "It sounds like you have no choice but to go. Please call me when you know more."

She assured him. "I will."

Before hanging up, he added, "Have a safe trip . . . and, Jaclyn, if you need me, call."

"Thank you, Steven. I will call you as soon as I can."

"Very well then, I'll be waiting."

They hung up and Jaclyn returned her attention to the road as Matt navigated through the increasing rush-hour traffic. Her mind wandered to New York. She tried to anticipate what she would encounter on her arrival. She thought back on her recent conversations with Carl. As hard as she tried, she could not think of one issue that Carl had mentioned as being at a critical juncture. That's why he felt comfortable leaving when he did. And although she tried not to worry or speculate on potential issues at hand, Stan's call weighed heavily on her mind.

CHAPTER 23
—◇—

Jaclyn walked into the Toner and Associates office building and was overwhelmed by a feeling she had not anticipated; she had come home. The familiar surroundings evoked thoughts of Carl in her mind and she instantly wished he were there and that she were coming back to welcome him home. As she walked down the long hall, she stopped briefly to greet several coworkers. Stan appeared outside Carl's office as she approached. When she was within arm's length, he extended his hand to greet her. "Jaclyn, thank you for coming."

She looked into Stan's serious face, trying to understand why she had been so urgently summonsed to New York. The dark circles around his sunken eyes told her that he had not had a good night's sleep. The stress evident in his face made it clear to her that something was terribly wrong. "Stan, how are you? What's going on?"

He took her by the arm as he replied and lead her toward the conference room. "I will be at liberty to explain everything to you in a matter of minutes."

She did not like waiting to be informed but she followed him as he made his way to the executive boardroom. He opened the door for her and she entered. As the room came into view, she could see the entire board of directors seated around the massive table. She looked toward Stan in silent request for an explanation, but he merely showed her to the seat at the head of the room. All eyes followed her. She felt uncomfortable being asked to sit in Carl's chair, but then she reminded herself that she was the one person who had the authority to act on his behalf. She quickly glanced around the table, silently greeting everyone with a nod of the head and a less than heartfelt smile.

When everyone was seated and the chatter in the room had subsided, Stan rose from his seat to call the meeting to order. As he opened his mouth to speak, he could not find his voice. He cleared his throat and took a few sips of water before trying again. "I want to begin this meeting of the board of directors by first thanking each of you for being here. I know it wasn't easy for you to rearrange your busy schedules at a moment's notice." He paused to look around the table, checking that he had everyone's undivided attention. When he was certain he did, he continued. "I'll begin by explaining the reason for this meeting." A heavy silence filled the room as Stan opened a file before him and picked up a document attached to a legal brief. He took a deep breath, looked at the faces before him and began. His serious tone sent Jaclyn to the edge of her seat. She hung on his every word. "It is with great sorrow that I convey the following news to you . . . " He stopped to clear his throat.

Sorrow? Jaclyn's heart skipped a beat. What business issue would bring sorrow . . .? Then it dawned on her...Carl...

" . . . I received word in the middle of the night that Carl has died."

A collective sigh filled the room and several people turned to one another in soft whispering. Jaclyn sat alone at the head of the table and began trembling uncontrollably. A series of thoughts ran through her mind . . .there was a mistake . . . Carl was on vacation . . What was Stan saying?

Stan tried to regain control of the room. "Please, may I have your attention . . .?" He paused, giving everyone an opportunity to settle down. Jaclyn waited nervously for him to continue and when he spoke again, she hung on his every word. "There is no easy way to say this, except to tell you what I know. From the report I received from local authorities, Carl was sailing . . . alone . . . and became ill. There was record of a call from his vessel, but at the time it was not clear why he had called the marina. Two young couples sailing in the same vicinity found him. They had approached the boat after watching it sail unattended between two islands." Stan paused to catch his breath. In almost a whisper, he continued. "The coroner's initial report states the cause of death as a heart attack."

Before proceeding, Stan waited a few minutes to allow

everyone time to digest the news. Each person shook his or her head in disbelief. Carl's longtime secretary, Gertrude, wept noisily in the corner. Jaclyn's head was pounding. She didn't want to believe what Stan was saying, but reality was beginning to set in. Carl was gone. Her heart was heavy and pooling tears threatened to stream down her cheeks. Her throat was dry.

Stan continued, "I have known about this since very early this morning. I have already spoken with the medical examiner at the hospital in San Juan, where they transported Carl's body. On his examination, he said that he strongly believes the cause of death was a massive heart attack, but explained that only an autopsy could conclusively confirm the exact cause. However, it was Carl's express wish never to undergo an autopsy, so we will have to honor his will and accept the judgement of the attending physician." Stan paused to allow time for anyone to speak, but a heavy silence continued to fill the room. "I have already made arrangements for Carl's body to be returned to New York tomorrow morning. Per his last will and testament, he requested a private wake followed by a burial alongside his parents in St. Joseph's cemetery. I have initiated all of his requests according to his will." Stan took a break and sipped from the glass of water before him. He looked momentarily at all the people around him, giving each a sympathetic nod. Besides the subtle sniffling sounds, the room remained depressingly quiet. "As for the business, I was with Carl when he changed his will to add a beneficiary to the company. Unlike his personal effects, which he has donated to a variety of places, mostly charities, his business, the one thing that truly meant something to him, is going to someone who also meant the world to him." All eyes in the room were fixed on Stan as he continued. Minds raced trying to anticipate who Carl had appointed. Several individuals seemed obvious choices, but with Carl having been extremely private in his dealings, his planning was a mystery to most of even his closest advisors. The anticipation was clear in the faces around the table.

Stan's mood lightened as he continued. "He has left Toner and Associates in the capable hands of Jaclyn Tate." The sound of her name jarred Jaclyn from a deep depressed state. She was not certain that she understood what Stan had said. Whispers filled the room. It was Joseph, the CFO, who was the first to speak up. "Jaclyn, congratulations. We all know how much trust Carl placed in you. I'm not the least bit surprised that you were the one he entrusted the business to."

The words still did not fully register. She felt as if she were in a trance. Stan recognized the glazed look in her eyes and cut off further comments. He moved toward her slowly as he spoke her name. "Jaclyn?" He waited for her to focus on him.

Slowly, she looked up at the man who was now standing by her side. "Yes?"

"Did you understand what I just said?"

She looked as if she were in a fog. "I believe so."

Stan leaned against the table so that he was closer to her. "Jaclyn, Carl has left Toner and Associates to you. I remember when he reached that decision a year ago. It gave him such a sense of security to know he would never have to worry about the future of his business. You gave him a great gift."

Jaclyn watched Stan intently as he spoke. Silent tears rolled down her cheeks as he recalled Carl's actions. Stan smiled at her. "In fact, when Carl asked me to prepare the paperwork, he said you were the daughter he always wanted. Carl asked me to add a letter he had written to you as part of his will. He instructed me to read it to you when you were told of his death. I will read it now if that is okay with you." Jaclyn nodded and Stan tore open the sealed envelope, unfolded the hand-written letter and began reading. The room was completely silent.

Dear Jaclyn,

I know this is a terrible moment for you. My only hope is that what I am about to tell you will ease your pain. Before you came into my life, I didn't know who would be the heir to Toner and Associates, but as our relationship grew and my respect for your talents deepened, I had no doubt you would be my successor. Congratulations, Jaclyn, on your appointment. You have earned it and you deserve it. I have all the confidence in the world that the board will fully honor and respect you in your newly appointed position.

As for what you have meant to me personally, I can not find the words to tell you how you have healed my soul and brought happiness into my otherwise lonely existence. You allowed me to enjoy life again. Not many people can have that effect on another person's life, but you did and I am eternally grateful to you for that. I'm going to ask you to do one last thing for me, and that is to be happy. There is nothing you can do to bring me back, but you can do something to make my legacy strong. I know that Toner and Associates will prosper in your hands. You can do it. Make it happen.

Love you, Carl

Jaclyn was looking up at Stan, smiling at Carl's words, in spite of the pain in her heart. And although she knew the repercussions of what she had just learned, she refused to think about the business and her new role. That would have to wait. For now, her mind focused on Carl. His image was indelibly etched in her mind's eye. The agony that gripped her heart and clouded her mind took over. At this moment she wasn't certain she would ever get over the loss.

***

It was hours before Jaclyn was finally alone. She was sitting in Carl's office in a chair facing his desk. She could picture him there. Then she stood and walked over to his sailboat collection. She picked up his prize antique wood schooner and thought of him in his glory sailing in the beautiful Caribbean waters. It pained her to imagine him falling ill all alone on the boat. If he had suffered a heart attack in New York and received immediate medical attention, would he still be alive today? She hated playing useless what-if games, but she wanted all of this to be a mistake. From the moment Stan dropped the bomb on her and the board members earlier in the day, everything had seemed a blur. She thought back on how numb she was as the board swore her in as the new CEO and chairman. She shook her head as if to wake from this crazy dream, but nothing changed. She was still in Carl's office, looking at his empty chair, when her thoughts turned to Steven. She leaned across Carl's desk, turned the phone toward her and dialed Steven's private line. Instantly, he answered the phone. Concern was obvious in his tone. "Cason."

Jaclyn couldn't help but feel good at the sound of his voice. He already had such an incredible calming effect on her. "Steven, it's Jac…"

He cut her off mid-sentence. "Jaclyn, I have been waiting by the phone to hear from you. What's going on?"

She sounded almost drunk. She slurred her words and spoke slowly and without energy. "I'm sorry I didn't call sooner, Steven... it's just that it all happened so fast . . . and so much has happened . . . I don't even know where to begin."

Steven jumped in. "Alright, take your time. Just tell me what's going on."

Jaclyn took a long, deep breath and then proceeded to give Steven a recap of the events of the day. With a strained voice, she sadly informed Steven of Carl's death. In disbelief, he listened to her account. She had spoken so dearly and highly of him. It was clear to Steven how much he had meant to her, so he could well imagine the depth of pain she felt as she learned of his passing. He shared his feelings with her. "Jaclyn, I am so sorry to hear about Carl. I could tell from your recounting of your relationship with him, that he meant a great deal to you. This must be very traumatic for you."

Jaclyn appreciated his sympathy. "Truthfully, I don't know how I am still able to speak coherently. My brain feels numb."

"I'm certain this is very difficult."

She then steadied herself to deliver the remainder of the news. "And that is just half of it." Steven listened attentively as she continued. "Carl left the business to me and appointed me CEO."

Steven was both amazed and impressed. Carl's decision to leave her his real estate empire spoke volumes about the accomplished professional and excellent businesswoman she was. Toner and Associates was a real estate powerhouse worth a fortune and it was now Jaclyn's. "Congratulations Jaclyn. This is an incredible series of events. I'm certain you have mixed emotions about your situation, but you must be honored by Carl's faith in you." Steven waited for Jaclyn to speak, but silence ensued. "Jaclyn, I want to be there for you. I wish I could be there tonight, but it's already late. If it's all right with you, I want to come to New York tomorrow."

"Thank you Steven. I could really use the support." She was grateful that he was planning to come. She had an incredible challenge ahead of her and having Steven's support would be a terrific help and comfort. Knowing he would be with her soon helped give her the strength to go on.

***

The next day passed in a blur. Jaclyn spent hours being briefed on the most pressing issues facing the firm. Although she was mentally tired and emotionally drained, she maintained her composure and handled all of the business issues with ease and competence. In her first day on the job as the new leader of Toner and Associates, she was earning the respect of her fellow board members. All of them had worked with her before but never in the capacity in which she now acted. Several of them told her they were impressed with her decision-making ability and excellent grasp of the industry as well as her savvy for maximizing opportunities. She was a brilliant star and now was her time to shine.

Periodically throughout the day she retreated to Carl's office. The sanctuary of his suite offered her a sense of peace and gave her strength. It was as if she could still meet with him, hear his words of wisdom and feel his presence. Connecting with him in the familiar surroundings gave her the will to go on, to continue his legacy and make him proud.

***

The man was out of breath as he spoke. "That's right. She left town. Her office verified that fact."

"Do we know the circumstances of her departure?"

"Yeah, some guy, Carl Toner, kicked the bucket. She's in New York at their office."

"Good job. Keep me informed of any further updates. I want to know immediately if you hear anything. Do I make myself clear?"

"Sure boss. No problem. I'll let ya know as soon as I hear anything else."

"Good. Keep in touch."

***

As Steven followed the chauffeur out of the terminal, he was surprised by the unseasonably cool weather. Jaclyn had arranged for a car service to meet him at the airport and take him into Manhattan. The driver expertly wove through the heavy traffic. As they ascended onto a bridge, Steven was taken aback by the amazing sight unfolding before him. Across the bay, magnificent in its magnitude, appeared a spectacular panoramic view of New York City. Steven was immediately in awe of this massive compilation of brick and mortar. It was a real estate aficionado's Mecca.

Before long, they were pulling up to the Plaza Hotel. A bellman opened the door for Steven and took his bags from the trunk. He then escorted Steven into the lobby and directed him to the reception desk. Steven walked up to the attractive young woman who was smiling broadly at him as he approached.

"Good evening." Steven said as he reached into his breast pocket for his billfold.

Her reply was courteous and friendly. "Good evening. Are you checking in with us this evening?"

Steven handed her his business card as he spoke. "Yes. I am Steven Cason, a guest of Ms. Jaclyn Tate. I believe Ms. Tate left instructions with you regarding my arrival."

The woman took Steven's card and looked up Jaclyn's reservation. She scanned the screen before her, then said, "Of course, Mr. Cason. May I please see your driver's license?"

Steven obliged her request and produced his identification. The woman took the card and verified the information. A moment later, she said, "Welcome to the Plaza, Mr. Cason. I trust that everything will be to your satisfaction. Should you require anything, please feel free to call upon any of us." She signaled to the bellman, who instantly appeared by Steven's side. "Mr. Cason is in the Vanderbilt Suite," she advised him. Then turned her attention back to Steven. "Scott will see you to your room, Mr. Cason. Have a pleasant stay with us and good evening."

Steven thanked her and turned to follow the middle-aged man as they walked over to the elevators. When they arrived at the suite, the bellman unlocked the door and held it open as Steven walked past him into the room. The bellman switched on the lights and Steven looked around. It was a luxurious room with many amenities and had a warm, welcoming feel. A basket of fruit and a chilling bottle of wine on a dining table in the corner of the enormous living room caught his attention. He walked over to the spread and caught sight of a note with his name written on it, propped up against the basket. Curious, he opened the envelope and pulled out the note. It read:

Dear Steven,

I am happy you arrived safely. Please make yourself comfortable and I will be there shortly. I expect to return to the Plaza between 8 and 8:30 this evening. Can't wait to see you.

Fondly,
Jaclyn

A smile crossed his lips as he read her note. He consulted his watch and noted it was nearly 8 o'clock already. The bellman interrupted his thoughts.

"Will that be all, sir?"

Steven nodded and crossed the room to tip the man.

Once alone, he explored the suite. He pulled back the sheer curtains, revealing large windows overlooking Central Park. As he stood enjoying the view, he heard a noise at the door. Slowly, Jaclyn opened the door and entered the room. Their eyes met and both of them moved eagerly toward the other. At once, they were entwined in a warm embrace. Neither spoke; they just held on tightly. When a few minutes had passed, Steven clasped Jaclyn's hands and held her out before him. "So this is what the CEO of Toner and Associates looks like. I am very impressed." Steven spoke sincerely. He was truly in awe of what Jaclyn had accomplished.

Jaclyn let out a nervous laugh. "Pretty amazing, isn't it? I still can't believe how much my life has changed in only a few days." She let out a heavy sigh before she continued. "But the most difficult thing for me to accept is that Carl is gone." Jaclyn looked down at the floor. "I guess I'm just refusing to acknowledge the truth. It seems impossible. One day I'm wishing him a good vacation and the next thing I know, I'm being informed of his death. It seems surreal. I mean, I still feel as if he's in the Caribbean, sailing around and having a great time. I find myself thinking he'll show up any minute, tan and well rested, ready to get back to work. I keep reminding myself that I better start admitting it's true. After all, his funeral is tomorrow."

When she finished speaking, Steven took hold of her chin and forced her to look into his eyes. He smiled at her, then took her in his arms and held her close to him as he stroked her hair and kissed the top of her head. After a few minutes of silence, Steven held her out in front of him again to see her face. He bent down toward her and spoke softly. "Jaclyn, everything is going to be fine. I know how difficult it is to lose someone you love and respect. Do you remember us talking about this last weekend? I told you about how I lost my dad when I was just a kid. If I allow myself to think back on that time, I can still feel the depth of the pain I endured. But you need to move past that and honor his life by being everything you can be. You know that's what he would want you to do."

She forced a smile as she replied, "Thank you for understanding the pain I'm feeling. I can't pretend that it doesn't hurt and right now the pain is so deep I'm having a hard time dealing with it. Today was a tough one. I heard the abbreviated list of critical issues facing the firm and assisted in the planning of Carl's wake and funeral. Carl's wishes were for a small and private wake with a funeral immediately following. Both take place tomorrow morning."

She paused to take a breath and Steven jumped right in. "I can imagine that trying to focus on the business when you are under such emotional strain must be nearly impossible."

She sighed. "Steven, I feel numb. I'm going through the motions, but I feel almost removed from it. I know that doesn't make any sense, but that's how I feel."

"I can relate. You need to give yourself some time. Now is a time to grieve. Later is the time to tend to business. Don't be so hard on yourself."

She laughed a nervous laugh. "You're right, it's just that I feel obligated to tend to the critical business issues, but it is so hard when your mind is not clear."

When she was through speaking, Steven led her over to a gold damask settee in the living room. She sat down and took off her heels as he sat beside her. She put her hand on his. "Thank you for coming. I can't imagine getting through tomorrow without you here." He smiled in reply. They sat in silence for a few minutes, Jaclyn enjoying the peace and security she felt being by his side and Steven uncertain what to say to ease her pain. Finally, he spoke. "Are you hungry?"

She looked up at him blankly. "Considering that I haven't eaten at all today, I should be, but my appetite is all but gone. Would it be awful on your first night in the Big Apple if I said I would love to have room service and just relax here with you?"

He took her chin in his hand and lifted her face to his. Softly, he planted a kiss on her lips. "That sounds wonderful to me. I came here to be with you, not to see New York. Can I order for us?"

She nodded and he stood to call room service. He found the room service menu on the secretary desk and placed an order. While he was on the phone, she walked into the bedroom to get changed. Minutes later, she returned wearing a plush, white terrycloth robe, her face washed clean and her hair pulled back into a tight ponytail. She looked twenty years old. Steven stood admiring her natural beauty as she walked toward him.

Self-consciously, she commented, "What's that look on your face all about? Haven't you ever seen a woman without makeup?"

He smiled at her as he replied, "I'm just admiring your beauty. Do you know that you look like a college student?"

Jaclyn curtsied to him as a thank-you, then made her way to the sofa once again. Steven excused himself from the room so he could change. As she sat there alone in the quiet of the moment, she tried to relax, but various thoughts plagued her mind. Unexpectantly, the phone rang, jarring her from her musings. She cleared her throat a few times before she could find her voice. "Hello?"

An unfamiliar voice said, "Ms. Tate, hello. I'm Michael Sturman of the *New York Times*. I was wondering if you have a few minutes for an interview?"

Jaclyn could not believe her ears. How did he know where she was staying? She knew that several newspaper reporters had called the office asking to speak with her, but she did not want to deal with the press until she was thoroughly informed of the business issues at hand. "Mr. Sturman, I don't know how you found out where I am staying, but I consider your call an invasion of privacy."

He was quick to reply so she would not hang up on him, his voice suddenly very sincere. "I am sorry, Ms. Tate. It's just that your story is of great interest to both the real estate community as well as your fellow New Yorkers. I didn't mean to disturb you. It's just that the public is eager to hear your story."

Jaclyn realized this man was obviously just doing his job and had not intended to do her any harm. She checked her tone. "Fair enough. But I'm not in a position to speak to the press at this time. Please call my office on Monday morning and we can set up a time to meet."

"Thank you, Ms. Tate. I'm sorry to have disturbed you. Have a good evening and I will call your office on Monday."

Before he hung up, she added. "Ask for Melanie. She will see that my first interview is with you."

Jaclyn could hear the appreciation in his voice. "Thank you, Ms. Tate. I will call Melanie first thing on Monday."

As Jaclyn hung up the phone, Steven entered the room wearing a matching white terrycloth robe with a gold Plaza emblem embroidered on the breast pocket. He captured her heart every time he walked into a room. She was instantly lost in his face.

"I heard the phone ring. Is everything alright?"

"Believe it or not, that was the press. They have been hounding the office trying to get an interview with me. I issued a statement yesterday saying that in light of Carl's death, I would not be in a position to speak to anyone regarding the business until next week at the earliest. That seemed to appease most of them."

"You have a lot on you right now. Try not to think about it anymore. If it's okay with you, I will ask the operator to block all incoming calls for the remainder of the evening."

Jaclyn nodded, but as Steven picked up the phone, she said, "Wait. Please ask them to allow calls from my parents or Stan Peters. I doubt either of them will call tonight, but just in case, I want them to be able to reach me if they need to."

Steven nodded and made the call to the operator. While he was on the phone, someone knocked on the door. Jaclyn went to the door to see who it was. She peered through the peephole and saw a waiter pushing a dinner cart. She opened the door for him to enter. He courteously greeted her, then silently went about his job and opened the sides of the cart to create a round table for two. He arranged the place settings, then opened the warming oven at the bottom of the cart and retrieved several silver dome-covered plates. Once everything on the table was set, he bowed and quietly exited the room.

As Steven completed the call, he walked over to the table, pulled out a chair and presented it to Jaclyn. She walked over to him and took a seat, then he sat across from her. He lifted one of the highly polished covers and presented the food to her. "Ms. Tate, your dinner is served."

She smiled at him as he continued presenting the food to her in the style of a waiter at a five-star restaurant, altering his voice to fit that of his assumed persona. "Madame, you have a choice of several entrees. The first is roast duck. Your second choice is beef medallions and a mixed green salad. Or you may fancy the chicken consume."

She was pleased with the selection. "It all looks terrific. I would love to start with the soup."

Steven covered the other dishes and served the broth for her. They enjoyed a tranquil dinner together, talking casually while they dined. It was the first time she had relaxed since her return to New York.

***

It had taken Andrew several phone calls to various hotels in New York before he remembered Jaclyn's saying she always wanted to stay at the Plaza. With a sense of urgency, he called the hotel and asked to speak with her. He was promptly informed she was not receiving calls. His temper rose as his resolve heightened. He pleaded with the operator, but she was unmoved by his words. He only gave up after she hung up on him and he tried again and got the same result with a second operator. He contemplated his situation. Perry Grant, a senior partner at Andrew's law firm, had called him into his office earlier that day. He recalled their meeting.

Andrew had been in a client briefing when his secretary came in with a note informing him that Mr. Grant wanted to see him immediately after his appointment. For the remainder of his time with his client, Andrew was preoccupied. It was a well-known fact in the firm that Andrew was up for partnership consideration, but equally recognized was Andrew's unwelcome marital status. He was single and never once in the history of the firm had a single or divorced person made partner. It was an unwritten policy that only happily married individuals had a place at the top. Andrew fought hard to cover up his breakup with Jaclyn. He lied about the status of their relationship, claiming that Jaclyn was only in Dallas temporarily and that on her return, they would wed. It was becoming, however, increasingly difficult to maintain his story. She had not been at any of the mandatory firm parties and the partners questioned him incessantly about her absence. He feared it would all come to a head now that

Carl had died and left Toner and Associates to her. Since he had heard the news earlier that morning, he began dreading the inevitable.

Unable to concentrate, he excused himself and left the client in the hands of his capable assistants. He made his way up to the executive floor and walked slowly to Grant's office. The whole time he was thinking of ways to explain his relationship with Jaclyn, but nothing short of continuing the string of lies made any sense to him. When Perry saw Andrew approaching, he stood and greeted him at the door. With a firm pat on the back, he showed Andrew into his office. "Andrew, how the hell are you? I heard the news about Jaclyn and Toner and Associates, incredible." He paused as if setting the stage for Andrew to continue.

Andrew paused while he formulated his thoughts. "Quite a shock, actually. Jaclyn is taking Carl's passing very hard."

Perry moved closer to Andrew, putting his hand on Andrew's shoulder in a show of compassion. "I'm certain it is very hard for her to accept. Why aren't you taking a few days off to help her through this time?"

His question caught Andrew by surprise. It was rare that any of the staff attorneys ever took a day off. "It's just that I had a client meeting scheduled for today, but I was planning to leave early."

Perry answered brusquely. "Nonsense, Andrew, you know how we feel about that girl. Now you assign one of your assistants to the meeting and you go take care of her. Please give her our condolences as well as our congratulations. Let me know if you need some time off next week. Bring her in for lunch at the private dining room as my guest, if she has time of course. I would like the chance to wish her well in person. She should be made to feel like family. See to it Andrew."

The pressure was mounting. Andrew understood Perry's interest in Jaclyn. It may have, at one time, been purely for Andrew's partnership, but now she was the decision-maker at Toner and Associates. His well-chosen words made it clear to Andrew; Perry wanted her business and expected Andrew to deliver it to him on a silver platter. Andrew felt more trapped than ever by his web of lies, but he was too far in to turn back. Somehow he had to fix everything, and with Jaclyn in New York, it was his only chance.

***

Following a sleep plagued by nightmares, Jaclyn moved about in a fog. She could not even eat the breakfast Steven had ordered for them and instead spent the extra time deciding what to wear. The only thing that felt right was her conservative black suit, black hose and black heels. She hated looking so morbid, but it was an accurate reflection of how she felt. Steven wore a black suit with a cream shirt and a designer tie. They made a strikingly handsome couple. As they prepared to leave the room, Jaclyn stopped Steven by the door. "Steven, I don't know if I thanked you enough for being here. It means the world to me."

Steven squeezed her hand and then opened the door. He held her hand tightly as they walked down the hall to the elevator. As they rode the elevator down to the lobby, he asked, "How are you holding up?"

There was pain and sorrow in her eyes, which she could not conceal. "This is very difficult for me, Steven, but having you here is making a world of difference." She was still looking up at him when the elevator doors opened. Suddenly, a man called out, "There she is."

The rude interruption diverted her attention. She looked into the lobby, shocked to see a crowd moving toward them. In a mad dash, several reporters converged upon them. Before Jaclyn realized what was happening, flashbulbs went off in her face and she was being forced back into Steven. He grabbed her hand, tucked her behind him and forcefully led the way through the crowd. He rushed her out the front door and to the waiting limousine. Having seen the commotion in the lobby, the chauffeur was waiting by the door to usher them into the vehicle. In one fluid motion, Jaclyn and Steven stepped into the backseat and were safely inside. Reporters continued to snap photographs as the limousine pulled away. Once they were on their way, Jaclyn took a sigh of relief. "Wow. I can't believe that just happened. What was that all about?"

Steven was amused by her humility. "You, Jaclyn. It was about you. Don't you understand? You are the CEO of one of the most prominent real estate companies on the East Coast. The public is hungry for your story."

Jaclyn looked at Steven in disbelief. "I liked living in obscurity much better."

Steven laughed. "Well, my dear, I feel as if your days of

private living are a thing of the past. Welcome to my world."

The press had momentarily distracted Jaclyn, but once she settled down, the reality of the moment set in once again. Her hands started shaking. Steven recognized the change in her. "Jaclyn, what's wrong? You're trembling."

She tried to steady herself as she replied. "I'm just a little overwhelmed."

Steven placed an arm around her and held her tightly. They rode the rest of the way to the church in silence.

***

Carl's wake was being held in a small neighborhood chapel in Westchester. Crowds of friends, family and associates crowded into the sanctuary. Jaclyn sat in the front pew with Steven and a few of Carl's relatives whom she had never met. The priest celebrated the mass then asked Jaclyn to come to the altar to address the congregation. As she heard her name being called, she rose from her seat and walked slowly to the podium, fearful her weak knees would not support her. She had to steady herself before she could find her voice. And as her words flowed, so did her tears and the tears of many in the crowd who shared her sorrow and felt her pain.

"I want to thank each of you for being here today. It would have made Carl very happy to see such a gathering of family and friends. Today we come together to honor a man who has touched each of our lives in a special way. For me, he was an incredible mentor and the truest of friends." She paused to dab her eyes of the tears that clouded her vision. She cleared her throat, then continued. "I know how much he will be missed both in the real estate community and within his social circle. It isn't often we are blessed with someone with as much integrity and caring as Carl. He was a man of incredible wisdom, foresight and compassion. He will be missed." Jaclyn paused to steady herself and regain control of her emotions. When she felt able to speak, she continued. "I am eternally grateful that he knew the depth of my love and respect for him. I am certain he is smiling, looking down on all of us gathered here today." She turned her eyes heavenward and spoke a few final words. "Rest in peace, my dear friend." It was such a heartfelt farewell that there was not one dry eye in the church by the time she solemnly took her seat next to Steven.

At the end of the service, the crowd silently emptied from the church and proceeded to form a mile-long procession escorting Carl to the cemetery by Long Island Sound. Carl had selected a plot overlooking the water. As they walked toward the burial site, Jaclyn was taken aback by the sound of waves hitting the shore where he would be laid to rest. It was rather unsettling to her that his love of the sea had cost him his life. Had he fallen ill in New York, he would have received immediate medical attention and could be alive today. She was lost in thought when Steven bent down and whispered in her ear. "How are you feeling?"

She turned to him and felt stronger by his presence. "I'll be alright. I just can't accept his passing. I know it will take some time."

Steven stood silently by her as she paused to reflect on the moment. He held her by the waist, letting her lean on him. They stood there quietly until almost everyone else had left. Without a word, she walked over to the flower-covered casket and knelt alongside the polished wood coffin. For a moment, it was just she and Carl, as it had been many times over the years. She spoke softly to him as if he were standing there before her. "Carl. I don't know yet how I am going to get by without you. I relied on you for so much." Tears filled her eyes and her vision blurred as she looked through her pooling tears. Her voice shook with emotion, but she was compelled to speak. "I loved you and I wonder if you ever knew how deeply. You meant so much to me. I will miss you all the days of my life." She paused to blow her nose and clear her throat. "Thank you for all you have been to me. I will do my best to make you proud. You keep an eye on me, you hear?" Overwhelmed by emotion, she leaned against the casket and wept.

Steven, who had been watching intently from a short distance, rushed over to her. "Jaclyn, I think it's time we go." He took a firm hold of her arm and helped her stand. She moved clumsily and Steven nearly had to carry her to the car. They drove the entire way back to the city in complete silence. Jaclyn cried until she fell asleep resting on Steven's arm. He watched her tenderly, wishing he could take away her pain.

CHAPTER 24
—◇—

Andrew opened his agenda to check his appointments for the week. It was filled with days of pretrial meetings. He needed to stay focused on this case because every win in court brought him closer to his coveted partnership. Jaclyn had caused a stir with her return to New York, but Andrew anticipated he could brush her under the rug one more time. Before he had even finished his first cup of coffee, the interoffice page sounded. He picked up the receiver and answered the call. "This is Andrew."

The man on the other end sounded annoyed. "Andrew, it's Perry. How did things go with Jaclyn this weekend?"

Andrew was surprised by the early morning call and he spoke slowly, buying time to organize his thoughts. "Perry, good morning. Well, what can I say, this type of thing is never easy."

The senior partner had lost his patience with this man. Andrew was obviously hiding something and Perry wanted straight facts now. "Come to my office, Andrew. I have a few things I want to go over with you."

Andrew had no choice but to oblige. "I'm on my way up."

As he walked through the empty halls, his mind raced. He tried to think of any possible situation Perry could come up with. If he could just hang onto this lie for a little while longer, then he would become partner. It would be too much of a public embarrassment for the firm to retract his partnership, so they would have to accept the truth when it eventually came out.

Andrew knocked on Perry's door and waited to be called in.

"Come in." Andrew stepped inside the room and came face to face with Perry, Tim Bosner and Sam Adams. It was the top rung, all sitting together at the conference table, looking at him accusingly. He swallowed hard as he said, "Good morning, gentlemen."

Perry replied on their behalf. "Come in, Andrew. We want to have a few words with you." Perry extended his hand toward the empty seat beside him and Andrew moved hesitantly toward it and sat down. When he was seated, Perry pushed the front page of the *New York Times* in front of him. Andrew scanned the page. His eyes came to rest on a picture of Jaclyn, partially shielded by a man he recognized from his encounter with him at Jaclyn's home. From what Andrew could ascertain, it appeared he was escorting her out of the Plaza hotel. Nervously, Andrew read the caption. "Jaclyn Tate, newly appointed head of Toner and Associates, is escorted to the funeral of Carl Toner by Steven Cason of Cason Properties of Dallas." Andrew continued to read the first few lines of the story. "Sources close to Ms. Tate inform us that she and Mr. Cason are staying at the Plaza. The couple has been linked romantically ..."

As if in shock, he looked up at the men before him. They waited for him to speak. "Gentlemen, I don't know what to say . . . I'm . . . I'm stunned."

The men seated before him looked quizzically at one another. They then looked back at Andrew. Perry was the one who chose to speak. "Can you explain why Jaclyn was staying at the Plaza? We expected that she would have stayed with you. What's going on, Andrew?"

Andrew straightened himself in his chair. "To be completely candid, I have many of the same questions. I received a call from Jaclyn last week and she informed me she was coming to New York but didn't explain why. I too expected she would stay with me, but she indicated she would be at the Plaza. You have to keep in mind that her father is a pastor. Knowing she would want to see her parents during her visit, I attributed her decision to stay at the Plaza to their being in town. I naively let it go."

Perry listened, but there was more to this and he wasn't giving up until he got the whole story. "And..."

Andrew appeared confused, "And?"

Perry clarified, "And what about the guy? The article says that they have been linked romantically."

Andrew tried to conceal his nerves. He had perfected a courtroom confident look and he called upon that skill to get him through the inquisition. "I am shocked. I feel rather betrayed, actually."

Tim chimed in, "You mean you didn't know about this guy until just now?"

Andrew looked down at the floor in a sign of embarrassment and humiliation. "No, Tim, I didn't. Jaclyn has been giving me the cold shoulder, but I attributed the change in her to Carl's death. I respected her decision to be alone during the past few days. I never expected that it was another man."

Perry's patience had been exhausted. "Why weren't you with her at the funeral?"

Andrew faltered. He never expected the partners would take it this far. This was certainly proving to be more intense than he had anticipated. "I had other commitments . . ."

Perry stopped him. "Listen Andrew, you've dug yourself a deep enough hole. I don't want to hear any more lies. Tim was at the wake, he knows the truth."

Tim's serious stare remained fixed on Andrew as he spoke. "Andrew, you may not be aware of this, but Carl and I went way back. In fact, I had a disturbing conversation with him several months ago." Andrew began to sweat. "We were seated together at a business development luncheon. The conversation centered on Jaclyn and her move to Dallas. He told me you were a factor in Jaclyn's decision to leave New York. He alluded to a bad parting between the two of you. He went so far as to question your integrity and our decision to consider you for partner." Tim paused, giving Andrew a disapproving glare. "I came to Perry to decide what to do with this information and we decided to give you an opportunity to advise us of the truth."

Perry added, "I had every faith in you that you would come to us."

Andrew felt his partnership slipping through his fingers.

The partners glanced at each other and nodded before Perry continued. "What do you have to say for yourself?"

Andrew cleared his throat then spoke. "I was hopeful I could turn things around with her. I did not see our breakup as permanent."

Tim interjected. "Then you don't deny what Carl suggested happened between the two of you?"

Andrew simply shook his head in reply. He was guilty and there was no way out of the mess he had created. He was being questioned by three of the top prosecutors in the country and his lies were no longer holding up. He was in well over his head and he knew it. All he could do at this point was try to think of a way to limit the damages.

"Then, Andrew," Perry said, "I'm disappointed to inform you that not only are you no longer up for partnership consideration, you're fired."

The words pierced through Andrew like a knife. For the past several months his life had been quickly unraveling and there was still no end in sight.

***

Jaclyn had a hard time seeing Steven off that morning. He had been a tremendous comfort to her and she hated to see him go. But she knew he had to get back to Dallas, so she didn't resist when he told her he had to leave. "You know, I don't want to go, Jaclyn, but I must. I expect you will be able to come home soon. But if that changes, you let me know and I will come to you."

She smiled at his words. "I know, Steven, but that doesn't make it any easier to be apart. Your being here has made all the difference in the world."

He took her in his arms one last time before he had to leave for the airport. He stroked her hair, gently caressed her arms and kissed her cheek softly. It brought back memories of their tender lovemaking the night before and he suddenly didn't think he had the resolve to leave. He found her mouth and they locked in a passionate kiss. They remained as one until a knock at the door announced the arrival of the bellman. Neither wanted to pull away, but Steven made the first move. He gently turned Jaclyn from him and walked over to the door. The man followed Steven into the room, grabbed his bag and informed him that his car was waiting in front of the hotel. Steven thanked the man and told him he would be down shortly. As soon as the man left the room, Jaclyn spoke. "I won't let you leave."

Steven smiled at her remark. "I don't want to leave, but I must. You and I both have work to do, but one way or another, we will spend next weekend together and that's a promise."

She looked up at him tenderly. "I will hold onto that promise. It may be the only thing that gets me through this week."

He took hold of her arms as he spoke, "I better be on my way. Take care of yourself. Call me if you need anything and keep in touch. I want to hear how things are going."

Jaclyn smiled at him and nodded in agreement. As he opened the door and exited the room, he turned back toward her. In almost a whisper, he said, "I love you, Jaclyn."

Tears stung her eyes. She knew she loved him, but to hear him say the words struck her. She smiled at him and then he was gone. The door closed between them before she could reply. She stepped back into the room, leaned against the wall, closed her eyes and remembered the warmth of Steven's touch. In such a short time, he had come to mean the world to her.

***

Jaclyn's day at the office moved at a frantic pace. She met with the press in a morning conference, answering questions about herself and the future of Toner and Associates. It was an exhausting process, but the result had been positive. Stan Peters, who stood by her side, commented later that he couldn't have scripted a better session. Immediately following, she met with the senior management team to discuss the organization of Toner and Associates and the distribution of duties. Although little needed to be changed, she did have to account for her periodic absences as she split her time between New York and Dallas. Jaclyn announced that ET Marsili, President of Toner and Associates, would work closely with her and be in charge during her time in Dallas. She had everyone's support and agreement on the plan. There was a positive charge in the air and Jaclyn was energized by it.

When she was finally able to take a break, she again retreated to Carl's office. As she was sitting at his desk, his private line rang. She hesitantly answered. "Jaclyn Tate."

An elderly gentleman spoke. "Hello, Jaclyn. I'm Tim Bosner . . .You may remember me . . ."

Jaclyn recalled the senior partner at Andrew's firm well. "Of course, Tim, how are you?"

"Fine, my dear. I am calling first to tell you how sorry we are to hear of Carl's passing. He will certainly be missed. As well, to give you our congratulations. I think you know how much you are liked by the partners at our firm and we know you are going to do a fantastic job for Toner and Associates."

"Thank you, Tim. I truly appreciate your call and well wishes."

"You're welcome Jaclyn. But I would also like to give you some good news."

"Considering last week, that sounds very nice."

"I wanted you to know that we have dismissed Andrew Thorton. He no longer represents our firm."

Jaclyn was at a loss for words.

"It came to our attention that Andrew may not have acted up to our strict conduct standards and was dealt with accordingly. Considering our clout in this town . . ." He left the rest of his sentence unfinished, but what he was saying was clear to Jaclyn.

"I appreciate the call Tim and I will certainly keep your firm in mind when I need legal counsel. I can say that I know my business will be handled with the utmost integrity."

When they ended the call, Jaclyn felt a great sense of satisfaction that Andrew had to pay dearly for his actions. He deserved what he got and she felt nothing but gratification.

CHAPTER 25
—◇—

Jaclyn walked away from Matt's desk smiling to herself. She had the final documents in hand for the closing of Thanksgiving Tower. It had all come full circle and she was now only a few hours away from finishing the deal. As she neared her desk, her private line began to ring. She sat down and picked up the receiver.

In an upbeat tone, she answered, "Jaclyn Tate."

Steven's voice sounded on the other end. "Good morning, Ms. Tate. How are you?"

A broad smile crossed her lips. In the past month, Steven had become such an important part of her life. The mere sound of his voice embraced her with warmth. "Good morning, Mr. Cason. I couldn't be better and I'm not certain if it's because of the way I was awakened this morning or the fact that the closing is today."

Steven purred into the phone. "I take it you enjoyed your massage this morning. I felt it was only fitting that you wake up in a special way on this important occasion."

Jaclyn responded sexily. "It was a fantastic way to wake up. However, I hope it doesn't only happen on special occasions. I could get used to that kind of treatment on a regular basis."

Steven smiled to himself. Jaclyn was becoming his obsession. He discovered in himself a preoccupation with her he had never anticipated experiencing. Her happiness and well being meant more to him than his own. "I'm counting on you getting used to it. I'm going to spoil you rotten." Jaclyn laughed at his playfulness. Then he continued, "Although I hate to change the direction of this conversation, I did want to check in to see if you have everything ready for the closing."

Jaclyn was confident. "The courier just delivered the final documents and now I'm ready and eager."

"Excellent. Then I'll see you at the title company in a few hours."

Jaclyn agreed. "I'll be there. Wouldn't miss it for the world."

***

Jaclyn stood at the immense windows looking out over downtown Dallas. It still felt like a dream that only a few months before they had closed on the Tower and fulfilled her longtime goal. She reminisced about the first day she had seen Thanksgiving Tower and what it had represented to her. So much had happened since then. In retrospect, it seemed a lifetime ago. The pain of losing Carl was bearable these days, Toner and Associates was continuing to flourish and her relationship with Steven grew more serious by the day. Over the past months, she juggled her obligations in two cities half a country apart seemingly effortlessly, but her heart remained in Dallas. As her budding romance with Steven grew, there was no doubt for either that their lives were forever intertwined.

As she stood there now, lost in thought, a truck several stories below her diverted her attention. She looked down at the commotion taking place in front of the building. Positioned at the entrance to Thanksgiving Tower was a large dais covered in a white tablecloth and decorated with red, white and blue bunting. The table was set for ten guests and immediately beside it was a podium with a microphone. Facing the stage was a sea of folding chairs set up for those invited to the dedication ceremony. A construction crew was adding the final touches to the platform and was checking that the audio was in working order. She watched Diana confer with the construction supervisor to ensure everything was in place and operational. With less than one hour remaining before the commencement of the scheduled event, the final preparations were well underway.

While they waited, Steven and Jaclyn entertained Jed, his wife, two daughters and their husbands, Sumitomo and two of his key staff members and JP and his guest, Maria. For the event, Steven had turned a conference room into a reception area and catered a lunch. Today was the event marking the public transfer in ownership of the building. As part of the deal, the skyscraper would remain known as Thanksgiving Tower, but it would be added to the impressive list of Cason Properties. It was to be the showcase asset for Cason and today was the culmination of an enormous amount of hard work and determination. Although the closing had been satisfying for Steven, having the public transfer and rededication of the building as a Cason-held property was fulfilling beyond description. The event would be heavily covered by the press and attended by many distinguished guests. Present were the Governor of Texas, the Mayor of Dallas, a senator and several congressmen, numerous prominent business associates, as well as representatives from every major newspaper and news station in town. It was an event of monumental proportion within the real estate community.

Diana walked into the reception room and sought out Steven. She waited for him to finish a conversation with Mr. Sumitomo, then pulled him aside. "Steven, I conducted the final check as you requested and everything looks perfect. The construction crew verified that everything is set and that the audio is in good working condition."

Steven pulled her close and whispered in her ear. "Is security all set?" Steven had heightened security following continued threats to him and Jaclyn. Although he had yet to uncover the reason or person behind the intimidation tactics, he was cautious. Especially today. There were many high profile guests in attendance and he feared that if someone were truly trying to hurt them, today they were sitting ducks. He took every precaution to ensure their safety, even going so far as obtaining permission to close off the street immediately in front of the building.

Diana nodded in reply.

Steven took hold of her arm. "Terrific Diana. Thank you for taking such good care of everything. You did a great job."

Diana smiled back at her boss, then left him and went in search of Al. She found him networking among the distinguished guests. As she watched him from a distance, she contemplated their relationship. To her surprise, their dating had become serious very quickly. Steven had also softened in his feelings toward Al once he knew Diana was seeing him. Steven had even offered to work with him on other deals and Al was rising to the opportunity.

Steven noted the time and called out to his guests. "Excuse me, may I have everyone's attention please?" He paused to allow everyone time to turn and look at him. "It is now only fifteen minutes before the ceremony is to begin. I think it would be best for us to make our way downstairs." At his words, the crowd gathered their belongings and moved into the hallway. Steven and Diana ushered everyone out of the room. Jaclyn held back and waited for the last person to leave before she followed them into the corridor. She met Steven by the elevators as he was directing the last guests. Jaclyn was about to enter the elevator, when Steven reached out to her and held her back. He told the others to go on and that they would join them shortly. When the doors closed, he turned toward Jaclyn and took her in his arms. He smiled at her broadly and took a deep breath before he spoke. "Jaclyn, I can't ever remember a time when I was happier. You are the biggest reason why. Thanksgiving Tower is just the icing on the cake." She smiled at him as he spoke from his heart. He leaned down toward her and kissed her. He then said excitedly, "Let's go celebrate!"

They entered the elevators and pushed the button for the lobby. Within seconds the elevator came to a halt and the doors opened again, and as they did, the crowd in the lobby turned and several people pounced on them. Reporters pushed their microphones and cameras in Steven's face and backed him against the foyer wall. Before Jaclyn knew what was happening, she had been separated from Steven and was being pushed and shoved by the crowd gathering around him. Instantly, several security guards took control over the converging mass of people and began directing them outside the building. As they exited, ushers escorted each of them to a seat.

Within a few minutes, the mob dispersed and Steven scanned the lobby in search of Jaclyn. Recognizing that she was not inside, he walked out through a side door and made his way toward the dais. He found Jaclyn climbing the steps to the stage. He came up behind her, put his hand on the small of her back and led her to the seat next to his. At the feel of his touch, she turned toward him and smiled. She sat and looked around her as the attendees noisily settled into their seats. She then looked down both ends of the long, narrow table. Starting from her left were Jed Hebert, Sumitomo, JP and Steven and to her right were the Governor, the Mayor, Senator Williams, Steven's real estate attorney and the vice president of Cason Properties. Everyone on the stage was seated and ready for the ceremony to begin. Steven waited for the crowd to quiet down. The assembly was larger than what Jaclyn had anticipated and as she looked out into the sea of faces before her, she recognized very few.

Seated in the last row, watching the events unfold, were Henry Hunter and his daughter Caroline. Henry had built that Tower as a monument to himself, and when he knew Steven had succeeded in buying it, he was more determined than ever to have it remain in the family through Caroline, but that dream was quickly fading. Henry's futile attempts to reunite Steven with Caroline had frustrated him to no end, but he had come to understand why. Although it was through friends that he had become aware of Steven's relationship with Jaclyn and had seen her at a few social functions, he had recently become fully aware of who she was. Where he had anticipated that she was just a pretty face, he later learned, much to his distress, that she was also the heir to Toner and Associates and was as a result, very wealthy and powerful. It was clear that she was formidable competition for Caroline, but Henry never gave up easily or without a fight. He still had a plan up his sleeve.

Caroline sat beside her father, bitterly watching the obvious warmth that existed between Steven and Jaclyn. She had hoped to work her way back into Steven's life, but none of her efforts or those of her father were proving successful. She felt defeated as she watched Steven and Jaclyn together. It was clear to her now that it was time she reset her sights. Even her father had to agree that Cason was apparently lost to another woman, one he knew instinctively he would not be able to get out of the picture as easily as he had once boasted.

A few seats away from Caroline was Andrew Thorton. He had not given up hope of mending his relationship with Jaclyn. He had lost her and his career in New York and he needed to get things back on track with his life. Although he took Steven's warning to heart and kept his distance from her, he had not forgone his goal to win her back. Through his contacts he remained well aware of her activities and knew today would be an important day for her. He wanted to share the moment with her, but as he observed her from afar, he knew that winning her back would be near impossible. Watching her interact with Steven made it clear to him that Jaclyn was in love with him. Andrew knew he had paid the ultimate price for his indiscretion. It had cost him everything that was important to him. As he waited anxiously for the right moment to leave, he noticed a tall blonde, a few seats away, staring and smiling broadly at him. He looked down the row at her and returned the smile. He noticed an elderly gentleman by her side, but he appeared too old to be her husband, more likely he was her father. Caroline continued smiling as their eyes met and held. She had been admiring his expensive suit and alligator shoes and noticed his Rolex watch and diamond ring. Money had a way of showing itself and Caroline had a keen eye for it. By the way she was smiling at him, Andrew was convinced she was interested in meeting him. He decided it was worth hanging around to find out. She certainly looked like she could fit the bill for the woman he needed by his side. Maybe this trip wasn't wasted after all, he thought, as he returned her provocative stare.

By the press box, but out of Jaclyn's direct line of vision, were her mother and father. Steven had sent for them to surprise her. She had commented to him on several occasions that she had been disappointed that on her recent trip to New York she was unable to see them. They did not like to travel into the city and she had been too overwhelmed with obligations to take the time to go to them. He wanted them there on this momentous day so they could be as proud of their daughter as he was. Since his relationship with Jaclyn was getting progressively serious, he also wanted to meet them. They were thrilled by his invitation and as they sat proudly among the distinguished guests, they admired their daughter. As they watched her up on stage, both of them were filled with pride. After all, she was their little girl.

Before long, Steven stood and walked over to the podium. He asked the audience for their attention before he began speaking. He started by introducing the individuals seated on the dais and thanked each of them for being a part of this historic occasion. He spoke at length about the Tower and its significance as one of the most recognizable buildings in the Dallas skyline. He then invited each of his partners to say a few words. Jed, Sumitomo and JP each took a turn expressing their excitement at being a part of Dallas history. When they were through, the governor and mayor also spoke about the Tower and the value and importance of men like Steven who believe in the great city of Dallas and continue to make it better. It was a tribute to both the Tower and the man behind the building. Steven was clearly in his glory. As the event came to a close, Steven took control of the podium once again to thank everyone for attending. He had a few special thank-yous reserved for last. He addressed the crowd. "If I may have your attention for a few final statements." He paused and waited for silence. When he regained the crowd's attention, he continued, "I would like to introduce you to a very special person, Jaclyn Tate." He motioned for Jaclyn to join him and she stood to a round of applause. When she reached him, he continued. "Ms. Tate is the agent responsible for putting together the buyers you see assembled before you and she deserves all the credit for the sale of this fine property. It was her hard work and dedication that made it all possible." Steven turned toward her and began clapping in recognition of her efforts and the crowd joined in. Jaclyn waved to the crowd in a show of thanks, then returned to her seat. Steven continued, "I want to thank each of you for being here today to join in our celebration and rededication of Thanksgiving Tower. At this time, I open the forum to the press."

As Steven addressed questions from the audience, Jaclyn scanned the faces before her. She smiled as her eyes came to rest on Matt. He was looking up at her with admiring eyes. A man in the rear of the congregation stood, stealing her attention away. When she returned her focus to the crowd, she spotted Andrew. She was angry until she followed his stare and saw him flirting with an attractive blond. Suddenly she recognized her. It was Caroline Hunter. Jaclyn laughed to herself. What a perfect pair, she thought, they certainly deserve each other. And as she sat there shaking her head, she saw them. They had been hoping to catch her eye. When her eyes met with her father's, he winked at her and she thought her heart would leap out of her chest. She quickly looked to his right and saw her mom, sitting up proudly as she watched her daughter. Jaclyn felt overwhelmed by emotion. Suddenly, Steven was back by her side. Lost in her own thoughts, she had not heard him end the presentation and thank everyone for attending. As he helped her up, she saw that the crowd was standing and exiting. He took hold of her by the waist and led her down the platform stairs. Her parents were waiting nearby as Steven directed her toward them. As soon as they came into her line of vision, she took Steven by the hand and hurried over to them. She flew into her father's embrace and held him tightly. She then turned to her mother and hugged her firmly. Steven stood smiling as he watched the reunion. She turned toward him as she held onto both of her parents. "Did you arrange this?"

He was pleased to admit he had. "Well, Jaclyn, I thought you would enjoy having your mom and dad here to celebrate this important day with us. When I called to invite them, they were more than eager to come."

She looked happily into both of their smiling faces. "When did you get in? I can't believe no one told me you were coming."

Her father was quick to speak. "We knew Steven wanted to surprise you and, besides that, we were well taken care of. We arrived last night and Steven was kind enough to have someone meet us at the airport and bring us to his apartment, where we spent the night. Waiting until today to be with you was difficult, but it was worth it knowing you would be surprised by our visit."

Her mother added, "Your father is right. Steven took excellent care of us. We couldn't have asked for a more gracious host."

Jaclyn was having trouble containing her excitement. She was celebrating a monumental business goal and was surrounded by the people she loved. Her heart swelled with joy. Steven watched her happily, as she basked in the moment.

***

Later that day, the four of them were enjoying a fabulous dinner at the Tower Club at the top of Thanksgiving Tower. They conversed casually over their meal, each enjoying the food and the company. They had been discussing Steven's business and Jaclyn's new responsibilities at Toner and Associates. It presented Steven the perfect opportunity to speak his mind. "Jaclyn, I hope you don't mind if I take the liberty of discussing in the presence of your parents, something I have been thinking about our businesses."

She was intrigued. "Feel free. You have my attention."

He smiled at her. "I have been thinking about you and Toner and Associates and I want to propose a merger."

She looked at him with a surprised expression. "A merger . . .?"

He explained. "If you look at the strengths and positioning of Toner and Associates together with Carl's vision for an expansion of the business to the Southwest, then it follows that a merger between Toner and Associates and Cason Properties would create a powerhouse real estate investment firm, second to none." He paused to read her reaction.

She studied the idea in silence for a moment, then chose her words carefully as she spoke. "A merger. Very interesting. I certainly can see the value in affiliating our businesses. How do you propose combining the organizations?"

He was careful not to sound too set with a plan. "The way I see it, there are strengths in both companies that we should capitalize on. And certainly we could study the best way to integrate the operations and facilities to maximize efficiency and minimize cost."

She could see he had spent a fair amount of time considering the proposal. "It appears you have given this a once or twice over already."

"It came to me one night when I couldn't sleep. My mind kept focusing on you in New York running Toner and Associates. I started analyzing your role and responsibilities. I realized I could relate to your situation. After all, our companies are of fairly equal net worth, operating within the same industry and with the same mission. If you plan to continue with Carl's agenda for expansion into the Southwest, we'll more or less be competitors. Considering the way you charm investors, I don't want us working against each other." Jaclyn smiled at his remark. "Take some time to think it through and if you're interested, we can start discussing the concept in greater detail."

She looked at her mom and dad before replying. Her parents listened intently but offered no opinion. "I'm very intrigued by what you are proposing, Steven. Your suggestion certainly has merit, however, it would be difficult for me to work closely with you if our friendship ever changed. I would be afraid to risk the stability of our businesses on our personal relationship."

Steven smiled at her. "I guess what I'm saying is I want to merge our businesses as part of a merger of our lives. I don't see it happening either if you and I aren't together on a long-term, permanent basis."

Jaclyn smiled warmly at Steven as she absorbed the sentiment of his words.

Jaclyn's father spoke up and both Jaclyn and Steven turned their attention to him. "I believe I just heard a marriage proposal."

Steven looked back at Jaclyn, whose expression questioned the accuracy of her father's assumption. Steven added, "Much has happened between us in a short time, but I know what we have and it is what I want for my future."

Jaclyn laughed as she spoke. "I guess I never imagined receiving a marriage proposal in such a formal, businesslike manner."

Steven corrected her. "This is not the actual proposal. It's my way of asking for your thoughts and to offer your parents an opportunity to give us their blessings. I have every intention of being down on one knee when I officially ask you to marry me."

Jaclyn couldn't believe what she was hearing. It was certainly sooner than expected, but it was what she had hoped for. She was also surprised by Steven's proposal of a merger of their businesses. Both ideas sounded exciting and promising. The four of them lifted their glasses in unison to toast to the occasion.

She smiled mischievously at him. "Well, on that condition, I agree to seriously consider your proposals."

Whatever Your Passion...

To fully embrace the greater community of women, Be Awesome Inc will donate a percentage of our profits to charitable and philanthropic organizations working to achieve significant progress in women's health and social issues. Be Awesome pledges to make a difference in women's lives, one book at a time. Your purchase of *The Deal* will contribute to these vital causes. Thank you for making a difference.

For more information, visit: beawesome.net

DISCARD

Printed in the United States
56232LVS00003BA/72